EVE SILVER

"Oh, how I have missed books like this!"
—*New York Times* bestselling author Linda Lael Miller

"Silver thrusts the classic gothic romance into the next century with the ideal merging of chilling and dark mystery elements and heated sexual tension."
—*RT Book Reviews*

"Hot romance and truly cool paranormal world building make Silver a welcome addition to the genre."
—*New York Times* bestselling author Kelley Armstrong

"[Silver] is going to be a force to reckon with in the future and look forward to reading her books as she heads up the bestseller chart."
—*ParanormalRomanceWriters.com*

"Silver's climb to the top is proving to be a rapid one!"
—*RT Book Reviews*

"Eve Silver makes magic!"
—*New York Times* bestselling author Cheyenne McCray

"This author is on a hot streak, providing a new gothic voice that infuses the traditions of the genre with updated twists and sizzling sensuality."
—*RT Book Reviews*

# EVE SILVER

# Sins OF THE SOUL

HQN™

Recycling programs
for this product may
not exist in your area.

ISBN-13: 978-0-373-77483-8

SINS OF THE SOUL

Copyright © 2010 by Eve Silver

This edition published by arrangement with Harlequin Books S.A.

For questions and comments about the quality of this book please contact us at Customer_eCare@Harlequin.ca.

® and TM are trademarks of the publisher. Trademarks indicated with ® are registered in the United States Patent and Trademark Office, the Canadian Trade Marks Office and in other countries.

www.HQNBooks.com

Printed in U.S.A.

For my boys
Sheridan and Dylan

## Acknowledgments

Thank you to my editor, Tara Parsons, for seeing
the magic and loving my books, and for having a
wonderfully skillful and clever editorial hand.
To my agent, Karen Solem, for her sage advice
and solid support.

To everyone at Harlequin who had a hand
in helping this book (and the other two in the trilogy)
along the way.

Writing is solitary work. Sometimes lonely.
Sometimes not. Because, after all, there are so many
imaginary people populating a writer's mind.
Thank you to my non-imaginary writing pals who
make this wild ride so much more fun: Nancy Frost,
Michelle Rowen, Ann Christopher, Caroline Linden,
Kristi Cook/Astor, Laura Drewry, Lori Devoti, and
Sally MacKenzie.

Thank you to my family. To Dylan, my light;
Sheridan, my joy; and Henning, my forever love.
They fill my heart and replenish my well.

And a special thank-you to my readers.

# SINS OF THE
# SOUL

*I stand and watch the clouds come. Angry. Rolling. Pewter and charcoal, they ooze one into the next, until there are not many clouds, but one. A single cold mass that chokes the stretch of beach and the water that churns at the shore.*

*I am alone, sucked in by the coming storm. Drowning. Both repelled by it and magnetically drawn.*

*Control is my liberator. My nemesis.*

*My father taught me to free my private demons when I must.*

*So I never do. Not anymore.*

*I have learned that his is not the only way.*

—Alastor Krayl

# CHAPTER ONE

*The Underworld, the Territory of Sutekh*

ALASTOR KRAYL LIFTED one impeccably shod foot, tipped up the toes of his Italian loafers and stopped the severed head as it rolled past him across the sandstone floor. Like trapping a soccer ball. Except the head wasn't quite round, what with the stump of the neck hanging off one side.

The free edge of the neck was messy and jagged, as though someone had twisted the head off like a screw cap. There was little blood, and what was there was dry, some of it flaking off, which meant the decapitation was not particularly recent. A day. Perhaps two.

From this angle, Alastor saw only a ring of closely cropped steel gray hair and the naked skin of the crown. He toed the thing over, stared down at the features—the broad forehead, the hawk-like nose—and masked his surprise as recognition dawned. Bloody hell.

His older brother, Dagan, spat the name, "Gahiji," at the same time as his younger brother, Malthus, leaned in and observed, "He's dead."

"You think?" Despite the situation, Alastor almost laughed.

Gahiji had died once before, some two thousand

years ago. Then he had been offered—and accepted—a second life as a soul reaper.

There would be no such reprieve this time.

This time, dead was dead.

"Which one of you killed him?" Alastor asked, reaching down to thread his fingers through Gahiji's hair and heft the head like a handbag.

He wished with all he was that he had been the one to exact revenge and twist Gahiji's head clean off. But he'd have done that only after he extracted information about his dead brother.

They needed to find Lokan's remains. They needed to find his Ka: his soul. And they needed to unite the two and reanimate him before he partook of the food of the dead and was lost to them forever, trapped in whatever limbo he'd been sent to.

Lokan's Ka was gone, not to any part of the Underworld they knew of, but somewhere else. Bloody hell, none of them even knew where to look. They'd waited for some sort of contact. The brothers had always had the ability to sense each other's pain, to know when one of them was in need. But no contact had come. Wherever Lokan was, he was lost to them, beyond their reach.

"Wish I could claim the kill," Dagan replied, his expression flat, his gray eyes cold as asphalt in winter.

Alastor didn't doubt it.

"Mal?"

His brother spread his hands and offered a casual shrug and a shake of his head.

Process of elimination had Alastor looking to the far side of the long, narrow room, to the fourth in their little private party: Sutekh, the most powerful of the

Underworld deities. He went by many names: Seth, Set, Seteh, Lord of the Desert, Mighty One of Two-fold Strength. Lord of Chaos. Lord of Evil.

The Krayl boys called him Dad. At least, Alastor did. His brothers preferred to shun any verbal claim of kinship, as though by avoiding the moniker they could avoid the relationship.

Their family dynamic was what pop psychology called *dysfunctional*.

Expression impassive, Sutekh regarded them with an unwavering gaze. He could choose any appearance that caught his fancy, and today it was the human face and form of Egyptian royalty. His skin was olive toned, his eyes large and dark, outlined in kohl. A narrow beard extended from his chin. The pleated folds of his head-dress framed his face, and the cloth of his royal apron was wrapped counterclockwise around his body. All of which meant they weren't here for shits and giggles. Sutekh meant business.

"Interesting locale," Mal murmured with a lazy glance at their surroundings. "Is there a reason we couldn't meet in your greeting room?"

"Gahiji was a traitor," Sutekh replied.

He was.

The bastard had been there when Lokan was tattooed with an inverted version of the mark of Aset, Sutekh's enemy. He'd watched while Lokan was skinned, butchered, his body hacked to bits, the parts scattered. Maybe Gahiji had even wielded a knife, a participant rather than an observer. Maybe he was the one who'd stretched Lokan's skin and set it in a black plastic frame, then sent it to Sutekh as proof of the deed.

Rage congealed in Alastor's gut. "If Gahiji could turn traitor, there are undoubtedly others among your minions."

"Yes."

Alastor glanced at the walls of solid sandstone block; the floor was more of the same. There was a single low, narrow doorway, closed off by a thick wooden door. No windows. No place for anyone to hide and listen.

"So this is your equivalent of the cone of silence," Mal said, drawing out the word *cone*.

Sutekh completely missed the tongue-in-cheek humor.

"Nowhere is safe," he said, his voice flat, his gaze sliding to each of his three living sons in turn, perhaps lingering on Dagan a millisecond longer than the others. "No one is trustworthy."

"Something you want to say?" Dagan asked softly.

Alastor stepped between his father and his older brother, heading off that discussion before it could begin. No sense hashing out the fact that Sutekh did not exactly approve of Dagan's mate, Roxy Tam. Alastor *did*. And though he wouldn't admit it aloud, a part of him even envied Dagan that he had found love. Romantic love. Chivalrous love—like Dagan could ever, by any stretch, be labeled chivalrous. In contrast, Alastor had been spoon-fed the art of chivalry since birth. But that had been when he'd lived in the world of man as a human, before he'd learned what he truly was. A soul reaper. Son of Sutekh.

He'd stopped thinking about courtliness and gallantry and love long ago.

Still, he was glad for his brother that he'd found it.

"Gahiji was *your* man for nearly two thousand years,

and he betrayed us all," Alastor pointed out. If blame was to be cast, might as well set it squarely where it belonged.

Sutekh's face remained expressionless, but the damp chill that suddenly seeped through the walls and floor reflected his mood.

"We are your sons." Alastor continued, letting the last word carry the weight of his message. The beings in this chamber were not the enemy. He cast a speaking glance toward Dagan. "All of us are your sons, loyal to you, whether you agree with our choices or not."

Yes, they were loyal. But everyone else in Sutekh's ranks or any other territory was suspect.

"So what now?" Mal asked with a nod toward Gahiji's severed head.

"We do exactly what we have been doing since Lokan was killed," Dagan said.

Alastor tamped down the surge of pain and rage that came at him as he thought of Lokan and what had been done to him. He wanted—needed—to find the rest of the sodding bastards who'd killed him. And he needed to return the favor. He owed all his brothers his life, but Lokan most of all, for all the times he'd scraped Alastor off the floor when things had been at their darkest.

"We bloody well need to step it up," he said, his tone hard. "Every whisper of information, no matter how far-fetched, gets assiduous attention."

"Assiduous?" Dagan and Mal chorused, then Dagan asked, "Word of the day?"

Mal snorted.

Alastor narrowed his eyes. "Sod off."

He lifted his head and found Sutekh staring at

them. He gave nothing away, but Alastor sensed his bemusement.

"You bicker," Sutekh observed.

"Often and well."

"Yet you smile."

"That's the point."

It was unusual for them to come to Sutekh's realm en masse, so he rarely had the opportunity to view his offspring's group interactions. Alastor suspected he preferred it that way, that their human tendencies confused him. If he was even capable of confusion. Hard to tell.

"Would you like this back?" Alastor asked as he hefted Gahiji's head and tossed it. His father's hand whipped up so fast it was no more than a blur, and he caught the head as it spun through the air. "What did you find out before you killed him?"

That had to be the reason for this summons: urgent information that Sutekh had obtained before he tore Gahiji's head from his body.

"I did not kill him." Sutekh's clipped words echoed off the walls.

Alastor felt his brothers' attention sharpen, as did his own. If they hadn't killed the bugger, and Sutekh hadn't killed him—

"Gahiji's head was delivered anonymously," Sutekh continued. "I had no part in his demise, and no opportunity to question him. He was dead, his darksoul taken, and this—" with a flourish, he held the head aloft so the filmy eyes stared out at them "—delivered without even a note."

"No gift wrap?" Mal quipped, but his tone was hard, devoid of levity.

"Who delivered it?" Alastor asked. That was the only important question.

"That, I do not know."

Taken aback, all three brothers fell silent. Sutekh knew everything that went on in his realm. It was impossible for someone to sneak in undetected. Which meant that an anonymous delivery was impossible.

Yet more proof that Gahiji hadn't been the only traitor in their midst.

Gahiji had revealed his duplicity when he'd attempted to kill Dagan's mate. They'd quickly learned that he had betrayed them, that he'd been part of the plot to kill Lokan.

But they hadn't known if he'd acted as leader or peon.

The delivery of his severed head answered that question, but raised another. Someone with enough power to kill a soul reaper had robbed both Lokan—and now Gahiji—of life.

Which meant Gahiji wasn't the mastermind.

So who was?

# CHAPTER TWO

*Burlington City, New Jersey*

NAPHRÉ KURATA SHOVED open the door of the Playhouse Lounge and almost hit some guy in the face.

And what a face.

His features were all angles and edges and hard, honed elegance. Clean-shaven. Honey-blond hair. Dark suit, perfectly tailored. Polished loafers. She noticed the details. In her business, it could mean the difference between life and a bullet in the head.

In this particular case she noticed for another reason. Something about him drew her gaze, demanded she look, made her feel like she never wanted to look away.

Great. She needed to remember to pick up batteries for her vibrator.

He didn't give her more than a cursory glance, just shifted a bit to the side and held the door as she passed. Interesting. This wasn't the sort of place where a guy held the door for a girl. But then, the action seemed almost automatic for him.

Tucking her chin, she walked on. She didn't want him to get a good look at her, just in case. Another trick in this biz. Notice the details, but don't let anyone notice a damned thing about *you*.

There was another man behind him, this one dark-haired with platinum hoops in his ears. She had the fleeting thought that guys who looked like them didn't need to come to places like this. Then she had to bite back a laugh. All sorts of guys came to strip clubs, for all sorts of reasons.

All sorts of girls did, too…maybe even one who needed to pick up the locale and front money for her next hit.

She cast a quick glance over her shoulder. The first guy held the door for the second, let him go through ahead. Again, interesting. Such neat and tidy manners.

The second guy was as good-looking as the first, but for some reason, as she reached the car and yanked open the door, her gaze slid back to the blond.

And caught him looking at her. For a millisecond, she held his gaze, and had the oddest sensation of recognition. Like she'd seen him before. But she knew with one hundred percent certainty that she hadn't. She'd remember that face if she had.

The sensation was more than a little unnerving.

She dropped her chin and tipped her head a bit to the side, hoping to rob him of a clear view of her features. Like he hadn't already gotten an eyeful.

When she looked up, all she saw was his back, disappearing through the door.

The crowd at the Playhouse Lounge was usually a mix of human and supernatural. For a second, she wondered if he was human. Then she shrugged. Not her business. But she was guessing he was because she hadn't sensed a supernatural vibe, and usually she was good at that.

Climbing into the passenger seat, she glanced at her companion.

"Making new friends, Naph?" Butcher asked.

"You know me better than that."

"Sure do." He offered a wheezing laugh.

She pulled the plain brown envelope Mick had given her from inside her jacket and tossed it on the seat between them. It was stuffed fat with bills.

"You count it?"

"What's with you and the bizarre questions tonight?" She dragged the shoulder strap over and buckled her seat belt.

Again, Butcher laughed. "Where're we going?"

"Ashton Memorial Park. Whitby. Tomorrow night. Mick said there'll be two open graves to choose from. Maybe more, if someone else dies before then."

"Hnn," Butcher grunted, and started the car. He stared straight ahead. "What else did Mick say?"

"That you owe him a bottle of scotch when this one's done. And that the client says you already have all the information about the mark that you need."

"That I do, Naph." Butcher put the car in drive, his expression thoughtful. "That I do."

"You plan on sharing anytime soon?" Not that she really needed to know. This was Butcher's hit. She was just along as backup. But she *liked* to know details before she made a hit. Her scruples were a tad more discerning than his.

As though he read her thoughts, Butcher said, "I know your rules, Naph. The mark's a killer."

"That's fine then." But of course, *fine* was a relative term.

Funny how no matter how hard you ran from destiny, it always caught up and bit you in the ass.

"Now *there* is a fine ass." The pounding music coming from inside the club nearly drowned out Mal's voice.

Thinking his brother was talking about the girl they'd passed on the way in, Alastor Krayl slapped his palm against the door, stopping it from swinging shut entirely, and glanced at the parking lot. He'd already noticed the sleek line of her long, jeans-clad legs, and the high curve of her arse on the way in.

Now, as he stood half-in, half-out of the club, he caught only a glimpse of her face: dark eyes, dark hair, lush lips. She quickly looked away.

Pretty girl, he thought. More than pretty. Memorable.

Better for her if he forgot her.

He hesitated for a few more seconds, feeling like he ought to go out and—

What? Ask for her number? That was Mal's style, not his.

Squelching the urge to stop her before she drove away, he let the door of the Playhouse Lounge swing shut behind him.

"Just look at that sweet booty," Mal said, and Alastor realized it wasn't the girl outside he was talking about. He followed Mal's gaze and immediately wished he hadn't.

The ass in question was anything but fine or sweet. Protruding above grease-streaked jeans was a large, white mound of quivering flesh bisected by several inches of deep crevice and adorned by tufts of wiry black hair. The owner of said body part was out of his chair, chest pressed flat to the stage, arms outstretched. On the stage, illuminated by the intermittent, flashing glare of the stage lights, a woman undulated and dipped with amazing elasticity just beyond his reach.

"Bloody hell," Alastor muttered. "Now that you've pointed it out, I'll carry that delightful image for the rest of the night." He wasn't certain his brother heard him because Mal was laughing like a lackwit and the music was pumping loud enough to shatter glass.

He glanced around. Before he'd even walked through the door, he'd felt a distinctive current crackle in the air, stronger now that he was inside. There were supernaturals here…where?

The place smelled like old beer and older sweat. Other than the stage lights, the lounge was dim. The outlines of tables and chairs blended with the shadows. There were few patrons: the group by the stage. Two teenagers at a round table, clearly underage and clearly trying not to draw attention as they looked around, wide-eyed. An old guy slouched in a booth in the shadows, three empty glasses in front of him, and a fourth well on its way. No sign of a barmaid. The barman was slumped on a stool, his face obscured as he flipped through a tattered motorcycle magazine. They were all mortal. But the supernatural vibe persisted.

His gaze shot to the far wall where two shallow hallways notched from the main room. One had a sign above it that read Restrooms, the other Staff Only.

"Are we here for a specific reason?" Alastor asked. Not sixty seconds in, and he was ready to leave. Already he suspected Mal might have fared better on his own. A distorted version of his own reflection stared back at him from the mirrored wall behind the bar. Alastor stood out here like a blue button on a white shirt. Which made him a poor candidate if Mal's intent was to blend in.

"Yeah, we're here for a reason."

"Tell me *she*—" Alastor jerked his head toward the stage "—is not it."

"She's not it."

The stripper was beautiful. Far more beautiful than such surroundings warranted. That fact alone cranked Alastor's suspicion from simmer to boil. Apart from a fine ass—which he couldn't help but notice—she had other assets, hidden ones.

With a sultry smile, she tossed her long, blond hair, and shimmied down, knees spread. The mortal male leaned even further onto the stage and waved a bill. His companions hooted encouragement, and one of them pulled out a bill of his own, clamped it between his teeth and shook his head like a dog.

Reaching into his pocket, Alastor withdrew an English toffee caramel, unwrapped it, and popped the candy in his mouth as he watched the stripper get up on all fours and crawl close enough to draw the bill from the man's meaty fingers. Close enough to let her hand linger on his, to lean in and let him stroke her hair. The average observer might see an unattractive man paying for the privilege of petting an unusually attractive woman.

Alastor saw something else entirely. "Looks like the Playhouse Lounge deals in something other than lap dances."

"It does," Mal agreed. "You got candy? I'm all out."

Alastor fished another from his pocket and offered it to his brother. Their half human, half god metabolism meant that their cells and tissues demanded massive amounts of glucose to convert to ready energy. Candy was a quick hit, but they'd been known to drink honey or eat refined sugar in a pinch. Not pleasant, but necessary.

"Succubus?" He glanced at the stage.

"You nailed it."

"No. Nor do I wish to." The thought of feeding a succubus was less than enticing.

Mal grinned, white teeth bright against day-old stubble. "Don't knock it till you try it, bro."

*Bro.* That word summed up a world of difference between them. Mal was a chameleon. As the centuries passed, he took on the trappings of the current world with ease: technology, fashion, music, slang.

And while Alastor adopted some—particularly technology—he chose not to adopt all. He was a product of his upbringing, appreciating the opera and fine tea, the art of conversation, a well-tailored suit, and a part of him had no wish to give that up. At some cellular level, he was still, and always would be, the titled gentleman.

Some three hundred years past, Sutekh had sired four sons by three different human women in an effort to further his power and extend it more fully to the human realm. Alastor and Dagan were born of the same woman, while Mal and Lokan both had different mothers. Sutekh had raised those sons in different worlds, keeping the eldest, Dagan, in the Underworld and fostering the others out in an experiment to see which would emerge the strongest.

Without question, Dad was one cold bastard, brutal in the manner of a scalpel rather than a club. And smart. Why choose one path to his desired outcome, and possibly err, when he could try four different approaches and quadruple his chances of success?

He'd sent Alastor to England to be raised as the heir to a title. The people he believed to be his parents were old enough to be his grandparents, the women he believed to be his older sisters already in their late teens when he was just a tot. He had been loved and pampered and happy, the sole male progeny in a sea of fussing females.

Then one day, Sutekh had blown in like a storm and ripped Alastor's sheltered, privileged world to shit. Alastor had gone from a gilded cage to the gutter. Then he'd gone to hell. And to his shock, he'd had company for the trip: his brothers, Dagan, Mal and Lokan.

They were the reasons he'd survived, the reasons he hadn't lost his mind to the bitterness and despair that had nearly swallowed him whole.

The succubus recaptured Alastor's attention as she shimmied and dipped. With a broad leer, the human by the stage straightened and looked around at his friends. For a second, Alastor had a clear view of his face. Their gazes met and he looked beyond lank hair and heavy brows, beyond the man's eyes to his soul.

And the darkness he saw made his lips curve in a faint smile.

"I take it he's her dinner?"

"Looks like."

"A bloody shame, that," Alastor murmured. "His darksoul is black as pitch." It took years of foul deeds to accumulate that kind of smut, and this man was wrapped in it like a sausage in a bun. "I wonder if the lady might be persuaded to forfeit her prior claim. I'm due for a kill."

"All work and no play…"

"…makes Dad happy." Sutekh had an army of soul reapers—his sons the princes among them—who harvested darksouls to satisfy Sutekh's voracious appetite for evil. Souls, dark and light, were the currency of the Underworld, the much sought-after prizes. Underworlders ran rackets in the Topworld of man: drugs, prostitution, weapons. But ultimately, it was the souls they wanted.

Mal glanced at him over his shoulder, his pale gray eyes assessing. "And we're all about making Sutekh happy."

Alastor cocked a brow, and after a moment, Mal continued. "I wouldn't try to con, wheedle or cheat Lillith out of a meal." He scraped his fingers back through his dark, sleek hair revealing thick platinum hoops—two in each ear—that glinted in the flashing light. "She's testy when she's hungry. And if you steal her dinner, you'll have to replace it."

"House rules?" Alastor asked, faintly amused.

"Only rule she's got. In this place—" Mal made an expansive gesture "—anything else is good to go. But she's territorial when it comes to her food. If you take Lillith's prey, you take its place." He shrugged, and then spread his hands, palms up. "Hey, you know me. If I can steal it, I will, but in this case, even I'll take a pass."

Which said a great deal. Mal was a thief and a pirate. Always had been, always would be. He liked his music loud, his liquor hard and his women hot-tempered and wild. And he never paid for what he could get, or take, for free.

"Then I'll make bloody certain to heed the rule."

Alastor had learned long ago that he far preferred the role of predator to that of prey. Control was his drug. "Right, then. If there's a reason we're here, mate, share. Else I'm done."

Mal looked at him, his expression hard. "Information, bro. Why else would we be here? Got a lead on someone who might have seen Lokan that night."

*That night.* The night Lokan was killed. The night someone made him their prey.

Rage and pain twisted in Alastor's gut, but he locked them down, refusing to allow even a small crack in his armor.

He meant to bloody well find whoever had done the deed, and make them pay, not with a bludgeon, but with small, precise cuts that prolonged the event and allowed him to savor the experience.

"Hey," Mal said. "Looks like a party."

A barmaid emerged from a room that cut off the Staff Only hallway. A black bow was tied around her neck. Young, pretty and human, she wore a skirt that revealed far more than it covered, a pair of black stilettos and nothing else. Her breasts were round and high—the size and shape making Alastor suspect a little surgical help—with spangled stars covering the areolas.

From behind her, light spilled out through the open door, and Alastor caught a glimpse of a female back and long, straight hair. The barmaid yanked the door shut too quickly for him to be certain, but he had a feeling he now knew exactly what they were doing here, and who they were here to see.

"Jackpot," Mal murmured, though if his reaction was

to the occupants of the room or the girl was anyone's guess.

Furtively, she looked around then froze when her gaze reached Alastor and Mal.

With a flash of white teeth, Mal waved her over. He flicked a glance at Alastor. "We're more likely to get information if you don't make her piss herself. At least lose the scowl."

Scowl? Alastor concentrated, attempting to organize his expression into something less off-putting.

"Never mind." Mal gave a short huff of laughter and shook his head.

The barmaid sauntered over, hips rolling, lips parting as she eyed Mal with blatant interest.

"Hello, darlin'." Mal grinned and shifted into easy conversation, comfortably playing her like an instrument—strum and pluck—as he worked at coaxing information about the private party behind the closed door.

Giggling and fluttering her lashes, the barmaid leaned closer, rubbing against Mal and dipping her chin in a kittenish move.

Alastor's patience frayed and quickly unraveled. There were more efficient ways to get a job done. He pulled out a C-note, flipped it into a neat fold and slid it between his middle and index fingers. The girl's attention wavered as he held it out toward her, the tip of her tongue sliding out to trace her lower lip. Avarice sharpened her features.

"Tell the blighters in the back that there are two more to join the party."

"There's no party," she said, a bit too hastily.

"There's no one back there." She caught her lower lip between her teeth. "I was just…"

"Checking the premises for…vermin?" He rubbed his fingers together, making the bill between them crackle.

She gnawed harder on her lip.

Letting her mull things over, he glanced at Mal, then jerked his head toward the stage. "You think Lillith will interfere?"

Mal shook his head. "Doubt it. She's interested in other things at the moment. So long as we don't mess the place up…" He shrugged and turned the full watt-age of his smile on the barmaid. "Your boss offering them protection, darlin', or just renting out space?"

The girl pressed her lips together. Alastor could almost see the wheels turning in her mind.

"Space," she answered after a moment, her eyes locked on the money in Alastor's hand.

"Mind offering introductions? Or we could always announce ourselves." Alastor slowly curled his fingers so the C-note disappeared inside his fist.

"They—" Raising her hand, the girl looked at the disappearing money, then shot a glance at the closed door, clearly trying to figure a way she could get the money and avoid stepping into the middle of a poten-tially sticky situation. "They don't like company," she said in a rush. "I think they have guns."

"Guns aren't a problem, and we're not company." Alastor pinned her with a hard look. "A smart girl would choose to make a few dollars off the interaction and then disappear." He offered a tight, close-lipped smile and let the edge of the bill peek out once more. "Are you a smart girl?"

Expression shuttered, she edged away from him, closer to Mal, who grinned down at her and said, "My brother's right, darlin'. We're not company."

Mal took the bill from Alastor and tucked it into the waistband of the scrap of cloth that passed for the girl's skirt, letting his hand linger on the flare of her hip.

"I'd say we're more like—" Alastor's lips peeled back in a parody of a smile *"—blood."*

The barmaid stared at him, wide-eyed, then she turned and muttered, "This way."

They followed. The sound of the music was less overpowering back here, away from the speakers. Stopping before the closed door, she hesitated, rapped twice, and called out, "Visitors," before scampering away.

"Private affair," a gruff voice replied. "Tell whoever—"

The words died as Alastor pushed open the door. A square wooden table was positioned in the center of the small room, illuminated by a naked overhead bulb. Around it sat three human men and one not-so-human female.

"Hey!" One of the three men at the table shoved to his feet, hand going inside his jacket. His chair clattered to the floor.

The female murmured a soft, "No," and rested her curled ebony talons lightly on his forearm.

The mortals saw her as a petite and pretty woman.

Alastor blinked, cleared the facade, and saw her exactly as she truly was.

She was both beautiful and monstrous, with small, fine-boned features and tiny white teeth, jagged as a shark's. Her skin had the smooth, supple texture of expensive leather, the color a deep burgundy red. A fall of straight, black hair cascaded in a smooth curtain down her back.

While the succubus out front explained a small measure of the supernatural vibe that had been crawling along his skin since he'd stood outside in the parking lot, the creature before him explained the rest.

The men were definitely human, Topworld grunts, inhabitants of the shady area that straddled Underworld and the mortal realm. They were hangers-on with delusions of catching a supernatural's favor and being welcomed to the club.

Alastor bit back a dark smile. He wondered if anyone had ever told them the price.

It was one the female had already paid. The essence of her being. She was one of Xaphan's concubines. A fire genie of some significant power, which meant she'd made her deal with the demon centuries past.

As a rule, mortals didn't get a free trip to go to the Underworld and, with rare exceptions, high-power supernaturals didn't get to come to the Topworld. The Underworld was divided in a manner similar to the way human crime families carved up cities, with everyone jealously guarding their own borders. The higher up the hierarchy an Underworld lord or god—Sutekh; Osiris; Hades; Izanami—the more confined. They couldn't travel to the mortal realm or to each other's territories, and they were forced to choose ambassadors, creatures of lesser supernatural power to move about and represent them. It was a way to balance things, a failsafe that had been set up six thousand years ago in a peace accord that had held until now.

The thing was, Lokan's murder threatened that accord. Kill Sutekh's son and he'd retaliate. Perhaps not right away. Perhaps he'd take his time, plan and plot. But in the end, Sutekh would find—and annihilate— the brains behind the deed, along with any who'd supported his efforts. And that would start a war.

Likely, that was the perpetrator's exact intent.

"Naamah," Alastor greeted the female before him. She was Xaphan's ambassador, his favored concubine. Alastor had met her before, when he'd stood by Dagan's side to battle a group of fire genies who had come for Dagan's mate, Roxy Tam.

The fire genies had lost that skirmish, which meant their fearless leader might be holding a bit of a grudge.

"Fancy meeting you here," she purred and drew a skein of silky hair back over her shoulder with a languid movement.

"You know each other?" Mal asked, clearly surprised.

"Not in the biblical sense." While Mal might not draw the line at bedding one, or several, of Xaphan's fire genies, Alastor did.

Naamah snorted. "We've…exchanged greetings."

"We had a bit of a row when she tried to barbecue Roxy," Alastor clarified.

"Had that truly been my intent, I would have succeeded," Naamah purred.

Alastor decided it wasn't a point worth arguing. He glanced at the table. In addition to the cards and glasses, there was an open bottle of Dalwhinnie and a bowl of unshelled peanuts.

"Pricey single malt for a place like this," Alastor observed, letting his gaze flick to each of the three humans in turn, and finally settle on the female once more. "This a special occasion?"

"What do you want, reaper?" Naamah asked at the same instant her companion snarled, "You see any fucking balloons, asshole?"

The guy turned to her with a frown. "Reaper? You know this guy?"

"Information," Mal replied, and Alastor kept quiet, letting his brother run with it. After all, Mal was the one who'd come up with this lead. Alastor was just along for the ride.

"Information about?"

Mal just stared Naamah down.

"Maybe we can do a trade," she said after an extended silence. "Did you find the kid?"

Mal answered in all honesty "No."

The kid she referred to was Dana Carr. And, no, they hadn't found her. In fact, by mutual agreement, they hadn't looked and didn't plan to. If anyone had asked Alastor a week past if he gave a fig about a mortal child, he'd have laughed.

Today, he'd say that even though he'd never laid eyes on her, he would kill for her. Start a war for her. Find a way to die for her if it meant her life.

Because he'd been hit broadside with the information that Dana Carr was his dead brother's daughter. Lokan's daughter.

Alastor's niece.

He thought it was impossible. Except recent events were making them all aware as never before that there were no such things as absolutes.

Soul reapers couldn't be killed, but someone had killed Lokan.

Soul reapers couldn't reproduce—not even Sutekh's sons—but Lokan had.

Soul reapers were enemies of the Daughters of Aset, yet Dagan had taken one as his mate, and trusted her as the sole being that knew Dana's location. Roxy Tam was the one who had discovered their link to Dana, and because of her unique tracking abilities, she was also the only creature living or dead who could find the kid and her mom.

Except she wasn't planning on looking anytime soon. She and Dagan were convinced that not knowing where the kid was, and therefore not being able to betray her location, was the only way to keep Dana safe. So the kid had disappeared somewhere in the world of man and, for the time being at least, would remain safely lost.

"If you haven't found the child, then you have no information that I want." Naamah waved a taloned hand in dismissal and leaned back in the chair.

"Why the fascination?" Alastor knew why Dana mattered to *him,* but he needed to know why she mattered to Xaphan and his fire genies. Sutekh had a lengthy history with the keeper of the braziers that light the lakes of fire, and it wasn't harmonious. Whatever Xaphan wanted with Dana, it could only be at cross-purposes with what the soul reapers wanted. "Why is this little human girl so important to you?" he asked, including the word *human* for a reason.

Naamah didn't blink. Didn't react at all. Which told him she didn't know the girl's secret, had no clue she was a soul reaper's progeny.

She made a sound of frustration. "Why is she so important to *you?*"

"She isn't." Alastor met and held her gaze. "We aren't the ones asking about her."

"Then what are you asking about?"

"What's your interest, darlin'?" Mal rested his hand on the back of her chair and leaned in close, his eyes locked on hers.

Naamah studied Mal, ignoring her human companions as they shifted and muttered. Finally, she answered, "She was with Frank Marin. She may have heard something. Seen something. I don't know the details, and I didn't ask. All I know is that Xaphan wants to know what she knows." Her mouth twisted in distaste. "And he wasn't pleased that we had a—" she shot a disgruntled look at Alastor "—disagreement with three soul reapers the other night. He's put the kibosh on anything similar, at least until after the meeting."

The meeting she was talking about had been called by Sutekh, ostensibly to promote peace, but every lord and god with half a brain was wary that Sutekh meant retribution for his son's murder. The logistics of getting all the attendees to neutral ground and the hostages in place—a convoluted safeguard that had gods and demigods offering lives as guarantees that ambassadors and emissaries wouldn't be annihilated on sight—had necessitated a postponement of the originally planned date, and the meeting was now set for two weeks hence.

It wasn't Sutekh who'd postponed it. He'd never do that; it would signify weakness.

The meeting had been pushed off by a request from Osiris, which in itself was suspect.

Studying Naamah's expression and posture, Alastor

chose to believe her explanation. She merely thought the child was a witness to whatever had gone down the night Lokan was killed. She had no idea exactly how important Dana was. Hell, up until a couple of days ago, none of them had had a clue. Lokan had never said a word about his daughter. Not a single word.

Why? Had he not trusted them with the knowledge? Or had he himself been unaware of the fact? Questions to ponder another time.

The issue at hand was why Xaphan was so interested in information about Lokan. Soul reapers were far outside his purview.

It made Alastor wonder if Xaphan's concern was motivated by culpability. It stood to reason that if he were the puppet master, he'd want to find—and dispose of—any witnesses before they could reveal him to Sutekh.

That explanation made perfect sense, which was exactly why Alastor wasn't convinced. It was too pat, too easy. If you hear hooves, think horses, not zebras. Except in Alastor's experience, sometimes the hooves did belong to zebras.

Mal asked Naamah another question, but Alastor wasn't listening because at that moment one of the humans reached for the bottle of Dalwhinnie. His sleeve pulled back, baring his forearm—and his tattoo. A scarab beetle. Nothing particularly noteworthy about that except, beside it, spelled out in hieroglyphics, was a name: Sutekh.

"Nice tat, mate," Alastor murmured. "Where'd you get it done?"

The guy just looked at him, dark eyes wary, a twitch setting off beneath the left one.

The scarab beetle. Sutekh's name. Alone, either one might mean nothing. Together, they pointed at the Setnakhts, a mortal cult of offshoot worshippers of Sutekh. In a bizarre twist, Dagan and Alastor had found evidence suggesting that the Setnakhts might somehow be involved in Lokan's murder.

Which meant this was Alastor's lucky night. The mortal with the tattoo might just have the answers Xaphan's concubine lacked.

"Mate?" Alastor urged.

Tension crackled in the air.

"Fuck off."

"Right, then." Alastor slammed his palm against the guy's wrist, pinning it in place. "Last chance."

Naamah leaped from her seat, hands raised, fingers curled into taloned claws.

Alastor shot her a hard look, his lips peeling back to bare his teeth. "Is he one of yours?"

She blinked, as though the question caught her off guard. She shook her head. "No."

"Then think carefully," Alastor warned.

She held his gaze for a second, and then sank back into her seat with a shrug, leaving the human to his fate.

One of the other men, the one who'd leaped to his feet when they first entered the room, surged forward, gun drawn, the scrape of his chair as he kicked it back loud in the quiet.

Alastor didn't hesitate. Without shifting his attention, he shot his free hand into the guy's chest, ripping through muscle, cracking bone. His fingers closed about the hot, beating heart. With a twist, he ripped it free. He tossed it on the table where it lay in a spreading puddle of blood, wet and pulsing.

He shoved his hand back inside the torso. The dark-soul came to him like a pet to its master, slithering up his arm, cold and slimy and dank.

With a grunt, he scooped up the dripping heart and tossed it to Mal, who caught it and tucked it away in the leather pouch he wore slung across his shoulder. Then he moved closer to tether the darksoul with a band of fire.

"Best to mind your own business." Alastor snarled the warning at the third man, who was frozen in place in an odd crouched position, halfway between sitting and standing, his expression a mask of horror. The guy sank into his chair and fisted his hands in his lap.

"Right then." Alastor caught the guy with the Set-nakht tattoo by the throat, lifting him from his chair. He struggled, closing his fingers around Alastor's wrist, trying to claw his way free.

"Shall we repair to the parlor for a bit of privacy, mate?"

Alastor hauled him out of the room and down the short hallway to the back door. He kicked it open and dragged the struggling human into the deserted alley.

"Let's have a chat, shall we?" He caught the man's jaw with his bloody fingers, and forced him to meet his gaze. "What's your name, mate?"

"Mick." It came out as little more than a rasp.

"Well, tell me something useful, Mick, and you might get to live."

## CHAPTER THREE

*Saru mo ki kara ochiru.*
Even monkeys fall from trees.

—Japanese proverb

*Ashton Memorial Park, Whitby, Ontario*

IT WAS A SIMPLE RULE. A basic rule. The first one Butcher had ever taught her. Always watch your back. Don't trust anyone else to do it for you. Naphré figured she had no one to blame but herself for her present unpleasant predicament, because she hadn't followed rule number one.

Butcher had a .40 cal Glock rammed tight against the back of her neck. And she hadn't seen it coming.

"Guess it's my lucky night," she muttered.

"How so?"

"You don't pack a .22."

Butcher grunted. "Good point."

Light bullet, high velocity, a .22 would ricochet around inside her skull like a pinball and percolate her brain into gray and pink goopy soup. She could quite possibly live through it, minus a few higher brain functions.

Not a welcome thought.

She preferred the Glock. Positioned as it was

between her first vertebra and the base of her skull, the barrel was directed at her brain stem. The bullet would go in through the back. Out through the front. Instant death. Nice and clean, if you didn't count the spray of blood.

Much more efficient than brain soup.

Only problem was, dying wouldn't be the end for her, thanks to a bargain she'd made six years ago on a cold, rainy night, with the sound of rending metal bright and loud around her, and the blood dripping off her hands.

She'd been such a stupid, naive girl back then, running from the frying pan into the fire.

"Hands behind your head," Butcher rasped.

She did as he instructed. Every minute she managed to stay alive was a minute to figure out a plan. "Butcher—"

"Job's a job, Naph. No hard feelings, huh?"

Right.

"No hard feelings," she agreed, doing a quick sweep of the parking lot and the road beyond, moving only her eyes as she searched for options. Her gun was still in its holster, her knife sheathed at the small of her back. Fat lot of good they'd do her there. Butcher would kill her before she could get either one clear.

She hadn't expected to need her weapons. Not quite yet. They'd driven here together, chatting about the earthquake in New Zealand that was all over the news. She'd thought they had time before they went after the mark. Guess she should have read between the lines last night when Mick said Butcher already had all the information about the mark that he needed. It was only when Butcher had pressed cold metal to warm skin that she'd realized *she* was the mark.

*Saru mo ki kara ochiru.* Even monkeys fall from trees. She could almost hear her grandfather's voice, low and even when he spoke Japanese, halting and accented when he spoke English, though he'd lived in the States for decades.

Unfolding events were proving her to be one dumb-ass monkey.

"Really am sorry for this, Naph."

"I know." She was sorry, too. Because one of them was going to die here tonight, and that just plain sucked.

Butcher slid her gun from the holster under her armpit and her knife from the sheath. She heard a dull thud, then a second, heavier sound as he tossed her weapons to the ground, and finally a soft shush as he toed them out of sight under the car.

He was doing exactly what she would do…what he'd taught her to do. Disarm the mark. Safety first.

"Bend nice and slow and get the knife from your boot," he ordered. "Then toss it down."

She followed his instructions, no sudden moves. Her second knife followed the first. That was it. All her weapons gone. And he *knew* that because in the car on the way over, he'd asked her exactly what she'd brought along.

"Look at the bright side," Butcher said as she straightened and put her hands back behind her head. "At least you didn't spend the last six years on your back."

"True." Instead, she'd spent the first three of those six bruised black-and-blue while she learned the ropes, and the next three snuffing lives. But, yeah, she supposed you could call that a bright side.

From the shadows, even a thin stream of light looked bright.

Butcher nudged her forward. She planted one foot in front of the other, taking it slow, buying precious seconds as she scanned the vicinity searching for any opportunity.

Maybe twenty yards away, the gates of the cemetery loomed before her, cold iron bent and twisted into intricate swirls. Beyond them was a narrow road flanked by grass, and by graves and stones and statues. The place was perfect, a cemetery forty minutes east of Toronto, run by management that tended to cut corners. There were no neighbors, no guards or dogs, and few working overhead lights.

"Between you and me, Butcher, isn't there another way? Maybe I take an extended trip to Tahiti? Maybe we both do? Always wanted to see Tahiti."

There was no other way. She knew that. But she had to ask. Had to try. She didn't want this to end with a corpse.

"Wish there was, girlie. Wish there was." Butcher nudged her forward with a shallow jab of his gun. Then he kept talking, uncharacteristically chatty. "You pissed off the wrong people, Naph. Called attention to yourself." He paused before continuing sorrowfully, "You screwed up big time."

*Screwed* being the operative word. She'd been hired as a Topworld assassin, not a whore. But when she'd declined Xaphan's prettily worded suggestion that she join the ranks of his concubines—*When I tell you I want to fuck you, bitch, then you get down on all fours, forehead to the floor, and say "thank you" and "how hard?"...or better yet, say nothing*—she'd left herself open to the worst sort of reprisal.

Xaphan was an Underworlder, a lesser god, the keeper of the furnaces and the braziers that light the lakes of fire. He had a chip on his shoulder the size of the pyramids. He was sulky and mean when he didn't get his way, and she'd thwarted him.

Which meant that out of the laundry list of names she could come up with of people who might have hired Butcher to kill her, Xaphan was coming up as the asshole most likely to take slot number one. Partly because she'd refused to take his jobs on an exclusive basis, but mostly because he was a petulant toddler who'd been denied the toy he wanted: her.

Nice one. Hire her own mentor to off her. A move like that took real class.

Butcher laid his fingertips on her shoulder as they walked toward the gates, a fleeting touch. "You were a good one, Naphré."

There was genuine emotion behind his words, and that just made this whole situation all the more bizarre. In his own way, Butcher cared about her. She knew that. So why was he pointing a gun at her head?

Because business was business. With Butcher, that was the *real* rule number one.

"A good one." She laughed, the sound scraping the quiet night, dull and dry, her breath showing white before her lips. "Naphré. My name. That's what it means, you know. Goodness."

"Goodness." Butcher grunted. "Another time, that'd actually be funny."

Yeah, it would be.

"Naphré…always thought that didn't sound Japanese."

"It isn't." Her Egyptian mother had chosen the name. Her *issei*—first-generation Japanese-American—father had allowed it, but insisted on a good Japanese middle name: Misao.

Perfect. Her name meant goodness, loyalty, fidelity. And her dad and grandfather had spoon-fed her the whole duty-above-all-else mentality her whole life, fostering some major shame and humility issues. As to her mom…well, from her mom she'd gotten the duty to the Asetian Guard that she'd denied. How was that for a craptastic combination?

Butcher had no clue. In all the years they'd been together, the most intimate conversation they'd ever had had been about the rash he got on his ass from the sand fleas on a Dominican Republic beach.

"Hnnn." Looked like Butcher had run out of words. He sighed, nudged her again, trying to get her moving. "I really am sorry about this."

"So'm I, Butcher." Because she *had* been a good one: he'd told her often enough that she was the best student he'd ever had. Ingrained humility kept her from completely believing him, but she knew she'd been good enough to suck up his lessons like a sponge and add a few fun twists of her own. Still, she'd never made the mistake of getting cocky. There was always something more she could learn.

Naphré took a few more steps, then stopped walking and stared straight ahead. There was nowhere for her to go; the gates before them were locked. Butcher was going to have to do something about that if he wanted to keep moving.

Breath suspended, she waited, waited...

The pressure of the barrel changed, a subtle shift. Her one chance. She moved. Spun. Dipped. Squatted low when he'd expect her to go high. Elbow ramming hard and sharp and clean into his nuts.

Butcher wheezed and doubled over. Fired once. But she was already moving, arcing back. The bullet whined past her head, close enough that it took off a lock of sleek, brown-black hair. From the corner of her eye, she saw it fall, felt it slither across the back of her hand.

*Kuso.* She'd dropped a fortune on this cut.

She swung and cracked him on the ear, open palm, speed and power. Enough to make him dizzy. Enough that he hesitated a fraction of a second before pulling the trigger a second time.

And that was enough for her to close her hand over his and change the trajectory of his shot by millimeters. The bullet was so close, she swore she felt it fly past her cheek.

Curling her fingers, she clawed at his skin, tearing bloody runnels in his flesh as she bounded back to her feet. He hissed, but held tight to the gun.

He backhanded her with his free hand. The force of the blow made her head snap back and her lip split.

But it wasn't enough to make her lose her hold. This was war. The prize was the Glock. And life.

With a snarl, she raised her knee toward his already abused privates, but he twisted to block her and she hit the side of his thigh instead. He made a sound of pain, but didn't back off.

He punched her, aiming for the underside of her chin. Moving on instinct, she deflected his fist, slammed his wrist a second time and a third, even as his fist skidded along the angle of her jaw.

Pretty stars and sharp pain.

Pulse racing, she kept her grip on the gun, rammed the heel of her palm into the underside of his nose, driving upward. Something crunched and his blood gushed over her fingers.

Another slam to his wrist and the gun tore free.

It jumped from her grasp like a freshly caught fish and she fumbled before she managed to get a solid grip.

Panting, adrenaline surging, she danced back several steps, beyond his reach.

That had been his mistake. He'd stood too close. He'd given her a chance. She had no intention of offering him the same.

But her instincts were screaming. Had he stood just a little too close? Had disarming him been just a little too easy?

Butcher was on his knees on the cracked concrete of the parking lot, swaying slightly, palm pressed to his ear, blood flowing from his nose over his lips and down his chin. His pants soaked up water from the shallow puddles, remnants of the storm that had howled through hours past. And he watched her, eyes narrow and cold. He would kill her if she let him.

There was blood on her tongue. Hers. Not his. She would never be that stupid. Swallowing human blood that wasn't her own was the last thing she ever intended to do. Six years ago, she'd chosen to leave the Asetian Guard, the secretive, elite organization that protected the interests of the Daughters of Aset and, when absolutely necessary, stepped up to protect mankind. She'd walked away from her heritage.

One mouthful of Butcher's blood—anyone's blood—and everything she'd done since that moment would all be for nothing.

And it was too late, anyway. Even a bucketful of blood wouldn't save her from the debt she owed.

She spat, then swiped her sleeve across her lower lip. The taste lingered.

If she lived through this, she knew what she'd be having for dinner tonight.

Steak. Closer to raw than rare.

The thought made the mark she'd carved into the front of her left shoulder tingle and burn, and the hunger in her belly twist and writhe.

Silently, she cursed the Asetian Guard for what they'd done to her. Choices made based on lies and obfuscation didn't count as *choices.*

*It is your duty, Naphré Kurata.*

Oh, yeah. They'd played the duty card, the perfect incentive for a kid who was half Japanese, raised by a traditional father who'd come to the States as a baby, and a doubly traditional grandfather. Duty, honor, humility. She was infused right down to a cellular level.

It had nearly killed her to walk away from her duty to the Asetian Guard. But what had followed had been worse.

"Tell me who hired you, Butcher." She was breathing hard, her heart slamming against her ribs, but her hand was rock steady as she leveled the Glock at his head. The iron grillwork of the cemetery fence threw barred shadows over his features. "Who wants me dead? Tell me, and I'll make it quick…" *Stay quiet, and I'll make it last.* He knew she would. Knew she could. After all, he'd taught her exactly what to do.

"You always was my best girl, Naph."

She knew that later she'd remember those words and the way he said them—a poignant combination of pride and resignation. Affection and acceptance.

But right now, she didn't dare buy into it and lower her guard. Maybe the hint of emotion was real. Maybe he faked it to lull her into complacency. When this was all done, the scene cleaned spit-shine perfect, the body buried, she'd pull the memory out, play it over and over, and let herself feel like shit. But right now, she'd do what she had to do.

"Tell me. Give me a fighting chance." She offered a faint smile. "For old times' sake." When Butcher stayed silent, she prodded, "Who hired you? Was it Xaphan?"

She'd learned never to assume anything in this business. Maybe it was someone else who wanted her dead. Over the years, she'd pissed off a few of the Underworld gods and demigods. Asking questions. Refusing the jobs that were just too crappy even for someone like her. She didn't do kids or teens. She didn't do parents in front of kids or teens. And she researched every job before she took it, making certain that she was satisfied with her choice. Basically, she stuck to killing killers.

But it seemed no one liked an assassin with scruples.

"It wasn't who you think. Not anyone you've done a job for." Butcher paused, then tipped his head and met her gaze, his expression blank. "You make it quick, Naph. I don't wanna hurt. That's what it's all about, you know?" He stared hard at her, and she had the strange thought that he was telling her something important. "I'd have made it quick for you," he finished softly.

He would have. She knew that.

"Yeah." Her voice was steady, her hand steadier.

He licked his lips, a quick, nervous dart of his tongue. "It's not an Underworlder."

Interesting.

"A Setnakht."

Even more interesting. The Setnakhts were a cult, offshoot worshippers of Sutekh—the überlord of chaos and evil. She'd never had any direct dealings with Sutekh. Not even indirect ones that she knew of. He had his own army of enforcers. Soul reapers who could pass between the mortal world and the realms of the dead. They harvested darksouls to feed Sutekh's insatiable appetite. And they harvested the *Ib*—the heart—of each victim to pacify Osiris and Anubis and the scales of truth.

"Why would Sutekh want me dead?" And if he did, why hire Butcher? Why not send one of his soul reapers to claim her? Surely he could have spared one for such a small task.

But the soul reapers had been occupied lately. Someone had butchered one of their own. Rumor had it they'd skinned the reaper and sent the tattooed skin, stretched in a shiny black plastic frame, to Sutekh as a gift. If the rumor was true, the reapers' energy was probably focused on figuring out the who, why and where. Was that the reason they'd gone looking for outside help with a kill? Hired Butcher?

"Didn't say nothing about Sutekh. He's got his own legion. He don't need the likes of me." Butcher coughed, turned his head and hawked a wad of phlegm on the ground. "I said it was a Setnakht."

"Okay. Let's say Sutekh isn't involved. What makes the Setnakhts want me dead?"

Was it personal? Had she killed someone connected to a Setnakht?

Suddenly it hit her. Bruised ego? No. Couldn't be. But it was the only connection she could come up with. She'd had lunch with some guy she'd met at the gym, Pyotr Kusnetzov. He was lean, handsome, attentive. He said all the right things. Smiled at the right times. She vaguely recalled a mention of the Temple of Setnakht. He'd wanted her to come to meetings, and he'd wanted to see her again. She'd declined. Not her type.

Was that what this was about? He wanted her dead because she wasn't interested?

That would be…insane.

Butcher shrugged. "Don't know. Didn't ask."

In all likelihood, Butcher honestly didn't know. His personal motto was: directions, no questions. He was only interested in the pertinent points, the ones with direct relation to the kill. Everything else was background noise. Clutter. He liked clients to tell him only what he needed to know and nothing more. And the reason behind the kill wasn't relevant in Butcher's mind.

It was one point they disagreed on. Naphré preferred to know that she wasn't offing the good guys.

Butcher didn't care, so long as he got paid.

"You taking this job… It doesn't make sense, Butcher." That was another thing he'd taught her. Things had to make sense. Naphré believed people always had reasons for the things they did. Motivations.

Usually simple ones. Greed. Hunger. Lust. So what was *his?* Why take a contract on her? "Why'd you take this job?"

"If not me, someone woulda." Butcher coughed. Spat. "They offered a nice, tidy sum. Man's gotta think of his retirement."

"Greed?" She shook her head. "I'm not buying it. Try again."

He snorted. "Ain't lust."

Yeah, she figured. Her coloring wasn't to his taste: dark brown eyes, straight brown-black hair. And she was too young—26—too tall—five-seven—too flat— her physique more athlete than porn star. Butcher liked them blonder, shorter, rounder and older. Which suited her just fine because apart from being almost twice her age, he was about as attractive to her as a slug.

"Does my motivation really matter?"

Not so much.

"That Setnakht that hired you…he got a name?" She huffed out a short breath. "Even better…a phone number?" She raised her brows. "Address?"

"Maybe a Web site?" Butcher offered a wheezing laugh at his own joke. The laugh turned into a bout of coughing that had him doubled over. When he got it under control, he continued, "Nah, not that I know. But *she* was high in the organization."

"She—?"

"Yeah. She. Had the signet ring of a priest. Onyx and gold. A scarab beetle with hieroglyphics underneath."

That information perked Naphré's interest. Pyotr had worn a ring like that on his pinky finger. She'd noticed its unusual design, but hadn't been interested enough in him to ask about it.

"And she had the bald head," Butcher continued. "Completely plucked eyebrows. No eyelashes. Not a single hair on her that I could see. Not even a nose hair. Dark eyes. Olive skin. I'm guessing not more than forty—" Butcher gave a lopsided leer "—'cause her tits still looked perky. She wasn't wearing no bra."

Trust Butcher to offer that pertinent observation.

"I was supposed to incapacitate you, then call her. I think she wanted to kill you herself. Told her I don't work that way."

Why would a Setnakht priest want her dead? And why would she want to handle the details? They were questions Naphré intended follow up on after tonight.

Butcher was giving her more than she'd asked for. More than he had to, given the situation. But he knew the score. One of them was going to die here in the cemetery parking lot with the moonlight casting long shadows and the smell of the earth, wet and rich, rising from beyond the iron fence.

She stared at him and blinked, wondering if maybe he'd meant it to be him all along. The thought came at her out of nowhere.

Nah. Butcher wasn't that selfless.

As though he knew what she was thinking, he said softly, "I woulda taken the shot, Naph. If you didn't manage to get the gun, I woulda made it clean, then buried you—" he jutted his chin toward the fence and the rows of stones that caught the moonlight, gleaming like teeth "—in an open grave they gonna put a box in tomorrow morning. Best place to bury a corpse you don't want no one to find—"

"—is under a corpse they expect to find," she finished.

His gaze flashed to hers. "Only one of us going home to watch *CSI* reruns tonight."

"I know," Naphré whispered.

Surging to his feet faster than his bulk ought to allow, Butcher lunged for her, limiting her choices. The gleam of a knife caught the moonlight.

Surprise bubbled and hissed. Not for the attack, but for the weapon of choice.

Everything seemed to move far slower than it should. The force of his leap propelled him forward. His hand brought the blade level with her heart.

And she thought, *Damn. Butcher never carries a knife.*


HE KNEW ONLY DARKNESS and pain.

Nothing else.

Not name or place. Not memories or dreams.

Rolling onto his side, he gritted his teeth against the agony that ground like glass shards into his muscles, his joints, even the marrow of his bones. Such pain was outside his experience. He felt as though he were starving, not just in his belly, but in the cells and tissues that formed him.

How long had he been like this?

Minutes. Centuries.

He had no way to know.

*Lokan.* A word without meaning sparked, then faded.

He reached inside himself, trying to form coherent thoughts. It was there. The wisp of awareness danced just beyond his reach. He tried to grasp it, to contain it.

Yes.

*Lokan.* The word did have meaning. His name. Lokan Krayl.

He had memories, a past that he felt he ought to know, if only he could scrape aside the layers of dust to find it.

He pushed up until he sat. At least, he thought he did. The place that held him had no such limitations as direction or space, and he was left disoriented, unable to differentiate up from down.

*The place that held him.*

Reaching out, he groped for the walls that were not walls, the bars that had no substance. Or perhaps he was the thing that had no substance.

He was a prisoner. He thought that he had tried to escape many times, and he had failed.

Panting, he fought against the crushing fog that obscured any spark of certainty. And then he saw it: a boat to cross the river Styx. A boat and a ferryman. There but not there.

So what *was* there?

He scrubbed the heels of his palms against his eyes. At least, he thought he did. He felt nothing save pain, endless pain.

"Push me, Daddy. Push me higher." The voice was sweet and high and happy. So happy. A little girl on a swing, squealing with joy as she flew higher and higher. His little girl. He missed her. His daughter.

But she was safe. Somehow, he knew she was safe. He'd done that one thing right. He had sent her to his enemies to keep her safe.

He frowned, certain that was wrong. But it wasn't. His enemies were the only ones who could keep his daughter safe. He'd sent his daughter to the Otherkin, to the Daughters of Aset.

*Dana*. Her name came to him with stunning clarity, so bright and wonderful it sliced through him, making him gasp. In his mind he saw every detail of her sweet face and denim-blue eyes, wide and trusting and full of love.

They were together in the sunshine. They were laughing. Then she was gone.

With a cry, he reached for her and found only darkness, and a spark in his core. A spark of memory.

There were others he cared about. Others he must warn. Dagan. Alastor. Malthus. His brothers. Cold dread unfurled in his belly as he thought of them. Dread *for* them, or *of* them?

Even in his confused state, he knew that made no sense.

He focused his thoughts on them, willing them to feel him through their blood bond. They had a connection, not a true ability to hear each other's thoughts, but an ability to sense when one was in pain or in danger or distress.

The knowledge made him cringe. They would have felt his death in vivid, brutal detail. Each slice of the knife. Each drop of blood.

Death.

Was he dead?

He thought he might be, thought he might have forgotten and just drifted here in the dark. How long? How long had he drifted?

Long enough that he'd forgotten his brothers, his father. His daughter's name. Until now. Now he remembered so many things.

He remembered that his daughter had been there the night they took him. That somehow he had saved her. He remembered that they'd taken him away, hooded, bound, his power held in check. By what? What would have made him, a soul reaper, son of Sutekh, the most powerful deity in the Underworld, so weak?

His own will.

He had chosen to give his life for hers. It was the only way. He had saved his daughter. He had sacrificed himself to keep her safe. And he had spared her the horror of witnessing what they had done to him.

Faced with the same choices, he would do it again.

He remembered their hands. Gloved hands. Knives. Blood. The smell of it. The taste of it on his lips. His blood.

Now, he pressed the flat of his hand to his chest, certain of what he would find: a gaping wound, the skin stripped from the surface of his muscle.

But he felt nothing. Nothing at all.

Who had taken him? Who had marked him and cut him? He knew their faces, human and supernatural, alike.

Rage came at him, a bitter, burning tide. He had been betrayed by his own kind.

*Gahiji.*

The name echoed through his thoughts. And the face. He remembered him. Gahiji. His father's trusted minion. Such treachery. Sharp as any blade. Gahiji had been there the night he was tattooed and skinned.

He thought he could feel their hands on him still, their knives, cutting only deep enough to separate skin from fascia.

They'd caught his blood in an oblong bowl. The image was sharply inscribed, clean about the edges, far clearer than his other thoughts.

He could *see* that bowl, and the hands that held it.

A ring. A scarab beetle. He knew that sign... He reached for the knowledge, but it hovered just beyond his reach, curling away like smoke, replaced by the vivid image of knives. Two of them. The blades black, dripping blood. His blood. His pain. Dripping in fat, red drops.

Had his brothers felt his pain? Had they known?

He could not feel them. Not now. Not then.

There had been someone behind him. Someone watching. Who? He could not see, though he struggled and writhed. That voice. He knew that voice. Horror congealed in his gut.

Betrayed, yes. By Gahiji. But not only by him.

He thought of his brothers, and white hot panic flared.

Urgency made him move, made him cry out in frustration and—

The memories sputtered and died.

And he no longer remembered names.

Not even his own.

## CHAPTER FOUR

*Asa no kougan, yuube no hakkou.*
A rosy face in the morning, white bones in the evening.

—Japanese proverb

NAPHRÉ DIDN'T STOP to think as Butcher came at her, knife raised, the long blade catching the moonlight. She took the first shot in the instant between inhale and exhale, the second partway through the exhale. Butcher's Glock Model 23 held thirteen rounds and one in the chamber. He'd let two go wild earlier. Now, she used two more. Double tap.

One shot to the forehead, leaving a neat, small hole. In the front, at least. The back would be messier. Second shot to the chest, maybe seven centimeters to the left of midline, the bullet slamming through muscle, tearing apart his left ventricle.

His whole body went rigid, then went down in a crumpled heap.

She allowed herself a single, slow breath. In through her nose. Out through her mouth. Grief or guilt—or whatever the hell that ugly knot in her chest signified—would come later. Not now. She couldn't afford to let it tear free now.

Survival of the fucking fittest.

Squatting by Butcher's side, she checked the carotid pulse. First on the right, then on the left. Nothing. Dead. Gone to…where?

She didn't even know who'd have a claim on him. Osiris? Hades? Satan? Maybe Hel, the Norse goddess of the dead.

Maybe no one.

Maybe he'd go to purgatory. Maybe he'd get eaten by Ammut and go nowhere.

Maybe. Maybe.

Didn't matter now. She was alive and he was dead.

She'd made her choice. Had she made any other, she'd be lying on the ground with all her sphincters released. She knew where she'd have headed then, straight to the demon that owned her soul, and that wasn't anywhere she wanted to be.

A quick rummage through the pockets of the shabby, old-school overcoat Butcher favored and she had his wallet, his cell, and…perfect: his car keys. Inside pocket. Right where he always kept them.

His car, a nondescript gray sedan, was parked at the opposite end of the lot. She jogged over, got down on all fours, and peered beneath. Her Glock and her knife were exactly where he'd tossed them, inches apart. Her second knife was about a foot away, near the rear tire. After settling her weapons back where they belonged, she tucked Butcher's gun in her belt, then popped the trunk.

It was neatly organized, and it didn't look much different than the trunk of her own car, a black Mini Cooper S with a white roof and stripes. There was his emergency suitcase, packed and ready to roll. A sleeping bag. A plastic bin containing water bottles and non-perishables. Butcher's idea of non-perishables was a massive bag of cheese puffs, some chocolate bars and a container of peanuts. Naphré went more for energy bars.

Off to one side was a shovel. That was Butcher. Always prepared.

So why was he dead while she was still alive?

A creepy sense of foreboding skittered across her skin, and her head jerked up. She took a slow look around, feeling like something was about to crawl out of the woodwork.

Squelching her unease she grabbed the shovel, slammed the trunk and walked briskly back to the body. For a second, she just stood there, looking down at him.

Butcher wasn't a small man. He'd had a fondness for meat-lover's pizzas and greasy onion rings. And an even greater fondness for the free weights he found at the gym. Which made him a daunting combination of muscle and fat. More than a couple of hundred pounds of it on his 5'8" frame.

From the way he'd behaved earlier, nudging her toward the gates, she figured his plan had been to make her walk to the side of an open grave, shoot her there, roll her in. That's exactly what she'd have done, given the choice. But she hadn't had that luxury. She hadn't been willing to risk walking Butcher all the way to the grave. There were too many things that could have gone wrong. Too many ways for him to turn the tables once more.

Besides, he'd pulled a knife and gone for her. That hadn't left her with much choice.

Which meant she was going to be working up a sweat.

Lifting her head, Naphré studied the stretch of empty road, the iron grillwork fence, the graves beyond, making certain there were no prying eyes. It was full dark, and there wasn't a whole hell of a lot of light here, just the moon when it peeked from behind the clouds, and a couple of working streetlamps far up the road. There weren't many places for someone to hide. She was as certain as she could be that no one was out there, despite the creepy sensation she'd experienced a few moments ago.

Supernaturals were less of a problem to detect than humans; they gave off some kind of energy vibe that felt like static electricity lacing the air. At least, that's what her sixth sense perceived it as. Humans were another thing entirely. She had to rely on good old sight and sound to pin them down.

She glanced at the shovel, then at Butcher. She needed both hands for this task. After a second's contemplation, she hauled on his belt to make space and thrust the shovel down his pants so the handle lay against his leg. Then she shoved her forearms under his armpits and started duck-walking backward, dragging him until her butt hit the cemetery gates. They were chained shut and locked.

Blowing out a breath, she dropped Butcher and turned to grab hold of the chain. She brought the butt of the gun down hard, then yanked on the lock. No luck. With a shrug, she shot it. No need to worry that anyone might hear. If the place was any more isolated, it'd be orbiting Mars.

She hauled open one side of the gate. The squeak

was like something out of a low-budget horror flick. Of course. This night demanded nothing less.

As she turned back toward Butcher, her senses sharpened and she froze. The wind carried a sheet of newspaper across the deserted road. It danced and swooped, but that wasn't what had caught her attention. There was something else. Something...

A shiver crawled up her spine on a million hairy little legs. She couldn't shake the feeling that someone watched her, and she couldn't forget what Butcher had told her about the Setnakht priest wanting to be there when he delivered the kill shot.

Her imagination was running wild. She didn't need this now.

The wind died and the paper fell flat.

Nothing else moved. Not even her.

Finally, she hauled Butcher's shoulders up once more and dragged him into the graveyard, pausing only long enough to nudge the gate shut with her foot. Just in case.

The narrow, paved road wended into the cemetery, past a willow tree, up a softly rolling hill. She paused. Cursed. Fucking hill. There had to be something closer. Butcher wouldn't have planned to walk her that far, and Mick had said there would be at least two open graves to choose from.

Mick...had he been in on this? Had he known she was the mark even as he handed her the envelope of cash?

Glancing around, she saw a much more appealing option than the hill. Maybe twenty yards in, set between two massive granite monuments, was an open hole just waiting for a casket.

Naphré headed for it, forearms looped under Butcher's armpits, posture hunched as she shuffled backward toward her goal.

Butcher weighed a ton. Growing heavier by the second.

She was out of breath and her arms were starting to feel the burn.

*Want some poutine, girl?* She blinked. Buried the memory. Butcher had loved his poutine. Among other things.

Why did he have to go and pull a gun on her? And a knife? Why the fuck?

Affection wasn't his forte—or hers—but taking a contract on his protégée? It made no damned sense.

But there were a lot of things about Butcher that hadn't made sense lately. A few weeks back, he'd insisted on doing a hit alone. Said he didn't want her with him. She'd been curious enough to wonder, but not enough to press the issue. Once in a while, Butcher had preferred to fly solo, likely because he was on a job he'd known she would turn down. Her scruples made her a bit more finicky than him.

The thing was, her gut told her something had gone wrong that night. Butcher hadn't been the same since. More paranoid than usual. More secretive. He'd said something about a temple and a sacrifice. And one night, after a full bottle of Crown Royal, he'd mentioned a name: Frank Marin. And something about Krayl, which could be a person, place or thing. He hadn't been in the mood to play twenty questions.

She'd been curious enough to do a little digging. Turned out, according to the Internet, that Krayl could be a lot of different things, including a starship commander in an online role-playing game set in the twenty-third century, a college basketball player or a demon. She hadn't been able to turn up much info on the demon. What she'd come up with on Marin hadn't offered any answers, either. He was scum. He'd done time in Australia for molesting kids. And recently, he'd turned up dead, killed in some seedy motel in Texas.

Had something gone wrong the night Butcher did that solo hit? Had Frank Marin been part of that? An accomplice? Not likely. If Butcher had wanted company, he'd have taken Naphré.

A witness?

Maybe. Probably. But at this exact moment, it really didn't matter. Right now, what mattered was cleanup.

She settled Butcher on the grass, and peered into the hole. There were bugs in there. The kind you could see—worms, maggots, centipedes—and the kind you couldn't—bacteria, fungi: saprophytes that thrived on dead flesh. She was okay with the former. Not so much the latter.

It was the bugs too small to see that always got you.

Touching her pocket, she felt for the mini bottle of hand sanitizer she carried with her wherever she went. The squared-off shape was oddly reassuring.

She grabbed the cold metal handle of the shovel and dragged it out of Butcher's pants. Then she squatted, rested her free hand on the edge of the grave, and hopped in.

Squelching her reservations about playing in the dirt, she worked quickly, methodically, digging down an extra few feet. Within minutes, she'd built up a sweat despite the cool temperature.

TWENTY MINUTES LATER, Naphré stood the shovel in the corner, clambered out and squatted by Butcher's side. With a grunt, she rolled him in. He hit bottom with a thud, sending up a small geyser of clods of damp earth. Then he lay there, arms at awkward angles, legs tangled, eyes staring unseeing at the blue-black sky.

Naphré stood looking down, panting, feeling like her lungs were wrapped in metal bands, or maybe it was her heart. It hurt. And she didn't want it to.

She sighed, then went back into the hole. Legs spread, she straddled Butcher's corpse, hesitated, and finally shook her head.

*"Kuso,"* she whispered, though she wanted to shout.

She tugged on Butcher's arms and legs. Rigor mortis wouldn't set in for a while yet, so he was still pliable and it took little effort to arrange him like he was sleeping. Better. But…

Bending over, she reached down and closed his eyes. Her hands were cold, his skin colder still.

She needed things. She knew that. Things to ease his way. God, she never thought about this stuff. She just did the job and moved on. But this wasn't a job. This was different.

Shoving her hand in her pocket, she rummaged for coins. Came up with three dimes and a quarter. Not enough. She needed six coins for the River of Three Crossings.

Bad enough to bury him like this. She wasn't sending him anywhere without those damned coins.

With a grimace, she went through his pockets once more. Nothing.

Okay then. Okay.

Ah. The inside pocket of his coat. And there they were. A handful of nickels and dimes. She couldn't recall exactly where they were supposed to go, but she knew he'd need two coins for each crossing, so she chose six dimes and tucked three under each palm.

Good…but not enough. She remembered something about putting a knife on the deceased's chest to keep away evil spirits, so she took the knife Butcher had tried to kill her with and laid it on his sternum, then clasped his hands over his chest, rearranging the coins to again lie beneath his palms, and finally, turned his head to the north.

Closing her eyes for a second, she tried to think of more funerary customs she'd witnessed. She knew the body was always washed and the orifices plugged with cotton or gauze. Yeah…not gonna go there. What else?

A hazy memory came to her of her great-aunt's burial, the casket, the dry ice, the traditional white kimono, leggings and sandals. There was nothing she could do about those. But a white headband was doable. Hunkering down, she used her own knife to slice away a length of Butcher's white shirt and folded it neatly, pinching the cloth between her fingernails to set the seam. It needed a triangle, dead center, but she didn't have a pen. She had no wooden tablet to inscribe his *kaimyo*—his posthumous name that would prevent his spirit from returning every time his name was called— and she had no way to cremate him, so burial would have to do.

Straightening, she glanced at the dirt she'd dug up already, piled in the corner of the grave. Best to finish the task and get going. She dug in and tossed shovelfuls over him, each one a layer between him and the world. She couldn't help but picture him the way he would look in hours…days…weeks. He'd turn first green, then purple and finally black. His body would bloat, his eyes bulge. His skin would blister and slough off. The bacteria in his gut would digest him from the inside out—

Bile burned the back of her throat, and she had a fleeting, horrific thought that she'd be sick.

She hadn't puked since her first kill, when she'd shot a man who in turn had shot many men—innocent men. She'd expected Butcher to rail and rant as she'd run from the body and fallen to her knees, retching and heaving.

Instead, he'd held her head and patted her back.

Tears stung her eyes at the memory.

This was not a good night. Not good at all.

Reaching into her pocket, she took out the bottle of hand sanitizer. Squirt. Rub. Rationally, she knew it wasn't going to wash away a damned thing. But as the last of the alcohol evaporated, she tipped her head back, stared up at the sky, took a couple of deep breaths and felt marginally better.

She killed people for a living. Didn't matter that she took only the jobs that didn't break her own code. She killed people. So what the hell was she doing feeling ill over a corpse? Butcher would have killed her if she hadn't killed him. She didn't doubt that for a second.

Disgusted with herself, she went back to hefting dirt. Once Butcher was covered, she patted everything down nice and tidy until the grave looked exactly as it had before she'd dug up the bottom.

She hauled ass out of the hole and rose, staring down, wondering if she ought to say something. A prayer. Over the body of her teacher. Her mentor.

The man she'd just killed.

Words danced through her thoughts, a series of ink-blots with meaning only if she bestowed it. And then they coalesced into some semblance of order. *The Lord is my shepherd, I shall not want. He maketh me to lie down in green pastures: he leadeth me beside the still waters...*

That was it. That was all she remembered.

They weren't the right words, anyway. Not for Butcher. He wasn't a fan of green pastures and still waters.

So she whispered something from the Egyptian Book of the Dead, instead. Two of the forty-two declarations of purity, ones she thought were fitting.

"He did not rise in the morning and expect more than was due to him." That was true enough. Butcher had been suspicious of everything. He hadn't trusted luxury or wealth. Hadn't trusted technology. He hadn't expected more than was due him, because he'd thought life was out to screw him, and he'd thought getting screwed was his due. "He has not brought his name forward to be praised."

"Tsk. Bastardizing the Book of the Dead?"

She had the Glock out and leveled in the direction of the clipped, masculine voice before she finished turning. Time enough later to wonder how he'd managed to sneak up on her unheard. Right now, she just needed to have him in her sights.

Only he wasn't where he was supposed to be.

He wasn't anywhere that she could see. There were

only shadows and grass and the swaying branches of the willow tree.

She scuttled back, behind its thick trunk, her gaze flashing from headstone to headstone, her gun tracking the same path.

"I wouldn't bother." His accent was English. Maybe. Or South African. Australian? Any or none of the above. But it definitely wasn't local. "With the weapon, I mean. You'll find it of little use."

So her gut had been right. She had sensed someone watching her earlier, but she hadn't felt electricity dancing along her skin then. She felt it now—a shimmer in the air, like a breeze towing in a storm, electric, wild—and realized he was right. She might as well put away the Glock. That voice didn't belong to anything human.

Which meant that a bullet might hit him, tear through skin and muscle and bone, but it wouldn't kill him. Probably wouldn't even slow him down.

She wasn't liking this situation. At all.

The night shifted, dark on dark. But he stayed hidden, blending with the shadows of one of the carved granite monuments. Which one?

"Come out where I can see you," Naphré crooned.

"Not quite yet." He gave a low laugh that echoed off the stones. "Why don't you step into the light where I can see you?"

"Not quite yet," she countered, and shifted deeper into the gloom.

He laughed again. Not a nice sound, more menace than mirth. It touched a nerve, making her feel predatory and aggressive and just plain pissed off. She tightened the noose on her baser instincts and focused on staying cool and logical. She had a feeling she'd fare better if she used brains over brawn.

"No matter," he said. "I can see quite well in the dark."

Of course he could. It was just that kind of night.

Who was he? Not one of Xaphan's lackeys. They were invariably female…unless Xaphan had hired outside help.

"You a demigod?" she asked. Any tidbit of information just might save her life.

"Not exactly." Neat, tidy consonants and vowels. Enough to allow her to pinpoint his location. There, beside the tall, narrow stone with winged angels carved on the sides. For all the good that did her.

"An enforcer?"

"In a manner of speaking." She could hear the hint of amusement.

The sensation of static electricity was crawling all over her now, and she decided she couldn't have missed it earlier. He must have dampened it somehow while he'd watched her bury Butcher. The possibility made her wary.

"I'm not playing your game," she whispered. She slid her gun into its holster, crossed her arms over her chest and said nothing more, only stared into the shadows that cloaked him. Then she saw the glitter of his eyes as he stared back.

"Bored already?" He stepped forward, away from the looming granite monument. "You have the attention span of a flea."

She'd have snarked back at him, except she was too busy mentally smacking herself in the head. It was the guy from outside the Playhouse Lounge.

Moonlight spilled over him, highlighting honey-blond hair. It was thick and expertly cut, neat and short except for straight, longish strands in front that fell to his cheekbones, framing an angular face. His arms were loose by his sides, his legs shoulder-width apart. Tall. Maybe six-one or six-two. There was a masculine grace to his posture. Deceptive. Dangerous.

A killer in a sleek designer suit and pristine white shirt. Open collar. No tie.

How had she read him as human last night? The electric charge he was generating now marked him as anything but.

"Not a demigod or an enforcer…" Which didn't leave a whole hell of a lot of choices because not many supernaturals could pass Topworld at will. He definitely wasn't a fire genie.

Which left only one being that could travel unhampered by rules, mute his supernatural vibe and pass undetected at will. Crap. "You're a soul reaper."

He inclined his head. "Excellent deductive reasoning."

There was definitely amusement in his tone.

"I'm not thrilled about being the butt of whatever asinine little joke you're enjoying," she said.

"Ah, but it is exactly your butt that I find so enjoyable."

She was actually speechless.

"Noticed it last night," he clarified. "Wasn't expecting to have the fine fortune to see it again, though."

She regained her voice. "Dick."

"Actually, no. Name's Alastor Krayl." He tipped his head to the side, studying the shadows that masked her.

*Krayl.* Her breath stopped. Person, place, or thing?

Guess now she knew. Krayl was a soul reaper.

There she'd been, not an hour past, wondering about Sutekh and the dead reaper, having no clue what the night would bring.

"You're not just any reaper. You're one of Sutekh's sons."

He didn't answer. Instead he asked a question, velvet soft. "What do you know of Sutekh, pet?"

*Kuso,* she knew better than to blurt her thoughts aloud. The fact that she'd done so only spoke to the shape she was in. This was definitely not a good night.

"I know he's the most powerful Underworld lord."

"Some would disagree on that point. Osiris, for instance. But Sutekh would be pleased to hear you say it." He paused. "Are you a Setnakht? Is that how you know his name?"

She swallowed, debating what would serve her better, truth or lie. Truth won. It would explain how she knew of Sutekh and soul reapers and Underworld lore. "I'm a Topworld enforcer."

"I know." His reply sent a chill crawling up her spine. She didn't want him to know a damned thing about her. The fact that he did was horrifying.

Was he here to kill her?

Fast as she was, she could never outrun a supernatural of his power. So she held very still as he prowled toward her.

Not strong enough to kill him. Not fast enough to flee.

But maybe smart enough to swing a deal. All she

needed to do was figure out why he was here. What he wanted.

Not her death.

At least, she didn't think so. If he'd wanted her dead, why not kill her when he first showed up? Right after she'd plugged Butcher. Or even last night when she'd brushed past him.

Clarity dawned. He hadn't known last night that he was after her, not until he'd gone inside the club and learned whatever it was he'd learned that had set him on her tail.

She tensed as he continued walking, thinking he meant to come for her, but he veered off course, away from the tree and her, toward the open grave. He bent and lifted the shovel, then turn to look at her once more.

His eyes were…blue? Gray? She couldn't tell from this distance in this light.

"Do you mind?" he asked, extending the shovel toward her.

*Mind what?*

"Surely you don't expect me to climb in there—" he waved the shovel toward the grave "—dressed like this?" There was an odd note to his question, almost a challenge.

What? He expected her to dig another hole? One where he could bury her after he ripped her heart out?

He made an impatient sound and answered the question she hadn't asked. "I hardly need to bury you, pet."

"Don't fucking call me *pet*."

He smiled tightly, his features accented by moonlight and shadow, his eyes cold enough to cry ice cubes.

"Foulmouthed little girl, aren't you? *Pet.*"

He wanted to get a rise out of her, and she meant to disappoint him. Pets had claws and teeth and tempers. She just needed to bide her time until she hit the right moment to show him all three.

He moved incredibly fast, beside the grave one second, right in front of her, a hand span away, the next. She didn't flinch, didn't even blink. If he meant to intimidate her, he'd have to do better than that.

Keeping her expression neutral, she met his gaze. Blue, she realized. His eyes were blue, framed by thick, curled lashes. The color was indescribable, like the turquoise and lapis lazuli in the ornate necklaces her mother had given her years ago. Her mother had called the color *wedjet.* Naphré still had those necklaces, but she never wore them. She didn't favor jewelry. Probably because her mother *did.*

"If I wanted you dead," he murmured, "you would be." *No doubt about it.* "And I'd simply leave you where you dropped. Unlike you, I have no reason to clean up after myself. Mortal laws are of little concern."

Wasn't he chatty? He'd just revealed a whole lot more than he'd probably meant to, lovely tidbits for her to store away for future reference, most important of which was the fact that if he didn't want her dead, then he wanted her alive.

Looked like they shared the same goal there.

"So what *do* you want?"

He smiled, baring white teeth and carving a long dimple in his left cheek.

"I want you to dig up the bloke you just buried."

It was her turn to laugh. "Why the hell would I do that?"

"Because he has something I need."

So he wasn't here for her. He was here for Butcher. Too late.

She shoved her hand in her own pocket and drew out Butcher's keys, cell and wallet. "I already emptied his pockets. Other than some change, this was it. Here. You can have them."

He didn't so much as glance down. "Those are not the things I need."

"Then what?"

Two vertical lines formed between his brows as he stared at her. She thought he looked more perplexed than annoyed, as though he wasn't used to questions.

Glancing down, he thrust the tip of the shovel into the ground and settled one foot on it, hands resting on the metal handle. Elegant hands, with long, strong fingers.

"He saw some things of interest to me—"

"Not like he can tell you about them." She flashed a too-sweet smile. "He's dead."

"His darksoul can speak volumes," he said softly. Then he looked up at her, all expression wiped away, his features a mask. "I'll need that, along with his heart."

Something about the way he said that made Naphré shiver. She shot a look at the open grave.

"Butcher's dead. I shot him—" she made a show of looking at her watch "—a little more than half an hour ago. Through the heart." He knew that, though. He'd been watching her for quite some time. "Which means his heart's probably not in particularly good shape."

"No?"

"Not unless you're looking for ground meat." She doubted there was much left of Butcher's heart. Then a thought struck. "Why the hell did you let me bury him if you were just going to make me dig him up again?"

The reaper's gaze roved restlessly over her features, to her neck, her breasts, her toes. And back again.

He held her gaze, and for an instant, she was snared in a world of deep blue. There were only his eyes, and the racing of her pulse, and while she told herself it was adrenaline stirred by the fear of being hunted by a reaper, a part of her thought maybe it was something else.

A sharp kick of awareness hit her, and a tingle danced through her. Attraction. To a soul reaper.

She huffed out a breath.

And here she'd thought this night couldn't get any worse.

"I like watching you move," he said.

"You—" Her eyes flashed to his. She clenched her jaw tight.

"Dig him up," he said, tossing the shovel at her feet.

There you go. The night *could* get worse.

"You'd best pray his darksoul is intact and that there's enough of his heart left to satisfy my needs, Naphré Kurata." He waited long enough for her to assimilate the fact that he knew her name. Crap on toast. "Unless you'd like to substitute yours?"

## CHAPTER FIVE

ALASTOR WATCHED NAPHRÉ doff her jacket, fold it neatly in half, shoulder to shoulder, and set it on the ground by the grave. Her brown-black hair gleamed in the moonlight, falling forward against her neck in a neat, blunt line as she moved. The little bumps of her spine caught his attention, and he wanted to trace his fingers from her skull, down along those bumps.

She was beautiful.

That was the second thing he'd noticed about her.

The first was her arse. Her high, round, gorgeous arse. He'd noticed it last night at the Playhouse Lounge. He'd stared at it in silent appreciation upon his arrival at the cemetery tonight as she recited her bastardized version of the declarations of purity.

He pushed the flap of his jacket aside and thrust his hand into his pants pocket. He couldn't remove the temptation, but he could control his reaction to it.

His reaction to her had been out of proportion since the second he'd laid eyes on her. Like a split lip he couldn't help but touch his tongue to again and again even though he knew he oughtn't.

Bad analogy. It made him think of touching his tongue to her.

She stared at him, her eyes so dark he couldn't discern between iris and pupil.

There was a knife at the small of her back, a gun in a holster under her arm, and a second one tucked in her belt. They posed little threat to him, so he didn't bother to take them away.

"Not interested in my weapons?" she asked.

"You won't get them free before I can disarm you." He paused, debated whether or not to finish the thought, then said, "And even if you do, you can't kill me." A warning, of sorts.

"Yeah. I figured."

"Then why ask?"

"You know what they say about assuming things."

Actually, he didn't.

She stared at him. Her shirt fit her like a second skin, long-sleeved, high-necked, black with a thin white stripe that followed the contours of her torso and arms. She rolled her shoulders and put her hands on her hips. Her movements made the cloth draw tight across her breasts. Nice, plump, round, not too large. A perfect handful. He could see the outline of her nipples, erect in response to the cold night air. He could almost feel them on his palms.

He fisted his hands in his pockets.

Lifting one hand, she snapped her fingers, and said, "Eyes up here."

He raised his gaze, then dropped it once more.

Her shirt was torn at her left shoulder, baring a section of skin.

Pretending that it was where he'd been looking all along, he dipped his chin toward the white logo that stood out against the black shirt. *Sugoi.*

"You're a runner."

"Am I?"

He'd bet she was, among other surprising things. He wasn't getting any sort of supernatural vibe off her. She was reading as strictly human. But the tear in her shirt revealed the lines of a raised scar that suggested otherwise. It wasn't a haphazard mark, but a specific design: an ankh with wings and horns. And it meant this entire evening had just taken on a whole new layer.

That mark—cut into her skin, etched there by her own hand—claimed her as Otherkin, a Daughter of Aset. Its presence raised a slew of questions, including what she was doing taking contract kills for Xaphan or some Topworld grunt rather than pledging her skills to the Asetian Guard, the elite forces of the Daughters of Aset.

Aset—Isis—was an ancient Egyptian goddess. Her Daughters were born to females of her line. Few knew insider details about them. They were secretive and private. But thanks to his brother's relationship with Roxy Tam, Alastor knew enough to recognize the mark, to know what it meant. Naphré Kurata wasn't just a Daughter of Aset, she was a blooded member of the Asetian Guard. They were the only ones who carved the mark in their skin, the only ones who took first blood and became pranic feeders, sustained by the life force—the blood—of others. They could feed without killing. And they usually fed from humans.

The Otherkin had been Sutekh's enemies for at least six thousand years, which by extrapolation made Naphré Alastor's enemy.

"Not one for chitchat?" He dipped his chin toward the grave. "Get busy then, pet."

"You're an asshole," she muttered.

"Blimey—" he layered his hands against his heart in mock dismay "—you cut me to the quick." He dropped his arms and hardened his tone. "Dig."

With one last, withering look in his direction she hopped into the grave and dug.

Her movements were spare and clean, and her running gear clung to her like a second skin. A good choice of apparel for her evening's activities. It wasn't confining. It'd be cool or warm as the situation demanded. She knew what she was about, this girl. She was prepared. He didn't know why that surprised him, why she surprised him.

The bugger in the back alley behind the Playhouse Lounge had offered up Butcher, telling Alastor where to find him, and hinting that his sidekick might be hanging about. But he hadn't shared all the information he could have because he hadn't said a word about the sidekick being a dark-haired, sloe-eyed, lean, mean distraction who'd pegged her own mentor through the head and the heart.

Peering over the side of the grave, Alastor said, "You're a cold-hearted one, you are. Figured you could kill him and take his jobs? Your own mentor? Or did someone hire you to do it?"

She stopped shoveling, but didn't look up at him. "Who said I was hired to kill *him?*"

Alastor digested that. *She'd* been the mark, and she'd managed to turn the tables. Funny, Mick hadn't said a word about that, either. "So the student surpassed the teacher. He ought to be proud."

"I'm sure he would be if he wasn't dead." Flat tone. Harsh words. She gave nothing away, but something made him suspect she didn't feel as unemotional as she appeared.

Then she went back to work, thrust and heft, her muscles moving with easy synchrony beneath her clothes.

He wanted to skim his palm up the swell of her calf to the curve of her thigh, and higher, to the smooth globe of her arse, and he wanted to do it skin to skin.

Bloody hell.

Glancing away, he scanned the vicinity, got his thoughts under control. The *chook* and *shush* of her shoveling provided a hum of background noise.

A couple of hundred years ago, he might have felt an avalanche of guilt for letting a lady sweat while he stood idle. He'd been raised in the sort of home where social calls and taking tea and handing a lady down from a carriage were the norm. The woman he'd believed to be his mother was the youngest daughter of a baronet; the man he'd believed to be his father was a baron. He'd sipped the milk of chivalry from a silver spoon, learned the intricate dance of upper-class manners when he was still in knee britches.

It was a world he'd left behind the day Sutekh blew in like a storm and tore it to shreds.

In *this* world, he felt not even a faint spark of guilt.

Taking his time, he studied the trees, the headstones and the narrow road as it disappeared over the hill. Then he turned to the cemetery gates and evaluated the road beyond. There wasn't much to see. Nothing but flat grass on either side that eventually fed into mixed forest.

Good cover for whoever was out there.

And there *was* someone out there. A human. Whoever it was had been watching Naphré since before he'd arrived.

He'd lied to her, of course. When she'd asked why he'd let her bury Butcher if he was only going to make her dig him up again, she'd clearly believed that he had been the one watching her all along. But the truth was, he'd only just arrived when she started her bastardized recital of the Book of the Dead. Whatever she'd sensed or suspected, he wasn't the cause of her hairs rising at her nape.

The human in question was perhaps a quarter mile off, settled comfortably in a tree, watching them through some sort of apparatus. Binoculars. Or a rifle scope.

Alastor wasn't concerned. Bullets weren't much of a problem for him, and as for Naphré, well, he could always get his answers from her darksoul if she were killed.

Oddly, the possibility didn't appeal.

"Who knows you're here?" he asked, reaching into his pocket and withdrawing an English toffee caramel. He unwrapped the candy, popped it in his mouth and shoved the wrapper back in his pocket.

She paused, tipped her head and turned it enough to shoot him a sidelong look through her thick, straight lashes.

"You. And some guy by the name of Mick, my liaison for this job." She paused and tapped the tip of her finger against her cheek. "Oh, but you already knew that. Because Mick's the one who gave me up, isn't he?"

"Actually, he gave up your companion. He barely

mentioned you at all. Called you 'the sidekick.' Mentioned that if I'd only been a few minutes earlier, I'd have run into you. I didn't bother to tell him our paths had crossed."

She nodded. "Is he dead?"

"When I left, he was alive and bleeding."

"Good." She hefted the shovel and slammed it into the earth. "Because I'm going to kill him myself when we're done."

Undoubtedly. But Alastor had a feeling someone else would beat her to it, the someone who'd sent Mick out as emissary in the first place.

A COUPLE OF MINUTES LATER, the shovel clinked against metal, likely a belt buckle. Naphré reached and stretched to stand the shovel in the corner, then got down and used her hands to swish the remains of the dirt to the sides, baring the dead man's torso.

"This good enough? Or you want me to haul him out of here as well?" Her tone was cold, unemotional, but he sensed the rage and resentment seething beneath the surface. And something else. Grief? The possibility surprised him.

Alastor leaned over the edge of the grave and saw that she'd bared most of Butcher's upper body. Certainly enough that he had access to his chest. Interestingly, she'd left the man's face covered.

"Good enough."

She nodded, rose and took a step back so she straddled the mound that covered Butcher's legs. There was a hill of dirt on one side of the grave where she'd piled it as she dug, making the confines down there uncomfortably tight for the task Alastor meant to perform.

Her expression cool and remote, her thoughts veiled, she looked up at him. He could guess that she was thinking she'd like to shoot him. Or stab him. Perhaps dismember his twitching corpse. Not that he blamed her.

"You have..." He made a vague gesture toward his own cheek.

She didn't blink, didn't move, but something shifted in her expression, so subtle he almost missed it. Slowly, she raised her hand to scrape her fingers along the delicate arc of her cheekbone, leaving not one, but three, neatly aligned smudges.

Her gaze dipped to her filthy hands and her eyes widened a fraction.

Tucking her chin, she rubbed her shoulder along her cheek, then looked up at him, eyes sparking with hate. Alastor figured it might be best not to mention the fact that the three neat lines were now one big, brown blotch.

Instead, he glanced into the grave, then down at his Italian loafers. The idea of climbing into the dirt didn't appeal, but he couldn't imagine how she'd drag the body out. "Shove over."

"Don't say you're planning to come down here with me." She glanced first at the damp earthen walls, then the partially uncovered body at her feet.

"The thought pleases me even less than it apparently pleases you, but I don't see an alternative. The body won't simply fly up here, will it?"

"What, your powers too paltry to levitate a corpse?"

"Telekinesis isn't in my repertoire." He arched a brow. "Yours?"

The tip of her tongue peeked out as she wet her lips. He watched the motion, thinking that he'd like to put his tongue where hers was.

She waved a hand to encompass the grave. "There isn't enough room. Let me get out first."

He kept his expression carefully blank and slowly shook his head.

To his surprise, she smiled. Close-lipped. No teeth. It struck him that the situation didn't call for a smile. Then he noticed her dimples. One in each cheek, peeking out at him like a gift. A man could be blinded to almost anything by that smile.

He supposed that was the point.

But her eyes didn't smile. They remained flat and cool and unreadable, like the dark surface of a placid lake with endless depths. Who could know what lurked in those depths?

Still, he stared at her for a second too long. Because she was truly lovely and there were so few lovely things in his life anymore.

The thought startled him, and he shifted back from the edge of the grave as though even a small increment of distance would rein in his wayward musings.

"Come on. Help me out," she said, impatient. She extended her right arm toward him.

"'Fraid not, pet." He was genuinely regretful. The confines were tight, he'd be the first to admit, and he had a feeling that getting all up close and rubby against her was a very bad plan. But he couldn't see an alternative because it was a given that the second he hauled her topside, she'd be out of here like a bat out of hell, and he wasn't quite ready to send her on her way. "No doubt you'll just give me your word that you'll wait up here like a good girl while I finish my business down there. But I have a bit of a problem with trust. Especially when it involves one of Aset's Daughters. You're a tricky lot, you are."

At his mention of Aset, she slapped her palm against her left shoulder.

"How—" Cutting off her own question, she composed her expression to give nothing of her thoughts away. He found her startlingly adept at that.

It clicked then. She wasn't pleased that he'd recognized her for what she was.

Interesting.

"What do you know about Aset's Daughters?" she asked.

"Not a great deal, other than that you're enemies of Sutekh." He studied her expression for any reaction to that, but she offered none. "Oh—" he snapped his fingers "—and my brother's bloody well shagging one of you." She winced. He supposed she wasn't fond of his word choice. "Her name's Roxy Tam. Know her?"

"No."

Now why did he think she was lying? He'd barely gotten the question out before she'd rattled off her answer. "Maybe know *of* her?"

She said nothing, which told him he'd hit the mark.

Distant, muffled footsteps alerted him that their mysterious voyeur was on the move, and trying to be subtle about it.

Naphré's posture tensed, her chin kicked up and she turned her head slowly from right to left. He wondered if it was just gut instinct making her wary, or if she was actually able to hear the footsteps. As a soul reaper, he had all sorts of tricks up his sleeve. As an Otherkin, did she?

He glanced over his shoulder and caught a split-second reflection of moonlight on metal. A gun, a zipper, a knife. The source didn't matter, the fact that it gave away the location of their uninvited guest did.

"I asked you earlier who knew you were here," he said. "You weren't exactly forthcoming, but it looks like whoever it is, they've decided to move. Which means I'm about ready to wrap things up."

With a pang of regret for his shoes—they were less than a week old—he leaped into the hole, crowding Naphré to one side, his chest to her back, her wonderful arse pressed against his groin.

She made a strangled sound of affront, which only goaded him to loop his arm around her ribs, just beneath the swell of her breasts, for no damned reason, other than he wanted to.

He expected a struggle, but what he got was the reaction of a professional. Tension hummed through her body as she stood rigid against him, waiting for his next move so she could counter with one of her own. Her head was cocked, as though she listened for any sound. Same as him.

But there was no sound. He hadn't expected any. Whoever was out there was in surveillance rather than attack mode.

He could feel the steady beat of her heart against his wrist.

He could smell her hair.

Leaning closer, he inhaled. Floral…but not really…. He brushed his cheek against the top of her head and breathed in again. Maybe fruity…it made him want to bury his face in her hair and just smell her for a while.

The urge passed when her head snapped back toward his face. He saved himself from a bloody nose only by the grace of inhumanly fast reflexes. But the head-butt was only a distraction. She pumped her hips forward, then back in a move that might have been construed as suggestive except for the fact that she employed significant force, akin to a battering ram. Her bum slammed him hard enough to shove him back against the earthen wall of the grave. He bit back a curse as he felt the earth's moisture seep through his clothing, ruining his suit.

But she wasn't done with him. Her heel hit his instep like a sledgehammer.

Damn it to bloody hell.

"Do whatever the hell you need to do," she ordered, her voice low and diamond hard. "Then get the hell out of here."

"Giving orders, pet?" he whispered against her ear.

"Tired of taking them. You want me dead, kill me. You don't kill me…then get the fuck out of my space."

"Such a potty mouth."

"Potty—" she turned her head to glance at him over her shoulder "—asshole. The two seem like a natural fit."

He could think of other things that would be a natural fit.

"Right, then." Catching hold of her wrists, he shifted her away from him. Earth sifted from the wall and pattered down as her shoulder hit the side of the grave.

"Squat," he ordered, his voice low.

She glared at him, dark eyes glittering, jaw set.

"Now if you keep looking at me like that, pet, I'm going to take umbrage. One would think you disliked me." He jerked her wrists forward and swept one leg sharply against the backs of her knees, hard enough to make them buckle. She went down with a huffing exhalation.

He expected her to swear, maybe to struggle a bit. It made him wary when she did nothing more than stare straight ahead. She was on her knees on a corpse, her arms extended above her head because he still held her wrists trapped in his hand, and she was regal as a bloody queen.

For some reason, it made him feel about an inch tall. She was the one who'd shot the last living witness who might have helped him find Lokan's remains. All he was doing was looking for answers. And feeling like a right bastard for doing so.

Not wanting to examine that feeling too closely, he shifted his grip so he held both her wrists in one hand. He spread his legs so he straddled the corpse's shoulders, and bent. Their faces were inches apart. He could feel her breath on his cheek.

For an endless second, he held her gaze, staring into her night-dark eyes. Beautiful eyes, even when she was glaring daggers sharp enough to draw blood.

He'd gone bloody daft. He was hunkered here in a wet, stinking grave, straddling a corpse, thinking about shagging the girl. The attraction was about more than her lovely face and sleek build. She fascinated him for some bizarre, inexplicable reason.

What had turned her into a killer?

The question brought a wry twist to his lips. Perhaps something similar to what had turned a titled lord into one. Heritage. Duty. Blood.

He had no business wondering about her. Or wanting her.

Bloody sodding hell.

He needed to finish his business here, take the dark-soul to Sutekh, then head home for a hot shower and a visit with Mary palm and her five sisters. That ought to settle the problem quite nicely.

With a sound of impatience, he looked down at the body, clawed his fingers, then rammed through muscle and bone. Butcher's chest tore open with a squelching sound.

A sharp hiss exploded from Naphré's lips, then she took a slow, deep breath, but she said nothing.

Alastor wiggled his fingers. Dead flesh, even freshly dead flesh, felt different than living muscle and skin. It was colder. The blood didn't run freely. The heart didn't pump.

As a rule, he did his reaping from the living. At least, they were alive until he got done with them. Robbing a corpse of heart and darksoul just didn't feel…sporting. But this situation broke the usual rules. Ends justify the means, and all that.

Reaching deep into the chest cavity, he felt around for the heart.

He glared at her as he hauled it out, tearing it free from the tether of the great veins and arteries. The left ventricle was pulp. "Blimey, it's chewed up more than a bit. Like a pound of mince."

"Mince?"

"Ground meat."

"I warned you." She gave an elegant, one shouldered shrug.

"Maybe I should be looking at you for answers, then, pet."

*"Hatake kara hamaguri wa torenu,"* she said softly, and smiled, curved lips, cold eyes. He wanted to lean in the last inch, press his mouth to hers, melt the ice.

He forced himself to lean back an inch. "Explain."

"You cannot take a clam from a rice field."

"Is that anything like *you can't get blood from a stone?*" He was practically snarling, and he couldn't fathom why he allowed her to get under his skin. He never let anyone get under his skin.

She took her time answering. "Exactly like."

He had the odd sensation that she was laughing at him. He didn't like it. He wanted her cowed and—

No. The second the thought formed, he recognized it for the lie it was. He didn't want her intimidated and afraid. He preferred her strength.

Bloody illogical. A cowed foe was an asset, a strong one a detriment.

"Not afraid of me, pet? Not afraid I'll take your immortal soul?"

Her lips parted. He thought that finally she understood her position. No such luck. She exhaled on a short huff of laughter.

"Forfeit my soul," she murmured, and jerked her wrists from his grasp. Since there was no longer any reason to keep hold of her, he let her go. "You might have a fight on your hands, *Alastor Krayl*." She said his name like she was tasting it, rolling the flavors on her tongue. "There's a prior claim. Might makes right." She paused. "Just how powerful is a soul reaper?"

Someone else had a claim on her soul, which meant he couldn't steal it.

"I assume you refer to your obligations to Aset."

"You ever hear the old adage about making assumptions?" Her tone held a tinge of bitterness. "Ass. U. Me. Get it?"

Actually, no. But he was interested in a different question at the moment. "If not Aset, then who?"

She didn't answer. He hadn't really expected her to.

"You owe me a shirt," he muttered.

"Excuse me?" Her tone dripped ice.

"You owe me a shirt. Got blood on this one." He made a gesture toward his stained cuff. "If I wasn't so busy making certain you didn't run off, I'd have two hands free and the job would have been far less messy."

Not waiting for her reaction, he reached into the gaping hole he'd made in Butcher's chest, let his thoughts coalesce and his energy focus.

In the distance he heard a sharp clap of thunder. He froze, glanced up. The sky was clear.

He refocused on the body, noting as he did so that the thunder seemed to have agitated the arthropods that lived in the soil, because they were crawling out of the earth. Centipedes. Insects. Worms.

A second clap of thunder followed the first, closer, angry, the sound unnatural. It left him feeling vaguely uneasy.

It must have affected Naphré in a similar manner. Her head tipped back, her gaze focused on some distant spot, and he could see she was funneling all her attention to listening for a repeat of that sound.

When the night stayed quiet, he returned to his task, summoning the darksoul to him. It came, cold and slippery, writhing into his hand and up around his forearm before slithering higher to caress his shoulder.

He was glad to see it. Given how long the body had been cold, there had been a moment or two when he wasn't so certain the darksoul hadn't left on its own journey to the Underworld, somewhere beyond Sutekh's reach.

Butcher knew things, had seen things the night Lokan was killed. Alastor felt certain of that. Unfortunately, he had no way to communicate with the darksoul directly. That was Sutekh's job. He was just the messenger service.

He tethered the oily, amorphous cloud with a band of pure energy that served as a harness. The darksoul writhed and twisted just above his left shoulder, jerking at its bond as though it understood its fate—to be consumed by Sutekh as a meal of pure power. To be robbed of any hope for rebirth and future life.

Thing was, this soul wasn't as dark as he'd hoped. Butcher might have been a killer, but he'd done some good in his wasted, mottled life, because there was still a hint of shine on him. Normally, this wasn't a soul Alastor would have bothered with. Sutekh liked them dipped in tar, dripping malice and malevolence like ice cream melting down the sides of a cone in the sun. A soul with a shine, even a tarnished shine, was one that held little interest.

Except this soul was different. Alastor hadn't harvested it as a meal. He'd harvested it for his father to read like a book.

As he raised his head, he caught Naphré staring

at the darksoul. He was surprised she could see it. Humans couldn't. But then, he already knew she was a Daughter of Aset, which made her not precisely human regardless of the fact that she presented as one, without even a hint of supernatural vibe.

The confines of the grave kept them as close as peas in a pod.

"Don't," she whispered.

"Don't what?" His gaze dipped to her mouth.

She wet her lips. "Don't take his soul."

There was anguish in her words. Genuine pain.

"You killed him," he pointed out.

"I know."

She didn't argue her case, didn't talk about how she'd had no choice or how Butcher had gone for her first, both of which Alastor suspected to be true.

Inexplicably, he thought of wrapping his arm around her, drawing her against his chest and just holding her. Bloody strange inclination.

He reached for her, meaning to touch her, just a single, fleeting touch. He froze when his fingers were just a breath away from her cheek. Time hung suspended. Finally, he dropped his hand, and said, "Oddly enough, if I could do as you ask, I would. But your friend here has a role to play, information to share that is important to me. So I'm afraid I must decline your pretty plea."

And damned if he didn't mean every word of that ridiculous little speech. If Butcher's darksoul hadn't potentially held the key to finding Lokan's killer, he just might have done as she asked. Such was the power of those incredible night-dark eyes.

"Be careful when you leave," he said. "There's some-one else out there."

"You're warning me to be careful?" She laughed, dipping her chin again in that way that was both allur-ing and oddly out of character. A demure killer. Naphré Kurata was a puzzle, one he'd like to take time piecing together.

Or slowly taking apart.

"The someone that's out there…you mean up the road?" she asked, her tone hard. "In the tree? Rifle scope?"

"Or binoculars. That's the one. But they aren't up the road anymore. They moved closer."

"Yes, I caught that."

His gaze dipped to her mouth and lingered. Her lips parted and her breathing hitched.

"Bloody hell." He leaned in, intending to taste her, to take a kiss, one kiss, before he headed to Sutekh's realm.

Her eyes widened. Her palm came up to flatten against his chest and he could feel the beat of his own heart.

"Don't," she whispered when he was so close that he felt her breath touch his lips. And the tip of her knife pierce his skin at the base of his throat.

Nicely played.

"You're very adept with that." He drew back enough that he could see the gleam of her blade in her hand. He hadn't even noticed her pulling it free of its sheath. Such inattention was utterly unlike him. "But you can't kill me, pet. Soul reapers don't die quite that easily."

"I know. But I can hurt you." She paused. "You try to take what I don't offer, and I *will* hurt you."

He opened his mouth to point out that she had offered. Maybe not with her words, but with the parting of her lips and the way she'd looked at him. Then he shrugged. Begging wasn't his style.

"If you're saying 'no,' then no it is, pet. My loss—" he rose, reached up and dug his fingers into the loose earth at the top of the grave, then kicked a toehold in the sheer wall; just before he scrambled up, he turned to look at her over his shoulder "—and yours."

# CHAPTER SIX

IN THE ALLEY ACROSS the street from Tesso's Bar and Grill, Dagan grabbed Roxy's arm and hauled her around to face him. He kissed her, hard and fast. The air around them was cool, but her lips were warm and welcoming.

"What was that for?" She looked at him quizzically.

"Making up for lost time."

He kissed her because he wanted to, because he could, because she let him. And because he'd stupidly wasted eleven years that he could have—should have—been kissing her.

Regret wasn't his thing, but neither was repeating his mistakes.

Dipping his head, he breathed in the scent of her skin. He skimmed his hand along the curve of her waist, pausing at the hilt of her knife where it protruded from a sheath on her belt. "You're gorgeous when you're stabbing things, Roxy Tam."

"So you've said before. But I'm not planning on stabbing things tonight." She cocked her hip, her posture all sass and challenge, but her lips curved in the hint of a smile. "Unless you're expecting trouble, reaper boy?"

"Depends on your definition of trouble." He paused.

"If it involves you and me, an absence of clothing, and a bit of a tussle over who gets to be on top, then that'd be a yes."

"Do tell." She leaned in, slipped her hand under his T-shirt and raked her nails along his belly, down, down, stopping at the waistband of his low slung, soft-as-butter jeans. "Then I'd best get my business here done quickly."

Yeah. The quicker, the better. The only thing was… she was thinking in the singular, while he was all about plurals, mentally converting her *I* to a *we*. She wasn't going in there without him.

As she headed down the alley toward the street, he hung back a step or two, for the pure joy of watching her walk. Sex and swagger. Fuck, he wanted her naked again right now.

"Business first, play later," she tossed back over her shoulder.

She made it to the mouth of the alley before she stopped and turned, her bronze-green eyes widening when she saw how close he stood. "No. You are *not* thinking of going in there with me. You're supposed to wait here. We agreed."

"Not exactly. You said you were going in alone. I didn't say anything. That's a hell of a lot different than agreement."

She glared at him. He glared back.

Being in love didn't change the fact that they still had a shitload of details to work out in terms of how to make things work day to day.

When they were alone and in bed—not to mention in the shower, up against a wall, on the kitchen table or the living room floor—there were no issues. But as soon as they left the cocoon, they had to deal with the fact that he was a soul reaper, son of Sutekh, and she was a Daughter of Aset. That he was hell-bent on finding his brother's remains and bringing him back to life. That up until five days ago, she'd been a member of the Asetian Guard with the assignment of making certain that the "dead reaper stayed dead," as she'd so eloquently put it.

Just because she'd mustered out of the Guard didn't mean she could put everything she'd stood for for ten years behind her.

And he sure as sugar wasn't going to put his goal of reanimating his brother behind him.

Stalemate.

He glanced over at Tesso's Bar and Grill. There were two burly guys by the front door, picking and choosing who got to go inside.

"They'll let me through," Roxy said, following his gaze. "You, on the other hand—" she arched a brow "—probably not."

The last time Roxy had been here to see Big Ralph, a Topworld grunt who ran prostitutes for Asmodeus, the Underworld demon of lust, he'd been talking about Xaphan and some guy named Butcher.

And not an hour ago, Mal had called to tell them he and Alastor had a lead on a guy who might have seen something the night Lokan was killed. Some guy named Butcher.

Now, what the fuck were the chances? Dagan didn't trust coincidences. Yet here he was, swimming in them.

Alastor was following up the lead he and Mal had dug up, and Dagan was here to have a chat with Big

Ralph, and through him, with Asmodeus. The demon was known for his lack of loyalty to any Underworld player other than himself. He offered information to the highest bidder.

Dagan was hoping that talk would lead to something—anything—to do with Lokan.

On the other hand, Roxy was hoping—

Fuck. He had no idea what she was hoping. She expressed sympathy over Lokan's death, and he knew it was genuine. But he also knew that she had grave concerns about his brother being found and brought back to life and fingering his killers. Because that would open the door to vengeance, which in turn could start an Armageddon that would spill into Topworld and leave a swath of dead in its wake.

Roxy might not be a soldier of the Asetian Guard anymore, but she had been for ten years, and her mandate of protecting the Guard at all times, and protecting humanity when she must, wasn't going to just disappear from her psyche.

He caught her arm again. Her gaze dipped to his hand, then rose to his face.

"Let's not worry about what we're going to do with the information when—"

"If," she interjected.

"—if we get it. Let's just find out what we can and then sort it out." He paused. "I don't want you going in there alone."

"I can take care of myself."

"I know." He offered a self-mocking smile. "But I can't handle waiting here while you do."

She sighed. "At least make yourself unobtrusive."

A decent compromise. Soul reapers could bend the

bonds between molecules, refracting light and hiding themselves from sight. He'd go into Tesso's with her, but thanks to his ability to be seen only when he wished, she'd be the only one who'd know he was there.

"Disappear," she said.

So he did.

"That's amazingly creepy."

He supposed it was.

She loped across the street and stopped only when one of the two guys guarding the door stepped directly in front of her path.

"Hey," she said.

He grunted. "Surprised to see you again so soon."

She wasn't a regular, but she'd been here often enough that he knew her face, if not her name.

"Just can't seem to stay away." She shoved her hand in her pocket and came up with a C-note. He palmed it then pulled the door open as she passed. The guy's gaze never strayed from her. He had no idea Dagan was there, right behind her, a beat away from ripping out the guy's heart if he didn't stop staring at Roxy's ass.

NAPHRÉ TOOK ALMOST AN HOUR to scour the grounds and make certain there wasn't a trace left behind to link her to Butcher's death. She knew she'd done her job exactly as she always did. No one would find him. Which meant no one would be looking for her.

Still, it was better to check twice than be sorry once.

Goosebumps prickled on her skin. Her gaze flitted to the gates of the cemetery. She knew now that whoever had watched her bury Butcher the first time, it hadn't been Alastor Krayl. And whoever had watched her do it the second time…again, not Alastor Krayl. He was long gone, the electricity he generated gone with him.

But she was still being watched.

She'd caught the quick flash of metal more than once. Binoculars or rifle. Her nature made her bet on the latter, but she didn't rush the cleanup because she figured that if whoever was out there wanted to shoot her, she'd have been dead hours ago.

Guess it wasn't her night to kick up her toes.

Which suited her just fine. She wasn't in any hurry to leave this mortal coil. She'd sold her soul to a demon. Which meant that her death ensured an eternity in the Underworld, her soul bound in service to that demon.

Taking a last, quick tour around the grave, she verified that nothing was out of place. So she hefted the shovel and headed back toward Butcher's car, eyes on the ground as she followed the exact path she'd taken when she'd dragged Butcher to the grave. She'd already done cleanup here and in the parking lot. This was her final check.

Along the way, she stopped and picked up a candy wrapper. March English Toffee Caramels. She blinked. The reaper. He'd smelled good enough to eat. She'd noticed that, but thought of it only now as she stared at the wrapper in her hand. She crumpled it and shoved it in her pocket.

When she reached Butcher's car, she popped the trunk and set the shovel off to one side. Then she hauled out a rag and a water bottle. She drenched the rag and made a big show of swiping it over her hands again and again, smearing the dirt. Casually, she slammed the trunk shut, and strolled around to the side of the car, still wiping. The car window reflected the road and the trees.

Shifting her angle, she checked behind her as she poured more water, did a little more wiping. Sure enough, there was the telltale flash of metal. Whoever was watching her wasn't trained, at least not in the art of camouflage.

A moment later, there he was. Maybe five-ten. Dressed in black. He slid from behind a tree just outside the cemetery fence.

Naphré's pulse kicked up a notch. She kept her limbs loose, her posture relaxed, not wanting the watcher to know he was watched.

She unfolded and refolded the rag so a clean square was revealed and poured out a bit more water. All the while, she kept her gaze on the window and the reflection it revealed, careful not to alert her tail to the fact that he'd been made.

Her knife was at the small of her back. Going for that would be a sure giveaway. Instead, she slowly shifted her hand and closed her fingers on the butt of Butcher's Glock where she had it thrust in the front of her belt.

She could kill him. Pull the gun, spin, aim, fire. No question she'd hit him on the first try, probably kill him with the first bullet. Then she'd take a second shot just to be sure.

But killing him wouldn't get her answers. And she wanted those, so she just held still and waited for him to make his next move.

Finally, the guy shifted forward, just enough that his bald scalp reflected the moonlight. He stood very still, staring at her so intently she actually felt like something was crawling on her skin. Her muscles twitched.

She watched his hands, waiting for even a whisper of threat. But slowly, carefully, he backed away.

As he turned, he was silhouetted by the moonlight and Naphré caught a full-body profile view.

Surprise. Not he. *She.*

Her watcher had breasts.

Looked like Butcher had made that call to that Setnakht priest who'd ordered the hit, after all. Either that, or she'd shown up here all on her own.

That meant the priest knew Butcher was dead, since she'd watched Naphré shoot him. And she knew Naphré was alive. Which was inconvenient.

But inconvenience could be turned to advantage. There was opportunity here.

Options played out in Naphré's thoughts. Kill the woman. Not a good way to get answers. Confront her. A decent option, but she was mentally and physically exhausted. She wasn't on point, and that meant she might make mistakes. Better to wait. Tomorrow was another day.

As she settled behind the wheel and started the car, she mentally prepared for a late night. Shower, then computer. She had some research to do about the Setnakhts and their High Priests.

AN HOUR LATER, NAPHRÉ was bundled up in her pink flannel pajamas, her hair wet, her heart heavy. She'd shampooed twice, conditioned once, washed away the dirt, but she couldn't shake the feeling that she wasn't quite clean.

Add to that the bizarre charge that kept lifting the

fine hairs on her forearms. She couldn't seem to shake the electrical vibe that she'd picked up from the soul reaper at the graveyard. Like a part of him was still with her.

She sank down on the couch and stared straight ahead.

Butcher was dead.

They'd been nearly inseparable for six years. They'd fought and laughed and worked together.

Now he was *dead*.

And she'd been the one to kill him. Not only that, but she'd let his soul go with the reaper, to Sutekh, the Lord of Chaos, the Lord of Evil. Didn't sound like a restful eternity to her. Crap.

Like she'd had a choice. Alastor Krayl, soul reaper extraordinaire, hadn't appeared to be in the mood to bargain. And she hadn't had any leverage.

For a second, back in the graveyard, she'd considered trying to summon the creature that owned her soul, to ask him to claim Butcher from the reaper. But there had been a few problems with that plan. To summon a demon, she needed a ring of salt and candles and a splash of her blood, not to mention the thin gold engraved wafer he'd given her the night she'd made her pact with him.

There in the graveyard, she'd found herself fresh out of all required elements, except her own blood.

Besides, she wasn't certain she *could* summon him. She'd never tried. Throughout the years, she'd left their meetings to his whim, not particularly anxious to see him any more often than she had to. He'd show up at her door, he'd give her a name, she'd do her research, and he'd come back a couple of nights later to find out if she'd done the job.

Sometimes she did, sometimes she didn't. It depended on whether the potential victim met the requirements on her mental checklist.

A killer with scruples. Yep, that was her.

He'd made it clear that that wasn't actually the way he'd have liked to play it. In fact, he'd been enraged the first time she'd turned him down. He'd stared at her, his small, dark eyes glittering in the candlelight, mouth turned down in a hard line.

"You will do as you are bidden," he'd ordered in an ugly tone.

"Yep. No problem," she'd replied. "Just as soon as I'm satisfied that your target is a sleazeball. This guy isn't. He volunteers at a food bank. Gives loads to charity. Is respectful to his mother. Helped his sister out when she needed it, and let his ex keep the house and the car, no contest. He cheats on his taxes. Owes nearly three grand in parking tickets. And he uses his mother's handicap sticker to get choice parking spots. He's barely a semi-creep. I'm not killing him."

"He is inscribed in the book of debts. His soul is promised to—" Whatever he'd been about to say, he'd changed his mind and amended it to, "I *will* have his soul."

"Then you'll get it yourself because I'm not doing this job. Find me a killer to kill." She'd folded her arms across her chest and stared the demon down. "Give me the name of a shitbag and I'll do the deed. Otherwise, you're on your own."

The demon had stared at her, his lips taut and almost white with rage.

*Demon.* That was another thing. She didn't know what she'd expected when she'd sold her soul, but it wasn't some short, stocky guy who, while butt-ugly, looked perfectly human. No forked tongue or tail. No lizard eyes. Just a scary-looking guy with a big head and a sneer.

After that, the demon had started bringing her only jobs where the target was acceptable to her sensibilities.

She didn't know whom he hired to do his dirty work for the jobs she declined. Maybe no one. When she checked a few months later, the guy she'd refused to off was still alive.

Now, edgy and tense, she rubbed her palms along her upper arms. Static electricity hung in the air. It reminded her of the way she'd felt at the graveyard, and that did not make her a happy girl.

She rose, crossed to the window and twitched the curtain to the side.

Her breath stopped. Her heart slammed against her ribs.

What the hell?

The electric vibe she'd been feeling wasn't her imagination conjuring memories of the reaper being with her. He *was* still with her.

Alastor Krayl was on the street below her third-floor window. He leaned one shoulder against the lamppost, his perfectly styled honey-gold hair catching the spill of light from the overhead bulb. His shoulders looked impossibly wide, his waist trim and narrow, accentuated by the cut of his dark, single-breasted jacket. His arms were crossed over his chest, and he scowled up at her, as though his presence was her fault and he was somehow here against his will.

Above his left shoulder, Butcher's darksoul dipped and bobbed.

Unease, confusion, anger. Emotions buffeted her.

She unlatched the window and lifted the sash. Resting her palms on the sill, she leaned out.

"What the hell are you doing?" she snarled, hoping like hell her neighbors weren't awake and listening.

"You chose an odd career path, pet."

"What?" She shook her head at his bizarre observation. He was a soul reaper, and he was commenting on *her* job? "Did you follow me?" How? *Why?* She'd thought he'd left the cemetery long before she did.

He shrugged and pushed off the post. "You were being watched."

"Watched," she echoed, and stared at him uncomprehending. He came here to tell her that? He'd already pointed it out back at the cemetery.

Suddenly she had the most bizarre thought. "You followed me home to make sure I was okay? Like we were at our high school prom? You're kidding, right?"

He opened his mouth, closed it, and in his silence, she had her answer.

It appeared that she'd acquired a supernatural stalker.

"Just wanted to make certain I knew where to find you if I decided we needed to have another chat," he said, voice soft and silky, eyes narrowed, jaw set.

"Right," she muttered.

"Right," he echoed, and something—his tone, his expression, the look in his eyes—made her think he was as baffled by his actions as she was.

Without another word, he turned his back on her and walked away, the darksoul trailing behind him.

"Wait!"

He stopped, but didn't turn.

"Don't take him. Whatever you think he has or knows, maybe I can help you find it another way. Maybe—"

He spun, his expression fierce. "I can't take a chance on maybes, pet. There's the small matter of a ticking clock."

"But the clock wasn't ticking so fast that you couldn't make a detour to stand outside my window?"

"That was—" He ran his fingers through his hair, stopped halfway through the action, then lowered his hand to stare at it like it belonged to someone else. Then he turned and kept walking up the road.

"See a doctor," she called. "There are medicines that might help. Or a padded room," she finished in an undertone.

He made a circular gesture with one hand and a dark, undulating oval of smoke and fog appeared before him. She felt cold just looking at it. There were no stars. No light. Just utter and complete darkness in that hole. He walked right through it, leaving her dumbfounded, staring at the spot where he'd disappeared long after he was gone.

She was left rattled and confused.

*He'd followed her home.*

He knew where she lived.

He could return any time he chose. And for some truly fucked-up reason, that didn't scare the crap out of her the way it should.

Pulling her head back in, she slammed the window

shut, flipped the latch and stomped back to the couch. Not enough that she had to be hounded by a soul reaper. No, she had to be hounded by a soul reaper who'd lost his ever-loving mind.

She grabbed her laptop, settled in and opened a browser. Three hours later, she had a whole whack of information about the Setnakhts, including a marginal grasp of their philosophy, a list of their places of worship worldwide, and the names of the High Priests in Toronto. Pyotr Kusnetzov—funny, he hadn't mentioned his exalted position when he'd been hitting on her at the gym. And Djeserit Bast, complete with a pretty picture that confirmed her identity as the woman Naphré had spotted at the graveyard, and ostensibly the High Priest who'd hired Butcher to kill her.

She closed the browser and lifted her head. Light crept through the crack in the curtains, casting pale-gray streaks on the floor. Every bone in her body ached, she was that tired. Tired in heart and soul and body.

One last task. She opened a new browser and checked her e-mail.

Her breath hitched and an icy chill touched her skin. There was one message in her inbox.

From Butcher.

Of course. How could this night be complete without a message from the dead?

Torn, she almost closed the browser. Almost didn't look.

Then she did, because she couldn't help it.

There was nothing personal there. Not a word. Not even a signature. Just a link.

She copied the link, pasted it into a new browser, and waited while it opened.

It was a medical site. Frowning, she leaned forward, eyes locked on the screen.

*Extensive small cell lung cancer.*

She shivered, suddenly chilled clear to the bone.

Metastasis. Treatment. Symptoms. The information was all there. She scanned it. Twice. The words were like little black bugs crawling on the screen, the form and meaning refusing to register.

And then she fixated on one section. Prognosis: poor.

*I woulda taken the shot, Naph.*

He would have. She didn't doubt that for a second.

But he'd counted on her to get the gun, counted on her to make it clean and neat and fast. Rather than slow and horrifically painful, lying in a hospital bed, his dignity tattered.

He'd taken the hit on her so she'd have a reason to kill him.

Damn it.

Damn *him.*

She closed the laptop with meticulous care and set it aside, then she sank back against the cushions, gut churning.

Letting her head drop into her hands, she did something she hadn't done in six long years.

She cried.

## CHAPTER SEVEN

*The Underworld, the Territory of Izanami*

"I WILL TAKE ONE HUNDRED SOULS for the one he stole from me," Izanami said, her voice soft and controlled, her rage like ice. She could hear the footsteps of the thunder deities echoing on the stone floor behind her, but she neither glanced back nor paused. They would match her pace; they would not fall behind.

Once, Izanami had been the Goddess of Creation. Now, she was the Goddess of Death, and Yomi-no-kuni was her realm. It was a place of shadows and darkness, an underground labyrinth fed by a raging river, blocked from the human world by a massive boulder that even the most powerful men or machinery could not move.

She had come to love Yomi's darkness, to cherish it.

For it was light—and a man's inability to keep his word—that had stolen her sole opportunity to return to the world of the living. That man had been her husband, Izanagi. He had come for her after death and he had promised not to look upon her, to allow the darkness to veil her from his sight until she could seek audience and free herself from the realm of the dead.

He had lied. He had conjured light in a place meant

to know only shadow, and upon seeing what she had become, he had fled. He had left her here.

She had trusted no man, whether mortal or supernatural, since.

"One of Sutekh's spawn took the soul."

She did not slow her pace as she asked, "Spawn? Not merely a soul reaper, but one of his sons?"

"Yes. I saw him myself. I warned him off. A single clap of thunder, and when he did not heed me, a second. Either he chose to ignore the warning, or he did not recognize it for what it was."

That stopped Izanami in her tracks. "Not recognize it for what it was?" Could that even be possible? Could the reaper have been unaware that the soul belonged to her? Could he have failed to understand the warning?

Despite her rage at having been robbed, she had to admit the possibility. She was confined to her realm, Sutekh to his. They did not mingle, and her minions knew as little of Sutekh's ways as Sutekh's likely knew of hers.

Years ago, she had done him a service, bringing to his attention a plot hatched by a pack of demons to infringe on his territory. In the centuries since, they had existed in uneasy truce because of that sole action, though she had not done it out of loyalty or friendship. She had done it for political gain, to ensure that though her loyalties lay with Sutekh's enemies, she herself was not regarded as an enemy, but rather as a distant and cool acquaintance.

In repayment for the forewarning she had given, Sutekh had offered her a boon all those years ago. She had yet to claim it.

Outside of that single event, they did not interact. Their minions did not interact, save for the rare political foray. She had sent an emissary to him a time or two, and his son, Lokan, had come to her on occasion. But that was the extent of their dealings.

Izanami had had quite her fill of males who lied and betrayed and failed to keep their word. Moreover, she had had quite enough of men who expected a woman to stay quiet and meek in their presence.

Look where such behavior had landed *her*.

The first time she had mated with Izanagi, her husband, she had been lured by his handsome looks. She had run to him and commented on his great beauty, speaking before he did. Her actions had caused the greatest deities to curse them. They had insisted that she must be docile, be silent, let Izanagi speak first or their mating could never be successful. Young and foolish, she had denied her own strength, denied her nature, and allowed herself to be subjugated.

She'd had thousands upon thousands of years to wise up since then.

Given her experiences, she preferred to ally with Osiris rather than Sutekh. At least he showed a measure of respect for his sister wife, Aset.

"Mistress," one of her servants whispered. "If the soul reaper was unaware, and no insult intended, perhaps it would serve you best if none were taken." She paused, then finished in a rush, "The grand meeting of allies is less than two weeks hence."

Izanami turned and waited for the girl to say more. She liked to weigh all views with unbiased care before making her final decision. So she spoke now without rancor or heat, and with genuine interest. "The soul of

Crandall Butcher belongs to me, not Sutekh. He was buried according to my custom, given coins for the River of Three Crossings, his soul pledged as mine. Do you disagree?"

"No, Izanami-no-mikoto."

Izanami noted the accord in her words, but in the hesitation and deference of her tone she heard all her servant did not say. The girl was uncertain, unwilling to overstep her position. She was fairly new to the Underworld, still finding her place. Izanami wished to draw her out; she wanted the opinion of one bold enough to speak. There was often wisdom to be found in the thoughts of others. It was no hardship to listen to varied perspectives before stating her own.

"Sutekh's soul reaper harvested both heart and darksoul, neither of which were his to take," Izanami said. "If I tolerate that insult, then I show the face of weakness to my enemy." She kept her tone low and even, allowing none of her rage to color her words. Her fury was not directed at this hapless servant, but at Sutekh's minion, the soul reaper who had stolen what was hers.

In truth, even he was not deserving of her wrath. It was Sutekh himself she must chastise.

"You may speak your mind without fear of repercussion," she urged when the girl held her tongue. "You believe I should deny my claim to the soul?"

"No, Izanami-no-mikoto."

"Postpone my claim?" What could possibly be in this child's mind? If the girl did not clarify her point soon, Izanami would move on.

"I believe you should have the soul that was stolen. But instead of rallying the thunder gods and going to battle, send an emissary to Sutekh and ask for what is yours. Present a logical argument rather than a threat."

*Ask.* A novel idea.

"Tact and politics," Izanami mused. Then she took the girl's point one step further. "And logic." That was a weapon in itself. Sutekh fed on malevolence and chaos. If she went to him with rage, geared for battle, it would only make him stronger. If she approached with calm deliberation, it would offer him no sustenance.

Which might well enrage him.

"A volunteer?" she asked, knowing there was a strong possibility that whomever she sent might never return.

*The Underworld, the Territory of Sutekh*

ALASTOR PAUSED ON THE sandstone gallery, wondering what the bloody hell he'd been thinking. His task successfully completed, the darksoul harvested, he'd meant to leave Naphré to rebury the corpse. Instead, he'd stayed and watched the High Priest slink from the shadows at the edge of the graveyard. Watched Naphré spot her, evaluate the threat.

Though he'd quickly ascertained that she needed no help from him, he'd been loath to go. In fact, he'd followed her home, and he had absolutely no explanation for the why of that.

Butcher's darksoul bobbed and twisted on its leash of fire just above his shoulder, then dipped to touch him before rising once more like a gas-filled corpse in a shallow pond. The damp chill of it settled on his skin even through his jacket and shirt as he studied those in the courtyard below, letting the angle and the shadows veil him. The line of supplicants snaked through the courtyard, then spilled beyond the walls to the rolling dunes of the desert sands. They were souls in search of entry to the afterlife and lesser deities who wanted to beg a boon of Sutekh.

He wondered if the souls understood the price.

Most of them would be denied entry. They were the lucky ones, sent off to roam the lakes of fire for eternity.

The unlucky ones would be lured by whatever guise of beauty Sutekh chose to don that day, they would be beckoned closer and offered soft words and encouragement. In this realm, Sutekh allowed them corporeal form, and they invariably took mistaken comfort in the familiar. They would pledge themselves to their own vile fate with willing lips and full hearts. They would think they had done something wonderful.

It was not that pledge or even the subterfuge of Sutekh's promises that sat heavy and ill on Alastor's shoulders. Truth was, Sutekh would choose to ingest only those with darksouls that were evil to the core. Hence, whatever fate they received was the one they'd earned.

No, it was the doom the unwitting fools heaped upon those they left behind—children, lovers, friends— adding names and generational debt to be inscribed in Sutekh's book. They doomed them just by uttering their names.

It was *that* betrayal that Alastor felt like a knife because once, a very long time ago, he had had a human family: father, mother, sisters and a horde of nieces to whom he played the doting uncle. Alastor had believed that the humans he left behind when Sutekh came for him had been the warranty of his cooperation in the early years, held in peril should he fail to follow Sutekh's will. That if he behaved, they would be allowed to finish out their mortal lives in full.

He'd been so foolish then. So naive.

In point of fact, Sutekh had never made that threat, or that promise. Not directly.

Time passed differently in the Underworld and Alastor's mortal family had been dead and buried for decades before he understood he'd been duped. He'd never seen them again.

He'd accused Sutekh of both lies and betrayal. In retrospect, he was surprised that he'd been that brave. Or perhaps only that stupid. But then, in the early years, when he first discovered what he was and what was expected of him, he had wanted to die.

But Sutekh had not granted him that. In his soft, calm voice, he had pointed out that he had offered a warning about the passage of time. Alastor had just been too new to the Underworld to understand exactly what it was that his newly discovered birth father was telling him.

Alastor pushed aside thoughts of the past. He was about to turn away from the stone balustrade that offered the perfect view of the line of supplicants when he caught sight of a figure, veiled and gloved and draped entirely in what appeared to be gray velvet. The woman—for despite his inability to discern either face or figure beneath the drapings, her movements made him believe she was female—was striding briskly up the line toward the front. She did not pause or look to either side, though the souls in line spoke out against her rapid progress.

She was not tall, not intimidating in size, and she made no menacing gestures. In fact, she appeared to completely ignore those she passed.

Yet they recoiled from her.

Not in fear, he realized after a moment. In disgust. Their revulsion was clear in both expression and body language. Even the lesser deities appeared repulsed.

His curiosity piqued, Alastor held his place and watched her approach. Once she paused, and her head tipped back. Her head was completely covered, so he could not see her eyes, but he knew she looked directly at him. Her glance pierced him. The sensation was chill and dreadful, not cold like fresh snow or clean ice. Not cold and clammy like the darksoul he held tethered, but rather like a slurry of fetid water that had stood through the winter then begun to rot at the thaw.

As she approached the gallery, the smell hit him so hard that he almost gagged. She smelled like rot, like fish left out in the heat for days, or like meat in a fridge that had lost power. The odor was so powerful that it was more than smell. He could taste it on the back of his tongue, and when he held his breath, it seeped through his pores into his skin.

She was directly below him now, and he saw that her raiment was not cloth at all, but a writhing, living drape of all manner of spiders and centipedes, insects and maggots that moved and shifted on her body, completely obscuring face and form. A veil and dress made entirely of crawling things. Even her hands and feet were obscured.

Or perhaps there were no hands or feet or face.

Perhaps the layers of writhing insects and arachnids were all that covered her bones.

He'd never encountered anything like her, and from the looks on the faces of the souls, and even the minor deities waiting in line, neither had they.

Her attention shifted to the barricaded gates that fronted Sutekh's palace. She was mistaken if she thought to enter his realm ahead of those who patiently waited their turns. Six servants guarded the gates, six of Sutekh's legion, souls who toiled tirelessly in the hopes of some day abasing themselves before their master and being offered the ultimate role of soul reaper.

They were fools. Their bodies had rotted long ago. There was no vessel left to force their souls into, and so they could be corporeal only here in the Underworld. They should know that. The fact that bodies rotted was no secret to anyone. Yet hope could obfuscate the most blatant truth.

Regardless, they did their jobs with efficiency and verve.

They would stop her and send her back.

SUTEKH'S GREETING CHAMBER consisted of more sandstone. More space, vast and mostly empty. The paired columns that spanned the length of the chamber were painted with bright colors to depict scenes of the delta, the river. The first time he'd seen them, Alastor had wondered if Sutekh had had them created to remind him of a time when he had lived Topworld, when he had walked in the sun and overseen the labors of his subjects and slaves, a time before the six-thousand-year-old ceasefire that ruled the Underworld.

He hadn't asked then, too new to his relationship with his father, too uncertain of his place.

He wouldn't ask now. The answer no longer interested him.

Continuing to the far end of the room, Alastor passed a small seating arrangement with chairs of Lebanese wood and a raised dais that contained a gilded throne. Never accuse Dad of subtlety.

His gaze slid to the spot behind the throne. It was empty, the chair that had been habitually positioned there removed the day Lokan was killed, because Sutekh could not bear the tangible reminder of his youngest son. It had been Lokan who sat a little behind and to the right of their father, Lokan who watched and listened and learned all about the political machinations of the Underworld lords and gods.

Lokan had thrived on the adrenaline high of Underworld politics.

And now Lokan was dead.

Alastor turned his attention to the far end of the room where the ornately carved wooden doors stood open. The burble of water over stone carried to him, and the scent of lotus blossoms. Darksoul in tow, he headed for the garden, then stepped through the doors into an oasis of palm trees that banked a tranquil pond.

On a large boulder beside the pond sat Sutekh. Today, his skin was sun-kissed, his hair honey-gold, trimmed close and styled. His jaw was clean-shaven, the second button of his single-breasted jacket left undone. Alastor might as well have been looking in a mirror.

But it was all a facade, a guise of humanity. And an amusement to Sutekh.

Alastor had no idea what his father truly looked like. Kemetic art showed a creature with a dog-like head, the snout of an anteater and a forked tail, but he had never seen his father take that form. No doubt the forked tail was accurate, at the least.

Head bowed, Sutekh appeared to watch the smooth glide of the exotic fish he'd had brought from the river Nile. In a perfect, calculated pose, he let one leg dangle along the face of the rock, his heel resting on the ground. The other was raised, knee bent, and his arm draped casually across. He did not look up, though Alastor was certain he knew his son had come.

"I've been waiting for you," Sutekh said, stirring himself at last, his movements languid as he lifted his head. "You are late."

And only then did the difference in their appearance become apparent.

Depending on the light, the color of his shirt and his mood, Alastor's eyes varied in shade from indigo to turquoise. Sutekh's were flat black, soulless, without depth or emotion, a sucking vortex.

Sutekh made no move to rise or draw near in greeting. That was Alastor's job. The prince pays homage to the king.

He wasn't about to stutter an explanation. He didn't owe one. And he didn't have one. He had no idea what had made him linger in the cemetery when he should have left, or follow Naphré home and stand about like a troubadour beneath her window.

But he couldn't regret his choice. There was something about her that made him want to look at her, tease her, spar with her. When she'd leaned out her window to demand answers, he'd simply enjoyed the sight of her in her unexpected pink flannel pajamas. Enjoyed the brief fantasy of slipping the round, white buttons free of the buttonholes to bare the skin of her chest, the swell of her breasts.

There was physical attraction there, true. But there was something more. By this point, he'd admitted that much to himself. He was far from done with Naphré Kurata.

"You have the patience of Job," Alastor offered in an undertone, knowing his father could hear him perfectly well. Sutekh offered no indication that the sarcasm rankled, but Alastor knew it did. How ridiculous that he enjoyed that knowledge.

He slung the leather pouch from across his shoulder and hauled the darksoul forward to offer both to Sutekh. His father made no move to accept either offering, only flicked a glance at the pouch, his lip curling in distaste. "You harvested from the dead."

"This wasn't a typical harvest. Say hello to Crandall Butcher. I believe he saw something the night Lokan was killed."

"You believe." Sutekh's head came up again with saurian grace; Alastor almost expected a forked tongue to flicker from between his lips. He waved one hand and said, "Continue."

Alastor glanced around the garden. "No security concerns today?"

"I have culled the ranks." There was no need to elaborate further. From that brief statement, Alastor understood exactly what his father had done.

"You found proof of involvement?"

The smile Sutekh offered was chilling. "Suspicion was sufficient."

Yes. That was Sutekh. Brutal in the manner of a scalpel rather than a club. Sutekh had destroyed any he thought might have been affiliated with Gahiji.

Some were beings that had been serving Sutekh far longer than the nearly three hundred years that Alastor had been alive. Soul reapers, servants, Sutekh would have shown no favoritism.

No doubt he had ingested their darksouls, no trial, no defense.

Nice reward for years of service.

"Tell me about Crandall Butcher."

"I believe he witnessed Lokan's murder."

"So you said." Sutekh raised his brows in an unsettling imitation of human expression, as though he was wearing a skin suit. "Witnessed? Or carried out?"

"I have no interest in guessing games. Easy enough for you to look into it." And by "look into" he meant that Sutekh would ingest Butcher's darksoul. Whatever memories it harbored would then belong to Sutekh as well.

"It's not quite that easy. You harvested from a dead man. The memories might be garbled. Or absent." There was no way to know for certain until Sutekh unhinged his jaws and took the darksoul into him. "Have you nothing better to offer?"

There was no mistaking the derision in his father's tone, and no doubt that his father meant him to hear it. They disagreed on how Alastor ought to manage his temper, and baiting him was Sutekh's way of making his point.

Alastor clamped down on the emotions that surged

deep inside him, the personal demons of anger and frustration squirming against the bonds he imposed. Sutekh sensed it. His head tipped up ever so slightly. His nostrils flared. A humming tension laced his frame.

"Free them," he ordered.

Which only made Alastor tighten the leash.

Chaos. Sutekh thrived on it, fed on it. And Alastor wasn't in the mood to provide it.

"I can offer my opinion," Alastor said, his tone even, his expression as impassive as he could make it. "The two witnesses we knew about were a bust."

"Frank and Joe Marin," Sutekh murmured.

"Frank was definitely there the night Lokan was killed. He admitted as much to Roxy." At the mention of Dagan's mate, Sutekh's expression tightened. Alastor ignored the reaction and forged on. "We know he was telling the truth because he described the tattoo the killers put on Lokan's chest." Then they'd cut it off him and sent it to Sutekh as a gift. "Frank claimed that he saw Lokan alive and that he left before the murder, and we have no way to prove or disprove that."

"You have discovered no further leads on who killed Frank Marin?"

"None."

"The Daughters of Aset…" Sutekh let the implication hang in the air. He was single-minded in his determination to pin Marin's death on them, and to hold them responsible for Lokan's murder. The enmity went way back. Sutekh had murdered Aset's husband, Osiris, and later, gone after her son, Horus. Which explained Aset's hatred of Sutekh.

But Sutekh never talked about what had sparked his

hatred of her. Mal liked to joke that it was because she'd spurned Sutekh for Osiris, but that was just a joke. At least, Alastor thought it was.

"The Daughters of Aset lost one of their own to the Marin brothers," Alastor pointed out.

"So you say."

"So the evidence supports."

They knew that Joe Marin had been there as well the night Lokan died, and that *he* hadn't left before the killing. In fact, the deed itself just might have been his handiwork. They'd found evidence that he'd practiced butchering and skinning his human victims until he had it down to a fine art. And they'd found proof that he'd killed at least one supernatural before, a Daughter of Aset, Roxy's mother, Kelley Tam.

The thing was, Daughters of Aset were a mystery. No one knew exactly how supernatural, or how human, they really were. Maybe it varied between individuals. Impossible to say given that they were so secretive that even their own acolytes often didn't know exactly what they were.

Proof being that Roxy Tam had spent over a decade thinking that Dagan had somehow turned her into a vampire. She was a Daughter of Aset, a member of the Asetian Guard, and she hadn't even known that she was a pranic feeder.

Unbidden, a recollection of Naphré surged in Alastor's thoughts. Through the tear in her shirt, he'd seen the mark of Aset that was carved in her skin.

How high up in the hierarchy was she? His guess was not very, given that she didn't give off any sort of supernatural energy. Despite her mark, the only read he got on her was purely mortal.

"What are you thinking?" Sutekh asked, rising from the boulder and striding closer, predatory, focused.

Alastor thrust Naphré from his mind. "Just pondering the enigma that is the Marin brothers."

Sutekh stared at him from behind a mortal mask, his eyes giving him away. Not human. No. Those eyes were ancient and cold, remorseless, pitiless, lacking even a flicker of humanity.

"You try to distract me, my son." Ah, never a good thing when Sutekh pulled the son card. "Your thoughts did not touch on the Marin brothers. You were thinking about something that brought you pleasure."

"Pleasure?" The possibility unsettled him. "You misread. Actually I was thinking about the connection between the Marins and the Daughters of Aset."

"Because they killed Frank Marin before we could question him?"

"We don't know that. Dagan's mate—"

"Consort," Sutekh interrupted, his tone less than complimentary.

Alastor didn't miss a beat. His father was baiting him, searching for the switch that would break his control. He wasn't about to be played so easily. "Dae prefers to call her his *partner*." He shrugged at Sutekh's dark look. "Roxy says it wasn't the Asetian Guard. She's still betting on Xaphan's concubines as the ones who took Frank Marin out."

"Regardless of who killed him—" Sutekh waved a hand negligently "—Frank Marin is dead, his darksoul and whatever knowledge he had is gone far beyond my reach. And his brother's darksoul was of absolutely no value. By the time you brought it to me, it was degraded beyond my ability to plumb." Sutekh flicked a glance at the darksoul bobbing above Alastor's shoulder. "Likely, this one is as well."

"Then perhaps you'd best get on with it."

Sutekh closed his eyes and inhaled deeply. He smiled then, lips peeling back from his teeth as he fed on Alastor's annoyance. "First, tell me how you found this...Crandall Butcher."

It didn't matter. But rather than waste time arguing, which was a futile endeavor, Alastor summarized the events in succinct detail.

"Mal heard about the possibility of a third witness from one of Xaphan's concubines. We ended up in a crappy back room at a crappier strip club, but Xaphan's pet had little of value to share. It was actually coincidence that there was a Topworld grunt there to play poker, a human with a tattoo that made me think he might be a Setnakht."

Sutekh held his index finger up. "What tattoo? Setnakhts are not habitually marked."

"A scarab beetle. And beneath it, your name."

Sutekh inclined his head in a short nod.

"After a brief chat in the back alley," Alastor continued, "Mick offered a name, Butcher, and a location where he was making a hit."

"Did this Topworlder give you a clear indication of Butcher's value?"

"He had no idea what he was telling me. He just spewed information in a desperate attempt to say *something* I might want to hear. But certain things he said made me believe that Butcher knew something about the night Lokan was killed. Either the guy was there, or he spoke with someone who was there."

"What made you think that?"

"Mick's story is that he got drunk with Butcher two nights after Lokan's murder. The wanker said that Butcher had taken to constantly looking over his shoulder and kept muttering about Underworlders who'd come after him if they knew."

"Knew what?"

"That's the question of the day. Mick got Butcher drunk, and Butcher rambled about something he'd seen that was going to get him dead and buried."

"And of course Mick couldn't supply details of what that something was." Sutekh's voice was low and smooth.

Alastor tried to ascertain the level of sarcasm in his father's questions, but found none.

"No. Maybe Butcher saw the killer's face. Or some other identifying feature. Why ask me when you can ask—" Alastor tugged the writhing darksoul forward "—him?"

Sutekh flicked a glance at the darksoul, bobbing on its tether of fire. "Barely a snack," he observed.

Alastor made no reply. Sutekh never changed. He fed on darkness and chaos and rage. Any tumultuous emotion was his succor. But Alastor had no intention of feeding his father anything but the darksoul he'd brought for that exact purpose.

Stepping closer, Sutekh inhaled deeply. Given that he had no need to breathe, the action was telling.

"The scent of a female clings to you."

Alastor fought the instinct to keep his father from knowing a single thing about Naphré Kurata. She was *his*. He didn't want to share even the most innocuous detail about her. Not with his father. Not with anyone. But he had to say something, so he offered the least he possibly could. "Butcher had an apprentice. She was there when I claimed the darksoul."

"And is she a witness as well?"

"No."

The silence hung between them. "So quick to deny the possibility. Are you so certain, then?"

Was he? Didn't matter. He was not harvesting from Naphré Kurata. No one was. He'd stand toe to toe with Sutekh on this one.

"Ask Butcher." He jerked the leash of fire so the darksoul bobbed and dipped. Sutekh was taking his sodding time about this, and Alastor's patience was wearing thin. Of course, that was likely his father's exact intent. The chaos generated by a down and dirty father/son row would suit him to perfection.

"His heart?" Sutekh prompted.

Alastor took the mangled heart from his leather pouch and set it on a gold dish that an unobtrusive servant rushed forward to hold before him. The man's eyes had been sewn shut, his ears removed. Sutekh's thoughts propelled him, guiding him though he could not see or hear.

If Gahiji could turn after nearly two thousand years, then none of the servants were trustworthy. So Alastor understood why Sutekh felt it was necessary to ensure that his closest personal servants had no way to hear or see anything that might be used to betray him. Still, he was repulsed by his father's brutality.

Sutekh's brows rose as he took in the state of the heart. Alastor offered neither apology nor explanation. It was what it was. Finally, Sutekh turned his gaze to the darksoul that bobbed and dipped above Alastor's shoulder.

"You could not question him while he was alive?"

"He was dead when I got there. And buried. I had to—" He paused, unwilling to divulge more information about the girl than was absolutely necessary. "I had to climb into the grave to retrieve his heart and darksoul."

That revelation elicited a rare and surprising flicker of response. Sutekh's brows drew together and the skin at the bridge of his nose crinkled.

"You took him from the grave?"

Wariness slithered through him at his father's uncharacteristically sharp tone. "Is that a problem?"

"It could be, as you well know. Was he buried by a religious cleric?"

"No."

"Were words said?" Sutekh pressed. "Was he consecrated to another?"

Alastor froze. Bloody hell. He hadn't even thought of that. He knew that if the darksoul was already pledged to another Underworld god or demigod, then he had no right to it. Usually, he didn't even bother with that issue because his victims were alive when he got to them and because it was usually Sutekh guiding his choice of harvest. But tonight had been different and he was only now realizing that he might have stepped on a live land mine, the rare sort that would explode whether he stayed on or climbed off.

In his mind, he ran through the events in the graveyard. He'd heard Naphré speak over the man's body, words from the Egyptian Book of the Dead. No problem there. She hadn't said the right things to actually award the kill's soul to anyone in particular. It could have gone to Osiris and Anubis or to Sutekh or even Ammut.

But what if she'd said things, done things, before he got there? Butcher's soul could be promised to pretty much any one of the Underworld gods and demigods, in which case, nabbing it for Sutekh was a major political no-no.

"I have no knowledge of any prior claim to this darksoul."

Sutekh's mouth curved in a hard smile. "No knowledge of a prior claim doesn't mean there isn't one. As always, you choose your words wisely, Alastor."

"Taught by the master," Alastor replied, his tone cold, his words clipped. His father knew exactly what he thought of him. Love. Hate. Admiration. Spite. Too many emotions to tally with mere words. They couldn't begin to describe the roiling cauldron of emotions Sutekh elicited not just in Alastor, but in all his sons. The only sentiment that Alastor could swear *wasn't* there was fear. Oh, it had been there in the beginning, cold and wet and dripping slime. But time had taught him that he could master his fear, and in doing so, break Sutekh's iron hold over him.

They'd helped each other, he and his brothers, and they'd made some progress toward freeing themselves from the scars of their father's yoke. But it had been Lokan, the youngest of the four, and oddly, the most wise, who had really helped them all find their way clear of the weight Sutekh had gleefully placed on their shoulders.

Lokan had taught them all to laugh again. For Alastor, it was relearning a skill he'd taken for granted as a child. For Mal, it was one he'd never lost. For Dagan, it was one he'd never before had the opportunity to learn.

Dragging his thoughts away from his dead brother, Alastor focused fully on Sutekh.

"What you have brought me here—" Sutekh gestured at the heart on the gold plate "—is not whole. And the darksoul is sluggish. You can see how it moves. This effort may be wasted."

Alastor had no idea why his father was wasting time. "Take the thing—" His demand choked off as a familiar smell came upon him, and he knew she was there even before she spoke.

"Stop!" The voice was both feminine and terrible. And the smell—bloody, fucking hell. Like dust. Like a crypt opened after a thousand years, stale and old and musty. And at the same time, like fresh blood and maggoty meat. He almost gagged.

He didn't need to turn to know who had joined them. The woman he had seen from the gallery. Incredibly, *impossibly,* she had passed the six guards at Sutekh's doors and made it through the corridors until she found them. No wonder Sutekh no longer trusted his borders.

Alastor turned and studied the creature before him. She stood no more than ten feet away, shrouded in layers of slithering, crawling things. There were tiny legs everywhere, and the round, white bodies of writhing maggots.

The figure glided forward, directing her attention and her words to Sutekh. "Your son has taken that which rightfully belongs to Izanami, She Who Invites, Goddess of Creation, Goddess of Death. Words were spoken. Customs followed. This soul is not yours. This heart belongs to another. Forfeit the soul—" her head turned toward Alastor "—or forfeit the thief."

# CHAPTER EIGHT

*The Temple of Setnakht, Toronto*

FROM HIS PLACE IN the corner, Pyotr Kusnetzov watched Djeserit Bast as she stood by the narrow, black granite bar in her private office, staring at the cut-crystal decanter.

She didn't know he was here, didn't think to look for an intruder in her private domain. She would not expect him to dare enter her territory. They were equals in the Cult of Setnakht, High Reverends both. For the moment.

But Pyotr had plans to change that. He meant to be a great leader, a supreme leader. An immortal leader. And he meant for Djeserit to be dead.

Djeserit splashed two fingers of whiskey into a tumbler, then bowed her head, gaze fixed on the glass. She'd turned on the recessed light above the gleaming black minibar, the bright circle of its limited reach the only light in the room. Likely, she was in the mood for shadows after this night's debacle. Though he lacked the nuances of Djeserit's plan, he knew she had plotted behind his back, and that she had failed.

Now, he had only to ascertain exactly what damage she had done.

Anger surged, and he fisted his hands at his sides,

throttling the urge to grab her by the throat and snap her neck. Not yet. It was the wrong time. The right circumstances had yet to be manipulated into place. But soon. Very soon.

Djeserit continued to stare at the tumbler, making no move to pick it up. Then she lifted the decanter once more and filled the glass nearly to the top. Her hand was shaking and a few drops splashed over the rim to lie sparkling on the gleaming black counter.

Lip curling in disdain, Pyotr watched as she lifted the tumbler to her lips. She drank, not in sips but in gulps.

The tableau—Djeserit here at the Temple instead of home in her bed, dressed entirely in black, drinking whiskey like water—was telling. Something had disturbed her greatly, and Pyotr knew exactly what that something was. Her plan had failed. Had she bothered to discuss it with him beforehand, he would have told her the outcome. But she had not, so he had not known about it until it was too late to stop her, and now who knew what unexpected complications she had created with her precipitous actions.

The worst part of it was, he had not seen it coming because Djeserit was never precipitous. Only through the man he had sent to infiltrate her elite team of bodyguards, a team she had chosen to dismiss for the night, had he even known that there was something special about tonight. It was one of the reasons he himself did not employ even a single guard. Trusting no one meant there could be no betrayals.

"Djeserit," he said as he disengaged from the shadows, enjoying her start of surprise and the way the liquor splashed over the rim and down her fingers to drip to the Persian carpet beneath their feet. He enjoyed unsettling her. It was a rare and unusual treat.

She spun to face him. She was a tall, imposing woman with piercing black eyes and a prominent nose. Like centuries of traditional Egyptian priests before her, she was completely hairless. Her scalp was bald. No eyebrows, no eyelashes.

"Pyotr." She spat his name like a curse. "What are you doing here? How did you get in?" She had spy cameras set in the walls and double locks with security measures in place to protect her domain.

"You left the door unlocked," he said with a mocking smile, knowing she wouldn't believe him and not caring in the slightest.

She stared at him, unblinking. Then she said, "You took my fish."

It was his turn to stare at her.

"I want it back."

"I have no idea what you're talking about," he said.

"You broke into my office tonight. You've done it before. I noticed yesterday that my fish, a priceless artifact, was missing." Her voice rose. "You took it."

"Djeserit, you sound unsettled. How unlike you." He offered a casual shrug as he fully disengaged from the shadow of the massive bookcase on the far wall. "Your artifact is not in my possession."

But its loss made him wonder if he was the only one who had discovered a way to pass through Djeserit's locks. The possibility of an outside intruder could not be discounted. But he had more immediate concerns.

Crossing to the glass and metal monstrosity that was her desk, he spread his fingers and dragged them across the top, leaving four neatly aligned smears in his wake.

"What were you thinking?" he whispered, stopping three feet away.

"What was I thinking?" She gulped the last of her drink, then turned and slammed the glass down on the countertop, before whirling to face him once more. Her expression was wily. "What exactly are you asking about?"

He despised her. But he was forced to ally with her until death freed him. Her death. Soon, but not yet.

"I know you went hunting tonight," he said, his tone flat and even. "You did not send a minion. You went yourself. I know you failed to obtain what you sought. And I know you may well have seriously harmed our cause. So I ask again, what were you thinking?"

"I was thinking that the girl you plan to use as a blood sacrifice has poor lineage. That at the rate we're going, we'll both be dead and buried before we can even begin to set the next step of the plan into motion."

He sucked in a breath, stunned by her words. If she knew about the blood, then she knew about the prophesy.

"Yes," she whispered. "I know you lied to me, spun tales about luring a soul reaper by killing innocents. It was the blood all along, Pyotr. But you choose poorly. They all have weak lineage. Too weak for the purpose you intend. Especially the latest lamb you intend to slaughter."

The lamb was Marie Matheson. She was a Daughter of Aset, but for centuries no one in her line had been part of the Asetian Guard. Her line was so weak, in fact, that she had no idea what she was. Her heritage was completely and utterly lost to her.

"The girl does have weak lineage," he agreed, refusing to confirm or deny whatever she thought she knew about the blood or the prophesy. He had plotted his course too carefully, and he had no desire to have her along for the ride.

"She is not enough. We must have better." Djeserit turned and sloshed more liquor into the tumbler. Pyotr watched her, both surprised and curious. He had never seen her abuse alcohol or drugs of any kind. She rarely even sipped wine with her dinner.

"And so you decided to go out and acquire a better victim?" he asked, her words sending a missing piece of the puzzle clicking into place. Now he understood. "With no discussion. No plan. No backup of any kind." Idiot. She was an idiot. Did she not think he had investigated all possibilities, worked all angles? If there was better than Marie to be had, they would have her.

"I know you approached Naphré Kurata. Attempted to woo her. Oh, do not look surprised. I know her name. I know many things about her." An ugly sneer crept into her tone. "If you'd been thinking with your head instead of your dick, we would have had her beneath our blades."

"Would we? Naphré *was* a better choice, for the reason of her lineage. On that point you are correct. But she was otherwise a poor choice. She is not malleable in the least. She is trained in the arts of death. And there is something else, something I cannot put my finger on...a taint of some sort." He shot her a dark look. "She is no lamb to be led to the slaughter. And she is no innocent. When I was with her, I sensed

something…off, like she's been touched by the hand of
another supernatural. A dark hand. We need the blood
of an innocent. One who has a pretty, shiny soul, not a
darksoul dipped in tar. I could not swear that Naphré
Kurata met our needs, so I chose elsewhere."

Fixating on one of his points and ignoring all the
others, Djeserit said, "I believed there were ways
around her training. I thought it a simple matter to
hire someone with more experience and at least equal
training."

"You thought…" Pyotr stared at her. No, it was too
incredible to even consider. Djeserit could not have
been so foolish. "Do not say that you thought to hire
her own mentor to kill her? You went to Butcher. Is
that what you did, Djeserit? Is it?"

"He wasn't supposed to kill her." She peeled off
her jacket and tossed it onto her obscenely expensive
ergonomic chair. Then, lifting a large envelope from
her desk, she began fanning herself. Sweat beaded on
her upper lip and her brow. "It's terribly hot in here,
do you not think so. Far too hot. I'll have to—"

"Djeserit." Pyotr imbued the single word with a full
measure of venom and a note of command.

She blinked, a slow lowering and raising of her lids.
It was a habit that annoyed him no end. Finally, she
said, "He was to render her insensate, then contact me.
I let him think it was because I wanted to witness her
demise. But in truth, I meant to bring her to you."

He heard the lie in the last part, but the truth in the
rest.

"If I understand your plan correctly, Butcher was to
summon you. You would then have arrived, killed him
and taken Naphré for our purposes."

"Butcher was uncooperative. He said he didn't work that way. That he wanted neither helpers nor witnesses." Again, the slow, exaggerated blink. "Still, I felt it was a solid plan, that I could work around his misgivings."

"Given that Naphré Kurata is not with you, clearly your plan was not solid enough. So tell me, Djeserit, did they join forces against you? Overpower you? Did you have not even one guard with you as backup? Or did they overpower him as well?"

"They were alone. Just the two of them. And *she* killed *him*. Two shots. One to the head, one to the heart."

Pyotr digested that. It was more than he had expected, and proof that his decision to choose another had been sound. If Naphré could terminate her teacher, then she would not have made a particularly good victim. Still, her blood was pure and powerful...

That Djeserit had gone ahead behind his back was irksome in the extreme, but the outcome was not unfavorable. Butcher had been a liability, a man who knew too much. Pyotr had meant to kill him regardless. But not yet. Not until he had no further need of him. Djeserit's actions had taken the choice from him, and he liked that not at all.

"So you are here sweating and guzzling liquor because your plans went awry?"

"No. I am here because my plan went far too perfectly. So perfectly that I was unprepared. He was there. In the graveyard. I saw him. Had I been braver, smarter, I could have touched him."

"Butcher? We have already established that he was there. And now he is dead."

"No, you pompous fool." Her eyes narrowed. "But

enough of my explanations. What of yours? You lied to me. The night Roxy Tam came here sniffing about. You spun a convoluted web of lies to make me believe it was all about killing innocents until we lured a soul reaper here to kill the killers. But that was a lie. A ploy." She was breathing heavily, her cheeks flushed. "I have found you out. I am aware of the prophesy now. Explain that away, if you can."

Anger surged, white-hot. If he moved even one step closer, he would beat her. He would beat her until her hated face was a bloody, bruised pulp. Until the skin on his knuckles was ripped open and raw. Until her bones broke and her breath eased out in a final sigh.

The thought brought a smile to his lips.

But he dared not indulge such fantasy. He was in control. He had long ago left behind the thug who used his fists rather than his brains. It had been decades since he'd used his fists like that. His weapons were more refined now. His intellect. His words. The beautifully honed edge of a knife when circumstances called for it.

Besides, he could not kill her. That was the fail-safe. They each knew too much. If he killed her, she would carry her tales to the Underworld. If she killed him, he would do the same.

Her lips curved and she smiled. Djeserit Bast was a woman who ought never smile.

"Who was at the cemetery?" he asked, his patience forced.

"*He* was there," she said. "The one we need. He was there. I saw him."

"What are you talking about?" But he knew. Deep inside, he knew.

She held up her hand, thumb and forefinger held an inch apart. "I was this close to the soul reaper. I believe he was another of Sutekh's sons." She pinched her fingertips together. "This close."

And with that revelation, Pyotr's control fragmented. She had jeopardized everything.

He lunged across the space and closed his hands around Djeserit's throat.

*The Underworld, the Territory of Sutekh*

COLD RAGE CURDLED IN Alastor's gut. At the situation. At himself.

The rules were clear. This darksoul had never been his to take. But if he gave up this harvest, then whatever Butcher had witnessed would be lost to them, his memories gone to another territory, beyond their reach. Just as Frank Marin's were.

And if he didn't give it up, by all laws and customs of the Underworld, the injured party could demand Alastor's soul as forfeit. Of course, *demand* and *obtain* were two completely different concepts.

"Does she speak the truth?" Sutekh glanced at him.

"I witnessed no ceremony that promised the soul to Izanami—" the creature made a sound of denial, and Alastor continued, not waiting for her to interject "—but there is a strong possibility she speaks truth. There was ample time for it to happen before I arrived."

"You ignored the warning of the thunder deity," she said flatly.

Sutekh stared at him impassively, as though waiting for a denial.

"I didn't realize it was a warning." Alastor paused for only a second, then barreled on, not waiting to consult his father, or even to think on what he proposed. Stepping into a political negotiation went totally against his character, but the situation was dire, and this was one time that might did not make right.

They needed Butcher's sodding darksoul and the information it might hold. He legally had no claim to it. There was no illegal recourse now that he'd been caught with his fingers in the pot. Negotiation was all that was left to him.

"I propose a trade," he said. "This darksoul for another. Would that be acceptable?"

He could feel his father's eyes upon him. And his censure. Or perhaps that was only what he expected to feel.

"A trade," the creature murmured, clearly startled by the proposition. "I received no instruction for that."

Alastor shot a glance at Sutekh. His father was impassive as always, his expression betraying nothing. It had been precipitous to make this offer, to jump in and preempt anything Sutekh might have done. But time was slipping away and, with it, hope of reuniting Lokan's body with his soul. If they had any hope of success, they needed to do that before he partook of the food of the dead and in so doing, sealed his eternity.

Sutekh stepped forward then and gestured toward the open doors. "Come, let us discuss this in comfort. May I offer refreshment? Honeyed cakes? Tea?"

Looking at the creature before him, Alastor could discern no mouth. There was only a gaping hole that opened when she spoke, quickly filled in by writhing centipedes and spiders the size of cherries, the legs as long as stems.

"No refreshment, thank you. But I have journeyed far. I will sit."

"Come." Sutekh led the way inside, and held the seat back as the creature arranged herself in one of the chairs of Lebanese wood. In seconds, the chair disappeared under an undulating wave of glistening bodies and innumerable thrashing legs.

Sutekh drifted to the pedestal that stood in the center of the great room, and the open book that rested there. Casually, he leafed through several pages then drew his finger down the list of names. At length, he paused, tapped the tip of his index finger against the page and nodded. He shot a glance at Alastor, and though his expression was utterly blank, Alastor's blood chilled in his veins.

He knew that look. His father was about to enact some nefarious scheme, one that would feed his need for rage and hate and pain.

Finally, Sutekh turned back to his guest.

Alastor watched all this from the place he had taken by the open garden doors, his shoulder propped against the jamb.

"Your name?" Sutekh asked as he seated himself.

She shook her head. "Unimportant. I am one of eight *Shikome*. I can be only what I am."

Alastor looked beyond the crawling things, beyond the smell, and he saw a fierce and proud creature, one of power. His father must have seen that as well, for he treated her with respect due a foe of value.

"How did you pass my guards?" he asked.

"With this." She drew from inside the writhing, undulating layers a wafer-thin oval of gold. Alastor recognized it. A cartouche. Sutekh's name encircled in a hieroglyphic representation of a doubled rope with its ends tied in a tangent line. It was a free pass. A card that could be traded for a favor. Sutekh was miserly about handing them out.

"Where did you get that?" Alastor asked, straightening off the doorjamb and crossing the space until he stood over her, looking down at the gold wafer she held in her bug-encrusted hand.

"Izanami and I have had dealings in the past," Sutekh said, never looking away from their guest, who perched at the edge of her chair, practically vibrating with leashed energy and tension. "I gave her a token of my appreciation for her assistance in a matter of delicacy some time ago. She has chosen this occasion to make use of it." Then he addressed himself to the *Shikome*. "Does Izanami stand with me at the meeting?"

"That is for you to ask Izanami, and of no relevance to our immediate discussion."

"I have asked her through an ambassador. She was coy in her reply."

"I am authorized to speak only about the darksoul your minion stole from Izanami-no-mikoto. Nothing more."

Sutekh inclined his head in acceptance. "What are your terms?"

"The return of the heart and darksoul." She turned her head toward Alastor and continued. "If you wish to negotiate some other satisfactory outcome, I can name only tentative terms. Should Izanami disagree when I advise her of our dialogue, then our discourse and agreement will be nullified."

"Of course."

"You wish to keep this particular darksoul?" She waved a hand toward the soul still tethered by a band of fire. Centipedes dropped off and scuttled along the floor.

"I do." With the smallest gesture of his pinky finger, Sutekh incinerated them, tiny flames flaring then disappearing, leaving minute piles of ash. Not merely a show of power, but a precaution. The *Shikome* could not be allowed to leave anything behind when she left. Not even a bug. One never knew what her connection was to the creatures that swarmed over her in waves.

"Why is this darksoul of such import?"

Alastor squelched the urge to interfere, to ensure that his father say nothing of the information they might learn of Lokan's death. It could well be Izanami who was the puppet-master behind Gahiji's actions. She was neither friend nor ally to Sutekh, after all.

But he needn't have entertained even a moment's worry. His father was an expert at declining the requests, demands, pleas of others.

"The darksoul is of interest to me. You know that already and that is all you need to know, and all I am prepared to reveal. I offer in exchange another soul, one inscribed in my book of debts. Not a soul promised to me by another, but one that made the offer directly."

"What soul?" the *Shikome* asked.

"Come," Sutekh said, and rose. "This way."

He led her to the book on the pedestal and with a languid swish of his hand flipped the pages open. Turning his hand palm up, he extended his index finger and let the very tip touch the inscribed name. The *Shikome* leaned close, stiffened and jerked away.

There was no expression for Alastor to read, yet read it he did.

She was incensed. The bugs that covered her seemed to swell like a tide, making her larger, darker. They grew in size, in volume, their movements frenzied, the effect disturbing, even to one such as him.

Why? What name had Sutekh shown her? What soul had he offered?

"You offer a soul with divided loyalties and tangled connections. I will need to speak with Izanami. This decision is beyond my reach." The insects that covered her made faint clicking sounds as she spoke, as though in chorus to her words.

Sutekh stared at her, saying nothing. His hand was yet extended, his finger resting on the name.

Though his father had not invited him to do so, Alastor strode forward and looked into the book. The page was filled by a lengthy list, the letters neat and tight. Yet, one name leaped at him, clear and defined. He not only read it, but felt it reach for him and catch hold of him, like a fist plunged in his chest.

Naphré Misao Kurata.

His Naphré.

He felt like he'd been kicked in the gut. The emotions he worked so hard to hold at bay shook the bars of their cage and howled.

Sutekh was speaking to him. "—the darksoul."

Raising his head, Alastor stared at the *Shikome,* wondering a million different things. How she had come at exactly this moment, robbing him of the opportunity to find out what Butcher had known about

Lokan. Why she had refused the alternate soul, Naphré's soul. What she meant by divided loyalties and tangled connections.

What the bloody hell Naphré's name was doing in that book.

"Where do you take this darksoul?" he asked, forcing the words past bloodless lips, focusing on the one question that demanded an immediate answer.

Izanami's ambassador turned to him and extended her hand, waiting for him to pass Butcher's darksoul—and its precious knowledge—to her. He had no choice. Even if he refused, Sutekh was the only one who could ingest the raw energy and glean the memories. If there were even any memories left to glean.

"To Yomi," she said.

Alastor nodded. "I wish to beg passage," he said. "I wish to speak with Izanami-no-mikoto." He could feel Sutekh's disapproval, but he didn't acknowledge it, didn't even glance at his father. He kept emotion and action under tightest restraint. "I would beg that you keep this soul safe until I have opportunity to present my case."

"You would trust me to keep my word?" Her tone was flat, cool, yet he sensed a modicum of amusement.

Alastor stared at her, wishing she had eyes he could look at, features he could read. But since she had neither, he relied on instinct, which was telling him she was a woman of honor. That her word had value. "Yes."

As a wave, the minute creatures that veiled her drew back then surged forward. He was left with the impression that his answer had surprised her.

"You have passage, then, soul reaper. Best find your

way there before the meeting of allies. Your invitation does not extend longer than that. Should you be caught in Izanami's territory once your welcome expires, your soul will be forfeit."

He could feel his father's displeasure buffeting him like breakers at the shore. He ignored it, keeping his gaze on the *Shikome*.

"Understood." Alastor inclined his head as he handed off the darksoul, controlling his expression as the foul chill of her touch permeated his body.

A centipede disengaged from the mass and crawled along the back of his hand. Another followed. And another. He did not shake them free or in any way indicate that he even knew they were there, though one of the centipedes crawled beneath the cuff of his shirt and up his arm with amazing speed.

And though she made no comment, he thought his reserve earned some small measure of the *Shikome*'s favor.

Sutekh waved his hand and the centipedes on Alastor's skin burst into flame. Unfortunately, the one beneath his shirt extended the flame to the cloth, and Alastor's entire sleeve erupted, scorching the skin of his arm from wrist to shoulder.

It was in Sutekh's power to make the burn disappear. But it was not in his nature.

He would let Alastor suffer for having overstepped.

Despite her lack of eyes, he sensed the *Shikome*'s gaze upon him. She rose, stepped forward, as though to offer either words or assistance. Although perhaps he misread.

Either way, he stalled her with a gesture. "I heal

fast." But the burn would hurt like the devil until he did, which was, of course, Sutekh's exact intent.

She inclined her head, towing Butcher's darksoul—and the secrets Alastor so desperately wanted—behind her as she walked toward the double doors of the greeting chamber. There, she paused and spoke without looking back.

"Bring the girl," she said. An order, not a suggestion.

The girl. She meant Naphré. Denial sprang to his lips, but he swallowed it, waiting to hear the rest of what she had to say.

"She will be offered safe passage along with you. And I will personally guarantee that she will be offered the chance to leave when we are done. But know that she is your free pass, soul reaper. Your key. Without her, you will be denied entry, this soul forever beyond your reach."

# CHAPTER NINE

*Kawara wa migaitemo tama ni naranu.*
A tile even though it be polished does not
become a jewel.

—Japanese proverb

*The Temple of Setnakht, Toronto*

STANDING ACROSS THE street from the Temple of Setnakht, Naphré leaned one shoulder against the wall
beside her, took out the little Ziploc baggie and shook
it to mix the ingredients. It was her own special trail
mix blend: edamame, chocolate-covered raisins and the
occasional cheesy fish cracker. She liked the salty with
the sweet. But she'd never met anyone else who liked
this particular blend. Her running buddies just gave her
a disgusted look if she offered them any during their
after-run chat. She gave a mental shrug. Their loss.

She'd been here for three hours. In that time, there'd
been a whole lot of comings and goings through the
chrome and glass front doors of the converted eigh-
teenth century factory that housed the Temple.

Looked like a party. Nothing fancy. No ball gowns
or suits—

Just the thought of a suit led her smack-dab to an
image of Alastor Krayl. It had been two nights since

she'd seen him last, when he'd been lounging outside her window, his insanely expensive suit accenting the breadth of his shoulders, white shirt bright against charcoal jacket. Top buttons open to reveal the strong column of his throat and just a hint of muscle at the top of his chest. Butcher's darksoul bobbing at his shoulder.

Yeah, the last bit sort of killed the appeal.

Which probably wasn't a bad thing. She had no business having a case of teenage hormone lust for a soul reaper. She thought she'd outgrown that. She *had* outgrown that. Which made this a case of adult lust.

Worse and worse.

She forced the thought of him from her mind. The last thing she needed was to be standing around in the cold mooning over a soul reaper with a pretty face. No…not pretty. Handsome. Lean. Hard jaw. Sculpted cheeks. Elegance and lethal, masculine grace.

She exhaled sharply and snapped her fingers, breaking her self-woven spell and shifted her thoughts back to the Setnakht party across the street.

Glancing down at her attire—denim jacket, gray top, black jeans and slouchy boots—she figured she'd fit in okay, so long as she didn't pull off her jacket and show off the knife at the small of her back. She hadn't bothered with a gun tonight. Surveillance didn't call for it.

Pinching her fingers, she ran them along the Ziploc seal and shoved the half-full baggie back in her pocket. Then she jogged across the street and grabbed hold of the door like she was expecting to get in, no problem, and pulled.

Except there *was* a problem.

It was locked.

Leaning in, she peered through the glass. The lobby was empty. All the people who'd arrived while she watched were in there somewhere, but not anywhere she could see.

She glanced to the left and saw a security guard striding her way. Good. Perfect. She plastered on a smile, one that showed a flash of teeth.

"Hey," she said as he pulled the door partially open. She angled her shoulder into the opening; he shifted to block her path. He was tall and skinny, with just a bit of a paunch. "I was worried that I was locked out of all the fun."

He didn't move to let her pass, though she took a half step forward. Keeping one forearm resting against the door, he blocked her way.

"Private function," he said.

"Right. Of course. But I'm invited. My date…his name's—"

Guess he didn't want to hear it, because he shoved the door shut and locked it before she finished. Then he turned and strode away without bothering to see if she stayed or went, making the clear statement that he didn't care either way. Which meant that if there was anything worth seeing in there, she wasn't going to see it from here.

*Kuso.*

Shoving her hands in her pockets, she turned away and headed back across the street to regroup and decide her next move.

She leaned against the wall, bent her knees and let herself slide down to an easy crouch. Her stomach rumbled; she'd missed dinner. She pulled out her little bottle of hand sanitizer, squirted a bit on her palm and rubbed it into her hands until it dried. Then she got out her trail mix again, munched a bit more and stared at the building across the street.

After a while, the security guard walked past the glass doors, pausing to shake each one and test the lock. Good man. He took his job seriously.

Choices, choices. She could look for a way to break in, or call it a night and contact the Temple in the morning and try again to make an appointment to see High Priest Djeserit Bast. The latter ought to be the more logical option, except she'd been trying to do just that for two days, without results.

But it looked like that was the option she'd have to take because she had one last item to cross off her to-do list for the night: make a call to a demon—her fourth in two days. Under the gauze bandage that she'd applied to her left forearm were three neat, parallel slashes. Soon to be four. *Yay.*

The night Butcher died had been a supremely shitty night. The whole shoot-and-kill-her-mentor-then-have-his-soul-taken-by-a-reaper really hadn't worked for her. Last night hadn't been much better, not with her staying up until the wee hours trying to summon the damned elusive demon who had dibs on her soul.

She'd followed the rules, sitting cross-legged on the floor, setting a circle of coarse salt, focusing her thoughts and energy. And, of course, splashing blood—her own—on the thin, engraved wafer of gold that the demon had given her the first night she'd met him, the night they'd made their blood bargain.

While her blood dripped and hissed and bubbled,

she'd waited. And waited. And waited. Repeats of the same process had yielded the same lack of results.

He wasn't answering. And he didn't have voice mail.

She wondered if the no-show deal was common. She had no clue. In six years, she'd never tried to summon him. She'd just gone about her business and waited for him to come to her. The longer he went between visits, the happier she was.

But right now, she wouldn't mind having a little chat. She wanted some answers, and he just might be the one to provide them.

Feeling a bit frustrated by her lack of success in that arena, she'd decided to be proactive about the High Priest. She'd come looking for Djeserit Bast rather than waiting for her to come hunting. But it looked like her luck was running pretty steady. No demon. No Djeserit.

But, hey, at least the soul reaper hadn't returned.

Which she ought to count as a positive. But she was kind of disappointed that he'd given up so easily. She'd enjoyed verbally sparring with him. And the way he'd looked at her, like she was an ice cream cone he'd like to lick, hadn't exactly been unpleasant. And...

"See...that is exactly what's wrong with my life," she muttered. "I'm actually considering Sutekh's son as potentially dateable." Or, if not dateable, at least shaggable, to steal his phrase.

How long had it been since she'd thought of anyone that way? Years. Years and years. Because she was an all-or-nothing kind of girl. Love with her whole soul, trust with her whole soul, or not at all.

Yeah, well, a soul reaper wasn't exactly a good

candidate for that. Offer him her soul—which actually wasn't even hers to offer anymore—and he was damn likely to take it. And not in a good way.

*Kawara wa migaitemo tama ni naranu.* A tile even though it be polished does not become a jewel. Her grandfather had told her that when her high school boyfriend dumped her the night before prom. And Alastor Krayl was no jewel. But then, he wasn't exactly a tile, either.

She needed to just stop thinking about him. About the way he'd followed her home to make certain she was okay after she reburied Butcher. Sort of nice, in a creepy stalker, soul reaper kind of way.

"Not thinking about him," she said in a singsong voice.

*Kuso.*

Glumly, she stared at the Temple of Setnakht, but there was absolutely nothing to see. Just a building, locked up tight. Anything interesting was happening inside, beyond her line of sight. She ought to head home. Get some sleep. But something inside her shivered and twitched, an insistence that she *needed* to be here.

Intuition was a powerful tool, one she'd learned not to disregard.

Might as well wait till the party broke up. How long could that be? Another hour? Two? If she was lucky, other opportunities might present themselves. She might even catch High Reverend Bast alone as she was leaving.

So she stayed where she was, her back propped against the redbrick building as the cold wind swept down the street, making her hair fly in her face and her skin prickle with gooseflesh. She watched and waited and pondered the whole demon/blood covenant predicament she found herself in. She didn't know how she was going to pay down her debt. How did one go about nullifying the sale of one's soul to a demon? She had no clue.

She could go to the Daughters of Aset, and their elite forces, the Asetian Guard. Ask for their help. But that would mean selling her soul all over again, to the exact group she'd run from in the first place because she hadn't wanted to give up who she was, to be swallowed by a hierarchy of secrecy and twisted allegiances.

To kill on command, without question.

The Daughters of Aset had three lineages. The Adaptive, the Keeper and the Guide. Predatory, aggressive, Guides were the vanguard, the ones who made sure the path was clear and safe. The ones who killed when they had to.

Naphré was a Guide, on her mother's side. She'd accepted that, trained for her post, even cut the dark mark—an ankh with wings and horns—into her skin. But in the end, she hadn't taken the final step to fulfill her duty; she hadn't tasted first blood. Which meant she hadn't stepped beyond human.

She'd run so she wouldn't have to kill just because the Asetian Guard told her to.

How fucking hilarious was it that she'd ended up doing exactly what she had been so morally opposed to. Only she was doing it for a different master.

Guess certain people were just born to do certain things.

Her attention sharpened and she pushed off the wall and straightened. Something had changed in the building across the street. For a long moment, she couldn't pinpoint exactly what that something was, then she saw it. Light. There was light bleeding into the side alley, suggesting either headlights or a security lamp turned on behind the building. She'd lay dollars to doughnuts that someone was making use of a back exit.

Back exits were always interesting.

Shoving her nearly empty baggie back in her pocket, she took off at a jog, casting a quick glance in each direction before she bolted across the street and down the alley.

NAPHRÉ PEERED AROUND THE edge of the wall, hugging the shadows, taking in the scene with a quick sweep. A steel door was propped open with a milk crate, spilling light onto the metal grate that served as a landing and the half dozen metal stairs that led down to the alley. A black sedan idled next to the stairs, no headlights, no interior lights. The back passenger door was open, as was the driver's door. There was no one inside.

Withdrawing before she could be seen, Naphré pressed up against the wall and listened. She heard the sound of footsteps on tile, then a heavier thud as feet hit the metal landing and, finally, the stairs. There was a muted moan, followed by a woman's voice. "Hey, I don't—" Another moan, and then, "Oh, please, don't hurt me. Oh...I think I'm going to throw—"

—up. Naphré mentally matched word to sound as the unseen woman did exactly as she promised.

A man's voice rattled off a litany of less-than-polite words. Then there was a thud, and an angry, "Do not move, you stupid cunt," then the sound of footsteps rushing off.

The voice was vaguely familiar.

*Kuso.* She did not need this. She was here to do surveillance. If she'd been lucky, she'd have found a way to crash the Setnakhts' party.

But whatever party this guy meant to have with a girl who was half-conscious and puking was not one she wanted in on. Of course, she couldn't leave well enough alone. The tattered remnants of her damned conscience wouldn't let her just turn around and leave.

The girl groaned again, the sound loud in the quiet alley.

Naphré took a deep breath and moved.

She rounded the corner and evaluated as she ran. The woman was slumped on the pavement against the bottom stair, legs sprawled, head bowed so her long, light-brown hair obscured her face. Beside her was a pool of vomit. She moaned as she tried to raise her head and push to her feet.

Drunk. Drugged. Sick. Naphré figured it could be any or all of the above. Didn't matter which, though. All that mattered was getting her out of here because there was absolutely no doubt in her mind that the guy who'd been carting her around was no Good Samaritan.

Black car. No lights. Back door. No prying eyes.

Her money was on nefarious plot rather than concerned date. Which meant she couldn't just leave the girl sitting in her own puke.

The car was running. Naphré dipped, shoved her forearms under the girl's armpits, hauled her up and dragged her toward the car. She winced as the girl's weight put pressure on the bandaged cuts on her forearm.

She was almost to the car when she raised her head and met the startled gaze of Pyotr Kusnetzov as he stalked through a door at the far end of the hallway.

For a frozen second, he just stared at her. Then he started to run, his hand reaching for something inside his jacket.

Naphré dropped the girl.

Heart pounding, she lunged up the stairs, two at a time, her gaze locked on Pyotr Kusnetzov, who was sprinting down the long, narrow hallway toward her. She hit the landing, kicked the milk carton out of the way and shoved the metal door. It slammed shut with a clang.

Spinning, she bolstered it with her back and anchored her feet against the metal rail. She needed a way to keep the damned thing shut. A quick look around revealed absolutely nothing useful.

*Kuso.*

Inspiration struck. She grabbed her spare knife from the sheath in her boot, rammed the blade under the door and trapped the handle in the metal grate of the landing. Then she straightened and turned just as a solid weight thudded against the door from the inside.

Pyotr Kusnetzov shook the handle and bellowed like an enraged bull. Damn. With the pretty manners he'd shown her, she really wouldn't have guessed he had that in him.

Her makeshift brace held. For the moment.

Heart pounding, she grabbed the railing, vaulted overtop and landed hard. The force of her landing echoed through her ankles and shins, despite her bent knees and neat gymnastic form. Guess that's what she got for a high dismount to concrete.

"Let's go," she muttered, grabbing the girl under the arms again and hauling her up. "Come on."

Naphré literally threw her through the open passenger door. She got no resistance, just a pathetic little moan.

She kicked the car door shut and skidded round the rear fender to get to the driver's side, one hand shooting out to rest on the trunk for balance.

Pyotr was still rattling the door and cursing.

There was a sharp snap and crackle.

Naphré turned, her gut sinking as she realized the knife might not hold.

She made a half turn back toward the open driver's door.

And got no further.

Rough fingers clamped on her upper arm, and she cried out, jerking away, only to find herself dragged against something solid and immovable.

Acting on reflex she spun as far as his hold let her, and punched, landing an uppercut to the underside of the immovable object's chin.

She heard a grunt, and felt the give as his head snapped back.

Shaking her hand to ease the sting in her knuckles, she glanced up and froze. Lapis lazuli eyes stared back at her.

"Oops."

"You think?" Clipped, perfect consonants and vowels.

Looked like the soul reaper was back, making a mess of her efforts just like he had when she'd buried—then unburied, then reburied—Butcher. So why, *why*, did a part of her feel a little electric thrill at the sight of him?

He grabbed her other arm, dragged her against him and kissed her. Lips, no tongue.

And damn if she didn't kiss him back.

His mouth was hard, demanding, maybe a little angry, like he was kissing her and didn't want to be kissing her and at the same time *did*. The feel of his mouth on hers tore through her, and then the kiss was over, his hard body a step away, his grasp on her arms gone.

The only thing that told her she hadn't imagined the whole thing was the taste of him on her lips and the way her whole body felt like it was singing.

His gaze locked with hers, his pupils dilated and dark, rimmed by a thin line of bright-blue iris. The effect was startling. Sexy.

"Get in the bloody car."

His tone, not so sexy.

A shot rang out and Alastor moved, so fast she didn't see a damned thing, only felt the air on her cheek. Cries came from far down the alley, and she realized that Pyotr had doubled back and found another way out of the building. And he'd brought company.

She was already moving when she heard a second shot, and almost simultaneously a grunt then a hiss. It took a millisecond to realize that Alastor was no longer in front of her, but behind. He'd moved with preternatural speed. And she was guessing he'd just taken a bullet in her stead.

He yanked open the rear driver's-side door, lifted her bodily with a solid forearm around her waist and threw her into the backseat. She skidded across the leather.

The door slammed. The car dipped as the reaper threw himself behind the wheel. A second slam and they were off, tires squealing.

Naphré's heart pounded against her ribs. She liked nice, clean, organized work. Clusterfucks like this one weren't really her scene.

Noise followed them. Shouts. The distinctive crack of gunshot.

"We need to get out of here," she said to the back of Alastor's head. "With the racket they're making, the cops'll be here any minute."

"We need to get out of here for reasons other than the local constabulary," he muttered, sounding incredibly proper, and incredibly put out.

"'Local constabulary,'" she echoed. "You from a different world?"

"Something like that," he clipped. "One with calling cards and copious amounts of tea."

She didn't think she wanted to know.

The girl on the seat beside her tried to straighten, and Naphré grabbed the back of her head, holding her down just in case the morons firing at them improved their aim.

"Bloody fucking hell," Alastor snarled, and slammed on the brakes. Naphré and the girl both went tumbling off the seat.

"…shooting at us…" the girl mumbled and tried to rise.

"No shit. Stay down." Naphré pushed the flat of her hand against the girl's back to emphasize her point. She had no idea why Alastor had stopped, but she knew she wasn't pleased that he had. What could be worse than trigger-happy Setnakhts?

She reared up just enough to see over the seat and out the front window. There was a group of women standing at the mouth of the alley.

"Beep at them," she ordered, slamming her fist against the back of Alastor's shoulder, practically feeling the breath of the Setnakhts on the back of her neck.

"What do you see?" he asked softly.

Like they had time for this. "A bunch of women out for the night," she snapped. "Beep. Make them move. Go." She shot a look over her shoulder and, sure enough, several dark shapes were racing along the alley toward them.

"Go!" She hit him again.

Lightning fast, his hand shot back and trapped hers. Her head jerked up. Their gazes locked in the rearview mirror.

All she could see were his eyes, incredibly blue, bright despite the darkness.

All she could feel was his touch. Electricity ramped through her, making the fine hairs on her forearm prickle and rise. The connection was startling, unsettling. It made her nerve endings feel like they'd been coasting until that moment, like they'd never experienced sensation until he'd touched her.

She had the crazy thought that she was like an electric circuit with a break in the flow, and he was the switch that completed her.

She tried to pull away, but he was having none of that.

"Look again, pet."

"What the f—" Her arguments died, because when she tore her gaze from the mirror and looked toward the group of women blocking their path, they appeared far different than they had a moment past. There wasn't much light—Alastor hadn't bothered to turn on the headlights—but between the moon and whatever ambient light leaked from the street, she got an eyeful. Those women didn't look like any humans she'd ever seen. Their skin was like dark-red leather, their hair black and sleek and their hands bore black, curved talons in place of nails.

*"Kuso,"* she hissed.

*"Kuso,* indeed," Alastor echoed. "Xaphan's concubines."

She'd met them in human form, negotiated more than one deal, but she'd never seen their true faces. This was enlightening, to say the least.

Had she given Xaphan a different answer when he so prettily invited her to his bed, she might be standing there shoulder to shoulder with them. A sobering thought.

From behind them came pounding feet and shouts. But no more shots. Guess the Setnakhts chasing them had finally realized that continued gunfire would draw a boatload of unwanted attention. Or maybe they, too, were seeing Xaphan's concubines as they truly were.

One of Xaphan's concubines brought her hand up like she was going to pitch a baseball and—incredibly—pitched a fireball. It sailed through the night, straight for them. Only it skidded along the roof of the car, buckling the metal as it went, and flew off the far side toward their pursuers.

Error, or intent? Hard to tell.

"They're fire genies," Alastor clarified, the poster boy for helpfulness. He slammed the car in gear, and reversed so fast the tires squealed.

"Thanks. Wasn't clear on that."

He hit the brakes, sending Naphré careening against the back of the seat. Beside her, the girl she was trying to rescue gagged and started to puke again.

"Leave her," Alastor clipped as he threw open his door. He got out, and hauled open Naphré's door. Then he reached in and grabbed her arm, bent on dragging her out.

Struggling against him, Naphré caught hold of the girl's long hair—the only thing she could reach as she fought against Alastor's superior strength—and as he dragged her from the car, she dragged the girl, who moaned and cried out.

"I said leave her," Alastor barked.

"No. It's her they want."

He blinked. "It's *you* they want."

"No. It's her."

"Leav—" He made a sound of incredible irritation, reached out and hauled Naphré up against him with one arm. Then, fisting his free hand in the back of the girl's shirt, he hefted her like a rag doll.

Guess he figured it was easier to *do* than to argue.

Another fireball sailed toward them, showering sparks on the hood of the car. From behind them came more gunfire, aimed not at them, but at the fire genies. Alastor turned so his big body shielded both Naphré and the girl as much as possible.

Naphré smelled burning wool, and reached up to slap at a few sparks that were smoldering on his suit jacket.

His lips thinned.

From behind them came the bang of hands and feet hitting the fender and trunk of the sedan. Their retreat was blocked by their pursuers. Their way forward was obstructed by fireball-slinging, leather-skinned genies in micro-minis and stiletto heels.

If she didn't know for certain that she was awake, Naphré would have been thinking she was having one hell of a dream after eating too much spicy koshary.

"Right, then," Alastor said, all matter-of-fact and genial. "Off we go."

He strode forward, dragging her along, carrying the semiconscious girl by her shirt.

"Go where?" Straight to hell if they kept moving into the genies' line of fire.

Abruptly, Alastor loosed his hold on her and made a gesture with his right hand. It was vaguely familiar. She realized that she'd seen him do that the other night, right before—

Naphré tensed as a great gaping black hole appeared before them, the edges writhing and twisting like smoke. He didn't even slow, just grabbed her again and kept on walking. Incredible cold radiated from the hole, like standing in a lake, naked, on the coldest day of winter.

"No fucking way." She dug in her heels, tried to backpedal. He meant to take her in there. Where? There was nothing but darkness.

All around them was pandemonium. The night lit up as the fire genies unleashed their power, the orange glow of their fire accenting the menacing darkness—the nothingness—of the hole Alastor had summoned.

From behind them came the retort of gunfire, too close. Alastor tensed and jerked against her.

He'd been shot, again. She could smell the metallic tang of his blood, calling to her, beckoning. Luscious. Like nothing she'd ever smelled before.

*Not now.* She almost snarled the words aloud as she battled her nature and the lure of his blood. Soul reaper blood. The scent made her mouth water. She'd been fighting what she was for years, but she'd never been quite this tempted.

Just a little taste and she would feed off his power. Just a little taste and she would step beyond her humanity.

Just a little taste and she'd give the demon that owned her far more than he'd paid for.

Another fireball sailed over them, so close she could feel the heat on her skin.

Frantic, she looked right, left. No way out.

Then she saw a woman behind the group of fire genies, walking toward them. She was completely enveloped in flowing, undulating gray cloth. Her hands. Her feet. Her head and face. Not even her eyes were visible.

Naphré froze and stared. There was something not right. Something—

"We need to leave. Now." Geniality evaporated. Alastor's voice was taut as an overwound guitar string. She glanced at him to find him staring hard at the woman in gray. The expression on his face was chilling.

He yanked her toward the gaping black hole.

She didn't know what she ought to be more wary of. The guns. The fire genies. The woman in gray.

Him.

She balked as he dragged her forward.

The frigid temperature of the black hole slapped her and she twisted away on instinct, but his grip was impossible to break.

Alastor stepped into the darkness, taking both her and the unconscious girl with him. The cold was worse than she'd expected, so bone-numbingly bitter that she felt like the skin was being flayed off her body. She tried to take a breath, but there was no air, only shards of ice, shards of glass, brutal cold that tore at her airway and lungs.

By comparison, Alastor's grasp on her felt like a tropical sun. She instinctively leaned toward him. The movement was a bad idea. Vertigo assailed her. She couldn't feel the ground beneath her feet, or even the weight of her limbs. There was no sensation of gravity. Only nothingness.

She didn't know where they were. Didn't know where they were going. Wasn't certain she would survive the trip.

The world tilted crazily to one side, then the other. She lost her sense of which way was up, lost any balance or coordination. Her stomach churned. Her head ached. Bile crawled up her throat.

She had the fleeting thought that she would never eat edamame, cheesy fish crackers or chocolate-covered raisins again.

And then came the sound of the unknown girl, barfing her guts out, doing exactly what Naphré felt like doing.

"Sodding. Bloody. Hell," Alastor snarled.

Yep, that about summed it up.

# CHAPTER TEN

"SHE BARFED ON MY Berlutis." Alastor stared woefully at his once pristine three-eyelet lace-up court shoes, now speckled with either the detritus of digestion or water droplets from one of the puddles that had dotted the alley. He could only hope it was the latter.

He glanced at Naphré, who was looking a bit peaky, and said, "I'm rather impressed that you didn't follow suit. I well recall the…unpleasantness I experienced the first few times I opened a portal." It was something that one had to acclimate to slowly.

Naphré held out a hand, palm outward, as though warding off even the sound of his voice. "W-w-w-whatever the hell you j-j-j-just did to me," she croaked, teeth chattering. "Do *not* do it again."

"I saved your arse, pet. Be thankful I did." She had no idea how thankful. Only two human days had passed, yet it seemed the *Shikome* had gotten tired of waiting for him to bring Naphré to Izanami. Or perhaps she had gotten tired of waiting for *him*.

Either way, her presence in the alley had been, in his opinion, the biggest threat of the evening.

Naphré's fingers curled into the fine wool of his jacket as she clutched at him for support. He gave her a minute, letting her lean her shoulder against him—

liking the feeling of having her close. He suspected she didn't even realize she was doing it.

She was competent. Strong. Intriguing—

She pressed her lips together, closed her eyes and inhaled sharply.

—and possibly about to hurl.

He took one giant step to the left. Just in case.

Reaching into his pocket, he withdrew a toffee caramel, unwrapped it one-handed—the other being full of unconscious female—and popped the candy in his mouth. He needed a sugar rush.

After a moment, Naphré squared her shoulders. She dragged her hair back from her face and turned her head to glare at him.

"Not an experience I'd ever want to repeat," she muttered.

"It was preferable to being shot, spitted and roasted, was it not?" Not to mention preferable to being taken by the *Shikome*. But he chose not to mention that. He took out another candy. "Here. Eat this."

Her glare ramped up to daggers of death. But she took the toffee. Then, to his utter stupefaction, she fished through her jacket pocket for a small bottle of clear liquid, squirted a bit in her hand and rubbed for several seconds. Only when she appeared satisfied did she unwrap and eat the candy.

"Hand sanitizer. It's the bugs you can't see that will get you," she murmured when she caught him staring at her.

"Right."

She shot him a suspicious glance, and echoed, "Right." Then she gathered herself, looked around, and froze. "We're on my street."

"Blimey. You don't say."

"What are we doing on my street?"

"We had to go somewhere."

"Not here. Somewhere else." Her tone was hard, brooking no argument.

So he didn't offer one. Why bother to argue when agreement would do just as well? "Fine. Suggest an alternative."

"How about your place?"

"Fine. I'll reopen a portal."

She turned pale at that. "A portal? Why? You live in the Underworld?"

That made him smile. "No. I live in Hilo, Hawaii."

"Really?" Her brows shot up. "I guess I expected you to live in England. I didn't picture you in a tropical climate, but that explains the tan. Why Hilo?"

"Weather is outside my control."

"Excuse me?"

"I dislike change. The weather in Hilo is consistent. It varies a mere five degrees throughout the year. I can arrive home on any day and find everything exactly as I left it."

Naphré opened her mouth, closed it and frowned. Finally, she said, "You have issues."

She had no idea.

"So do you," he murmured, and she laughed.

"You have no idea."

For a second, something shimmering and delicate stretched between them, an instant of connection. It lured him. It repelled him. Connecting with anyone was dangerous. Losing them ripped open too many wounds. And he was bound to lose Naphré because she was hip-deep in a load of shite. She was a Daughter of Aset who'd apparently turned her back on her kind and prostituted her murderous skills to the highest bidder. She was indebted to Sutekh, hunted by Izanami. She was trouble in a dark-haired, dark-eyed, incredibly alluring package, and if he had half a brain, he'd get as far from her as he could.

Unfortunately, he was beginning to doubt that he had even half a brain.

"Let's get her inside." Alastor hefted the unconscious woman and draped her over his shoulder like a coiled garden hose, her long hair hanging toward the ground. She chose that moment to moan and roll. On instinct, he slapped his hand against a handy body part to steady her. The handiest part just happened to be her arse.

Raising his head, he caught Naphré staring at him. Her expression was utterly blank, her dark eyes giving nothing away. Bloody hell.

"You probably clean up at poker," he muttered, shifting his grip and settling his palm on the small of the girl's back instead.

"You know it."

"Is your flat the main floor or the first?" he asked, his sole interest at the moment in divesting himself of the unconscious girl.

"Main floor. First floor. Aren't they the same thing?" He gathered she'd like to add a *duh* to the end of that question, but somehow refrained.

"No, they are not the same thing."

He started walking toward the front door of the tall, narrow house set between two other tall, narrow houses. It was an upscale downtown street, one where the homes looked to be about a century old, but were all well-tended and maintained. He'd guess mostly single-family residences, with the occasional conversion to a multi-unit dwelling. "The ground floor is exactly what it sounds like. The floor that is level with the ground. The first floor is the one above it."

"No, that's the second floor."

"No—" He cut himself off and turned his head to look at her over his shoulder. What was it about Naphré Kurata that drew him into an argument one might hear between children in short pants?

Worse still, what made him...*enjoy* it?

"Keys," he said very softly. An order.

She studied him for a long moment, her expression neutral, revealing nothing of her thoughts. But then, he didn't need to read her expression to know what she was thinking at the moment. He could practically hear the word *asshole* echoing down the deserted street. Finally, she shoved her hand in her pocket and came up with a set of keys. Pushing past him, she led the way up three wide stairs to the front door—frosted, etched glass set in an oak frame.

"Pretty," he said, not bothering to mask his sarcasm. "But not particularly safety-conscious."

She didn't bother with a reply.

"How many flats?" he asked, wanting to form an estimate of how many people might be in the building.

"Flats? Oh, apartments. Three." Naphré unlocked the front door and pushed it open. There was a small entry hallway. Directly ahead was a narrow staircase, and to the right of that, a heavy door with a peephole: the entry to the ground-floor flat.

"This way," she said, and headed up. "There's a student who rents the basement. And a business guy who rents the first—" she laughed softly and amended "—*ground* floor. He travels a lot."

"Rents from whom?" he asked.

"Me."

Fascinating. "Nice house. Nice neighborhood. The assassin business pays well."

"You ought to know. I'm guessing you have a lovely little place in Hilo."

*Little* was not a term that applied. And he didn't get paid for his kills—at least, not in dollars. He earned his money through wise investment. "Touché, pet." He couldn't help but smile. "Each flat is separate?"

"Yes."

They reached the top of the stairs. There was a small landing, large enough for only one person, so Alastor remained a couple of steps behind.

"You live alone?" he asked as she slid the key in the lock.

"I have a roommate." There was an interesting undercurrent to her reply. Amusement, perhaps.

He had the fleeting, rather intense, thought that he didn't want her roommate to be a man. Unless he was gay. That would be acceptable.

Naphré pushed open the door and stepped inside, then half turned toward him.

"May I come in?" he asked.

A tight smile tugged at her lips. "What…you can't come in unless I invite you? Like a—" she lowered her voice and whispered "—vampire?"

"No such thing as vampires, pet." His gaze dipped to her left shoulder where they both knew the dark mark was cut into her skin. "But that's an interesting word choice, don't you think, what with you being Otherkin.

Daughters of Aset are pranic feeders, right? You drink the life force of others. Drink their blood."

She gasped, and her eyes widened a fraction before she locked down her expression once more. She didn't blurt out questions or denials. She was one cool player, his Naphré.

*His* Naphré. Bloody hell. He was losing his sodding mind.

"Interesting what one can learn when one's brother is shagging a Daughter of Aset." He stepped forward, using his size to try and crowd her back. When she refused to yield an inch, they stood toe to toe, glaring at each other. "As to your question about not coming in unless you invite me...I can do anything I please," he murmured. "I was just being polite."

"Daughters of Aset don't *shag* soul reapers."

"No?" He let his gaze take a leisurely meander down her body. "We shall see."

She jerked back, rallied and said, "I suppose we shall."

Stepping back, she flicked on the light, held the door wide and let him in.

Her flat was larger than he'd expected. The house might not be wide, but it was deep. Directly ahead was a long, narrow hallway. To the left was a staircase that ascended to the next floor and to the right was a large, arched opening that led to a living room.

Stepping to the right, he took a quick look about. The rooms flowed one into the next, spaces demarcated by furniture placement rather than walls and doors. Living room at the front, then dining room. His gaze drifted to the rectangular wooden table. Big enough to seat eight or ten. That table told him a great deal about her. She had a social life. She entertained family or friends. She'd said she had a roommate, but one didn't have a table that size to serve one. Or even two...

There was a half wall at the far end of the dining room, then the kitchen. It was a good size—cherry cabinets, granite counters, stainless appliances—and beyond that a small sitting room with an enormous television.

Returning his attention to the living room, he looked for a place to dump the unconscious woman he held. The space was neat, clean, everything in its place. He liked that. His home was the same. No clutter. Few knickknacks. He liked the minimalist look, and from what he could see of Naphré's flat, so did she.

He blinked as he realized he was mapping out common ground, common habits. Looking for a connection with her. Which was, quite simply, mad.

Thrusting those thoughts away, he refocused on assessing his surroundings. The furniture was almost uniformly white. The accents were black and, here and there, a splash of blue. The pieces were clean and strong, almost masculine. He cut a glance at Naphré, wondering again if her roommate was male. The oversize television and strong decor suggested he might be, and that possibility rankled.

The woman he held stirred once more, and Alastor headed for the couch under the large front window, intending to divest himself of his burden.

"Do *not*," Naphré said in a furious whisper.

"What?" He looked back at her over his shoulder. She still stood directly beside the door, an odd, pained look on her face as her gaze dipped to his feet, then back to his eyes.

The look she settled on him left him feeling like he'd been judged and come up lacking, and blimey, but he had no clue what it was that had got her hackles up.

"What?" he asked again.

"She barfed. And she was sitting on the ground in the alley. Who knows what seeped into her clothes. Do not put her on my white couch. Wait." She closed and locked the door, then leaned down to remove her boots. She worked swiftly, taking off one, then the other, and lining them neatly side by side on a mat by the door. She slipped her feet into a pair of plain black slippers, then she straightened and sent him another one of those pained looks, her gaze sliding from the woman he held down his legs to his feet. She stared at his Berlutis a second too long, and for some reason he was left feeling like a barbarian.

Then off she went, up the second set of stairs, and he saw her pull that little bottle of hand sanitizer from her pocket once more. She returned with a flannel sheet, unfolded it, laid it over the couch and said, "Okay, fine. You can put her down now."

"Your wish, my command."

"Really?" The look she gave him spoke volumes. "Then I wish you could disappear and take puke girl with you."

"*You're* the one who decided to bring her along."

"What was I supposed to do? Leave her there?"

"Why not? They were after *you*. She would have been perfectly fine."

She stared at him, brow furrowed, then she dipped her head toward the sheet-covered couch and again said, "You can put her down."

"Right." He'd almost forgotten he was holding

her, he'd been so focused on Naphré. Leaning in, he dropped his shoulder, letting the girl slide off.

"Is that really what you thought?" Naphré asked. "That they were after me?"

Her tone made him wary, made him feel like he'd missed some key part of this picture. "Of course. Why do you think I stepped in? For some strange woman I care nothing about?"

"*I'm* a strange woman you care nothing about."

There was absolutely nothing in this world or the next that would tempt him to answer that.

She stared at him, then said slowly, "You stepped in because you thought you were protecting me. What the hell do you think you are? My big brother?"

Definitely not. In no way did he ever want to think of himself as her brother.

Liquid, dark eyes stared back at him. Shell-pink lips parted. A faint flush tinged her cheeks. So pretty. She was so damned pretty.

Her gaze dropped to his mouth and enough seconds ticked past that he felt that look like an arrow to his groin.

Bloody hell. She got him hard with just one look.

He'd kissed her in the alley, a hard, quick press of his lips on hers. He wanted to kiss her again, slow, take his time. Put his tongue inside her and taste her. Peel her clothes off. Touch her smooth, golden skin.

Put his fingers inside her. And then his cock.

Locking down his control, he asked, "Are you saying they weren't after you?" The words came out a little rough.

She shook her head. "I told you...they were after

*her.* It was looking like a date rape. Or worse. They drugged her."

"Did they? I thought she was drunk and in the wrong place at the wrong time." He paused, shrugged. "And I didn't give a damn. Playing the knight for human females is not a priority."

"Yet you played the knight for me." The softly voiced assertion hung between them. "What were you doing in that alley, anyway?" she demanded.

"I saw you get turned away by the security guard." He'd figured she would give up then. But, no. Not Naphré. "When you took off around the back of the building, I thought you'd gone to reconnoiter. You didn't reappear out front—" he shrugged "—so I followed." And by then, she'd already grabbed the girl and stirred up a mess of trouble.

"You—" She closed her mouth and frowned. "What were you doing at the Temple?"

"I followed you."

"You followed me? From here?" She sounded affronted. Appalled. "How did I not see you?"

"Soul reapers are seen only if they wish to be seen, pet."

"What, you're like the invisible man?"

"I can shift the bonds between molecules so I refract light."

She blinked.

The woman on the couch moaned, drawing his attention. She was sprawled with one leg hanging off the edge, and one arm extended awkwardly off to the side and down so her fingertips skimmed the floor. The other arm was tucked beneath her at an extremely uncomfortable-looking angle. With a shake of his head,

Alastor rearranged her limbs, then shifted her head so her neck wasn't twisted to one side.

When he looked up, Naphré was watching him, brows delicately arched over dark eyes. He could drown in those eyes. Not because he could read her thoughts there, but because he couldn't.

He *couldn't*. It hit him then. He ought to be able to look into mortal eyes and see the shine or the tarnish of their soul. That's the way it played out with every mortal he'd ever encountered. But with Naphré, all he saw was *her*. Her secrets and her soul were veiled.

It was as though she wasn't purely human, though the energy signature he got from her said she was. A puzzle. One that had warning bells clanging.

"You've had experience taking care of unconscious women," she said. Her gaze shifted to the woman on the couch, then back to his face, and he felt inexplicably defensive.

"It was an automatic reaction."

He did have experience, but not the sort she thought. Unbidden, memories of his adoptive mother flickered through his thoughts, not the way she had been when he was small—which was the way he preferred to remember her—but the way she had looked lying in her bed near the end of her life, feeble, weak, insensate most of the time. He remembered slipping his arm behind her back and lifting her so she could sip a cup of water.

She'd died shortly after Sutekh took him. She'd never had the chance to see him one last time.

He'd never had the chance to say goodbye.

Hell, he hadn't had the chance to say goodbye to any

of them. His family had died and turned to dust before he ever made it to Topworld once more.

Resolutely, he thrust the memories aside.

"She'd have a horrible crick if I left her like that," he muttered as he turned away from the girl on the couch.

Seconds ticked past and Naphré made no reply. Then she offered one of those enigmatic, incredible, close-lipped smiles, more predatory than pretty. And blimey if he didn't feel like the sun had come out.

She moved past him and rested her fingertips on the girl's neck, checking her carotid pulse. Apparently satisfied, she turned away and called, "Niko? You here, baby?"

Then she went to the bottom of the stairs and called up, but again, there was no reply.

Niko. The roommate. Something dark uncoiled inside him, something possessive and territorial.

As though she sensed the rising tide, she glanced at him over her shoulder. Too late.

SHE DIDN'T EVEN SEE him move. One second he was five feet away, the next, he was crowding her back against the door, danger and heat, a perfect predator.

"We have a bit of unfinished business, pet." He flattened his palm against the door by her head and stared down at her. She could see every feathered lash, and the faint gold stubble that told her he'd shaved hours past.

"I don't think so." But she did. He'd kissed her in the alley. And now he was going to kiss her again. She was going to *let* him kiss her again.

He leaned in and brushed the side of his nose against

hers. She ought to move away. But the part of her that was balking at the danger he presented was far weaker than the part of her that was wildly attracted to it.

Closing her eyes, she let sensation ramp through her as he moved his nose along her cheek and down to the angle of her jaw. The smell of his skin—like sunshine and tropical breezes—lured her, and the feel of his lashes fanning her cheek as he blinked.

She was trapped between the solid contours of his body and the door at her back. And she liked it. Liked the sensation of him looming over her, and the light touch of his lips on her throat.

With a little moan she arched her neck, wanting his mouth on hers. Her lips felt swollen. Her breasts felt swollen. She was aching for his kiss and the touch of his hand.

Lust. Only lust, she told herself.

But then she thought of the strange sense of recognition that she'd experienced the very first time she saw him at the Playhouse Lounge, and she wondered…

He drew back. She almost whimpered.

"So impatient, pet." His smile was primitive. Bright white. "The tease is part of the pleasure. I like to take my time." Something flickered in his eyes. Something dark and a little frightening. "Priceless art. Precious gems." His lashes lowered, lifted. "Fleeting moments of pure joy. These things are meant to be savored, not rushed."

Her breath caught. Was that what he thought she was? A fleeting moment of pure joy?

He lifted his hand and ran the backs of his fingers along her cheek. His touch made her skin sing.

And then he kissed her. He swooped in and took

her, slanting his lips on hers. His tongue pushed inside, tasting her, claiming her. No tentative touch or gentle breach. He took what he wanted, and something deep inside her unfurled and answered.

With a moan, she caught hold of the fine wool of his suit jacket, crushing the material in her fists, trying to drag him closer. He let her feel only his kiss when she wanted more, wanted his body full against her, skin to skin.

This was crazy. On some level, she knew that. But she stamped that thought beneath her heel and met the thrust of his tongue with her own.

Taking her lower lip between his teeth, he bit her, then sucked on her. The sensations that rushed through her were like nothing she'd ever experienced, nothing she'd ever imagined.

He'd strummed her to a near frenzy with barely a touch and one kiss.

When he pulled back a little, she followed, her mouth seeking his.

He fisted his hands in her hair, tipping her head so he could kiss her deeper, taking what he wanted.

With a gasp, she shoved her hands under his suit jacket and skimmed her palms along his back, feeling the heat of him through his shirt.

He caught her wrists, dragged them up over her head and held them there with one hand, the other stroking slowly down her arm, her shoulder, her waist.

She couldn't breathe. Didn't need to breathe. There was only the feel of him, the taste of him. Everything else fell away.

Coming up on her toes, she molded herself against him, wanting to be closer, pressed tighter. She wanted his clothes gone, and hers. She wanted to feel him moving naked against her.

Something inside her clicked. A sense of self-preservation. What the hell was she doing?

Kissing a soul reaper. Inviting him in.

This was not a good plan. This was not any plan. It was basic and raw. And it was far into the danger zone.

With a gasp, she jerked away, turning her face toward her shoulder. She didn't dare look at him. He was temptation wrapped up in a well-tailored package, and she was way too close to the flame.

Slowly, she dragged her trapped wrists from his grasp, a little surprised that he let her.

His thigh was pressed high between her own. And his taste was on her tongue.

A kiss. Just a kiss. But really, so much more than that. A claiming. A stamp of ownership.

But she couldn't say with any certainty exactly who had been stamping whom.

# CHAPTER ELEVEN

"BACK OFF." SHE SHOVED hard against his chest.

She was breathing hard and avoiding his gaze. Alastor figured that unless he wanted all-out war, he'd be wise to do exactly as she asked. So he stepped back and let her go, though the primitive thing inside him was writhing against the restraint. He wanted her. She wanted him. Simplicity itself.

"You're making things complicated," he murmured.

"This isn't—" She broke off, shook her head.

He wanted to push, to demand capitulation, but he had a feeling that with Naphré, patience would serve him better.

She shot a glance through the archway into the living room, made a show of sniffing the air and wrinkling her nose.

"I smell like puke," she said, her tone flat. She didn't, but as far as excuses went, it was innovative. "She got me when she hurled in the car. I need a shower." She jerked her head toward the woman sleeping on the couch. "You get to stay here and play nursemaid if she wakes up. There's a bucket under the sink in the kitchen. If she throws up again, it better be into that, or you'll be the one mopping the floor."

"According to whom?"

Ducking around him, she headed for the stairs. With her hand on the banister, she paused, head bowed, shoulders tight.

"According to me," she said without looking back.

And she clearly believed she could enforce her threat. It was a novel experience, having a woman treat him as an equal. Not a coddled son or brother. Not a knight or savior. Not a threat. Exactly as an equal. He couldn't think of a time in his life where that had ever happened before.

Then she bolted up the stairs, her slippers slapping wood.

Alastor stepped forward and watched her gorgeous, round arse sway, appreciating the view. Then she was gone, and a moment later, the sound of running water carried down to him.

He fought the urge to follow her.

Naphré Kurata was a conundrum. She was a Topworld assassin who double-tapped without blinking, but she caved under a single kiss.

Bloody fascinating.

Making his way along the hall, Alastor discovered a powder room beneath the stairs. He assessed his clothing and was pleased to note that it was spatter-free. There were a few scorched holes at the shoulder, as well as a long, narrow rent on the left sleeve where the first bullet had winged him, and a hole in the back to the right of midline. His white shirt was bloodstained. His arm was gouged. His right side striped where the second bullet had taken out a chunk.

Overall, he had fared well.

And the burns he'd sustained when his father incinerated the centipedes were almost gone now. Rapid healing was one of the benefits of being Sutekh's son. Getting the wounds in the first place was one of the downsides.

He used a damp tissue to wipe his shoes clean. Not vomit. Water stains from the puddles. Still, they were ruined.

As he tossed the tissue in the trash and washed his hands and then his bullet wounds, he recalled the look on Naphré's face as she'd stared at his shoes. She'd lined her own boots up beside the door.

Perhaps the shoes-on, shoes-off issue was important to her. No, not perhaps. Definitely. He put his shirt back on, then his jacket. Heading back to the front door, he left his shoes neatly lined up beside hers.

That done, he wandered through the living spaces in his stocking feet. He could hear the water running in the bathroom overhead. Naphré was in there. Showering. Naked.

His lips curled as he wondered what she'd do if he went up and joined her, backed her against the wall, kissed her—

A loud bang carried from the upper floor, followed quickly by a second and a third. He heard her curse, then, "Damn, you're fast."

Tipping his head back, he stared at the ceiling, wondering whom she was talking to. The mysterious Niko? An unpleasant kernel of jealousy unfurled in his gut.

He focused, but picked up no sense of anyone in the building save Naphré and the unconscious girl.

There was no more banging. Just the pounding of the shower. He imagined the water sluicing over her smooth skin: shoulders, breasts, belly. She'd be soaping her hands now, trailing them up her arms—

No, she wouldn't be trailing anything. She'd be scrubbing swiftly and efficiently and finishing the shower in record time.

There. The water turned off. She'd been in there less than five minutes.

He pictured her stepping from the shower stall, her hair wet and slicked back from her face, the water beading on her lips. He wanted to lick those droplets from her skin. He wanted to turn her against the wall with her palms flat and her breasts pressed against the cool tile. He wanted to slide his fingers between her thighs. Tease her. Push one finger, then two, inside her. Seal his teeth against the nape of her neck and bite. Make her come for him. Make her scream.

For that single shining moment, he didn't want them to be equal. He wanted to master her, mate her. Mark her as his.

PYOTR FOLLOWED DJESERIT into her office, unwilling to invite her into his own. He wanted nothing of her to taint his private domain, not even a molecule of her scent, or a single shed cell of her skin.

"The police?" she demanded as she whirled to face him, her voice hoarse and jagged. "They're out there, taking names and contact information of every congregant who was at the party."

"It's been taken care of," he replied.

She made a dismissive sound. "Your assurance is worthless."

He stared at her, his gut churning with hate and anger. He wanted to kill her. And that was an impossibility. They were like conjoined twins, each unable to separate from the other without risking his own demise.

They were constrained by circumstance, by the secret knowledge they each held.

Secret even from themselves. The identity of the puppet-master behind the soul reaper's murder was locked in their psyches, to be released only upon their deaths.

"The police have investigated to their satisfaction," he replied at last. "They merely follow protocol, taking names. There will be no further investigation." It had taken only three phone calls to make the issue disappear. Phone calls to highly-placed individuals to head off any but the most cursory investigation of the gunfire and flaming wreckage that Naphré Kurata and her unexpected savior had left in the alley.

Nostrils flaring, Djeserit took a long, slow breath, as though girding herself against the urge to attack. "And Xaphan's concubines?" she asked. "What role did they play?"

In all truthfulness, he replied, "I have no idea. They arrived. They flung fire and burned the sedan until it was a charred, twisted hulk. But whether they meant their actions as allies or enemies...how am I to know?" In the melee it had been impossible to tell whose side they were fighting on. Had they aimed their fire at the reaper or the Setnakhts? Both had been singed. Perhaps that had been their intent.

Djeserit was breathing hard, her nostrils flaring, her hands fisted tight by her sides. She wanted to kill him.

Just as he wanted to kill her.

"Go ahead," he whispered. "Try."

He so wanted her to try. That would give him leave to retaliate.

Of course, neither of them could break their unholy pact and complete the act. But he would enjoy the process of bringing her close to the brink of death once more.

The other night, when he had wrapped his hands around her throat and held on until her tongue protruded like a swollen purple snake, he had ached to finish the deed. She had given as good as she got; he had bruises on his arms where she had pummeled him and a lump on the back of his head where she'd cracked him with a crystal vase.

But her struggles were not the reason he had refrained from killing her. He could not take her life without risking his own, along with any potential immortality. If he sent her to the Underworld, she would only betray him to whatever god or demigod claimed her soul. Word would get out, and then those who wished to avenge Lokan Krayl's death would come for him.

So he had been forced to take his hands from her neck, to settle for the small joy he got from the sight of the marks he had left on her skin.

Then she had stolen even that paltry pleasure by covering them with the turtlenecks she had worn since.

"You asinine fool!" Djeserit advanced on him, her dark eyes narrowed. Despite her olive coloring, her face was a pale oval framed by the black turtleneck and black knitted cap she wore. Her lips were pale and bloodless, while two bright red flags stained her cheeks. "You lost them both. Two Daughters of Aset in one place, and you let them get away."

"I? I lost them?" His anger was so rich and thick that his voice trembled with the force of it. "I did not hire

Naphré Kurata's mentor to kill her. I did not stalk her when he failed. I did not let her see me at the graveyard and open us up to all manner of difficulties, including her very presence here this night. It was not me that she sought when she attempted to talk her way past security. *You* are the reason Naphré came here tonight. Hence, you are the reason Marie has escaped our grasp."

He made no mention of his own involvement in this night's debacle. He had no idea what madness had allowed him to leave Marie unattended in the alley even for a moment. But she had been insensate. He had not imagined she could get very far.

He certainly had not imagined that Naphré would leap to the girl's rescue. His research indicated she had broken with the Asetian Guard years ago. And Marie was not even on their radar. Yet here were two Daughters of Aset, the one saving the other. Was his intel wrong? Was his contact within the Asetian Guard unreliable? Were Marie and Naphré both secret members?

He could not credit it. His contact in the Guard was well situated and in a position to have access to all manner of classified information. A mole at one of the highest levels. It had taken him a decade to cultivate that connection. She had confirmed that Naphré had no contact with the Guard, and that Marie had flown under their radar.

But even more alarming than Naphré's presence was the fact that it was a soul reaper Pyotr had glimpsed dragging them both off. Two Daughters of Aset in the company of, if Pyotr was not mistaken, not merely a peon, but one of Sutekh's sons. Having had a hand in the murder of one, he could not mistake another.

What gave these two women such value that the
reaper exposed himself in order to nab them, breaking
the custom of avoiding being seen by humans? One
more question to add to his ever-growing list.

"What do the police believe occurred?"

"It will be recorded as three deaths due to a drunk
driver, and a car with an exploding propane tank in the
trunk."

Quite inventive, if he did say so himself.

"Three?"

"Yes." The three men who had backed him up in
the chase had all died, incinerated in the raging inferno
that had consumed the car. A sad and tragic loss. And
incredibly convenient that their deaths rendered them
unable to share with Djeserit the information that they
had seen the soul reaper in the alley.

Djeserit did not—and would not—know of the reaper's  presence, because she had arrived after he had
disappeared. She had seen nothing but the aftermath,
and Pyotr was not about to enlighten her.

Pyotr sucked in a sharp breath. A soul reaper. In the
company of Daughters of Aset.

It was impossible. Soul reapers and Otherkin did not
work together. Yet they *had* been together, not once,
but twice, tonight, and the night Djeserit had seen him
at the cemetery.

He needed to think. He needed to plan.

What if the secrets of the Setnakhts—his secrets—
had been betrayed?

Impossible.

Mastering his rising panic, he kept his expression
neutral, revealing nothing of his thoughts.

Djeserit whirled away from him and walked around

her massive glass-and-metal desk to settle into her ergonomic chair, a luxury paid for by the congregation at the astonishing cost of nearly ten thousand dollars. For a chair.

Pyotr knew she wished to make a statement by her action, to make him stand before her like a subordinate while she sat in luxury, to show him she was the one with the greater position and power. A week ago, he would have let her because it amused him.

Tonight, he stepped forward, swept his arm across the glass surface and sent pens and papers and laptop sailing through the air before plummeting to the ground.

She cried out, then mastered her reaction and simply glared at him in silence.

"Unfortunately, we are bound by the blood of our greatest kill," Pyotr spat. "We have no choice but to work in tandem. We are the two who know the truth of the soul reaper's death." A truth that was buried beyond their conscious reach, a fail-safe to protect them, they had been told. Of course, it was truly there to protect the identity of whoever had sent Gahiji to them.

He reached across the desk and rested his fingers on her throat, thin cloth separating him from the bruises he had already put there. She stared at him, her expression utterly composed, but her eyes reflected her fear. Good. She should be afraid.

He lowered his voice to a whisper. "I cannot sacrifice you without betraying my own involvement, and you cannot kill me without betraying yours. So we are stuck with each other, until our plan is complete."

"Sutekh will come," Djeserit murmured. "He will

live again and walk in the sun. The prophesy foretells it. 'The blood of Aset. The blood of Sutekh. And the God will pass the Twelve Gates and walk the Earth once more.'"

Pyotr inhaled sharply. She'd said she knew of the prophesy. He hadn't expected her to quote it verbatim. But hearing the words spoken aloud brought clarity to his thoughts.

"The blood of Aset," he murmured.

"Mixed with the blood of Sutekh's son. The blood of Sutekh to summon Sutekh." Djeserit paused. "We need Marie back. You are the one who lost her, so you must find her."

Pyotr drew back and stared at her. Marie's blood was weak, but they access to another...he shook his head. "Perhaps I was too hasty in discounting Naphré Kurata."

Djeserit stared at him, then offered one of her irritating, slow blinks. "That is a quick about-face."

"An about-face, yes. But not one made without due consideration. We have yet to find a true enough Asetian bloodline. We keep collecting from weak progeny and waiting until we have enough. Yet it seems that there is never enough. Naphré's line is pure and powerful, the most pure and powerful we have yet discovered—"

"Stumbled upon," Djeserit interjected.

Pyotr ignored her, his good humor somewhat restored as possibilities unfurled. "Her blood may well be worth the extra effort."

And with the help of his contact, a traitor within the ranks of the Asetian Guard, perhaps there was a way to get it.

BATTLING THE INSTINCT TO TEAR up the stairs and lick the water from Naphré's skin, Alastor scanned the walls, the shelves, searching for a distraction. He was supposed to be luring her to the Underworld, not his bed. Business was business. He'd be wise to keep that thought front and center.

On a high table were two framed photos: one of Naphré in what appeared to be her teens, standing beside an unsmiling, white-haired man. Another of a younger, dark-haired man who looked enough like the first that Alastor guessed them to be father and son. And Alastor thought the nose, the chin...Naphré's father and grandfather?

On the wall was a photograph of a young, smiling girl, long hair in pigtails, dark eyes fringed with straight lashes. She was flanked by the younger of the two men and a beautiful brown-haired, brown-eyed woman with a Mediterranean cast to her features. A family portrait.

Alastor looked away, feeling a bit like a voyeur, though he wondered at the sentiment. The portrait was out on public display for any guest to see.

But that was just it. He wasn't exactly a guest.

He felt like he had no right to look at her family.

Probably because he'd hate for anyone to pry into his memories of his own. The mortal family he'd lost.

It had been centuries, but a part of him would always mourn them and the loss of the life he had expected to be his. He had been the pampered golden son among a flock of women: mother, sisters, nieces.

But the greater part of him relished the fact that he was Sutekh's son. Immortal. In the beginning, he had been tortured by the knowledge of what he was. He was no longer conflicted. The soul reaper part of him had won.

Now his brothers were his family.

And one of them was gone.

Pulling out his cell, he rang Mal. As usual, the call went to voice mail. *"You got Mal. Talk. If I like what you have to say, you'll hear back from me."*

"Wanker," he muttered and disconnected.

The phone rang almost immediately.

"If you're there, why didn't you just pick up?" Alastor asked, annoyed.

"I had company. Just seeing her out, in fact. Hang on a sec." Alastor heard the murmur of goodbyes, a feminine voice, the sound of a door closing, then Mal asked, "Feeling a bit pissy, bro?"

"Pukey, if you'd really like to know."

"What?"

"I just rescued a drugged human female."

Mal was silent a moment. Then he said, "Mazel tov."

"Funny." Alastor paused. "There's a point to my call. You're tight with Xaphan's concubines—"

"Only about a dozen of them. I've yet to seduce the rest. But hope springs eternal."

"Sod off. Look, I want you to see if you can find out why they're so interested in Lokan's death." He did a quick rundown of the events in the alley and the fact that the fire genies had been unexpected additions to the melee. "It's nagging at me, and you know how I am with things that don't fit in their proper place."

"That I do, bro," Mal said. "Exactly what were you doing in that alley?"

"Reconnaissance." Alastor brought him up to speed on Butcher's darksoul and the *Shikome*.

"Centipedes?" Mal asked at one point, then fell silent as Alastor explained the rest.

"I hope to go to Izanami and find a way to gain access to the information locked in Butcher's bloody sodding darksoul." In order to do that, Alastor needed Naphré to accompany him. "The way the *Shikome* showed up tonight in the alley makes me think time is of the essence."

Which made no sense. Though days had passed Topworld, in Izanami's realm it would be more like minutes. So why the bloody hell was the *Shikome* so anxious?

"You're actually planning to go there? To Izanami's territory?" Mal asked.

"Yeah, I bloody well am." He'd been following Naphré tonight, trying to decide whether to ask nicely if she'd like to go on a little trip to the Underworld, or just grab her. He still hadn't made up his mind as to which approach was best. "You're planning to go to Osiris's realm," he pointed out.

"Different situation entirely."

True. Mal was being sent to Osiris by Sutekh's decree as part of the hostage exchange for the meeting of allies, whereas Alastor had no doubt that Sutekh was feeling less than jolly about his own intent to visit the *Shikome*.

"Besides, Osiris is part of my grand plan," Mal said.

"And it appears that Izanami is now part of mine," Alastor said. "You share your plan with Sutekh?"

"Did he share his with us?"

Of course Sutekh had a plan. Alastor had no doubt of that. But he hadn't shared it with his sons. Not yet.

"Speaking of plans..." Alastor said. "I got to thinking about the boxes of bones and frozen body parts, and the photographs of the victims that Dagan and I found in Joe Marin's basement. What if those murders weren't the work of one man alone? What if they were sanctioned?"

"You're thinking that maybe none of this was about Joe Marin's personal proclivities? That maybe what you found in that basement was bigger than that? Say, the size of a worldwide cult."

"I think it's a possibility. Unfortunately, the gentleman in question is unavailable to confirm." Joe Marin was dead, his heart and darksoul harvested by Dae. They hadn't pried much information out of him before the kill, and Sutekh hadn't found anything coherent in the darksoul when he'd taken it inside himself. "But then, I come across this drugged girl," Alastor continued, "and I get to thinking, what if there's someone else out there doing the Setnakhts' dirty work?"

"So you think there's a Setnakht murdering human women. What does that have to do with Lokan?" Mal asked.

"We know there's a link between Lokan's death and the Setnakhts. That Xaphan and his concubines are inordinately interested in Lokan's demise." They also knew that Lokan's daughter, Dana, had been in Toronto the night her father was killed. But that last point he didn't voice aloud. He was taking no risks that somewhere, somehow, he would be overheard.

"So what you're really saying is that we know squat,"

Mal said. "The puzzle pieces don't fit." He paused. "I went there, you know. To their Temple."

Alastor was surprised that this was the first he was hearing of it. "What did you find?"

"Not a damned thing. Though they did have some lovely artifacts."

"You didn't."

"Shiny, pretty things. I found a lovely little glass perfume bottle in the shape of a fish just sitting on a shelf in one of the offices. Genuine. Created long before glassblowing was invented..."

"You stole it."

"I prefer to think of it as borrowed on a permanent basis. Couldn't help myself. You know how I am with baubles." Mal laughed darkly. "I hoped I'd walk in and find a neon sign that said, Lokan Krayl's remains, this way."

Alastor heard his brother's pain. It matched his own.

They were both silent for a moment, then Mal said, "If Dae had his way, we'd just kill them all. Anyone who qualifies even remotely for the suspect list."

Dagan had expressed his preference several times. Kill the Setnakhts. Go to war with Xaphan. Annihilate anyone who might have been even remotely involved in Lokan's death.

"But that won't get us answers. And Lokan would still be dead." His soul would still be missing, his body somewhere none of them could find. And while killing everyone—both human and supernatural—that they suspected might be involved would certainly be satisfying, it wouldn't in any way help to bring their brother back. In fact, it might kill all hope of doing so because those souls would be claimed by other deities, just as Butcher's had been. Which meant Sutekh wouldn't have a crack at getting information out of them.

The one consolation for Alastor, and, he suspected, for Dagan and Mal as well was that Lokan's daughter, Dana, was hidden in plain sight in the mortal realm, with no one able to find her save Roxy Tam. In a bizarre twist of fate, it was Roxy who'd figured out what Dana was to them, and Roxy was the only one who could find her if she chose to.

She didn't choose to. Not right now. It was the best way to keep Dana safe. If no one knew where she was, then no one could find her. Or betray her location.

A Daughter of Aset, Sutekh's enemy, standing as protector for the daughter of Sutekh's son.

What a bloody convoluted mess.

Alastor ended the call, and glanced at the girl on the couch. She was curled on her side, her hands tucked beneath her chin. If Naphré was right and she'd been drugged, she'd be asleep for hours.

He crossed to the shelves that lined the opposite wall. There were more pictures of Naphré, one with her arms looped around the shoulders of two women— friends, from the look of it—and another with a group of women and men all wearing running gear. He scanned the faces of the men, then froze as the realization of what he was looking for sank in. The face of the mysterious Niko.

What the bloody hell was he doing?

Annoyed with himself, he turned away from the photos and wandered through the dining room and the kitchen to the den at the back of the house. There was a leather couch there and a low coffee table. But it was what the table held that gave him pause: a bag of coarse salt. A curved knife with a gold handle. Five white candles.

Looked like someone was carrying out a ritual summoning.

He inhaled sharply. Was this related to the fact that Naphré's name was inscribed in Sutekh's book of debts? Was she trying to summon Sutekh himself?

If so, she was in for disappointment. Summoned or not, Sutekh was locked in his own realm as part of the six-thousand-year-old ceasefire agreement. He couldn't come Topworld, though no doubt he'd love to. That was one of the main reasons he'd sired half human sons. He couldn't come Topworld, but they could.

Something thudded against the floor above him. There were a few seconds of silence, then a second thud, louder than the first, and Naphré's voice, hard and low. "Get the fuck off me."

Alastor didn't think. He acted. With preternatural speed he was up the stairs and at her door. He didn't knock, just threw it open, senses alert, his gaze flicking to the corners, searching for threat. Finding none.

She was standing by the dresser, a drawer open, a small pile of folded items on the top.

She spun to face him, her body tense, her posture defensive. She was lean and taut, dark hair swinging damp and loose almost to her shoulders, eyes watchful.

His gaze lingered on her left forearm. There were three gashes there, lined up side by side. Blood for the summoning, no doubt.

"What are you doing?" Her voice was low, controlled. And incredibly sexy. He wanted to shake her control. Shatter it.

Stepping into the room, he approached her slowly.

"I heard you fighting...something."

"Fighting?" Her brows dipped.

"You warned whatever it was to get the fuck off you."

"Get the fu—" She shook her head. "I was chasing a centipede. There were two in the bathroom. Fast little buggers that made it down the drain before I got them. Then a spider here in the bedroom. The thing was the size of my fist."

He shot her a look.

"Okay, maybe not my fist...but it was big."

Bugs. He'd rushed in to save her from bugs.

She looked around. "Niko show up yet?"

Niko. The roommate. Bloke was either sleeping like the dead, or not here. Lucky for him if it was the latter, because Alastor was in no mood to meet him.

She scraped her fingers back through her damp hair. Her black tank top bared a lovely amount of fresh-from-the-shower flushed, naked skin: her shoulders, her arms, an expanse of her chest and the top swell of her breasts.

The primitive part of him, the part that ripped out hearts and harvested souls, reared and snarled. Something about her roused him, and he felt the power turning dark and strong as it flowed through him.

Hunger.

Naphré turned to face him once more, and she gasped as she saw the expression on his face.

"What?" she demanded. "You look positively feral."

"Do I?" He offered no explanation, just kept looking his fill.

She appeared confused for a second, and then—smart girl—her eyes widened and she took a long, slow breath. She knew he was looking at her, knew he liked what he saw. Hell, he figured she knew he wanted her.

There was an answering flicker of awareness in her gaze, a widening and darkening of her eyes, a parting of her lips.

He almost went to her, pulled her against him, the urge was that strong. He wanted to taste her, to push her, to make her give up a measure of control. No, not a measure. All. He wanted her to give up all.

He glanced at her bed, and pictured her there, her dark, straight hair spread on the white pillow. Her hands grasping the bars of the headboard. Better yet, her wrists tied there with dark-red ribbons, pulled taut as he licked and kissed and bit his way down her body.

In that instant, he was glad for the length of his suit jacket.

Her eyes widened even more. Her breath caught.

He wanted her naked. He wanted her willing.

If she took even one step, he would kiss her.

Then her gaze slid away, over his left shoulder, toward the door.

"Niko," she breathed, looking past him.

*Niko.* Jealousy swelled, a dark, ugly tide, and he felt his control slipping away. He tightened the chains, holding it in check.

"There you are, my sweet girl," Naphré cooed.

*Girl.* Alastor pivoted on his heel. Two enormous green eyes peered at him from the top of the armoire on the opposite wall. Then a sleek, black cat leaped down and sauntered out the door and into the hall.

For an instant, he said nothing at all, then, "I was picturing someone larger. Someone Greek. And male."

"Excuse me?"

"Niko. Your roommate. I was expecting a man."

She blinked. "N-E-K-O. Neko. Her name is Neko. It's Japanese—" she shook her head and turned away "—for cat."

Of course. What would Naphré Kurata call her cat, other than *cat?*

The dresser drawer was still open, and she'd knocked over the pile of folded items when she'd spun to face him. He walked over and lifted a scrap of cloth. Panties.

"White cotton?" he asked, rubbing them between his thumb and index finger. "Sensible. You wearing a pair like these right now?"

Her shoulders tensed. She turned very slowly, eyes narrowed, lips taut. "No."

"Take down your pants, pet, and let me see," he ordered softly.

For a second, he thought she'd come at him, hackles raised, claws bared. When she turned away, reaching for another garment, he realized that was exactly what he wanted. He wanted to decimate her control while he kept his intact.

So he caved to instinct and stepped toward her.

# CHAPTER TWELVE

ALASTOR STALKED HER, one step forward for each step back. Naphré crossed her arms over her chest and contemplated avenues of escape. Not because she was afraid that Alastor would come even closer. Because she was afraid that she wanted him to.

A strand of hair curved along his cheek, the color of pale ale. She drank in his features, clean and strong, and then he snared her gaze and she was drowning. Lost.

The moment spun and stretched.

He took another step forward. She took another step back.

The wood of the dresser pressed against her and she froze, pulse kicking up a notch as she realized there was nowhere left to go.

She stared at him as he shucked his jacket and tossed it on the bed. Naphré noticed the fit of his shirt. Made to measure. As he moved, it accented his shoulders and chest.

Then she noticed the blood. On his sleeve and at the side of his waist.

*"Kuso,"* she hissed, reaching out to touch him, freezing with the tips of her fingers only millimeters away. He'd been shot in the alley. How could she have

forgotten that? "You're bleeding." And this close, she could smell it, so wonderfully delicious.

Pure temptation for one such as she. Never had she been more aware of what she was, and what she had chosen not to become. His blood was a dark flower against the pristine white of his shirt.

"Are—" The word caught, and she tried again. "Are you okay?"

"I am." His lips curved at the corners, his smile predatory, knowing. "Are you?"

No. She stared at the blood on his sleeve, tempted, so tempted, then slowly dragged her eyes back to his. Her heart was racing. Her legs felt wobbly.

It wasn't just his blood that lured her.

Attraction. So inconvenient. So dangerous.

He leaned closer and rested his hands on the dresser, one on either side of her, trapping her, but not touching her.

She looked first at his right hand, then at his left, then she raised her head and met his gaze once more. Her heart slammed against her ribs. Common sense told her to push him away. But she seemed to have lost her grasp on common sense. Instead, she stood exactly where she was, feeling the heat of his body across the space between them.

"What about...?" She offered the only protest she could think of.

"She's been drugged. She'll likely sleep for hours."

Of course he was right. For all intents and purposes, they were alone.

Staring straight ahead, she struggled for emotional distance. But straight ahead meant that she was looking at the V of naked, tanned skin revealed by the open collar of his shirt, the strong column of his throat and the clean line of his jaw.

She needed to focus on something other than him, the gorgeous, rich scent of his blood, the lure of his lips, his hard body, so defined under the tailored lines of his shirt. On a purely physical level, she wanted him.

The scent of his blood calling to the part of herself that she denied ramped that attraction up to danger zone.

Eyes glittering, he stared down at her, and she saw in that instant something animalistic. Not human. Here was the soul reaper, the otherworldly creature, peeking through the carefully cultivated veneer of humanity.

A predator in the guise of smooth sophistication.

The most successful predators were all about control, all about waiting for exactly the right moment before they pounced. Too early or too late, and they'd lose their prey.

"Don't," Naphré whispered as his chest brushed hers, a wild shock to her senses.

Panting, she held very still, and with each breath her nipples grazed his chest, layering sensation on sensation. They'd been dancing around this all along. And now, the moment had arrived.

His fingers were warm on the skin of her wrist. She wanted to pull away. She wanted to lean closer.

"Don't what?" he asked, and trailed the backs of his fingers down the side of her forehead to her cheek, her chin, her throat. "Be specific, love. I'm all about the details."

Her breath stopped when his fingers reached her

collarbone, and she hung there, suspended, her pulse tripping like a bird caught in a snare.

He was gentle. And a part of him didn't want to be. She saw that in his eyes, saw the part that wanted to push her down on the floor and spread her thighs and thrust deep without thought or care for her pleasure. He held that part back with cage and chains.

She'd thought him cool, controlled, and now she saw that she'd been wrong. Beneath the layers of ice was a beast, untamed and urgent, held in check by his will alone.

She wanted to free that beast. Wanted to touch it, taste it, make it roar.

The pads of his fingers rested against the wildly pounding pulse at her throat. He splayed his fingers and dragged them slowly along the curve of her shoulder and down her arm, her forearm.

She had time to jerk away. Time to protest. She did nothing other than stand there, heart racing, as he closed his fingers around her wrists. He walked her sideways, then back, guiding her with the weight of his body until she felt the wall, cool and smooth.

Lowering his weight, he pinned her there, and dipped his head to the hollow of her shoulder. She felt his breath against her ear, and then his teeth, catching the lobe and nipping gently.

"Don't what?" he asked again, his voice low and thick.

She swallowed, her mouth dry, her lips feeling full and swollen.

"Don't stop." The words were more thought than sound. It didn't matter. He heard her. And he took what she offered.

His mouth claimed hers, tasting her, the kiss deep and hungry. His tongue pushed inside her mouth, teasing, twining, tormenting. He used his teeth. He used the pressure of his body. He let his hands roam at will, skimming her breasts, her belly, the curve of her hip, then sliding up into her hair, angling her head so he could kiss her more deeply.

He cupped the weight of her breast, his thumb brushing her nipple through tank top and lace bra. A sigh escaped her, then a gasp as he pinched her nipple and rolled it between thumb and forefinger.

His hand dipped to the curve of her waist, then slid around to her ass, kneading and squeezing. She followed his lead, grasping his buttocks, the muscles beautifully curved and hard.

Lust slammed her, sharp and dangerous.

He pulled back just a little, teasing her, making her come to him. And she did. She chased the kiss and pressed against him and offered herself with the thrust of her tongue and the pump of her hips.

Dragging his mouth from hers, he laughed low, the sound so erotic it was like a physical caress.

"I want you to take off your tank top and your jeans," he murmured. "I want to watch you. I want to see your naked skin."

Neither a request nor an order. He only stated what he wanted, knowing that she would give it to him.

He stepped back, not far, just enough that he could do exactly what he'd said he wanted to do: watch her while she peeled her black tank top up over her head. The cloth slipped from her hand and pooled on the floor with a soft shush.

She shivered at the expression in his eyes as he

looked at her. So hungry. So dark. Blue glass held to a flame.

Then he raised his gaze to hers and said, "Your jeans." His voice was like smoke, like velvet. Like sin.

She skimmed her palms along the black lace cups of her bra, down her waist to the button of her jeans. Slowly, she slid it free, then lowered the zipper partway.

"Push them down, pet. Nice and slow."

Somewhere inside her was a seductive creature that wanted his eyes on her, hot and voracious. She'd caught him looking at her ass, more than once.

So she turned her back to him, pushed the zipper down, then pushed the denim over her hips to her thighs, arching her back as she leaned forward very slowly. She heard the hitch in his breathing. She shot him a look over her shoulder, bent all the way forward and slid off first one leg, then the other, knowing that the only thing he was looking at was her behind, now clad only in a pair of see-through black lace boy shorts.

He caught her hands and drew them forward, arranging her palms so they were flat against the wall, and she was bent at the waist, facing away from him.

"Not white cotton," he murmured.

His hands skimmed her ass, squeezed, then slid lower to her thighs.

He was close at her back, leaning over her, his breath touching her nape. Then his teeth. She felt them on her skin. She felt them close on the swell of muscle where her neck met her shoulder.

With a gasp, she tried to straighten, to move.

"No," he rasped. "Stay exactly as you are." His hands moved on her skin, reinforcing his command.

She wanted to turn to him, touch him, pull the clothes from his body and run her tongue along his hot skin. But something in his tone made her stay exactly as she was, hands against the wall, bent forward. A part of her was appalled that she was letting him do this. A part of her was darkly excited.

His fingers freed the catch of her bra, and he pulled the scrap of cloth along her arms so it dangled at her wrists and her breasts were free, the nipples erect. From behind, he slid his hands around her, teased her breasts. She could feel his erection against her buttocks, thick and hard, confined by his clothing.

She arched into his touch, her nipples aching, and that served to press her ass tighter against him.

The way he touched her was mind-drugging. She was aching, wet. She wanted him right now, inside her, full and thick, stretching her, filling her, but he took his time, enjoying her body at his leisure.

"Beautiful," he murmured as he traced his tongue along the bumps of her spine. She believed him. In that moment, she felt incredibly beautiful.

Then he looped his fingers in the top of her panties, and slowly, so slowly, he drew them down, trailing along her thighs, her calves and—oh, God—his tongue followed the path of his fingers.

As he nudged her, she lifted one foot then the other, and then she was bare before him.

"Turn around."

She did, the straps of her black lacy bra sliding off as she dropped her hands from the wall. He looked at her, his gaze lingering on her breasts, her dark nipples, then dropping lower to the apex of her thighs. She was naked. He was clothed. A sexy little power play that made her shiver.

"You are gorgeous. Perfect."

With his eyes avid and hot upon her, she felt both gorgeous and perfect. God, the way he looked at her.

Reaching out, he dipped the tip of his finger into her navel, then dragged it down, lower. Her breath hung suspended.

His mouth curved in a faint smile; his eyes were dark and hard with lust, the blue preternaturally bright against the thick, curling fringe of his lashes.

His fingers slid between her thighs and rubbed at her opening, slick and swollen.

"I don't—"

He pushed his fingers inside her, and her breath slid away in a sharp hiss as she grabbed hold of him. In that second he was her anchor and her buoy. She needed him to stay afloat.

"You're so wet, so tight." His voice was low and rough with desire.

Looping his arm around her back, he held her close and she could smell his hair, his skin, luscious and tantalizing. She could feel the hard, lean lines of corded muscle through his clothes. Strong thighs pressed against hers. Muscled forearm against the small of her back. His lips were hungry on hers while his fingers moved inside her, his palm shifting to press against her clitoris, and she arched into his touch.

She shoved her hands under his shirt, her palms flat against the solid ridges of his abdomen, then her nails scraping his skin as she dragged her hands lower, wanting—

"No." He caught her wrist.

"I want to touch you," she rasped.

"Not yet."

His fingers slid out of her and she cried out in disappointment.

Pushing her back until she was pressed to the wall once more, he dipped his head and ran his tongue over first one nipple, then the other. Then he pressed his palms to the insides of her thighs and spread her legs.

"Wait…" Her protest was barely a whisper as he sank down before her to kiss her belly, and lower, taking her out of her comfort zone. This was too fast. Too intimate. "Wait—"

"No." He splayed his fingers on her thigh, gently pushing her back against the wall.

The plaster was cool against her naked skin. He slanted her a glance through his lashes, then dipped his head and ran his tongue along her center in a slow glide, making her gasp. Again he licked her, and again. Her knees buckled. She slid down the wall, legs splayed, his hands on her buttocks, guiding her descent until she lay with her shoulders propped against the wall, which meant she could watch him lick her, suck her—

He used his teeth, not hard, just enough to make her arch and cry out in pleasure, in need. Then he used his tongue, slow and lingering, then faster, working circles and lines. He made her sigh his name. He made her gasp. He made her whisper, "Don't stop. Don't stop. Oh, God. Please, don't stop."

Closing his hands on her hips, he held her still as she thrashed and struggled, trying to get away, trying to get closer. Closer. *Please. Yes. Now. So close.*

Her fingers tangled in his hair and held on like he was the only stable thing in a wild, pounding storm.

"Come for me, Naphré. Now. Let me watch you come." He pushed his fingers inside her again, stretching her, filling her. He put his mouth on her clit.

She was so close.

He reached up and stroked his thumb over her nipple, then pinched just hard enough to take her to the thin line between pleasure and pain.

She tore apart. She screamed as she climaxed, hips thrusting up from the floor, back arched, every nerve in her body chasing the pleasure. He held his tongue lightly against her clit, making her release go on and on in endless crashing waves.

Her heart felt like it would beat right out of her chest.

As though from far away, she felt him disengage her fingers from his hair, felt him move away from her and she thought he would strip off his clothes and come to her, heavy and hard. The thought made her shiver.

She lay there, drifting, waiting, and then she realized he was taking too long.

Forcing her lids open, she saw him sitting on the edge of her bed, fully clothed, his eyes hot as he watched her. His gorgeous mouth was curved in a masculine smile.

"I'd love to have a photo of you, just like that."

She pushed up on her elbows and felt a flush creep into her cheeks as she looked down at herself. Her legs were spread wide, offering him a very clear view of anything he might wish to see.

She straightened her legs and brought them together, feeling strangely shy.

"Aren't you going to…" She shook her head, not certain how to ask, *what* to ask. He'd made her come. One of the wildest orgasms of her life. Maybe *the* wildest. Now he was sitting there in his charcoal pants and impeccably tailored—if somewhat rumpled and bloodstained—white shirt, with a hard-on so obvious she could have seen it from the moon. And he wasn't making a move toward her.

A pained expression touched his features, and he reached down to rearrange himself as he shook his head. "Unfortunately, no. There's the small inconvenience of a drug wearing off."

The silence was deafening. She stared at him, uncomprehending.

And then she heard what he'd heard. A moan, followed by the shush of cloth on cloth. Like someone was shifting restlessly in the moments between wake and sleep.

Looked like puke girl was waking up early.

# CHAPTER THIRTEEN

ALASTOR WATCHED AS Naphré reached for her underwear, enjoying every small movement and the play of
sleek muscle under her smooth golden skin. He almost
groaned as she slid the straps of her bra up her arms
and positioned the lace to cup her breasts. He found
the sight of her putting things on as intensely erotic as
watching them come off.

She slanted him a glance from beneath her lashes.

He didn't bother to pretend he wasn't taking in the
view. Instead, he reached down and shifted his cock
to a less uncomfortable angle. Didn't help. He was so
hard, he felt like his skin would split.

Her gaze dipped to the front of his slacks. She wet
her lips.

"I should have left her in the alley," she said, her
voice rough with both lust and regret.

"No argument." He held out his hand. "Come
here."

She crossed to the bed and stood over him, holding
his gaze, a million questions in her eyes.

Catching her hand, he drew her closer, between his
spread thighs. Then he reached up, curled his fingers
around the back of her neck and drew her lips toward
his.

"I don't want to…" Her voice trailed away, but he

knew what she meant to say. *I don't want to kiss after oral sex.*

"I do," he said. And he put his mouth on hers, opening his lips, tasting her, letting her taste him…and herself.

A second of resistance, and then he felt it melt away.

She leaned one knee on the bed, bending in closer to him, her hand sliding down the front of his shirt along the planes of his chest and the ridges of his abdomen.

Catching hold of her wrist, he broke the kiss and drew back.

A little sound of frustration escaped her. "What are you, the prince of mixed messages?"

The faint creak of the couch carried from downstairs. He shook his head. "No mix intended. I want you. But a sixty-second bang doesn't appeal. When I have you, I want to take my time. And right now, we have little of that."

"But…" She made a vague gesture toward his straining erection, then dropped her hand and scraped her nails along the length of him, through his pants, sending lust crashing through him like a breaker, nearly shredding his control.

"We have company, pet—" he dipped his head toward the door "—and I don't like an audience."

He sank his teeth into the fleshy part at the base of her thumb. She inhaled sharply, and just the sound of that fanned his interest. Bloody hell, she was so damned hot.

"I want you to think about the way I touched you." He let his fingertips drift along her underwear. She gasped, but didn't pull away. "The way I kissed you."

He ran the pad of his thumb over her lower lip. Her tongue darted out to taste, then her pretty white teeth nipped his flesh.

He felt it like a jolt of electricity, straight to his cock. His reaper hearing let him pick up the sounds of the girl stirring downstairs. They didn't have the luxury of time. So he locked down the urge to push Naphré back on the bed and push himself deep inside her.

"I want you to think about *me*," he finished. "Anticipation is half the fun."

"Do you always get what you want?"

He rose to loom over her.

"Yes." His mouth curved, and he let the word hang for a moment before he asked, "Mind if I use your toothbrush, pet?"

"And if I do?"

"I'll use it anyway." Without waiting for a reply, he crossed to the door of the ensuite bath.

But apparently he wasn't the only one used to getting his way. In a flash she ducked in front of him, flicked on the light, and opened the mirrored door of the medicine chest.

"No, you won't." She took out a new, wrapped toothbrush, slapped it against his chest, and ducked out the door.

He leaned back and watched her pull on the rest of her clothes, then she left the bedroom without a backward glance and headed down the stairs.

When he was done in the bathroom, he followed and found Naphré in the open archway of the living room, arms crossed over her chest.

The girl was awake, up on all fours, her back arched

like a cat, every muscle in her body tense. Her brown eyes were wild and unfocused.

"You're okay," Naphré said, her voice low and calm.

"Stay away from me."

"We're away." Alastor gestured at the space that separated them. "There's at least six feet between us and you."

"Don't freak out," Naphré said, and when the girl swallowed convulsively, she finished, "and do *not* throw up on my rug."

Alastor gave her a second, then asked, "Name?"

The girl just moaned, sank down onto her haunches and lowered her head to her hands.

*"Name?"* Naphré muttered, and shot him a look. "Not much into foreplay, are you?"

"Sometimes quick and rough works best."

She met and held his gaze. "Or slow and rough," she said, very low.

Her words made him think about all sorts of things that were completely inappropriate at the moment. With a start, he realized that had been her exact intent. Shift the balance. Shift control. Naphré wasn't one to let someone else call the shots.

The girl on the couch raised her head. They both turned toward her. Her eyes widened. What little color remained drained completely from her face. With a scream, she looked beyond them and skittered back as far as she could go, her back pressing into the corner.

Alastor whirled, searching for the threat. Beside him, Naphré did the same.

"Centipede. Skateboard-sized centipede," the girl

said in a high, panicked voice. She was breathing fast as she pointed at the wall.

Alastor followed the direction of her finger, but there was nothing there. Still, he didn't relax. Perhaps Naphré needed an exterminator, or perhaps the centipedes had nothing to do with an infestation.

"Oh, God. It went under the rug."

He toed the edge of the rug back. Nothing there either.

"Well, it's gone for now," Naphré said, obviously trying for placating, though the words came out with an edge. She shrugged. "It must be centipede season. I saw two in the shower. Tried to get them with the shampoo bottle but they were fast. Made it down the drain in a blink—" She broke off at the horrified look on the girl's face.

"I hate bugs."

Naphré lifted something from the bookshelf and held it out toward the girl. "Hand sanitizer? It's the bugs you can't see that you have to worry about."

At that sage advice, the girl hugged herself and started to cry.

Blimey.

NAPHRÉ LOOKED UP TO FIND Alastor staring at her, frowning. She didn't like the look on his face. A worried Alastor made for a worried Naphré, though why a discussion of bugs should cause him concern him was beyond her.

"You see centipedes here often?" he asked.

"Do *not* tell me you're afraid of bugs, too."

He said nothing. She gave in. "Often enough. The

place isn't infested or anything. Every old house has them, right?"

His eyes narrowed. His lips tightened. "Right." He turned to the girl. "Let's start with introductions, shall we? I am Alastor. This is Naphré, and you are…?"

She looked back and forth between the two of them, then said, "Marie." She swallowed and grimaced. "Marie Matheson."

Alastor was utterly still, his expression impassive, his body relaxed. But something—a sharpening of his attention or a subtle shift in the pattern of his breathing—made Naphré think the name meant something to him.

Pressing one hand to her forehead, Marie eased down from the defensive pose she'd taken and deflated against the couch as though she'd been poked with a pin. She rubbed her temples. "My head hurts."

"You were drugged, Marie. That's why your head hurts," Naphré said. "And why you puked. You want some water?"

Marie took a second before answering, as she either processed the question in her drug-hazed thoughts or processed the information that she'd been drugged. Finally, she whispered, "Please."

Naphré went and filled a glass, and when she returned, Alastor said, "Give it to me." Then he slid his forearm behind Marie's upper back and supported her as she sat forward. She was rigid, and she darted nervous glances at him from the corner of her eye.

"Sip it." If he noticed her unease, he ignored it. He brought the glass to her lips, and Marie did as he ordered, then he eased her back again and handed the glass back to Naphré.

"Aren't you an interesting case?" Naphré murmured, studying him speculatively. She didn't know what to make of him. He was a soul reaper. He killed people. Those who had once been *her* people—the Daughters of Aset—in particular. At least, so she'd been indoctrinated to believe.

And yet, here he was playing nurse to Marie.

That, along with the fact that he hadn't killed *her,* made the doctrine suspect.

As she watched him now, Naphré wanted to ask whom he'd taken care of in the past, because there was no doubt in her mind that he'd offered comfort to someone at some point. Which made no sense. He was a soul reaper. He took lives; he didn't make life easier. But someone had mattered to him enough that he'd nursed them and learned the ropes. Who? A woman?

The second the question—and, with it, the tinge of jealousy—surfaced, she thrust them aside.

"Marie," Alastor said, his voice soft but commanding. "Who drugged you?"

"Drugged—" She wrapped her arms around herself and held tight, as though that was the only way she could hold herself together.

"Do you remember?" Naphré asked.

Marie made a sound somewhere between a gasp and a sob. "I remember the party. I remember feeling sick and…scared." She turned her head and stared at Naphré. "I remember your voice. But not from the party. From after." She frowned. "That's right, isn't it?"

Her tongue darted out to wet her lips. Naphré felt a pang of sympathy. She handed her the glass. Marie's hand shook so badly that water sloshed over the rim to splash the front of her dress. Alastor reached forward as though to help her again, but she shot him a nervous glance and said, "No. I'm fine." Raising the glass to her lips, she sipped the water. "Just give me a minute."

Stepping back, Naphré gave her a bit of space. Alastor moved to stand at the foot of the couch.

"Who drugged you, Marie?" Alastor's tone, while still soft, had changed to one of command, demanding a reply.

"I don't know." She looked around for somewhere to set the glass, and when Naphré took it from her she brought her hands together and laced her fingers so tightly that the knuckles showed white. "It could have been anyone."

"It could have," Alastor agreed. "But you know who it was. Tell me."

Marie made a sound of distress.

"Tell me," Alastor said again, his voice still low, still commanding.

"The High Reverend," Marie blurted.

"Djeserit Bast?" Naphré asked.

"No. High Reverend Kusnetzov."

Bastard.

"Why did he drug you?" Alastor asked.

"I—" Marie shook her head and her eyes darted to the left. "I don't know."

"Guess." His tone was hard.

Marie pressed her lips together.

"Right, then." Alastor shot a look at Naphré. "I'll just take her back to the Temple now." The man who'd so solicitously tended to Marie moments past was gone. In his place was an emotionless creature without expression, jaw set, eyes cold and flat.

"No!" Marie struggled upright on the couch and pressed her fingertips to her temples. "It was High Reverend Kusnetzov. He put something in my wine. When I first started to feel woozy, I knew what he'd done, and I thought at first that it was because…well, because he wanted to…" She shook her head. "But that didn't make sense." Her expression shifted to one of pain. "I mean, I was attracted to him."

Naphré didn't doubt that, despite the fact that Pyotr Kusnetzov was probably two decades older. He worked out. Stayed in shape. His face was unlined, with pleasant, even features. He was an attractive man. Which was why she'd had lunch with him. But there was also something off about him. Which was why she hadn't had lunch with him a second time.

"He didn't need to drug me," Marie said. "I would have…slept with him. And I know he knew it."

"So why the drug?"

"I don't know." At Alastor's disbelieving look, she amended, "I'm not certain. I think it might be because of something I saw. A few weeks ago, I left my purse at the Temple. When I went back for it, the doors were locked. I rang the bell. No one came. Not even the security guard. I was about to leave, and then I thought I'd just check the side door.

"I stumbled on Pyotr and a group of men I didn't recognize. They weren't from our congregation. One of them was different. There was something about him…" She looked at Alastor. "You remind me of him. He had blond hair and he had the same sort of…electric energy about him."

*Electric energy.* Not something most humans ever picked up on, because humans weren't attuned to the supernatural as a rule. Which meant Marie wasn't purely human.

Naphré got a bad feeling in her gut. She narrowed her eyes as she studied Marie, searching for a sign, a clue. Searching for the dark mark of the Daughters of Aset. A long shot, but she had a feeling about this one.

"Go on," Alastor encouraged, his voice low and even. But Naphré thought there was leashed tension in his body, as though Marie's story was important to him.

"There was a little girl there, and she ran to him and hugged his legs. The expression on his face...I know it's crazy—" she gave a soft laugh "—but I remember thinking that he would die for her."

The tension left Alastor's body. It was as though he thrust it away, summoned a level of calm detachment and put it in place with deliberate care.

In Naphré's mind, that solidified the importance of the information Marie was sharing. Alastor was so invested in what she was saying that he was forced to ice his emotions against it. She recognized the tactic. It was one she tended to employ herself.

"Pyotr was there," Marie continued. "He spoke to some of the men. And then he looked up and saw me, and it was terrible. The way he looked at me. The way it made me feel." She shuddered. "I was so afraid. And then he smiled and I thought I imagined it. He went inside the Temple with me and helped me find my purse and sent me off. And after that night, he was so nice to me." She looked at each of them in turn, her eyes wide. "I really did think I'd imagined it. All of it.

"But then I met this guy at a bar." She looked at

Alastor and frowned. "And you remind me of him, too, but he had dark hair and earrings. His name was Mal. Anyway, he asked me to go for coffee. He was unbelievably hot—" she looked at Naphré and raised her eyebrows "—so I went. We talked for hours. He was…nice. Funny. Entertaining. I remember telling him about that night and my purse and everything. He really listened.

"And then he put me in a taxi. You know, I thought he might call me after that. I gave him my number. But he never did." She sounded wistful. "Funny thing, though. Just before I got in the taxi, I looked up and I thought I saw one of the security guards from the Temple across the street. Then a bus went past and when I looked again, he was gone."

Alastor was quiet, his body relaxed, and Naphré had the odd impression that what Marie was telling them was not news to him.

Then an image clicked. Dark hair. Earrings. The guy Marie described was a ringer for the one Naphré had seen with Alastor that night outside the Playhouse Lounge.

"Did Pyotr ever talk to you about the night you forgot your purse?" Naphré asked. Whatever Pyotr had planned for Marie tonight, Naphré suspected it had something to do with what she'd seen.

"No. Not a word. But after that night, he paid special attention to me. Always there. Always chatting me up. And then tonight, he was so kind, so attentive…" Her voice trailed away, and she sounded young and lost.

"Indeed," Alastor murmured.

"Oh, God," Marie whispered. "What do I do now? I can't go home, can I?"

"No," Naphré agreed, thoughts spinning. Marie most
definitely could not go home. "The night you went back
for your purse," she prompted, instinct guiding her, "did
you hear any names? Recognize any other faces?"

"No…" She frowned. "No. I told Mal that, too. He
kept asking me the same thing. I told him, all I heard
was something about going to the butcher."

"The butcher," Naphré echoed, every muscle in her
body snapping to alert. She was hyperaware that, beside
her, Alastor was reacting the same way. So *this* was
new information to him. "You sure about that?"

"Yes. I'm sure."

Naphré glanced at Alastor. She'd suspected that
Butcher had been at a hit that went wrong. A hit on a
soul reaper. Alastor's brother. Damn. It was one thing
to suspect it, another to have it confirmed. No wonder
Alastor wanted Butcher's darksoul.

"And what was special about tonight?" Alastor asked. "Why did the wanker decide to drug you
tonight."

A tear leaked from the corner of Marie's eye to trace
a path along her cheek. "I don't know. We've been cel-
ebrating, preparing for a sacrifice of a sheep." Marie
turned and looked at Naphré, eyes wide, more tears
leaking. "It isn't as terrible as it sounds. The sheep's
going to be killed at a slaughterhouse, like any other
sheep, and the meat distributed to the poor." Her voice
wavered and she didn't look like she believed her own
reassurances.

Alastor's lips curled in a dark smile. "I have no doubt
the good Reverend was planning a slaughter. But my
bets would be on a lamb," he said. *One with big brown*

*eyes and long, wavy hair. One that happened to be in the wrong place at the wrong time,* he didn't say.

And Naphré would lay bets that he was right.

"Oh, God! Another one!" Marie pointed at the wall.

Naphré spun, lunged and slammed the heel of her palm against a centipede that looked a good three inches long.

"Gross," she muttered as she used her nail to scrape up the edge, then peeled the thing off her skin and dropped it in Marie's nearly empty glass of water. A couple of legs were stubborn, and she had to rub at them before they fell free.

Lifting her head, she found Marie staring at her, face chalk-pale with a tinge of green.

"Hall," Naphré barked and used her index finger to point the direction. "Turn right. Bathroom's under the stairs on the left."

Marie was already up and stumbling.

"What?" Naphré asked as she caught Alastor staring at her with the oddest expression.

"Four centipedes—"

"Five."

"—in less than hour?" His voice was darkly soft. "Thought you said you didn't have an infestation, pet."

"I—" What was with him and his bug fixation? Guess everyone had their issues. She shrugged and headed for the kitchen to wash her hands. He followed.

"What do we do with her?" Naphré asked once she'd finished soaping and rinsing. Alastor was leaning against the pantry, arms crossed over his chest, looking disgustingly masculine and appealing. She huffed out a breath. "You have something against standing on your own two feet?"

He ignored the second question and addressed the first. "What do you mean, 'do with her'?"

The yoke of responsibility loomed, heavy and confining. "She can't stay here."

"Then send her home."

"They'll come for her."

"We can't have that," he murmured, and she wasn't sure if he was serious or sarcastic.

"Okay, good. Glad we're thinking along the same lines."

"What lines would those be, pet?" He slanted her a glance, eyes bottle-glass blue against dark, curled lashes. He stared at her like he looked through her... no, like he wanted *her* to see clear through *him,* to see the hard truth of his words, though his tone was soft. "Do not think I am swayed by altruism or sympathy of any kind. I have my own reasons for wanting little Marie to stay alive. And they have nothing to do with her and everything to do with me."

It seemed important to him that she view him as a coldhearted bastard, and she could only wonder why.

Maybe because he *was.*

"If this is your way of telling me that it was just sex...you don't need to bother. Because—"

"It isn't. Because it wasn't." His tone was hard. His eyes were hot, and the way he looked at her made her want to look away.

Which she didn't. Turning your back on a predator wasn't such a good plan.

Alastor reached into his pocket and pulled out his

cell phone. Naphré couldn't help it. She laughed. How funny was that? A reaper who used a cell phone.

He shot her a quizzical glance as he placed the call, but made no comment.

"I have a situation," he said when someone answered. "Bring Roxy. The situation is female." He was silent for a second, listening, then his lips turned in a faint smile, revealing just a hint of the crease in his left cheek. "No, not mine." Then he hung up without even saying goodbye.

Roxy. Well, it looked as though she was about to meet Roxy Tam. She knew of her. Naphré had left the Guard a couple of years after Roxy came to them. They'd never met, but sometimes you heard things. Names. Stories. Roxy Tam was supposed to be one tough chick. And if Naphré had stayed with the Asetian Guard, they would have shared a mentor, Calliope Kane.

"Whoever you just called is going to have a heck of a hard time bringing anyone," Naphré observed. "You forgot to give them the address."

"They won't need it." Alastor stepped closer, until he stood maybe a foot away. Her gaze slid to his mouth, and unbidden, the memories of the way he'd kissed her...kissed her mouth and then—

It took her a second to gather her thoughts. "Why won't they need my address?"

"My brothers and I have a link," he said, his attention wholly focused on her, his accent a little more pronounced than before. "We can...sense...each other. Mostly, when one of us is in trouble." Another step closer, almost like he were lured by an unseen line. "But also if we need to find each other in a hurry."

"Do all soul reapers have that link? The one you share with your brothers?" She realized that she sounded breathless, *felt* breathless, as she waited for him to bring his weight full against her, to kiss her.

His lips pulled back to reveal white teeth, and that dimple that creased his cheek.

"Looking to find out all my secrets, pet?"

Dipping his head, he brushed his cheek against her hair and inhaled. She froze, a rabbit in a field. Stupid rabbit, just sitting there waiting for the wolf to pounce.

"If I can." She barely got the words out. "Knowledge is power."

"Size is power," he whispered against her ear, resting his hands on the granite counter, caging her. "And strength. And intellect and allies. Power is not determined by only one thing."

She turned her head just a little, just enough to catch the lobe of his ear between her teeth, and she bit him, hard enough to get his attention. Not such a stupid rabbit, after all.

He went utterly still. Then he laughed low in his throat and said, "I share that link only with my brothers."

Of course, she had no doubt that he'd meant to tell her that all along.

He drew back and studied her. His eyes glittered. His brows lifted almost imperceptibly, like he was asking a question. By letting herself remain exactly as she was, plastered against him like caramel on a sundae, she was giving him an answer.

Slowly, so slowly, he leaned in, his mouth inches

from hers. She arched up, tipped her head back, aching, offering.

The sound of the bathroom door opening made her freeze. She pushed down on his forearms. He released her. But he didn't step away. She hadn't really expected he would.

He only watched her, expression hard, eyes heavy-lidded, as she sidled away and strode back to the living room. She couldn't hear his footsteps, but her heightened awareness of him told her that he followed.

Marie came back into the room, and looked back and forth between them, likely sensing the tension that made the air crackle and spark. She said nothing. Alastor said nothing. And Naphré found she could think of nothing but the feel of him up against her.

"Tea?" she offered brightly, and danced away toward the kitchen before anyone could answer.

But she felt him watching her, eyes hungry, tension humming around him like a live wire.

# CHAPTER FOURTEEN

*Fuku wa uchi, Oni wa soto.*
Bring good fortune into the home and send out
the demon.

—Japanese proverb

TEA FOR THREE WAS awkward, at best.

Alastor's insistence on doing the brewing and
pouring hadn't made the entire procedure any more
comfortable.

"Control freak," she'd shot at him under her breath.
From the kitchen. While he was in the living room.

"Without a doubt," he'd replied.

Damned reaper hearing.

They finished the tea—he added three teaspoons
of sugar to his—and he ate the entire plate of sugar
cookies she put out. Which was fine, because neither
she nor Marie were interested.

When he caught her staring at him, he shrugged and
said, "Sugar," like that was supposed to explain his
overboard sweet tooth. Or the way he kept so incredibly lean despite the amount of sugar he packed away.
She'd seen him without his jacket, seen the way his
shirt hugged his muscles and lay flat on his belly.

Thinking of that made her want to peel his clothes

off, lay her hands on his skin and feel the steely strength of him.

As she piled the plates and cups on the tray, Alastor rose and went to the window. He stood leaning one shoulder against the wall, arms crossed over his chest. He'd put his suit jacket back on, which was likely a good thing, given the bloodstains on his shirt. She doubted Marie would be blasé about those.

Some time later, he said, "They're here." Then he strode to the door and went down to street level to let them in.

Naphré waited by her open door, straining to hear any bits of dialogue that might float up to her, but none did. Then she heard feet on the stairs.

First came a woman with long brown-black ringlets and a knife strapped to her jeans-clad thigh. She looked up and caught Naphré staring. Her eyes were bronze and green, and the best descriptor that sprang to mind was *fierce*. Like a tiger.

Naphré dipped her chin toward the knife. "You're a girl after my own heart. I'm Naphré Kurata."

"Roxy Tam." Roxy climbed the last step to the landing and offered her hand. Her handshake was firm and quick, and Naphré got the most bizarre energy vibe off her. Definitely Otherkin, but…something else, as well.

She was wearing a pair of faded, torn jeans, a dark-green T-shirt and a dark denim jacket with the sleeves pushed back on her forearms.

Naphré's gaze flicked to Roxy's bare forearm and the mark etched in her skin. An ankh with wings and horns. The location marked her lineage as the Keeper, just as the location of Naphré's marked her as a Guide. They'd each been born to their line, to their duties.

Would Roxy judge her for walking away from hers? Would it present a problem?

"Look familiar, pet?" Alastor asked as he stepped up behind her.

She gasped, spun. "You were downstairs. How did you—" She shook her head. "Never mind."

"I have a feeling you two are going to get on just like sisters," Alastor said to Roxy, then offered a taut smile. "Or Daughters."

"Witty." The smile Roxy offered Alastor was a mirror of his own. "What's that word you like to use? Oh, yeah—" she snapped her fingers "—lackwit." Then she turned her attention back to Naphré. "You left the Guard?"

Despite the tone and the cutting edge of their words, or maybe because of it, Naphré got the feeling these two actually liked each other. "Wasn't my thing," she replied.

"Do tell." Roxy sent her a measured look. "I suspect there's quite a lot to that story."

Yeah, there was. *Quite a lot* being a demon who happened to hold the ownership papers on her soul, but that was not a story she was interested in sharing.

"Quite a bit to your story, as well, I think."

Roxy's brows rose. "Touché."

"Come on in." Naphré pulled the door more fully open and stepped back. Roxy entered, and then, seemingly appearing out of the darkness, came a tall man dressed in faded, worn jeans and a brown leather jacket that was scarred and scuffed.

Naphré couldn't help but stare. He was the bad boy

version of Alastor's masculine elegance. He had the same honey-gold hair, but he wore it long and loose to his shoulders. His face was a bit narrower, his features sharper, his jaw slightly more squared, but she had to look closely to note the differences. And she was pissed off at herself as she realized that she'd noticed enough about Alastor to pinpoint every subtle nuance.

The most glaring difference was the color of their eyes. Alastor's eyes were blue, the shade changeable, depending on his mood. This man's were gray. Flat and cold. Until his gaze slid to Roxy, and then she saw a flare of emotion. Possessive. Hot. Not mere lust. It was more than that. He looked at Roxy like she was *his*. Like he would fight for her. Die for her. Like he… loved her.

She glanced away. Because that look was private.

And because some crazy part of her wondered what it would feel like to have Alastor look at *her* that way.

"Dae." Alastor stepped up beside her.

"Your brother," she murmured. Not a question.

"What gave us away?" Dagan asked, unsmiling.

"You're both such sharp dressers," she shot back.

Dagan's brows rose, and he shot a look at his brother. "Feisty."

"You're not English," Naphré noted.

Dagan shrugged. "Same mother. Same father. Different lives."

"There's a story there," she said to Alastor.

"We all have one, don't we, pet?" Alastor glanced at his brother. "Shoes," he said.

"What?"

"Shoes," he repeated.

Naphré looked at him, startled. In that second she realized that his own shoes were off, lined up next to hers. He must have done that while she was in the shower. She was oddly touched that he'd noticed her preference. Doubly touched that he asked his brother to follow her custom.

Once everyone was in stocking feet, they moved into the living room and found Marie crammed into the corner of the couch, knees up, arms wrapped around them, like she was trying to turn herself into an invisible little ball.

"Marie," Dagan echoed when Alastor said her name, and shot his brother a cool, speaking glance.

"Marie Matheson," Alastor clarified.

Alastor quickly explained the situation. As he talked, Marie shot more than one wary glance at Dagan, and Naphré couldn't say that she blamed her. At least Alastor appeared partially civilized because of the elegant way he dressed—of course, look a little closer and you couldn't help but see the predator beneath the polished exterior.

But Dagan didn't even try.

When Roxy offered Marie a place to stay until they figured things out, Marie just chewed on her lower lip and slanted sidelong glances through her lashes. Still, Roxy's reassurances proved enough to convince her that she'd be safer with them than anywhere else, and within half an hour the three of them were leaving.

"Dae." Alastor stopped his brother as he went to follow the two women out. "You caught her name, yes?"

Dagan paused on the stairs and turned. He reached into his pocket and pulled out a red lollipop, took his time taking off the wrapper and, finally, popped the sucker in his mouth. What was it with these guys and sugar? Then he folded the wrapper in half, then in half again before shoving it in his pocket.

"Mal mentioned her." Dagan's gaze met Naphré's, then returned to Alastor. "He mentioned some *information* she shared."

"I suspect she has more, though she doesn't know it. She was there. She saw Lokan. She says she didn't recognize anyone other than Kusnetzov, but I think you and Roxy might want to spend some time chatting with her. Get a description, even if she can't name names."

"You think we ought to call in Mal to talk with her?"

"Your call. She wasn't one of his conquests." Alastor offered a wry smile. "But I'm guessing she's wishing she had been."

Dagan nodded. "I'll let him know she's staying with me. No doubt he'll make himself scarce."

"You and Roxy find out anything from Big Ralph?" Alastor asked. When Dagan looked at Naphré again, as though suggesting they might not want to talk in front of her, Alastor said, "She worked with Butcher."

Dagan stared at her, his eyes flat gray, like a cold lake under a winter-storm sky. Before he could say anything, Alastor stepped in front of her and said, whisper soft, "Don't think it, mate. She's mine. Any questions she gets asked come from me."

Ordinarily, Naphré would have taken umbrage with the proprietary air, but the thought of being the bug under Dagan's microscope didn't exactly appeal, so she kept quiet.

"Tell me about your meeting with Big Ralph," Alastor said.

"All we found was a lot of hearsay and rumor. Apparently Xaphan's offering one hell of a reward for information about Lokan's killer."

"Which suggests that the killer wasn't Xaphan or his crew," Alastor said.

"Or it suggests that Xaphan's wily enough to offer a reward for information that would implicate him, just so he can find out if such information exists," Naphré offered, and when all eyes turned to her, she shrugged. "I've done a lot of jobs for Xaphan. I know a little bit about the way he thinks."

"Lucky you," Dagan murmured, then he turned and headed down the stairs.

NAPHRÉ HAD BARELY CLOSED and locked the door, when a knock sounded, firm and quick.

"They must have forgotten something," she said and swung the door open just as the most horrific smell hit her and Alastor yelled, "No."

Too late.

Naphré didn't have time to think, to react, to do anything other than jerk back, jerk away.

Only she couldn't move. Her mind cried out against the horror of what was before her and the complete and utter paralysis of her body. Her mind screamed *run* and in her mind that was exactly what she did.

But in truth, she stayed planted in place as though her feet had grown roots and the floor beneath them was soil.

The creature standing just outside the door was

draped in what appeared to be shimmering velvet. But was not.

Before Naphré's appalled gaze, the velvet pulled in on itself, drawing tight to the woman's body, then it swelled and grew, pushing outward like a great balloon filling with water. But it was no balloon. It was a swell of maggots and centipedes and spiders, skittering and moving, crawling one over the next, swelling toward her like a horrific tide. She swore she could hear them, the sound of their mandibles clicking.

Somewhere in the distance she could hear Alastor yelling her name. Far away. She had thought he was right behind her.

Again, she tried to move, a Herculean effort that failed. And then they were on her, on every exposed bit of flesh. On her hands, her face, crawling on her skin, and through her hair. She slammed her eyes shut and pressed her lips tight, but she could feel tiny legs at her nostrils and her ears.

*Not afraid of bugs. Not afraid of bugs.*

But they were more than bugs. They were a living, writhing, crawling cage that held her in place and tormented her with the scrape of tiny feet and the wriggle of tiny bodies. All over her. They were everywhere.

She wanted to scream.

She didn't dare scream. They would have a way to get inside her then.

Her fear swelled, choking her, demoralizing her.

"Naphré. Bloody hell, Naphré!" Alastor's voice coming at her from so very far away.

She should look for him, reach for him.

No. If she opened her eyes, they would crawl inside. And as soon as she thought it, she swore she could feel it, the slither of the maggots and the million tiny legs of the centipedes, inside her lids, scampering across her eyeballs.

She opened her mouth to scream and they poured in.

ALASTOR HADN'T EXPECTED HER to come here.

Foolish, really.

Because here she was.

And he'd had ample warning. The centipedes that Naphré had seen in her bathroom and the one that had terrorized Marie in the living room. Harbingers.

The *Shikome* had found them. What had he bloody well imagined? That she'd slink off and wait patiently after she'd missed her opportunity in the alley earlier tonight?

As the surge of legs and shiny bodies swelled toward them, he reached for Naphré, tried to grab hold of her, but his fingers slipped and slid as though he was grabbing oil. He couldn't get a firm grasp. There was only a writhing, twisting tide of tiny creatures flowing like a river, like lava, obscuring the space she had occupied only a second past.

His gut clenched. Fear. It had been so long since he'd felt that emotion that he almost didn't recognize it. And then he did. The taste of it was strong, bitter, stinging his tongue.

He wouldn't lose her. Not like this. Not subsumed into this wriggling mass.

Alastor dove into the writhing, clicking sea, searching for the *Shikome*, intent on attack. But he could no more get a fix on her than he could on Naphré. Thousands of tiny legs touched his skin. Thousands of tiny bites erupted, small stings that swelled to burning pain. He surged forward, and still he got nowhere. He closed his hands and insects oozed between his fingers, but he couldn't find Naphré no matter which way he turned.

Jerking back, outside the tide, he tried to figure out an effective approach.

A single centipede dropped from the mass and scampered toward him. And then was gone.

He stared at the spot it had been. There was only dark, polished wood and shadows. And no centipede.

With a snarl, he dove into the fray once more, eyes open, lips peeled back. They crawled on him, bit at him and his skin prickled and swelled, then split, his flesh scored raw. Blood and ribbons of skin hung from his lacerated fingers and palms, and still they bit and burrowed into him.

He flung his hands and watched the centipedes and spiders fall. They moved and wriggled, and in a blink, were gone.

But that was the thing. He hadn't blinked. Hadn't looked away.

Illusion.

The pain, the blood, the writhing mass that enveloped them, all illusion.

Were those that veiled the *Shikome* illusion as well?

He surged forward, pushing against the moving, squirming wall of them, and reached deep into the mass. He couldn't find her, couldn't feel her, but he closed his fingers tight and pulled back with a sharp yank. The force of his action threw him off balance and he slammed hard against the wall.

The centipedes swelled and grew, until they were as

long as his arm, biting out massive hunks of muscle and skin, leaving raw gaping wounds in their wake. They crawled all over him.

"Enough," he snarled, and pulled on his reserves of control, seeking the icy calm that had kept him sane for nearly three centuries. Control. All he needed was control.

And the tide ebbed.

Naphré was in his arms, trembling, gasping, eyes shut tight, hands opening and closing as though she crushed something in her fists.

She crushed nothing. Only air.

But in her mind, she crushed the waves of insects that overwhelmed her. She used whatever resources she had, and she fought. And something inside him roared in recognition and awe.

Panting, he spun her to face him, pressed her head against his chest and wrapped his arm around her back. He had no name for what he felt, no context for it. She was a woman he barely knew. She was a Daughter of Aset. She was nothing to him.

*But she could be everything.* He didn't know where that thought came from. Didn't want to know. Didn't want to think it.

He pushed the emotions that battered him into the plain beige box he kept for them in his mind, closed the lid and wrapped it in chains and a padlock.

Better. He could breathe now, he could think now.

If he didn't acknowledge the fact that he was starting to care about her, then that caring couldn't pose a threat to his control.

He raised his gaze to the open door, and there

was the *Shikome,* only standing there on the landing, covered in her living, writhing garments.

He had a suspicion about the *Shikome*'s presence, and in a moment he would test it, but first, information.

"Release her," he ordered, clipped consonants and taut vowels.

"As you wish, son of Sutekh." The place where her mouth should have been opened to form a round black hole that was quickly filled in by squirming, writhing things. She lifted then dropped one shoulder, and Naphré drew a shuddering breath.

"Hey," he said softly, lowering his gaze to hers. For an instant, she looked at him with absolute relief, which quickly faded. He recognized the exact second that she came to herself, realized where she was and what she was doing, leaning on him, letting him hold her.

Her expression smoothed, all evidence of her thoughts and emotions wiped clean, the terror and turmoil locked down where she could control them.

He almost smiled. Maybe that was the attraction. Like to like. Both of them so determined to hold everything on a tight leash.

She pushed away to stand on her own feet, and he felt a pang of...what? Loss? Regret?

Slowly, she turned to the open door.

"What do you want?" Calm voice. Clenched fists.

The *Shikome* turned her head so she was fully facing Naphré, and said, "Did he not tell you?"

There were no features to express her emotions, no eyes to reflect her thoughts. But Alastor thought there was a certain malicious glee in the *Shikome*'s question. As though she wanted to show him for a liar and betrayer.

"Did he—" Naphré glanced at Alastor, her gaze wary now. "He told me nothing about you. Quite an oversight, it seems."

Alastor fixed his gaze on the *Shikome*. "Why are you here?"

"Time passes. You dawdle while Izanami waits. You show disrespect." A particularly large spider crawled into the orifice as she spoke, hanging there for an instant before scuttling inside.

"No disrespect was intended." *Izanami waits?* He'd only been following Naphré for a couple of days. That was minutes in Underworld time. "Didn't realize there was quite such a need for haste."

"Did you not?"

On his part, yes. He was anxious to find out Butcher's answers. But on Izanami's part? He didn't trust her urgency. Something was off here.

"You seemed so anxious to know the secrets of the darksoul you were forced to forfeit. Has that changed?"

Naphré shot him a look at the mention of Butcher's darksoul. "You don't have it?"

"No, and no," he answered both their questions as he tried to figure the angles. What was she doing here? He was the one who wanted Butcher's darksoul, so why was she so anxious for him to come and get it?

Because they'd agreed that he wouldn't be coming alone.

Which meant that the *Shikome* wasn't anxious to give up Butcher's darksoul; she was anxious for him to bring Naphré to Izanami's realm. Why?

"Bring her to me, and I will intercede for you with Izanami," she said, and he could swear he heard the bugs that crawled all over her clicking in anticipation. "You will speak with Izanami. You will present your case and petition for the darksoul to be returned to you. I will offer what support I can. All you need to do is come as we agreed, and bring the girl."

Everything she was saying was true. Yet there was an undercurrent to her words that made him think she was as twisty as a pretzel. As though she chose her words to both present the facts and obscure them.

She promised everything, and nothing.

He'd spent enough years picking up Sutekh's evasions that her technique felt stale.

Naphré's eyes narrowed. "By 'the girl,' I believe you mean me?" She shot Alastor a scathing look and to his shock, he realized there was hurt and disappointment there as well. "All that crap about following me to make certain I was okay…" She shook her head and stepped away, her gaze sliding back to the *Shikome*. "What do you want with me?"

He reached out and caught Naphré's wrist, drew her back, kept her from stepping out into the hall. He gave her credit for having the guts to face the figure on the landing after what she'd just been through. Naphré was no shrinking violet, though he'd already known that. This was just one more bit of proof.

But then, she had said that she only feared the bugs that were too small to see.

She glanced down at his fingers curling around her wrist and shook him free. He released her, not liking it, but respecting her right to make her own choice.

His gut was telling him to grab her by the hair, yank her to safety and beat his chest at the threat. Lovely. He'd regressed to the Pleistocene.

"I make it a habit never to go to the Underworld with strangers," Naphré said.

The *Shikome* offered what Alastor suspected was meant to be a laugh. "I am Yomotsu-shikome. One of eight."

"Divine fury," Naphré murmured.

"Not divine. I am but a servant."

"According to legend, you are more than that." Naphré slanted a glance at Alastor, her eyes like ebony, polished and cool, revealing nothing of her thoughts. "You were going to trade me for Butcher's soul." Her tone was devoid of inflection, her expression flat, but he felt her pain. She believed he had betrayed her. Lied to her. Tricked her.

And he had. If not by direct lie, then certainly by evasion.

Means to an end.

So why were guilt and remorse biting at his arse? Why did he hate that he'd been the one to put that fleeting look of betrayal in her eyes?

"Naphré—"

"Answer me." An order that was little more than a whisper.

"Bloody hell. There was no specific mention of a trade. I want Butcher's darksoul and she—" he tipped his head toward the *Shikome* "—offered me passage in order to dialogue with Izanami if I brought you along for the trip. No one said the trip was one way. I figured you'd walk in with me, then walk back out."

Naphré stared at him for several seconds, saying nothing, then she turned back to the *Shikome* and asked, "Why does Izanami wish to see me?"

She didn't question him. Didn't indicate whether

she believed him or not. And on this point, he wasn't exactly lying. Not about this, at least. He hadn't understood from his original dialogue with the *Shikome* that he was expected to trade Naphré for the darksoul.

A flicker of unease ignited in his chest. What had he thought? That he was supposed to bring her for a visit and then they'd leave together after they took tea and watercress sandwiches?

Had he become so adept at lying that he was able to fool even himself?

The truth was, he *had* known, or at least suspected. If he took Naphré to an Underworld territory, there was a bloody good chance she wasn't coming back, regardless of any assurances the *Shikome* made.

He supposed he'd thought he was okay with that. Now, he realized he wasn't. Things had changed. He wasn't willing to trade Naphré for information. Nor was he willing to forego what information Butcher's darksoul harbored.

Impasse.

And he didn't understand why he was even arguing with himself. There ought to be no question. Butcher likely had answers about the night Lokan was killed. He could be Alastor's only hope of finding his brother's Ka.

He ought to see Naphré Kurata as dispensable.

He didn't understand exactly what he felt for her, but she was something to him. And still, he lied to her, if not outright, then at least by omission, because he'd seen her name in Sutekh's book and he hadn't said a word to her about that, either.

He had his reasons. Naphré hadn't exactly bared her secrets; she was cagey about the demon that owned her soul. Why? Did she even know it was Sutekh? He didn't think so, for a number of reasons, not the least of which was the fact that the summoning remnants told him that she truly believed she'd sold her eternity to a *demon.* And Sutekh wasn't. He was a god. The most powerful god of the Underworld. Alastor was fairly certain that Naphré was in the dark about exactly whom she'd made her bargain with.

Until he knew the why of that, the reasons behind Sutekh's subterfuge, he wasn't about to reveal the truth. That might just send him stumbling into a real viper's nest.

"Izanami wishes you brought to her. I do not question Izanami's wishes," the *Shikome* said. Which could either mean she had no idea why Izanami wanted to see Naphré, or she wasn't willing to part with that information. Either way, Naphré wasn't getting answers.

*Izanami wishes you brought to her.* The words swirled through his thoughts, and alarms started clanging. Because the *Shikome* had come to Sutekh's greeting room, not Izanami. The *Shikome* had demanded the return of Butcher's darksoul, and the *Shikome* was the one he had made his offer to: a soul for a soul. She was the one who had seen Naphré's name in Sutekh's book. She was the one who had demanded that Naphré accompany him.

Not Izanami. Izanami hadn't been there. She hadn't been part of the picture. She'd never seen Naphré's name in the book. So how could she have demanded her presence?

Something here wasn't right.

It was on the tip of his tongue to point all this out, and then he rethought. Why give away the game for free? Let the *Shikome* think he had no clue that something was manky.

"Izanami's going to be disappointed if she wants me to stay for an extended visit," Naphré said, her tone flat. "I belong to another."

"We are aware." The Shikome gestured toward the mark of the Daughters of Aset, partially visible under the strap of Naphré's black tank top. Centipedes dropped from her extended hand and skittered away to be lost in the shadows.

Naphré glanced down as they came closer, then she raised her head and looked directly at where the *Shikome*'s eyes should have been. Lifting her slippered foot, she brought it down hard as one centipede ran past, then she ground her heel back and forth.

A smile tugged at Alastor's lips. He had to admire her moxie.

She moved her foot. Where the dead centipede should have been, there was only gleaming wooden floor. Alastor glanced around for the others that had dropped from the *Shikome*'s hand, but they were gone, swallowed by the shadows or the baseboards...

Or not.

Suspicion unfurled.

"Izanami is aware of your heritage. Your choices—" the Shikome paused "—and your mistakes."

One of those mistakes being that she'd pledged her soul to Sutekh. He'd seen the fury that had swelled in the *Shikome* when she'd seen Naphré's name inscribed there.

"You are no longer part of the Asetian Guard," the *Shikome* continued.

Alastor knew that Roxy had walked away from the

Guard when she'd taken up with Dagan, though she hadn't made that choice solely because of her relationship with his brother. She'd said it hadn't been a good fit for her all along. Something about not doing well with blind obedience. Now it seemed that Naphré hadn't found it a good fit, either.

Which told him that, like Roxy, she'd been merely a foot soldier with no access to classified information. Otherwise, they wouldn't have let her go.

"If she comes to Izanami's realm willingly, can she choose to leave?" Alastor asked, drawing the attention of both Naphré and the *Shikome*.

"I cannot presume to speak for Izanami."

An answer that wasn't an answer. Being adept at those himself, Alastor wasn't inclined to settle. "Make an educated guess."

"If she does not partake of the food of the dead, she cannot be held permanently in the realm of the Underworld."

"Still not an answer. You ever consider politics?"

"It is the only one I can offer."

Torn, Alastor weighed his options. Take Naphré to Izanami and risk that she could never come back. Leave her here, go alone and risk that he'd be denied access to Butcher's darksoul and the secrets he might have known in life. He wasn't liking either one.

"Then she won't be joining us." He said the words without intending to, yet once they were out, he felt like they were the only answer he could give. Risking Naphré's life, her soul, wasn't something he was willing to do. But risking his own was. "I'll offer myself in her place."

An empty, gaping slit appeared in the undulating

mass that was the *Shikome*'s face. Alastor realized it was her version of a smile.

"That is not an option. The meeting of allies draws near. Should Izanami take you, Sutekh's son, the outcome of that meeting is assured."

True enough.

A fat, white maggot wriggled along the Shikome's foot and dropped to the floor. Alastor blinked, and it was gone. He frowned, staring at the place it had been. He inhaled through his nose, tentatively at first, then deeply.

Where was the smell that had been here earlier?

"*You* are not offering anything in my place," Naphré said with a hard look in his direction. Her hands were fisted at her sides, her shoulders tense, but her tone was neutral and even. "I am right here, despite the fact that the two of you are discussing me like I'm not. And I make my own decisions. You have no jurisdiction over me, Alastor Krayl, though you seem to be making a habit of acting like you do."

Alastor opened his mouth to reply, then snapped it shut. Something deep and primal unfurled inside him, whispering that he had every right. That she was his. He locked it down, focused on the *Shikome,* turning her words over and over in his mind.

Understanding clicked like tumblers in a lock. *Bring her to me, and I will intercede for you with Izanami.* She hadn't said "give her to me" but rather "bring her to me," even though she was standing not three feet away. And the smell…other than the initial aroma of rot and decay, the scent the *Shikome* carried with her had dissipated. All he smelled now was a faint hint of Naphré's floral shampoo.

He prowled forward onto the landing, crowding the Shikome back toward the stairs. "How is it that you're walking around Topworld? A rare skill, that."

The *Shikome* said nothing.

Lunging forward, Alastor sliced the side of his hand down from the *Shikome*'s crown clear through to her belly. Centipedes scattered, crawling up his arm and skittering along the ground, and then like smoke, they were gone. *She* was gone.

Like she had never been.

But the threat she'd carried with her lingered.

# CHAPTER FIFTEEN

SILENCE HUNG BETWEEN them as Naphré spun to stare at him, eyes wide. "She was never here."

"But she was, pet, in all but substance. She is as real as this wall." Alastor reached out and knocked on it. "And the threat she presents is real, as well. Do not make the mistake of thinking otherwise."

"How did you know she was here...but not here?"

"The smell. Her power is such that she could maintain a visual and auditory representation. She couldn't divert enough power to maintain the smell. And she never managed to conjure substance."

He shoved his hand in his pants pocket and fisted it there because what he really wanted to do was grab her, hold her, touch her, and he didn't need to be a mind reader to know that Naphré wouldn't welcome that right now. She was wound tight as a top ready to spin.

"She has something you want."

"She does. Butcher's darksoul."

"Butcher's really making the rounds." She huffed out a breath through her nose and shook her head. "I thought you had his darksoul."

"I did." He offered a humorless smile. "And then I lost it. It seems that whatever you bloody well said and did before I arrived in that graveyard guaranteed Izanami his soul. My harvesting it stepped on some toes. She sent the *Shikome* to Sutekh's realm to claim it."

"And you want it back. Is Sutekh that hard up for souls? Just go…harvest another."

"I need *Butcher's* darksoul, pet."

She nodded. "Yeah, you've been giving me that impression."

"I believe he witnessed something the night my brother was killed. Given what Marie said, it appears that he did. Whatever he saw, it could be the key. It could help me bring Lokan back." He struggled to keep his voice even, to hide the depth of his emotion at the thought of reanimating his brother, but he failed. The endless well of darkness, the pain and rage, and even the hint of hope colored every syllable.

She heard it. He could see that in the way she was looking at him, her eyes shimmering with understanding. Then her brows drew down and she visibly steeled herself, the emotional withdrawal evident in the subtle changes to her body. She shifted her shoulders back, tipped her head away, drew her lips taut. She was clearly fighting against feeling either sympathy or empathy, and he couldn't blame her.

"So, this whole time, the way you said you were keeping tabs on me to protect me…you're a fucking liar. All along, it was about using me to get what you want." The words were accusatory, but her tone was flat. She wouldn't offer him even her rage. "Even what happened…what I let you do to me on my bedroom floor…the whole time, you were manipulating me."

Expressionless now, utterly controlled, Naphré stared at him. Where was the woman he'd kissed? The woman who had melted beneath his touch? Gone. In her place was a warrior, hard and cold and focused. And damned if he didn't like her ice as much as he liked the burning heat of her sun.

"Do you want me to make excuses? Make a pretty plea for forgiveness? Not sodding likely, pet. My brother is dead." He'd lost one family, his human family, centuries ago. He wouldn't lose another. "If there's something, anything, I can do to bring him back, I'll do it."

"Including sacrificing me."

Yes. No. Bloody sodding hell. "It started out that way."

The admission startled them both. Her gaze flashed to his.

"*Started out that way.* But isn't that way anymore?"

"No." He wanted to take her hand. He wanted to draw her to him and kiss her, stroke his palm down her back, peel her black tank top over her head and feel her skin. Show her what he could not tell her. Because he didn't know what to say. How to explain something to her that he couldn't even explain to himself. *I think you matter to me. I think that on some level, I've been waiting for you for centuries.*

It sounded like rubbish in his mind. He imagined it would sound even more ridiculous if he set the words free.

"Does she want to kill me? Take my soul?" She fell silent for a few seconds. "Or…she wants *you* to kill me? Is that it?"

"I can tell you only what I know. You have a free pass to enter Izanami's realm. I can't promise that you have a free pass to leave it."

"Suddenly honesty's the best policy?"

"Which is why I'm leaving you here," he continued as though she hadn't interrupted.

He could make no other decision. He couldn't risk her life. Couldn't risk never seeing her again. Because that was the way this would pan out. Sutekh had offered her soul in exchange for Butcher's. Which meant that if she died in Izanami's realm, if her soul was trapped there, he'd never see her again. The thought of that sat like acid in his gut.

Her lids dipped, then lifted, and she looked at him as though plumbing his soul. She exhaled in a rush.

"I need to go," he said.

"Not just yet." She blocked his way.

He could push her aside, but he didn't dare touch her. If he touched her, he would kiss her. If he kissed her, he wouldn't stop. The taste he'd had of her had been a morsel, an appetizer, whetting his appetite for the meal. He wanted her to be his meal.

Bloody hell.

"You don't make my decisions for me, Alastor. And before I make one for myself, I need more information. Why would I have a free pass to Izanami's realm? Tell me exactly what the *Shikome* said to you."

"She told me to bring you. That you were my ticket in. That without you accompanying me, I'd be shit out of luck."

Naphré tipped her head a bit to the side and the corners of her mouth twitched. "Those were her exact words?"

"I'm paraphrasing."

"But I'm the key?"

"So she said."

"And you don't find that odd?"

Oh, he found it exceedingly odd. Just as he found it odd that Naphré's name was in Sutekh's book of debts, though she claimed to have had no dealings with him. And he found it odd that she'd been summoning a demon that didn't exist, when she was indentured to a god. And odd that she was a bloody Topworld assassin. Everything about her, about *them,* about this situation, was bleeding, sodding odd.

"Odd or not, the circumstances are what they are."

"Then I'm going with you—"

"Too dangerous." He spoke so quickly he drowned out her declaration.

Her lips curved, but her smile didn't reach her eyes. "How is that your call to make?" The softness of her tone only accented her anger. He'd stepped on her toes. Hard.

"Do you understand nothing? I'm trying to *pro-tect* you, and I'm bloody well sacrificing a great deal in order to do it." Possibly sacrificing his entree into Izanami's realm, his chance at Butcher's darksoul, his chance to gain information about his brother. Of course, if he couldn't get in legitimately, he could always find a back door. Sutekh wouldn't be pleased because it would set Izanami solidly against him, but Alastor would deal with that difficulty when the time came.

"I didn't ask you to protect me."

"And I didn't ask to feel this urgent drive to do so," he snarled. "I haven't been able to get you out of my mind since the night I saw you at the Playhouse Lounge."

She inhaled sharply. "What are you talking about? You barely glanced at me."

He wanted to shake her. Instead, he grabbed her arm and pulled her against him. Her head fell back as she held his gaze.

"Black jeans," he rasped. "Bomber-style black jacket. Black sweater. Black hiking boots. No necklace. No earrings. No rings. You tried to make yourself as unobtrusive as possible. And your round, sweet, delectable arse made that bloody impossible."

For endless seconds, he just stared at her, waiting for her to rail at him, hit him, pull away.

"My arse?" She frowned and shook her head. Then, "I forgot about the boots."

"I didn't. I didn't forget a bleeding thing."

He ought to let her go.

Instead, he lowered his head and kissed her, lips and tongue and teeth. A kiss of claiming and taking and need.

She kissed him back, her lips clinging to his when he pulled away.

"You're staying here, pet."

"She'll just come for me again." She was breathless, her lips wet from his kiss. But she didn't give an inch. "The fact that you want to fuck me…oh, sorry, I mean shag me…gives you the right to decide my actions? I don't think so."

She stood toe-to-toe with him, glaring up at him, daring him to try and make her submit to his will.

Shag her? He wanted to do far more than that. He wanted to claim her. Own her. Some uncivilized thing inside him was screaming for him to mark her as his and let no one dare trespass. He shook his head, kept his tone cool and even. "This has nothing to do with wanting to shag you."

"Then what does it have to do with?"

"With…" He raked his fingers back through his hair, caught himself halfway through the uncharacteristic action, froze, then dropped his hand. "It has to do with needing to know you are safe. That you're here—"

"Waiting for you barefoot in the kitchen?"

"Yes. No. Bloody hell." How was he supposed to explain this to her when he didn't understand it himself?

She huffed out a short breath, pressed her palms against his cheeks and rose up on her toes so her mouth was inches from his. "I won't wait here for you, Alastor, pacing and wringing my hands. Another girl, maybe, but not me," she whispered, her breath fanning his lips. "I won't take orders from you—" she caught his lower lip between her teeth and bit down, hard enough for him to feel it, not hard enough to break skin "—except, maybe, in bed."

He caught her wrist and jerked her arms down so they were by her side. She didn't struggle, just held his gaze, her eyes fathomless, so dark he could drown in them. "This isn't a game, Naphré."

"It is. Everything in life, and probably in death, is a game. The wisest person knows that, recognizes it and plays it. Like chess. Look ten steps ahead, Alastor. What happens when your knight moves on the queen? What happens when you show up alone at Izanami's door and she won't let you in because you don't have the key? Apparently that key is me."

He didn't want it to be.

"And see, that's another thing. I need to go with you

because I need to know why she's so interested in me, why she wants me there at all. My soul is not hers. I belong to another."

"Another," Alastor echoed. "But not Aset."

Her lips compressed in a taut line. "No."

"Who?" He knew the answer, but he wanted her to say it. He wanted her to trust him. "Who owns your soul?"

He wanted to own it. Her soul. Her body. Her mind.

But Naphré Kurata was a woman who would never let herself be truly owned. Not by him. Not by anyone.

He suspected that was part of her allure.

"Who owns my soul? I'm starting to wonder that myself." The laugh that escaped her was hard enough to scratch a diamond. "Maybe Aset owns a piece. Maybe Izanami thinks she does. I'd like to say that I own it. Me. Only me."

"But you can't?"

"No." Her tone was flat and emotionless. "I sold my soul to a demon in order to survive. Stupid, really. Because in the end, I didn't gain a damned thing. I ended up in exactly the place I was running from. Only instead of working for the devil I knew, I ended up working for the devil I didn't. How's that for irony?"

"Explain."

"No." She offered a tight smile. "It doesn't matter. It's a long and stupid story. And we have places to go. People, or rather, maggot-infested deities, to see."

So many powerful Underworld deities appeared to have some sort of claim on her: Aset, Sutekh, Izanami. And those were only the ones he knew about.

Yet she remained independent, strong, her claim to herself the most powerful of all.

"You have no idea what Izanami wants with you?"

"None." She met his gaze, guileless, open. No evasion. But layered deep, he read a flicker of concern. She didn't like this any more than he did. Or maybe that concern reflected a lie. "But once we get there, I'm sure we'll find out."

"Well, color me a jammy git."

She shot him a cool look. "Speak English."

That got him. He laughed. She had a way of making him do that. "Jammy. Lucky. Git. Person. That *English* enough for you, pet?"

"Lucky because...?"

"I won't just have to watch my own arse on this trip—" he raised one brow "—I'll get to watch yours."

She didn't dignify that with a reply.

"PACKING A PICNIC?" He asked several minutes later as he watched her align little plastic baggies on the kitchen counter. He stood with one shoulder propped against the wall, arms crossed over his chest.

She glanced at him. "My walls stay up even if you don't prop them. I promise."

Opening one of the little bags, she then filled it with shelled sunflower seeds. Then she yanked open the fridge, took out a diet soda, and shot a glance at him over her shoulder.

"You want one?"

"Do you have something that isn't diet? Something with a hit of sugar?"

"What's with you and sugar?" She looked back into the fridge. "I have orange juice."

"That'll do." He paused. "My metabolism runs at an abnormal rate."

"Yours, or all soul reapers?" She got out a glass and poured the juice, then slid it across the counter toward him. He reached for it. Their fingers brushed. She jerked away, flipped the tab on her soda and took a long, deep pull. Following her lead, he drank his juice, feeling the sugar hit him with the needed lift.

"My brothers and I. We have a unique physiology."

"What about food? Doesn't that give you the energy you need?"

"Not all food is converted to glucose at the same rate. Sugar does the trick."

"You're getting into science territory, and that's a place I don't want to go." She went back to filling little plastic bags. He watched her move, watched the cloth of her tank top pull tight to her breasts as she lifted her arms, and the sway of her hair, strands falling forward to accent the smooth curve of her cheek.

"You planning on bringing a wheeled cart to tote all of that?" he asked.

"I like to be prepared." She counted out four energy bars and slid the box back in the cupboard. Then she filled another Ziploc with raisins and almonds. Finally, she retrieved a small black backpack from the hall closet.

"Don't expect me to offer to help you carry that about."

"Don't expect me to let you even if you offer." Again, that cool, dismissive look that she managed so well.

For some reason, it made him feel anything but cool. The more she rebuffed him, the more he wanted to grab her, haul her against him, push his tongue in her mouth and taste the heat she worked so hard to conceal.

Blatantly ignoring him now, she headed up the stairs. He followed, arriving on the landing just as she disappeared into the bedroom. Through the open door, he watched as she pulled a dark-red T-shirt over her black tank top, then pulled open a drawer and began to collect clean socks and...panties. As she piled things neatly on top of the dresser, she lifted her head and caught him watching her.

Holding her gaze, he walked toward her and slowly pulled a pair of panties from the top of the pile. White cotton panties. So unsexy that they were sexy.

She froze. Then her gaze shifted beyond his shoulder, her expression locking down. He didn't need to turn to guess at what she saw.

"Spider," she said. "The size of a Hummer."

She picked up the pace, pulling out leggings, a sports bra, a long-sleeved shirt, underwear and socks. She rolled each of them into a tight cylinder, tucked them all in a freezer baggie and stuffed it in the bottom of the pack.

"Preparing for a tsunami?" he asked.

She shrugged. "You never know. I like to consider all possibilities."

"So competent," he murmured. "I like that."

She ignored him.

"I like the way you can switch gears, screaming my name while you come, then pulling it together, all business."

His emotions were unsettled while she appeared

cool as a cucumber. He wanted to shift the playing field, put her squarely on the side having trouble with control.

She glanced up, night-dark eyes and thick, straight lashes. He waited for her to react to his teasing. Instead, she asked in a calm, even voice, "You have any idea of climate? Terrain? Anything you can tell me about Izanami's territory?"

As he watched her lush mouth form the words, he imagined her on her knees in front of him, her gorgeous lips wrapped around his cock.

He glanced away. Took a slow breath. Right, then. None of that.

It had been his choice to stop earlier. The right choice.

He couldn't say what had come over him, what had made him kiss her and taste her...

Yeah, he could. She had come over him. The scent of her hair. The bravery she'd shown in the alley. Her wit. Her guts.

He watched her push those thrice damned panties into another Ziploc bag.

"Izanami's territory?" she prodded.

"Never been there," he said into the growing silence. "Know nothing about it. I'd suggest layers, that way you can peel off whatever you don't need." Wrong choice of words. They only made him think of peeling off her clothes and laying her on the bed and taking her over and over again for hours. Days.

She stared at him, frozen, her hands deep in the bag, her lips slightly parted.

Bloody fucking hell. He'd like to keep her in bed, naked and panting, for a week.

And maybe she knew that, or maybe her own thoughts were running along the same lines, because she spun away and pulled a gray, long-sleeved lightweight fleece from her drawer, rolled it into a tight cylinder and tucked it in the bag.

"You're yanking my libido like a chain," she said, her head bowed. "You need to stop."

"Or what?"

"Or you might not like what I do in return."

She closed the pack, hefted it onto her shoulder and strode toward him. He expected her to turn sideways and sidle past him so their bodies touched as little as possible. Instead, she walked straight toward him and, when she reached him, pushed full against him. He felt the connection like a jolt of electricity.

"I like to keep things even," she said, head tipped back as she stared up at him. "Right now, I feel like things aren't so balanced." She leaned a little closer, dropped her voice a little lower. "You had your mouth on my clit. Seems only fair that I wrap mine around your cock." Her nails scraped him through the cloth of his slacks. The cock in question lifted its head and waved. "Unfortunately, someone has other ideas."

She jerked her head at the wall. He glanced over and saw that the spider had been replaced by centipedes, and they were multiplying. There had to be thousands, skittering up and down from floor to ceiling.

Illusion? Possibly. He had only to walk over and touch one to know for certain. But either way, it didn't matter. They were an expression of the *Shikome*'s—and Izanami's—impatience.

Time was running out.

Naphré pushed past him and headed down the stairs, leaving him to adjust himself in private. Again.

This was going to be an exceptionally long trip.

Bloody hell. He couldn't think straight around her.

"You can still back out," he offered.

She glanced back, and gave a dismissive shrug. "They'll only come for me once you're gone. I figure I stand a better chance with you watching my back than I do alone."

"A valid point." It was. He was only fooling himself if he thought that leaving her behind would save her. If Izanami wanted her, she'd find a way to have her. He knew that better than most, given that he was the thing Sutekh sent to collect those *he* wanted. "Trusting me to watch your back, pet?"

"Trusting myself to watch it if you don't."

Once downstairs, she poured food and water for Neko. Then she grabbed the phone and dialed. "Hey," she said when someone answered, "it's Naphré. Neko's going to be here alone for a few days, maybe longer. I need to go out of town. Can you check on her?" A pause, then, "Thanks."

"Friend?" he asked, annoyed by the surge of possessiveness that made him want to know the sex of that friend.

"My mother."

He blinked, startled. He hadn't thought her mother was alive. Somehow, he'd expected Naphré Kurata, Topworld assassin, to be an orphan, a loner.

"What?" she asked. His expression must have given him away.

"I have no idea why, but I assumed your mother was deceased."

"You know what they say about assumptions…" She shrugged. "My mom took off when I was little." She jerked her head toward the photo on the wall, the one with the smiling family, *her* smiling family. "Right after that picture was taken. My dad and my grandfather raised me. Then, one day, I…found her again. She'd made her choices. I made mine." She shrugged. "By then, I was well on the path to what I am now. I figured I had no right to judge her."

"You have a good relationship, then?"

She laughed, not with bitterness, but with genuine amusement. The sound slid through him like hot chocolate on a cold day. "I'm guessing it's as good as you have with your dad." She huffed another laugh at his expression. "Works that well for you, does it? Being son of the überlord of chaos?"

Then it was his turn to laugh, a startled burst of sound. "Peachy. Is that how you see your mother? As a lord, or rather, lady of chaos?"

"No. I see her as a woman who thought she was doing the right thing but made a horrible mistake. It cost her everything." Sadness crept into her eyes, then flickered away. "But I understand the whole duty thing. She felt it was her obligation to—"

She cut herself off, obviously concerned that she was about to reveal too much. But he could fill in the blanks even if she didn't say it. She was Otherkin, a Daughter of Aset. Which meant her mother was a Daughter of Aset. A member of the Asetian Guard? He was going to guess that the mother had chosen to honor that heritage while the daughter had chosen to turn her back on it. Why?

He was appalled that the answer mattered to him.

EVE SILVER                                        271

He didn't want to feel a damned thing for her, didn't want her to matter. If he didn't care, it wouldn't hurt when he lost her.

When she didn't elaborate, he prompted, "And that obligation was...?"

"I share, you share." Slanting him a glance through her lashes, she asked, "You up for that, Alastor?"

No. No, he definitely was not, and that seemed to be the answer she expected because she didn't wait for him to say it aloud. But just before she turned away, he thought he saw a flicker of disappointment.

She went to stand in front of the framed picture on the wall. Clearly, their moment of intimate revelation was over. She reached up and slid her fingers along the side, releasing a hidden catch. Then she pulled back one side of the frame, and it swung open like a door, revealing a niche in the wall about eight inches deep. There were several weapons anchored there. Guns. Knives. Shuriken. Nunchaku. A pair of tonfa—wooden batons with side handles that were used for both defense and attack.

"What's that?" he asked as she reached for a different baton about seven inches long.

"Keibo," she said. "A flick of the wrist and it extends to twenty-one inches. Good for confined spaces."

She took it down, along with the tonfa. Then she took down two knives, a thick-handled one with short curved blade, and a second one with a longer blade and a finger hook.

"No guns?" He was interested in her choices. They were all close-contact weapons. But more than that, they were all useless. If she needed to fight in Izanami's realm, then she was destined to lose, because they were

Underworlders, dead but not dead, dead but immortal. Eternal. And she was only human.

"None of my weapons will be of significant value in Izanami's realm," she pointed out, surprising him as she said exactly what he'd been thinking.

"Then why bring them along?"

"Habit." She went to the front door, opened the closet and took out a pair of hiking boots. She bent and sheathed the longer knife inside the left boot, then straightened and settled the shorter one in the utility belt she'd buckled at the curve of her hips.

He followed, pausing only when he spotted a crystal dish of hard candies on a shelf. He grabbed it and emptied all of them into his jacket pockets to supplement the toffee caramels he had left. He'd been caught a time or two without adequate sugar. The hunger had been powerful, gnawing at him from the inside out, not just in his gut, but in every tissue and cell and tendon. Rather unpleasant.

Setting the now empty dish back on the shelf, he raised his head and found her watching him.

"Ready to visit the realm of the dead?" he asked.

"As long as it's just a visit and not a permanent move."

"I won't be leaving without you," he said. Because he couldn't outrun the suspicion that Izanami meant to keep her there.

# CHAPTER SIXTEEN

ALASTOR DID THAT THING with his hand and conjured another portal. As she stared at the undulating, smoking hole and felt the chill creep through the air toward them, Naphré made her displeasure known.

Quite clearly.

"How did you think we'd be traveling?" he asked.

"I don't know. Plane. Train. Anything other than the vomit-coaster."

He laughed, that same low, rumbling laugh that she'd first heard in the graveyard. It enveloped her. Made her hyperaware of everything about him. The scent of his skin. The way his mouth curved to reveal that long, sexy crease in his left cheek. The hint of darkness and promise and…raunchiness in that smile.

There was no doubt in her mind that Alastor Krayl didn't have many rules in bed.

Actually, no, she had the feeling that he loved rules, as long as he was applying them to others. He was all about control.

And she didn't want to examine the reasons that she found that appealing.

Without any warning, he took her hand, twined his fingers with hers and dragged her into the icy blackness of the smoky, undulating hole before them. Cold. Mind-numbing, skin-flaying cold. Tiny ice crystals formed on her skin, her lashes, her lips. Every breath was an agony. Every small movement a nauseating flip.

The trip through the portal, as he called it, wasn't any better the second time than it had been the first. The bone-deep chill, the feeling of disorientation, the horrible sensation that there was only this dark pit of nothing and the whole world was somehow gone, were all exactly as they had been when he'd dragged her into the portal in the alley.

Up became down, right became left. She lost all sense of time. She couldn't see Alastor, couldn't feel him, except for the firm hold of his hand on hers. That was her anchor and she held on to it with everything she was.

They hit their destination and the hole disgorged them. She stumbled, and almost fell, Alastor's quick lunge and the steely band of his arm around her waist the only thing that kept her from going down.

She heard the crumple of a candy wrapper and opened her eyes to find that he was holding one of his ever-present toffees out toward her.

"Here. This'll help."

Popping the candy in her mouth, she closed her eyes and let the sugar melt on her tongue.

"Where are we?" she asked once her teeth stopped chattering enough for her to speak.

"Japan."

Of course they were. "Your black hole certainly beats airport lineups."

He glanced down at her, his eyes so blue it nearly took her breath away. His lips lifted in a delicious, shiver inducing curve. "Done much traveling, pet?'

"A bit. Japan. Egypt. I went to the Dominican

Republic once. Mostly, I've just traveled around North America. For work."

"Work," he echoed, then laughed. "Is that what you call the assassination business?"

"You ever hear the saying about pots and kettles?"

He stared at her for a long moment, and then he said, "We make a pair, don't we?"

"We do," she said softly, and he held her gaze as seconds ticked past.

Finally, he stepped away, glanced about, and tossed casually over his shoulder, "You said North America. Not South America?"

"Nope. Not my turf. Topworlders there have their own territorial teams they like to use. The top team in South America are the Ramirez brothers. Butcher never wanted to step on their toes. He said it was bad business. So we stuck to our own continent."

"Just as Underworlders stick to their own territories."

"Just as."

"Bad business," he mused, mouth grim, eyes hard.

"What is?"

"Being here is bad business, pet. You stick to me like glue, right? You do not leave my side. You do exactly as I say."

"You'd like that."

His gaze dipped to her mouth. "Yes, I would."

She rolled in her lower lip, swiped her tongue across the surface, trying to ignore the little shiver that chased up her spine. "I'll follow your lead. You're the expert."

"What makes you say that?" Exasperation tinged his words. She didn't like that. It made her uneasy.

"You're a soul reaper. You can pass to the Underworld at will. You've been here before, haven't you?"

"If by here, you mean the Underworld, then yes, many, many times. If you refer to Izanami's realm, then I'm afraid I'll have to disappoint."

She digested that. Of course, it made sense. She knew that Topworlders were territorial. She imagined Underworlders were as well. There was really no reason he'd be familiar with realms other than Sutekh's. "So you really have no idea what we're up against? No idea what to expect?"

"None."

"Dandy."

"Think of it as an adventure." He stared down at her, his jaw set, his eyes glittering. Then he reached out and caught her upper arm, dragged her against him and lowered his head until his mouth was inches from her own. Her heart skipped a beat, then raced.

"I thought you don't like change," she whispered. "I would have thought that means you don't like adventure."

"Depends on the adventure." His mouth was on hers before she could even think to protest. Not that she was thinking of protesting. He kissed her like he wanted to own her, devour her, his tongue in her mouth, his lips hard on her own. Life sizzled through her. When he kissed her like this, it was like she'd never been kissed before.

She hadn't.

Not the way Alastor kissed her.

Lifting up on her toes, she molded her body to his, feeling hard planes and ridges pressed against her breasts, her thighs.

Heat poured through her. Electric heat.

With a moan, she reached up, tunneled her fingers through his hair and shifted her lips against his.

Closing his hands around her waist, he held her a little away from him. He dipped his head so his lips pressed to the hollow where her neck met the curve of her shoulder. He was breathing hard, and she felt a kick of satisfaction at that. She wasn't the only one affected.

He lifted his head and stared at her. Blue like the sky. Blue like the ocean. Blue like the heart of a flame, framed in those dark, thick, curling lashes.

"Before we go in again, I need an answer to a question, pet. And I need you to tell the truth." Not a request, a demand. She nodded, but offered no promises. She'd wait until she heard the question before she decided whether or not to answer. "You were summoning a demon recently, yes?"

Unease skittered through her as she wondered if he'd been watching her every second since the night she'd shot Butcher. And then she sifted through the possibilities and realized he must have seen the salt and the candles that she'd left out. She hadn't been expecting company.

"Yes," she said.

"Why? You're a Daughter of Aset. Why not go to the Asetian Guard if you need help with something?"

"It's complicated."

"Complicated is just another way of saying 'none of your fucking business.' I have no fondness for euphemisms."

"Fine. I'll say it outright. None of your fucking business."

His eyes changed color. They were the blue of a glacier in the deepest Arctic now, pale and so cold they were almost gray.

"Oh, but it is, pet. Everything about you is my business. You're trusting me to keep you safe in there, to get you in and get you back out. I need to know what surprises I might run into."

She took a deep breath, let it out. Moment of truth. Only she didn't need to share all her secrets, in all their ugly, tattered glory. She could share only what he truly needed to know.

And why was she so hesitant to reveal her truths? He was a soul reaper. He tore out hearts. No one could ever accuse him of being warm and fuzzy. He was certainly no better—or worse—than she. So why was she so afraid to reveal herself?

Because she'd seen the way his brother looked at Roxy Tam, and she'd coveted that look, that connection. She'd seen the faintest hint in Alastor's eyes as he looked at *her.* She didn't want to snuff that spark before it ever had a chance to grow.

And she'd seen what had happened to her parents. How the truth had driven them apart, driven her mother to leave all she loved behind.

So she offered a small truth in place of the larger. "I never took first blood. Do you know what that is?"

"Daughters of Aset pledge themselves by carving the dark mark in their skin, and fully claim their heritage by feeding off the life force of others. Usually by taking sips of human blood. First blood is the first taste, the taste that initiates."

She was taken aback by how much he knew. "How—"

"You met Roxy."

"Yes, but for her to divulge all of that to you…a soul reaper…that's like the Russians telling the Americans their secrets during the Cold War."

"The circumstances of her revelation were life or death, and she didn't exactly tell anyone. It was more of an accidental discovery." He held his hand up, palm forward. "That story is not relevant at the moment. But it might interest you to know that Dae was Roxy's first blood."

"What? You mean…they…" She shook her head, completely mystified. Roxy Tam had taken the blood of a soul reaper. She couldn't imagine that. From the second that she'd understood what she was, she'd been told that Sutekh and his soul reapers were the ultimate enemy. The purest evil.

Except Alastor wasn't.

He'd saved her ass. Saved Marie's ass as well, though if she was honest she'd have to admit that was more by happenstance than intent.

She wasn't going to paint him as a saint when she knew he was a sinner.

"Now that we've established my knowledge of first blood, give me your story. Make it clear and concise." He was back to ordering her around. "I am not going into Izanami's realm unprepared."

No. Of course he wasn't. He liked to be in control. No doubt he planned for every possible contingency. Alastor didn't like to simply run with things. If she'd figured out anything about him, she'd figured out that much.

And really, what did her secret matter? He was

Sutekh's son. It wasn't like he could judge her for the company she kept.

"I sold my soul to a demon so I could survive."

"So you said before." Something indecipherable flashed in his eyes. Whatever it was, he hid it quickly, and it left her feeling uneasy, like there was something he knew and wasn't sharing. "You said that instead of working for the devil you knew, you ended up working for the devil you didn't. Explain." His tone promised that now was not a good opportunity to ask him any questions. More of a time for her to be offering answers.

She blew out a breath. "About six years ago, I had some shit go down. I left the Asetian Guard."

"Why?" Clipped. Cold. He expected an answer.

"They wanted me to step up, and I didn't like the smell of the shit they were asking me to step in. There are three lineages of the Daughters of Aset. Keeper. Adaptive. And my lineage, Guide. We're aggressive by nature. Predatory." She huffed out a breath. "Once blooded, Guides kill people. Those who threaten the hierarchy of the Asetian Guard."

"And you appear to be extremely competent at it. I fail to see the difficulty."

"Yeah, me too." She took a deep breath. *"Now."*

"Naphré." A growled warning. Alastor Krayl was growing impatient.

"I didn't *want* to kill people. I didn't want to be an assassin. I'd already carved the dark mark in my skin, but hadn't taken first blood. I tried to explain that I wanted out, that I wanted to do something different. I was young. I was torn. Duty against morals." She gave an ugly laugh. "That's funny, isn't it? Me talking about morals now."

"Go on."

She did. The words came in a rush now. "It was a mess. A big fucking mess. *I* was a mess. My dad and grandfather raised me. You know what it's like to be raised with those expectations, those traditions? The Japanese culture is all about respect and duty. *I'm* all about duty. That's who I am…was…and I ran away from who I was supposed to be. Like a coward."

He didn't argue. Didn't reassure. Just listened.

"I was twenty years old. I was freaked out and afraid. I tried to go to my superior, to tell her how I felt. She was away on a retreat, so I went to her superior.

"You know what I found? My *mother!* I found that her superior was my mother. My missing mother. The one who'd left me. *She left me.* For the Asetian Guard. Put duty over her daughter. And you know what? The worst part of it was, I hated her for that, but I understood, too. I understood. She gave up everything for them, her daughter, her husband, and I *didn't want to.*

"I freaked. I ran. And got caught in what amounted to the perfect storm. I was in the middle of fucking nowhere. I hitched a ride and made it to a gas station. Called my father. He came for me, even though I'd left him without a word or an explanation. Hours later, there we were, in the car, all buckled up nice and safe, driving down the highway. A gravel truck came at us from the opposite direction. A car turned out in front of it. That was the perfect storm. The truck swerved to miss the car. Hit us instead.

"I was hurt. Broken ribs. Fractured thighbone. I was

bleeding. Weak. And there was a horrible pressure low in my belly. I think I must have been bleeding inside. But my dad was worse. His chest was ripped open and blood was pulsing out in spurts. On my hands. On the seat. He was going to die. I think maybe I was going to die, too."

Her heart was racing and she felt sick as the memories took her. Alastor brushed the backs of his fingers along her cheek. Just that. It was enough to steady her.

"I was sobbing, praying, begging for help. Promising anything if my dad could just live. The car was a twisted mess. There were sparks. The smell of gasoline.

"I look up, and there he was. The demon. 'Save yourself,' he said. And I knew he meant first blood. I couldn't. I wouldn't. I didn't want that life.

"He stared at me, then he said, 'I will save him from these injuries. And you. For a price.' I told him to do it. I told him I didn't care about the price. So he saves my dad. And the price is me. He gets my soul, and he turns me into a fucking assassin. I ran so fast and hard from the Asetian Guard that I ran smack-dab into the thing I was running from." She gave a bitter laugh. "And that's the end of the story."

"And your father?" But he already knew the answer. She could see it in his eyes.

"Died two months later. Legionnaires' disease. He went on a business trip to Belgium and two weeks later, he was dead, along with five other people who stayed in the same hotel."

"Legionnaires' disease?"

"It's a rare…deadly…kind of pneumonia. Caused by a bug. *Legionella pneumophila*."

"It's the bugs you can't see..." Alastor echoed the things she'd said to Marie, and his gaze dipped to her pocket where she kept her ever-present little bottle of sanitizer.

"Yeah. Stupid, I know. You can't even get Legionnaires' disease by direct contact. You have to breathe it in from the air-conditioning system or something." She shrugged, uncomfortable with the topic.

"Do you believe the demon lied to you?"

"No. I believe I was too stupid to read the fine print. He did exactly what he promised to do. Saved my dad from the injuries he got in that car accident. He never promised that my dad would live forever."

"The demon's name. Tell me." His voice was edged with tension. As though the name really mattered. Maybe it did. Maybe different demons had different levels of power. Maybe some were even a match for a soul reaper.

"I don't know. I never knew."

"Then how could you summon him? You need a name for a summoning."

"That's what I thought, but apparently not. He said I didn't. And I never summoned him, not before now. I just waited until he set me a task. And in between his visits, I tried to...just live."

"Describe him."

"Butt-ugly. Stocky. Big head. Balding, with a ring of gray hair. His eyes scared the crap out me. Small, dark, soulless."

A muscle jumped in Alastor's jaw. That small, tell-tale sign made her uneasy.

"When was the last time you saw him?"

"Couple months ago. I've been trying to summon

him since the night I shot Butcher. No luck. No answer."

"And you won't get one."

Something in his tone chilled the blood in her veins. She swallowed, backed up a step.

"Why not?"

"Your demon's name was Gahiji. And he's been terminated."

"What? Terminated? Dead? Do you mean *dead?* How can a demon be killed? I didn't even know that was possible."

When he offered no reply, she fell silent for a moment, digesting the shocking information, trying to figure out exactly what it meant. "What about my debt?" she asked, the words almost choking her. It'd be nice to think the demon's death set her free, but she knew way too much about the Underworld's workings now to let herself think that for even a second.

Alastor just stared at her, his eyes chilled to that flat blue-gray that made her feel like taking a step back. Maybe two. Just in case his amazing control finally blew. Something about this situation stirred his emotions. It didn't take a genius to figure that out. But what was it…anger? Something else? And the big question was: why?

"Talk to me," she said. "Tell me what you know. Does this demon's death negate my debt?"

"What I know," Alastor echoed, his tone completely flat. "See, that's the thing, pet. I *don't* know, and not knowing is not a good thing."

He was lying. Or if not exactly lying, not sharing the whole truth.

"And…" she prompted, waiting for him to fill in

the blanks. When he said nothing, she tried to free-associate things on her own. "Maybe that's why the *Shikome* is interested in me. Maybe the demon's death somehow transferred my debt to her. Maybe—"

"She wants you for some other as-yet unknown reason. There was no transfer. Your debt is still owned by the same entity that has owned it all along." Bitterness leached into his words, and she wondered at that. "The question is, why the bloody, sodding subterfuge?"

"What subterfuge? And how can I still owe the debt to the demon I've owed it to all along if he's been, as you put it, terminated?"

"You don't."

"I don't what?" Frustration surged. "Either explain what the hell you're talking about, or shut up with the cryptic comments."

Talk about cutting off your nose to spite your face.

Alastor chose option two. He shut down. No matter how she phrased the next question and the next, he refused to say another word about the demon. And that left her with a greasy ball of unease churning in her gut.

## CHAPTER SEVENTEEN

THEY HIKED DOWN A steep slope, Alastor going first, Naphré bringing up the rear. She shook her head, thinking that if there was anyone out here watching them, they definitely made an interesting looking pair, what with Alastor turned out in his suit and Naphré in her more activity-appropriate jeans and layers and hiking boots and pack.

At points, the slope was so steep that Naphré ended up on her thigh and one ass cheek, doing a controlled slide, her feet forward to slow her descent.

She had no idea how Alastor stayed on his feet, given that his fancy dress shoes had zero tread. Every once in a while, he'd stop and look back at her, and every time he did, she had the impression that he wanted to say something.

Finally, when they were about halfway down the slope, he did. "I'll carry you." He turned and waited as though expecting her to scramble up and leap into his arms.

"Just try," she snarled, as a particularly sharp stone embedded in the ground scraped along her thigh as she skidded past. "I can do this on my own."

"You sound like a two-year-old," he said, then pitched his voice higher. "'By myself. Do it by myself.'"

That froze her in place. His inflection was perfect.

He actually sounded like a two-year-old. She **knew**, because the house next to hers was home to **twin**s, and they invariably spent hours outside on the sidewalk, scooting along on their ride-on toys, yelling some version of exactly that as their frazzled mom tried to keep coats zipped and shoes tied. And since two-year-old twins didn't exactly share a similar schedule to a Topworld assassin, they usually were out there exactly when she was trying to get some sleep.

From his perfect impersonation, she could tell that Alastor knew kids. He knew how they sounded and what they said.

The thought shocked her. And made her wary.

She was a killer, but she drew lines. Please, please, let him draw lines, too. Don't let the guy she was falling—

Whoa. No. Not going there, even in her private thoughts. He'd given her a great orgasm. She could get one of those anywhere, including her vibrator. If she ever remembered to pick up batteries for it. She was not going to confuse sexual release with actual emotion.

"What do you know about two-year-olds?" she asked.

"What are you really asking, pet? If I harvest from babies? The answer is no." He turned away and resumed walking while she minced her way behind him, pebbles and loose earth falling away beneath her boots. Then he turned his head and spoke over his shoulder. "But don't get all warm and fuzzy on me. The darksouls I take are dipped in slime, blacker than pitch. Babies haven't had a chance to accumulate that sort of darkness."

She was quiet for a moment, following in his wake, then she said. "Next time, if you want me to believe the 'I'm an arsehole' speech in order to avoid answering a question, you'll have to do better to make it sound convincing. Tell me how you know what little kids sound like."

"A half dozen nieces," he muttered. Clearly annoyed with her.

"And they're how old?"

He just kept moving, silent now.

Topic off limits. But she pressed anyway. The terrain leveled out a bit and she managed to stay on her feet as she jogged a few steps to catch up to him.

"Alastor?"

"Chatty all of a sudden, pet?"

She caught hold of his arm.

He glanced down, then up.

He didn't loosen her fingers or pull away. He didn't need to. He was already far, far away from her, his walls firmly in place. She felt the rebuff. It stung, and she had no idea why it should.

"My human family is dead. My parents, my sisters, my nieces are dead," he said in a low, controlled voice, as though reciting a bit of information that had no meaning to him at all. "They were significant fixtures in my life. My human life. My sisters brought them to visit often. They grew to womanhood. I later learned that they had nieces of their own, and great-nieces...several generations of them, while I was gone. I never knew them."

His nieces were dead. Several generations of them.

"Generations," she echoed. How many years was that? Confusion assailed her.

*My human family.* She hadn't thought about it, really, but now she did. He was Sutekh's son. Not human. Somehow, she'd overlooked the varied and layered ramifications of that. He was an Underworlder, one of the few who could pass into Topworld at will. But that didn't make him human.

She almost asked, *what are you?* A soul reaper, yes, and Sutekh's son. But what exactly did that mean? And then she read the subtle tension in his frame and she thought she must tread lightly, or she would destroy whatever seed the two of them had managed to plant.

She shouldn't care about that seed. She had no business caring about it. She'd forfeited the right to many things the night she'd sworn herself to a demon. One of those things was affection. And lov—

Don't even think it.

Keep it light.

"You said generations. How old are you?" Oh, yeah. That was light.

"In mortal years?"

"Umm...sure."

"Watch that boulder," he said, and circled around it. She followed, thinking that their conversation was over.

Only after a long time did he say, "I was born nearly three hundred years ago."

She sucked in a sharp breath.

Well, there was a lesson. Don't ask if you can't handle the answer.

THEY REACHED A GULLY. On either side of them the mountains rose, tree-covered and green. The ground beneath their feet was sandy, dotted with stones and rocks and boulders. There were small pockets of muddy water here and there. Alastor figured it must have rained recently.

He'd had the perfect opening, and he'd chosen not to use it. They'd talked about his family. It had been the ideal opportunity to talk about Sutekh, to tell her that the demon that had tricked her into signing away her soul was, in fact, no demon at all, but his father.

But he'd held his tongue.

He didn't know why her name was in Sutekh's book of debts. He didn't know why his father, out of all the souls he had claim to, had chosen to offer her, Naphré, to Izanami. And all those unknowns kept him from the big reveal. Because he couldn't betray his father. Loyalty to his father, his brothers, was ingrained in who he was, who he had become.

Until he knew more, he couldn't tell her a bloody thing. And that was eating him alive, because the omission felt like a betrayal.

The ground before him wasn't smooth or flat. Their going was slow and arduous as they skirted boulders and deep grooves in the ground. Alone, he would have traveled the distance in perhaps one-tenth the time. But he wasn't alone.

"Dry riverbed?" Naphré asked from behind him.

"Looks like." He didn't say more, though a part of him wanted to. Wanted to just hear her voice. He liked the sound of it, calm and smooth. Feminine.

"Do you actually know where we're going?" she asked.

He snorted. "To Izanami's realm."

"Do you know how to get there?"

He stopped, turned. "Why do you ask?"

"You're striding along so purposefully, I'm trying to figure out if it's because you know where we're going, or because you don't."

"I do." In a manner of speaking. He knew the general location but not the exact coordinates of the entrance to Yomi. But he'd detect the subtle vibrations of the molecules in the air that signaled the supernatural when they approached Izanami's door.

"Lead on, Macduff."

"Misquote," Alastor said, walking on.

"What?"

"The actual quote is 'Lay on, Macduff, and damned be him who first cries 'Hold! enough!'"

She walked silently behind him, and then, "Well, they mean the same thing."

He laughed. "Close enough."

"Must you always have the last word?"

"Whenever possible."

She didn't complain, though he set a brutal pace. For her, anyway. For him, it was a stroll.

"Let me take the backpack," he offered for what must have been the tenth time.

And again, she said, "No. It isn't heavy."

"I was raised never to let a lady carry something when I could carry it for her."

She laughed, a deep, throaty sound that made him feel like he was standing in the sun. "What on earth gave you the idea that I'm a lady?"

He opened his mouth to offer a pithy reply, when his instincts started screaming and he stopped so abruptly that she slammed into his back.

"What's wrong?" She shifted so her back was against his and they presented the most advantageous configuration against any threat. He suspected it was an ingrained, automatic response.

"I don't know." Nothing. There was no noticeable change in their surroundings, not in temperature or the scent of the air or the ground beneath their feet. No hint of supernatural energy. Yet, it was all wrong. "Stay close enough that you can hear my pulse," he ordered.

She pressed tight against his back, her pack digging into his shoulder, and a quick glance told him that she had her knife in her hand. For all the good it would do her against a *Shikome,* or anything else Izanami might send.

He looked down at the ground beneath their feet, almost expecting a veritable army of creeping centipedes to be swarming out of a crevice and skittering up their legs. There was nothing there. A quick scan of the surrounding slopes yielded no clues. There were no supernaturals about, and no humans.

But he wasn't fooled. They were a step away from disaster.

"We need to move. Now." He grabbed Naphré's hand and set off at a jog. She kept up, no questions, no arguments.

As they rounded a bend, the gully sloped down and they followed it to where an enormous boulder blocked their way.

A blind end.

Every instinct Alastor had told him this was not a good place to be. But Naphré resisted when he started to walk away, their arms extending the full distance between them as she refused to move, and he refused to let go his hold on her hand.

"This is it," she breathed, laying her other palm flat against the boulder that towered over them.

"It? What?"

"The story of Izanami and her husband, Izanagi. She died. He followed her to Yomi, wanting her back. When he got there, things didn't work out as planned."

"In what way?"

"She had already partaken of the food of the dead, and her body was decomposing. He swore to her he wouldn't look at her while she begged the deities for release from death and the chance to return to life." She shrugged. "He lied."

"Doesn't everyone? What does that have to do with this boulder?"

"He ran from her once he saw her rotting corpse. He escaped and pushed a boulder to block the entrance to *Yomotsuhirasaka*."

"Which is?"

"The cavern at the entrance to Yomi."

Alastor glanced up at the rock face. "You think this is that boulder." And now that she'd so succinctly recapped the story, so did he. But that didn't negate the fact that he felt like jumping out of his skin, every sense and instinct screaming that this situation was wrong.

He did a quick evaluation of the boulder, running his fingers along the edges, squatting to feel along the base. He clambered up the stone face of the rock wall that bordered it, just to see if the way in was at the top.

Nothing.

"Izanami!" he called. The wind picked up and blew down the gully, but that was the only reply he got.

From his place some twelve feet up the rock face,

he looked down at Naphré. She was hunkered down, running her fingers along the base of the boulder.

He had to smile at that. Trust her to not trust him.

As though sensing his regard, she tipped her head back and her lips curled in that mysterious, close-lipped smile.

"Double-checking, in case I missed the secret lever?" he asked.

She shrugged. "The *Shikome* said I'm the key, right?"

And he was an utter and complete moron.

Izanami wanted nothing from him, had no reason to let him into her realm. She wanted Naphré. And he had only the *Shikome*'s intimation that he'd be allowed to come along for the ride.

Bloody sodding hell.

He leaped down, landing so close that his thigh skimmed her shoulder. She was already rising, and he closed his fingers on her upper arm and hauled her the rest of the way up.

"It's a sodding trap," he snarled. Rage curdled in his gut. He was a thrice-damned fool. The *Shikome* had played him, using the darksoul he so clearly wanted as the bait, Naphré the prize she sought to bag.

Why? Why the fuck did they want her?

Time to figure out those answers once he had her somewhere safe.

He laced his fingers with Naphré's, as tight as he dared without risking breaking her bones. She didn't argue or struggle or ask a single question. He focused his attention on summoning a portal, grabbing the energy that surged between Topworld and the Underworld and momentarily combining them to create a fracture between the realms, an icy doorway that would allow them to escape.

Too late.

From behind came a booming, echoing roar, and he spun to see a massive wall of water chasing along the riverbed toward them.

OBLIVION. IT CALLED TO HIM.

The cold sliced him open like a scalpel, flaps of skin pulled wide to lay bare the flesh and bone beneath. He was normally immune to cold. Yet this numbing chill nullified the part of him that was Sutekh's son and left only the human part to face the tiny crystals that formed on his lashes, his skin, flaying him raw.

Death by freezing. By drowning. By loneliness and self-loathing.

Where were these thoughts coming from?

He'd left them behind long ago.

He opened his eyes and looked into hers. Naphré. Eyes like an endless lake. Dark. Fathomless. She was there in front of him. No, inside him. She could hear what he heard, know what he knew.

He didn't want her to know what a coward he had been. To know the many ways he had tried to take his own life. The first time he'd taken a soul. The darkness inside him. The part of him that reveled in harvesting souls and hearts. The taste of that, the rush of absolute pleasure.

It wasn't the knowledge of what he was that made him hate himself so. It was the knowledge that he liked it.

He'd wanted to die. To kill himself.

He'd tried. He'd failed.

Lokan had saved him. And Mal and Dagan. Though they always insisted that in the end, he'd saved himself.

It had taken him a very long time to learn to cage his demons.

All the souls he'd claimed. The memories he'd buried. The parents who'd raised him, the sisters who'd loved him, gone so long he could only remember their features if he pulled out the faded miniatures he'd found in the back of a curio shop after years of searching. They were there with him now, looking at him with such hate and loathing.

And then they fell away, one by one.

Time had no meaning. He only knew that there was no bottom to this endless well. His body tumbled and turned in air that wasn't air. No gravity. No resistance. Water. He was in water so cold it should have been solid ice.

Clenching his fingers, he tried to feel Naphré's hand in his. But he felt nothing, not even his own fingers curling against his palms.

Did he have her? She was his anchor, his buoy.

"Naphré!" A scream that echoed to the vast and infinite dome of the black sky. A scream that was heard only in his own mind as the water slammed them against rock—was that the boulder they hit?—and she was torn away. Lost.

And then he was alone. Alone with the promise of death. Once, he would have reached for it, welcomed its kiss like a lover. Once, he had believed it was all he deserved.

"Naphré!" Her name echoed back at him again and

again, until the sound coalesced with the roaring of the water.

A river.

He had to find her. She could drown. She could die. And if she died in Izanami's realm she would be lost to him.

Fear suddenly became part of the journey. He didn't want to lose her. He'd only just found her.

Naphré.

Again, he lost all sense of time. He knew it passed because the deep ache that warned him he needed a sugar hit was coming on him, doubling him over. Pain, sharp and bright. In his cells.

In his heart.

The pain of memories surging at him like a swarm of locusts. The face of the woman he had thought was his mother, her eyes rheumy, her skin parchment-thin and folded in neat wrinkles at her neck and chin. She smiled at him and beckoned him near, then she rested her hand on his head and said, "You are a fine gentleman, my Alastor. Remember that in the years to come. You are your father's son and heir."

His father's son? Undoubtedly.

But not the father she referred to. Not *his* heir.

He was son to another. Heir to a different sort of title entirely. Killer. Monster. Soul reaper.

And he was truly a monster, because he reveled in his new role.

How was he to reconcile the monster with the man?

More images. Dead whores in St. Giles. Dead sailors in the Rookery. But not by his hand.

"Father, why have you forsaken me?"

His human father. An old man when Alastor was yet in swaddling. Still, Alastor had loved him, loved them both, the elderly people he thought were his parents. Loved the sisters who had helped raise him, so much older than he, with children of their own.

And he wasn't about to love again. Not ever. Never. Except his brothers.

Again, he tumbled, again and again, more memories flashing. Lokan laughing. Lokan dead. No body for them to hold. Only his blood soaking the ground, and the mark of the Asetian Guard burned there.

Naphré.

Again, he flexed his fingers and this time he felt them, felt his nails dig into his palms.

And knew with soul-searing certainty that he hadn't imagined it. He'd lost her somewhere along the way.

He couldn't lose her. She was his salvation.

The second the thought formed he thrust it away.

There was no such thing as salvation. There was only what he was. Sutekh's son. Sutekh's minion. Sutekh's soul reaper for eternity.

His thoughts were wandering to dangerous places. He needed a sugar hit and he needed it now. Forcing himself to move through what felt like setting concrete, he got his hand into his pocket and closed his fingers around a candy. He focused only on that, the hard little shape of it, and somehow he removed the wrapper. He felt the familiar shape of it and smelled English toffee caramel. The candy was his own, brought with him from Topworld, safe to eat. Somehow, he got it into his mouth and the sugar hit him.

He closed his eyes. Did he sleep? Or was it only a blink?

And then two red lights gleamed in the utter blackness. Which was odd in itself because he could see as well in the dark as the light, but he couldn't see a bloody thing here.

Except those two lights.

No, not lights. Eyes. Red eyes, glowing like coals. A flash of teeth so white they shot off a glare. Sutekh. Come for him. Alastor saw him as a hellfire demon, though Sutekh had worn the guise of a man the day he came for his son. The day he blew in like a storm and ripped him from everything he knew, showed him that he wasn't the good son, the gentleman his parents had raised. He was a monster, a demon in his own right.

How many years until he stopped seeing himself that way?

Decades. It had taken him decades, and by the time he got his head screwed on right, his parents, his sisters, even their children were all nothing more than ashes. Dust. Memories.

He hit bottom. At least, he thought he did, his knees bending into a deep squat to take the force of the landing. Icy water filled his ears, his nose, his mouth, and he realized he was in a river. He had been all along.

The flow was turbulent, frothing and foaming as it rushed through the darkness, carrying him with it, and then he was falling again, the sound of the water a roar all around him, above him, below him.

A waterfall. He'd gone over the edge. He was falling, tumbling, spinning in midair.

Bracing himself, he waited for impact, but when it came, it wasn't what he expected.

His shoulder slammed against hard ground, followed by the rest of his body. His breath left him in a rush. Pain echoed through his shoulder, to his collarbone to his sternum. His was breathless from the strength of it.

Pushing himself up, he rested back on his haunches and slicked his palm over his eyes, wiping away frigid water.

He took note of his surroundings. Overhead was a crimson sky that stretched as far as he could see in all directions. The terrain was flat. No mountains. No trees. Not even a rock. The only break in the monotony was the water that picked up the color of the sky, reflecting a river of blood. It flowed fast and hard, sections frothing pink where the turbulence broke the surface.

But there was no cliff, no tumbling waterfall, no sign of the place he'd just been.

Illusion or reality? In the Underworld, the former was likely, but that latter was possible. Having never been to Izanami's realm before, he had no way to say with any certainty.

His cell phone rang, the ring tone set to the Grateful Dead's "Friend of the Devil." Funny. When he got his hands on Mal, he'd throttle the wanker.

It took a bit of effort to wriggle the thing free of his pocket. His clothes were drenched, and wet slacks didn't exactly have a great deal of give. Finally, he barked, "Yeah?"

"Alastor?" Naphré's voice, flat and dull. His alarm bells went haywire. The more tense she was, the flatter she got. "I didn't know if we'd even have reception here."

"Yeah, I'm a little surprised myself, though I'm not quite certain where here is—" He broke off. "How'd you get this number, pet? I don't recall giving it to you."

Silence, then, "I don't know. I pulled out my phone, saw there was service. I just returned the last call, and you answered."

Returned the last call. But he'd never rung her up.

"Where are you?"

Silence, then, "I'm not sure. It's so dark I honestly can't see my hand in front of my face. The only light is from my phone."

Alastor strained to hear her, not through the phone, but in the surrounding vicinity. How far was she? Was she even in the same realm?

"Move the phone away from your mouth, and say my name, nice and loud," he ordered.

She was silent for a second, then, "Okay."

He moved his own phone away from his ear and listened. He could hear his name drifting from the phone, but not from anywhere else. So she was nowhere nearby.

Moving his cell back into position, he called, "Naphré!"

She must have heard him because she came back on the line.

"Wherever I am," she said, "it's nowhere near you."

"I'd say that observation's bang-on. Move your phone around and see if it gives you enough light to tell you anything."

He heard her moving, heard a footstep and a soft grunt, then a louder thud. "Naphré?"

"There are bodies," she said, her voice tight.

"Bodies?"

"In various stages of decomposition. Maggots. Lots and lots of maggots." She gave a tight laugh, and he figured she was close to the edge.

"What else?" He almost called her *pet,* but something stopped him, some unease with the unexplained. Something here didn't add up.

Her footsteps echoed through the phone, which told him she was walking on something hard, maybe stone. Then another sound carried to him and he identified it at the same second she said, "A river. It's flowing pretty fast."

Alas  stared at the river. Was she upriver? Downriver?

"What color is the water?"

"I can't tell. It's too dark."

"Is it cold?" Alastor asked.

He waited, imagining her hunkering down and dipping her hand in the water.

"Colder than your father's heart," she reported.

He laughed, relieved that she still held fast to her sense of humor despite the circumstances. And then his laughter died.

Colder that his father's heart? How would Naphré know anything about that?

"Listen," he said. "I'm just glad you brought a couple of pistols with you. They'll serve you in an emergency."

"So am I."

Which told him all he needed to know. Illusion. The cell didn't work here. And it wasn't Naphré on the other end of this line. She had brought knives and other close-range weapons, but no guns.

Illusion. A trick. Like the *Shikome* that had come to Naphré's door.

Izanami was fucking with his mind.

With a snarl, he hauled back then flung the phone as hard as he could. It went sailing end over end to crash to the ground on the far side of the river.

# CHAPTER EIGHTEEN

*The Underworld, the Territory of Izanami*

MALTHUS KRAYL COULD see as well in the dark as he could in the light. But not here. Here he was running blind, and he didn't like it. This was Izanami's realm, a place Sutekh didn't dare venture. Actually, Mal was more than a little cocky to think he could walk in and walk out himself. Sutekh's progeny wouldn't be any more welcome than the überlord of chaos himself.

But Alastor was here somewhere, and there was something wrong. Mal and Dagan had both sensed it. A quick visit to Sutekh had confirmed it. Alastor had come after Butcher's darksoul. The only argument Mal had with that was that he'd gone without one of his brothers at his back.

Had he learned nothing from Lokan's death?

Mal had drawn straws with Dae to see who got to come after their errant brother. Dagan won. Mal argued. Roxy stepped in. Mal got to come.

He'd had to laugh at that. Amazing the things Roxy could do. Like get his arrogant older brother to sit down and listen to reason. It had boiled down to the simple point that Dae was an asshole and Mal wasn't—or, at least, he knew how to give the impression that he wasn't. Not-an-asshole stood a better chance of success in a negotiation. Period.

So he'd opened a portal, crossed his fingers and leaped. Perhaps not the most solid of plans, but hey, that's the way he rolled. He wasn't about to change his modus operandi now.

The thing was, he hadn't gone directly to Izanami's realm. Not the way he did when he'd followed Sutekh's directive and gone to see Osiris. That time, he'd arrived at what amounted to Osiris's front door: the long corridor that led to the Hall of Two Truths. No such luck trying to get an audience with Izanami. He'd stepped out of the portal into…he had no idea what.

He walked on, using sound and touch to guide his way. It was more than little unsettling, if he was honest.

How long had he been here? Hard to tell. There was something twisty about Izanami's realm, not just the usual shift and dip that marked the transition from Topworld to Underworld. It felt like time was warped here, moving outside of any expectations. But maybe that was just because it was utterly and completely dark. Black as a gangrenous limb.

He thought he was walking on solid stone, but he couldn't be certain. His footsteps didn't echo. It was more the way his boots met the ground with each step.

After a time, he stopped, his senses searching for what was different. Something had changed. He felt as though he'd just pushed through Jell-O.

"Malthus Krayl," a cultured, feminine voice greeted him. A beautiful voice. Like chimes. Like a soft wind dancing through branches. That voice lured and promised, and he didn't trust it one damned bit.

He stopped dead, not wanting to accidentally land in her lap. "Call me Mal. And you are…?"

Laughter, so pretty it made him smile. He shook his head. Focused. Refused to be led.

Silence, and then she said, "I am Izanami." He thought there was a hint of wariness, or perhaps surprise in her tone.

"A pleasure." He almost teased her, almost tried his usual charm. It was on the tip of his tongue to make a flip comment about it being a shame to hide beauty in darkness. But something stopped him. Some gut instinct that warned that Izanami was not the sort of female to fall for his wooden-nickel charms.

She was a powerful deity. She would expect the respect due her.

"I brought you a gift," he said, suddenly wondering if maybe he shouldn't have. Too late. Done was done.

"A gift," she echoed, and he thought he heard a faint note of surprise.

"Moonflower. *Ipomoea alba.* They bloom at night."

Silence, and then he felt a cold touch on his hand and the flowers were gone.

"Why are you here, Mal?"

"I've come for my brother."

"And he came for something that does not belong to him. A darksoul that was pledged to me."

He squinted into the darkness, trying to see her face. Her voice lured him, called to him, so soft, so soothing. But he could see nothing, and some honed instinct deep in his gut whispered that that was probably a good thing.

"He brought the girl, though. The one you asked for." For some reason, Sutekh had been a fount of information, sharing the knowledge of the *Shikome*'s request. Mal had been a little surprised by that. Cooperation wasn't his father's strong point.

"Did he?" There was genuine surprise in her tone.

That couldn't be good. He'd thought she knew. Sutekh always knew exactly who was inside his borders. Why would he think otherwise for Izanami? Something stank like fish out in the sun.

Unease skittered up his spine on a million little legs. Then crawled along his shoulder blade. Reaching back, he scratched at the spot. Then he felt them, tiny creatures crawling all over his flesh. Up his neck, into his hair.

He could almost taste Izanami's anticipation, could definitely feel it vibrating in the air.

He threw back his head and laughed.

"I grew up eating maggot-infested bread, sleeping in a rag pallet that was made up more of fleas than cloth. I grew up with rats gnawing at my toes and bedbugs drinking my blood. You trying to creep me out, Izanami? I don't creep easy."

Laughter, so sweet and pretty.

"Your brother is not here, Malthus Krayl. I thank you for the flowers. They are not enough to earn my favor, but they were enough to keep you from my wrath."

Then the floor fell away. The world fell away.

He found himself spinning through an icy portal, disgorged into a back alley in a Dumpster filled with rotting food.

As he grasped the rim and vaulted out, he thought he heard a final tinkle of her laughter carrying on the wind.

"Fuck." He raked his hair back off his face, froze mid-motion and looked at his hand. It was striped with filth from the rim of the dumpster. "Fuck."

Grabbing his cell, he dialed Dae's number.

"That didn't go so good," he said when his brother answered. "I think I fucked up. I'm not sure he's actually even in Izanami's realm. I don't think she knew that Naphré Kurata was with him. And for some reason, I'm thinking it's not a good thing that she knows it now."

THE DARKNESS WAS ABSOLUTE. Not like night or a darkened room, but like a cave deep in a mountain, with the entrance blocked. Naphré couldn't see the water, but she could hear it rushing along with unstoppable power and intent. She'd been in it, and now she wasn't, and she couldn't recall exactly how she'd crawled from the churning depths, though she could swear she remembered Alastor's hands on her ass, pushing her to safety.

She remembered tumbling in the frigid rapids, not knowing up from down, her chest screaming, her lungs threatening to burst. She remembered gasping a breath, Alastor's hand holding hers, and both of them going under.

She'd thought she could hear him inside her head, hear him talking about his life, his family, his brothers. His nearly overwhelming wish to die.

What the hell was that all about?

Maybe it was her own memories that she'd shoved

on him. She'd thought she wanted to kill herself. When she'd first realized that in running from the Asetian Guard, all she'd accomplished was trading one hell for another, that she had indentured herself as an assassin for a demon rather than killing for the Guard, she'd wanted to die.

Then she'd done her first kill, her first job, puked all over the place with Butcher rubbing her back, and she'd known she'd survive. A part of her had died that night, but a different part was born.

So maybe thinking she had been inside Alastor's head was only her own memories coming back to haunt her.

Either way, she had more immediate problems. She was cold. So cold. And dripping wet.

Teeth chattering, limbs shaking, she wrapped her arms around herself and curled into a tight ball, willing herself to get warm.

She could swear that she remembered Alastor heaving her out of the water and screaming at her to breathe.

"Alastor." Her teeth were chattering and clacking and she doubted he'd recognize that word as his name. She tried again, louder, same results. His name was mangled, and silence was the only reply.

Again she yelled. Louder. Again. The act of shifting and moving and calling out was having a small warming effect.

"Alastor!"

He wasn't here. She was alone.

No one to rely on but herself. As always.

But she was so cold. Even breathing felt like more of an effort than she could handle.

She needed to get dry. That was the priority.

Her entire body shook with rhythmic shudders. She wanted to curl up even tighter. Instead, she got up on her knees, stretched out her hands and swept them back and forth in wide arcs, inching forward as she sought her pack.

She didn't dare hope it was nearby. But she didn't dare give up on it either.

She had no idea how long she searched, moving forward on her knees, then sideway, then back again, mentally measuring how far she crawled each time so she could retrace her movement and end up exactly where she'd begun.

That seemed important, having a baseline to work from in the endless, sooty darkness.

Counting the distance gave her a measure of confidence. Which was actually ridiculous, but hey, she needed to take her comfort where she found it.

Then she became aware of a weight pulling on her shoulders, like it had suddenly appeared there when, of course, it had been there all along. The backpack was exactly where it had started out. On her back.

Gratitude and relief surged. She closed her eyes hard, and clenched her teeth against the urge to sob. She dropped her forehead to her crossed arms and crouched there, slowly counting to sixty, letting herself have that much time, and only that much time, to wallow.

Then she pushed herself up onto her knees and painstakingly dragged the pack off her shoulders.

It took her a few tries to get the plastic fastener open, and another few tries for her trembling, numb fingers to work the zipper. Then the bag was open and she pulled out things. A sopping wet fleecey. Sealed plastic baggies of snacks. A water bottle. She was careful to pile everything nearby. It was dark. She couldn't see a thing. And she had no desire to lose any of her treasures to the blackness.

At the bottom of the pack was the plastic bag with her running gear in it.

Stripping off her sopping clothing was painstaking work. Her jacket. Her T-shirt. Her jeans took forever. She didn't even have the strength to worry about what the darkness concealed. She figured that if it was so dark that she couldn't see whatever might be out there, then whatever might be out there couldn't see her either.

And if it could…well, it would get an eyeful.

At last, she was out of her wet clothes and dressed in her dry ones.

Exhausted, her only thought was sleep. But she forced herself to spread her wet things flat so they had a hope of drying at least partially while she rested. Then she rummaged for a protein bar, tore it open and bit off a hunk. Chew, swallow, repeat, until about half was gone. She rewrapped the remains and tucked them away in the pack. Curling up to conserve heat, she fell into an uneasy sleep.

When she awoke, the sky was a red saucer, smeared with clouds limned in burgundy. The ground stretched flat in all directions, a dry, cracked, red-brown plane sliced by a crimson river.

There was no sign of Alastor. She didn't want to let herself think about that. About him. But worry nagged at her.

She laughed grimly. He was a soul reaper. He wasn't the one she should be worrying about. He'd probably opened one of those portals and headed for home the second the going got rough.

Unfortunately, there was no part of her that actually believed that. She wished she did. It would take away one worry. But in her heart, she knew he wouldn't just leave her here.

He'd fought to save her. Jagged memories of the river came to her, of him clinging to her hand, keeping her head above the swirling torrent, dragging her up again and again and telling her to breathe.

She swore she remembered him heaving her out of the water, pushing her to dry ground before the current tore him away.

But maybe that was all a pretty fantasy.

Either way, he wasn't here now and she was the only thing she could rely on.

Same shit, different day.

How long had she slept? She glanced at her watch. It wasn't working. With a laugh, she hauled out her cell. No reception.

No surprise.

She didn't think she was Topworld anymore.

Hell, she almost expected to see some food and drink with little signs attached that read, "Eat me" or "Drink me." Or maybe a white rabbit would run past muttering about being late. Nothing would surprise her now.

Tipping her head back, she looked at the sky. No sun, so no way to measure time. The way her stomach was growling made her think she had been out of it for quite a while.

She ate the rest of the protein bar and some nuts and raisins. Brushed her teeth using a bit of her bottled water. That made her feel better...almost normal, in fact.

She checked her wet clothes. Dry now. The jeans were stiff, as was the jacket. Another indicator that she'd been asleep for hours. She rolled everything into tight cylinders and tucked what she could into the plastic freezer bag before shoving that into the bottom of the pack.

Then she took measure of her situation. She had the water bottle that she'd already opened. She had one other in her pack. She had enough food that she could stretch to last her for a few days, but the water might be a problem.

Her gaze slid to the river, bright-red water under a bloodred sky. Was it drinkable? Did she dare?

Something niggled at the back of her mind, something bad. But she couldn't think what it was right now, so she didn't focus on that, but rather the question of whether to stay put or to walk.

Staying put meant she was waiting for something. Or someone. Playing the pathetic princess holding out for rescue wasn't her style. Besides, she had no idea what had happened to Alastor.

There was a really good chance that rescue wasn't coming.

"Okay," she said aloud, just to hear a voice, any voice, even her own. "Walking it is. Which way?"

The water was coming from her right, which meant that was probably the direction she had come from, carried here by the massive wave that had caught them up like a giant, brutal fist.

She looked to her left. "Left it is," she muttered. Might as well follow the water. Alastor had pushed her out, as far as she could recall, which meant the river had carried him farther along. She might walk for a bit and find him. Which would be a very good thing.

Or she might walk for a bit and find out where the river went. Likely, to Izanami.

A less good thing, but still an option.

She was wearing the running gear that she'd pulled out of her pack, but she hadn't brought spare shoes, which meant her hiking boots were her only option. Sitting back down, she grabbed them and dragged them closer, then shoved her hand inside to see how wet they still were.

Not wet at all.

She frowned, glanced at the sky. Right. No sun. No way to tell time. But her stomach was rumbling again, making her think she'd dawdled here a lot longer than it had seemed.

Aware that her rations were limited, she took a handful of almonds, a couple sips of water, and started to walk.

And walk.

Hard to tell how much ground she covered, or how long she kept going. She walked until exhaustion took her and she slept. She awoke, ate, drank, walked some more. Time was meaningless. The scenery was meaningless. Everything looked the same. The river never changed. The land never changed. There wasn't so much as a stone to mark her way. For all she knew, she was walking in circles, passing the same point again and again.

She didn't let herself admit that she was afraid. That something was very wrong. She was out of food, and almost out of water. Yet, she thought she'd only been walking for a few hours.

The passage of time was warped. Altered. She thought she remembered Alastor saying something about that happening in the Underworld. Then she thought maybe she imagined it.

Everything was becoming a blur.

Stopping dead in her tracks, she hunkered down and took stock. What she'd been doing up till now hadn't worked. She needed to do something different.

Or she would die.

She opened the pack and evaluated her supplies.

She had a lighter she could use to start a fire, but there was nothing to set alight and nothing that she could boil the river water in to make it safe to drink. She shot a glance at the water, considered all the possible deadly microorganisms—the bugs she couldn't see—that might hide in its red depths, and shuddered.

The point was fast approaching when she was going have to decide if she was willing to scoop it up and drink it as is.

But just the thought of that made her so afraid that her gut clenched and her heart raced. Why? What was it about drinking the water that was so wrong?

Then it hit her. The food of the dead. If she ate or drank anything in the Underworld that had not been brought with her, then she would never be able to leave. Partake of the food of the dead, and you're dead. That's why the thought of drinking the water was so abhorrent.

Damned if she did. Damned if she didn't.

Either way, she would die.

A nice thought to accompany her on her endless trek.

Again, she slept.

When she woke up, she felt so weak she could barely move. There was no more water. No more food. She couldn't remember how long ago it had run out.

Pushing herself to a semi-sitting position, her legs stretched out to the side, she stared at the river. Was he here somewhere? Alastor?

The river had carried him away. She remembered that. She was certain of it.

But she was so weak. She was out of options. She was going to die here on this hard, red ground and she'd never get to say goodbye.

*He'd* never get to say goodbye.

In her mind, she heard the tone of his voice as he talked about his human family: dead parents, dead sisters, dead nieces. Somehow she knew it would hurt him unbearably to lose her without even a goodbye.

A sharp pain blossomed in her chest.

She'd never made love with him. She was so angry with herself for that. She was going to die and he was going to be left without even a memory of her. She should have pushed it, should have insisted, should have punched through that damned icy wall he wrapped around himself.

"Fuck you and your control, Alastor Krayl," she whispered. It was little more than a rasp.

Then she pushed up on all fours, head hanging down, the world spinning around her. All the "should-haves" of her life seemed to spiral down toward her, and she was bowed beneath the weight of them.

Forcing her head up, she stared at the river and the

white-capped swirls of water that broke around the rocks.

Wait. The rocks. She stared at them, their size, their shape, and she knew in her gut that she hadn't really taken a single step. No matter how long she'd walked, no matter how much time had passed, those were the same damned rocks.

Only the water moved here. Only the water could carry her forward.

Maybe the river would carry her to Alastor. *Kuso,* she should have dived in before, when she had been strong enough to actually be able to swim.

She pushed to her feet, staggered and stared down at her backpack. There wasn't much left in there that was of use to her, and the pack would only be dead weight in the river. Weight her flagging strength couldn't carry.

She fished out her little bottle of hand sanitizer. Empty.

Her decision made, she left it behind, left the pack behind, and staggered to the water's edge. It ran fast and wild and as she squatted to let her fingers trail in the water, she realized that it ran damned cold.

What the hell was she doing even entertaining this idea?

"Got a better one, Kurata?" She stared straight ahead. She could sit down and wait. But waiting was the same as giving up. She was out of water, out of food. If she was going to die, might as well die as a warrior, fighting for her life with whatever she had at her disposal. In this case, that was one cold, scary river.

"In for a penny," she muttered and let her whole

hand dip into the water. Cold as ice. Cold as a winter wind. Cold as the grave she'd buried Butcher in.

*Kuso.*

She couldn't remember how long until hypothermia set in. A couple of minutes? Ten? Twenty?

Whatever it was, she was about to find out.

She closed her eyes, thought of Alastor, the way he'd kissed her. The way he'd touched her. The way he'd looked at her with a bit of what she'd seen in Dagan's eyes when he looked at Roxy.

Thinking of that, his eyes so blue and bright against the dark fringe of his lashes, she leaned forward and let herself fall.


TIME WAS DISTORTED. ALASTOR paced along the bank of the river, sensing that weeks had passed, though in the human realm, it was less. He was certain it was less.

He'd spaced out his candy, making it last as long as he could, managing the pain when it crashed over him in waves. It was only pain. Pain was finite. He could control it.

He glanced at his open palm.

Only three pieces of candy left.

He dropped them back into his pocket.

The river rushed toward him and he kept walking. He remembered shoving Naphré out of the water and onto the bank. He'd yelled at her to breathe. Then the water tore him away as though intent on separating them.

Maybe it had been.

Maybe Izanami had her already. Maybe the *Shikome* had snatched Naphré the second they were separated.

The thought coiled in his gut, in his heart, like a poison worm, spreading acid in all directions.

Naphré might be out here, alone, afraid, hungry... dying.

He could survive without food or water, the deity part of him keeping the human part alive. It wouldn't be pleasant. He was already clawed by agonizing pain that stole his breath and made him want to howl. It was only pain. He could survive for a very long time.

She couldn't.

How long would her supplies last?

He could summon a portal and get the hell out of here. Problem with that was, it was a one-time deal. He could open a doorway and leave, but it was highly unlikely Izanami would allow him to make a return trip. And he wasn't leaving without Naphré.

Another wave of pain hit him hard, every cell in his body screaming for sugar. Panting, he doubled over, then forced himself upright, mastering the agony.

Finally, he straightened.

He walked along the river in the opposite direction of the flow, his eyes fixed in the distance, searching for Naphré. He was determined to find her. To save her.

To tell her what he should have told her before they ever came here.

That she was his. Call it destiny, fate. Love. The name didn't matter. *Naphré.*

THE WATER WAS COLDER than cold, the force of the current so strong that Naphré was whipped along, pulled under, spun upside-down and over—arse over tits, as Alastor would say—until she bobbed up to the surface, grabbed a desperate breath, then was sucked under and the whole thing began once more.

She was crazy to have risked this.

But her gut was telling her there wasn't time for any other option. She had no idea where she was, but she was sure that if she stayed long enough, there'd be no going back.

People weren't meant to cross into the Underworld. It was a one-way trip. And she wasn't ready to give up on life just yet.

Her lungs were screaming, the urge to inhale nearly too strong to fight. But she had no idea which way was up. There was only the frigid water and the greedy current, pulling at her, carrying her along.

She didn't fight, though she wanted to kick for the surface with all her might. Problem was, she wasn't sure were the surface was. She could just as easily kick her way to the bottom of a watery grave because there was only darkness. All around her there was only darkness.

The sensation was horrific, doubly so because the water in her ears dulled all sound and she couldn't tell if the roaring she heard was the river, or her own heart pounding so hard it was close to bursting.

She fought to stay conscious, fought against the sharp-edged instinct to inhale, and then her head broke the surface once more. She gasped, coughed, fought to keep her head above water. She couldn't feel her limbs. They were like dead weight, dragging her down along with her clothes and wet boots and the general lethargy that was sapping her strength.

Fear was her enemy.

Fear was all she knew. Cloying, clawing, overpowering fear that both enveloped and gouged at her as she bobbed along in the dark. Where had the red sky gone? Where had the baked earth gone?

There was nothing there. Nothing.

Then she was catapulted into space, the water sluicing past her, the river roaring so loudly she couldn't hear the desperate gallop of her heart anymore.

She fell. The air whistled past. No more water. Just a vacuum of empty space, devoid of smell or sound.

When she hit, she cried out. Her landing was anything but soft. She came down on her back, her legs jolting up, her head hammering back against the ground. She saw stars and halos and wild flashing lights, then she saw nothing, heard nothing. Her world went black.

## CHAPTER NINETEEN

"DON'T YOU FUCKING die on me. If you die, I will kill you myself." Kneeling beside Naphré, Alastor shook her again, his fingers digging into her shoulders. But she only lay there, eyes closed, skin pale and cold. He pressed his mouth to hers, willed his strength to be hers. "Don't you bloody well die."

One minute he'd been alone and the next, she been there, tossed at his feet like a broken doll.

Tossed by whom? From where? The terrain hadn't changed. The only difference was that Naphré hadn't been there before and now she was. Every instinct screamed that someone was playing with them, toying with them. He'd seen Sutekh play similar games often enough.

It didn't matter at the moment. All that mattered was her. He couldn't lose her. He'd lost much and survived. But he couldn't lose her.

He reached out with his inner senses, meaning to summon a portal and get her to safety. He touched the energy that surged between Topworld and the Underworld, two separate streams that he needed to combine for a fragment of a second. He reached.

His senses brushed it, almost grabbing it.

He wasn't strong enough. That was the drawback to his half human, half god metabolism—the need for a constant supply of energy. Glucose. And he hadn't had that in days. Maybe weeks. He didn't know how long they'd been trapped here.

Shoving his hand in his pocket, he took out one of his precious mints. Unwrapped it. Popped it in his mouth. The sugar slammed him like a drug, giving him a split-second rush. He reached for the streams of energy with all he had, stretching his power.

What should have been easy—a parlor trick for him after all these years—proved difficult. Impossible. The streams danced beyond his reach.

Something was blocking him. Something that didn't want them to leave. Something that for the moment was more powerful than he was.

Looked like the portal wasn't going to be their way out.

He let it go, and focused on Naphré, who lay pale and quiet on the ground. His gut clenched as he looked at her.

She was human. Purely human.

And she was dying.

Desperation and anguish bubbled inside him. He didn't like the place his fear was taking him, but he couldn't seem to get his walls in place.

"Naphré." He gathered her into his lap, held her and rocked and tried to think of what the bloody hell he was supposed to do.

His pulse raced. His thoughts whirled. He'd become so accustomed to relying on his supernatural gifts, he was at a loss to figure out how to save her without them.

Not that he used those gifts to do much saving.

He looked around, frantic. He needed things. Water. Food.

*Yes, food.*

*Feed her.* The whisper came from deep in his soul, a dark slither of enticement. *Feed her and make her yours.*

Feed her his blood. That's what Dagan had done to save Roxy's life. It had worked for them. It would work for Naphré.

How long since she had eaten? How long since she'd had anything to drink? If he didn't feed her his blood, he was letting her die.

But Naphré had chosen not to take first blood. She'd told him that in no uncertain terms.

If he gave her his, he was robbing her of that choice.

What right did he have to do that to her?

*Might makes right,* his instincts whispered, insidious, powerful. *You have the means to control this situation. Do it. Control it.*

There were so many ramifications.

*Open a vein. Feed her.*

He stared at her, traced the tip of his finger along her lower lip, felt the faint gust of her breath on his skin.

"Fuck," he snarled. "Fuck."

If he did this, the choice would be his, not hers. If he did this he would be in control. If he did this he could bind her to him, because if he gave her his blood, her physiology would be altered. She would forever be a pranic feeder. She would need to regularly take the blood of another to survive. A human? He thought not. Once she'd sipped from his life force—a soul reaper's life force—he doubted a mere mortal would satisfy.

Would she want this? Would she choose it?

No. She didn't want this. She'd chosen a different life than this.

He would be forcing an existence on her that she had walked away from. She had the dark mark of the Asetian Guard in her skin, cut there by her own hand, but she had chosen not to complete her transition. She wasn't blooded. She'd specifically told him she didn't want to be.

Did the choice she'd made six years ago reflect the way she felt now?

What the bloody, sodding hell did he care? *He* wanted her alive. He wanted her with him. His blood would ensure that.

He thrust his hand in his pocket, closed his fingers on one of the hard, oval mints he'd taken from the crystal dish in her flat. Only two left. He unwrapped one, stuck it in his mouth, closed his eyes as the sugar melted on his tongue. Precious seconds ticked past. Then the glucose hit his stomach and was absorbed into his blood.

It wasn't much. It wouldn't last. He needed to work fast.

Reaching down, he slid her knife from the sheath in her boot. It caught the light of the crimson sky and reflected it back, making the honed edge look like it was already dipped in blood.

He leaned down and pressed his lips to hers. They were glacier cold, unyielding, unmoving.

Horror closed its fist around his heart, squeezing, choking. She wasn't breathing. He was too late.

He would not be too late.

With a snarl, he yanked up his sleeve and slashed

the blade across his forearm, deep. Blood welled in a neat red line, then ran in rivulets down his wrist to his palm before dripping down his fingers.

He brought his hand toward her, brought his blood to her lips.

She *was* breathing. Barely. The faint huff of her breath touched his skin.

Panting, he froze, blood dripping from his fingertips to splash her cheek.

She didn't want this. She hadn't chosen this. She'd run from it, denied it.

"Bloody, fucking hell."

He had no right. His pain, his loss weren't justifications. He couldn't take her choice the way Sutekh had taken his. The fact that, in the end, he liked being a soul reaper didn't change what his father had done, forced him to take on a role whether he wanted it or not.

The way he felt about Naphré meant he couldn't do that to her, not even to save her life. Love didn't give him that right.

With a roar, he buried the blade in the rock-hard ground, all the way to the hilt.

Dropping his face into the hollow where Naphré's neck met her shoulder, Alastor fought to rein in his raging emotions. But they were free, flowing through him, the pain terrible and sharp, mixing with the agony of his starving cells.

All he could think was that he would lose her. That she would be gone and he would know the agony of that loss. That he would have to live with the eternal circle of guilt and might-have-beens.

But living with the knowledge that he had stolen her humanity without her permission, that he had robbed her of the life she had expected would be hers the way Sutekh had done to him, was worse. He would not perpetrate such evil on Naphré.

"Alastor." His name was no more than a breath.

He jerked back and stared down at her. Her eyes were open but unfocused, her lips parted. Slowly, she glanced to the side, her gaze locking on his hand where he balanced his weight against the ground.

His blood dripped from the deep gash to the parched earth. Where each drop fell, a dark stain spread.

Her eyes widened. Her lips parted. Her nostrils flared and he realized she could smell it.

Her gaze locked on his, hot, frenzied.

"Yes," she breathed.

Hope unfurled, and he didn't trust it, didn't want to feel it. Couldn't bear to be crushed when it died.

"Do you understand what you're asking? What it will mean?" he rasped. He didn't want to offer her the choice. He wanted to grab her and squeeze his blood into her mouth and force her swallow. He wanted to make this decision for her. And he had no right.

"I...understand."

An eternity passed in a millisecond, and he didn't dare examine the emotions that surged inside him, primitive, dark. Outside his control.

Cupping one hand behind her head, he lifted her and brought his slashed forearm to her lips. She clamped on the lacerated flesh, sucking, pulling.

The sensation was lush, sensual, pain mixing with pleasure. He hadn't expected that, the erotic element to her feeding from him.

She arched toward him, her head and shoulders coming up off the ground, her hands clamping on his forearm. Widening her mouth against his skin, she swept her tongue across the cut, lapping at his blood.

The pull of her lips teased his senses.

Arousal stirred, base and instinctual. All the restless parts of him exploded into life. He wanted to claim her. He wanted to take her, feed her his blood as he thrust his cock deep inside her.

She gave a final hard, sucking pull, then tore her mouth away from his forearm, breathing hard, as though it cost her much to give it up.

He pushed her back onto the ground. Eyes locked on hers, he ran his hands along her arms, her breasts, down her belly to her legs.

Panting, she watched him, her lips red with his blood, a line of it trickling from the corner of her mouth to the angle of her jaw. With a groan, he leaned in and licked her, tasting his blood. He nipped his teeth along her jaw and then down, along the muscle and tendons of her neck.

He kissed her mouth. Wild. Imperative. The last, tenuous thread of his control was severed, his lust and pain and fear set free. All that mattered was that he hold her, taste her, take her beneath him and drive into her until the demons eased.

"I thought you were gone," he rasped. The words were insignificant, inconsequential. Too small to express what he felt for her, the great, writhing balloon of his emotions that swelled and swelled until he thought it would burst. More words were there, right there in his throat, stuck like a fishbone.

But she must have understood, because she reached for him and laid her palm against his cheek and looked at him as though he was the most precious thing in her world.

Maybe he was.

Somehow, she'd become the most precious thing in his.

NAPHRÉ RESTED HER PALM against Alastor's cheek and tried to think of a way to explain what she felt, to say it, to make him understand. He'd made her care. He'd stood outside her window with Butcher's darksoul bobbing because he'd had to make certain she wasn't followed…by anyone but him. He'd weighed the merits of her arguments and brought her with him on this journey, though he hadn't wanted to. He'd shown her the respect of letting her make her own decision. He'd stepped in to save Marie in the alley, though he *definitely* hadn't wanted to do that.

He'd made her care.

But it was more than that. What she felt was elemental, the caring mixed with, if not precisely a sense of ownership, a sense of possession and *right*. He was *hers*. Hers to love. She would kill for him. Die for him.

And she need only be brave enough to reach out and grab him.

Emotion mixed with instinct in a bubbling slurry, frightening, powerful. Logic told her such depth of feeling was impossible. That she didn't know him. Hadn't spent enough time with him to build such nuanced feelings.

But logic was weak in the face of the onslaught that surged inside her.

Somehow, he'd made her love him.

She'd known him for only days. She'd known him forever. Like a stop-motion picture, she relived that moment when she'd first seen him outside the Playhouse Lounge, the way she'd felt as though she *knew* him.

And he knew her.

Hungrily, her gaze roamed his face now. His jaw was shaded by several days' growth of dark gold beard, his features etched with lines of tension and fatigue. He looked raw and wild. There was nothing left of the controlled, impeccable facade he preferred to present. He was stripped bare, primal and male and so beautiful Naphré's heart ached.

"I didn't know if I was ever going to see you again," she whispered. "I couldn't bear not seeing you again."

His gaze locked on hers; his eyes darkened, the pupils going wide, leaving only a thin rim of blue.

The way he looked at her made her shiver. There was something inside him, something dark and animalistic. The walls had come down; the beast was free.

She wanted to say something. She didn't know what.

He didn't offer her the chance.

His mouth was on hers, hard, hungry, demanding. No gentle kiss. A claiming. A marking. His teeth nipped her lower lip. His tongue stroked the hurt. She moaned and reached for him, her hands fisting in his hair, her body responding on a level she hadn't even known was part of her.

She'd had his blood. She wanted his sex.

They were alive. What better way to celebrate than to take him and let him take her?

He dragged her up against him, his hands working their way under her wet T-shirt, his palms wonderfully warm on her icy, wet skin.

Drawing back, he dragged her shirt from her body, working it over her head and along her arms, snarling in frustration when the wet cloth caught and held. It refused to pull free. He simply tore it in half and tossed it aside.

She surged up, twisted her fingers in his hair and brought his mouth to hers. Her kiss was urgent, wild. They both tasted of his blood, metallic and salty and so delicious that she wanted to sink her teeth into his flesh and feed and feed.

"Fuck," he rasped, his hands working her wet pants, shoving and yanking until he wadded them at her calves. She thought he would tear them, too, but finally he dragged them free.

She was naked, panting as he came over her, the weight of his body pinning her to the ground, the heat of him sinking through her. He slanted his mouth over hers, kissing her hard and deep.

He was hungry. He was anxious and euphoric. She could feel all the wild emotions that tumbled through him, turbulent as the river, feel them deep within as though they were her own.

This was nothing like the controlled tease he'd offered in her bedroom when he'd stroked her and licked until she'd unraveled beneath his touch while he remained a step apart. Remote. Distant.

This was raw and stripped bare. He fed from her mouth like a creature starved. She was thrilled by his elemental hunger.

She would have this moment. She would have this shining chance to take him deep inside.

No hiding what she was. No running. Not this time.

She felt like all her life she'd been running as hard and as fast as she could and always staying in exactly the place she started.

Hands moving restlessly over her body, raw passion in every stroke, he put the claim of his touch on her, his blood smearing on her skin. She turned her head and licked his blood from her shoulder, then she surged up and kissed him, sharing the taste.

There were no words. She didn't need them.

She cried out as he cupped her breasts, his hands a little rough. Urgent. Her nipples were hard and swollen. Again, she cried out when he dipped his head and took the tip of her breast in his mouth with a hard, sucking pull. Then he moved to her other breast and did the same.

Sensation arrowed through her.

Frenzied, she pushed aside his clothes, tearing at buttons, fumbling with the zipper. He helped her as she made a sound of impatience and then, finally, he was naked. Hot skin, hard muscle. Ridges and planes put together to form perfection.

He was beautiful. He was sinuous and strong, long limbs, corded muscle.

Breathing heavily, he looked down at her, his eyes glittering blue flame, his expression hard, his mouth taut.

Without finesse or warning, he pushed her thighs wide, parted her sleek folds, and pushed his fingers up inside her. She was wet and ready. Pleasure spiraled through her and he captured the sounds of her cries with his mouth on hers.

She met every stroke and touch with her own, her hands roaming his body, broad shoulders, lean hips, the chiseled planes of his chest and belly.

Scraping her nails down his chest she toyed with his flat male nipples, liking the way he sucked in a breath.

Then she reached lower, tipping her head to watch as her fingers curled around the thickness of his shaft, too long to fit in her fist, too wide for her fingers to fully circle him. He was heat and velvet skin, smooth and full.

She *wanted* to lick him, to pull the length of his cock into her mouth.

But she *needed* to have him inside her. Now.

Shifting her hips, she tried to entice him, lure him, make him thrust inside her. She was hungry for him. Aching. With a little wiggle, she tried to get on top.

He pinned her hands above her head. He pinned her legs with his. He let his weight come full on her now. So wonderfully heavy.

He kissed her, tongue, teeth, power and need. The kiss poured through her, reached deep inside her, turned her inside out, turned her liquid and lost.

His knees nudging her thighs apart, he reached between them, the back of his fingers stroking her swollen folds as he positioned himself and then finally, finally, the broad head of his cock pushed at her opening. So good. She shimmied down, trying to bring him inside.

From low in his throat a sound escaped him, pleasure, almost pain as he pushed deep. A smooth thrust, slick, wet. She was on fire. She was soaring, sensation layered on sensation.

Then there was no more control, no more holding back. There was only pounding need. His. Hers.

He flexed and moved over her, his muscles surging beneath his skin, supple, strong.

Her fingers dug into the muscled globes of his ass. Her eyes closed. She felt like her entire body was attuned to his every thrust, her every cell poised to explode. Desperate yearning clawed at her.

She couldn't breathe.

She could only move. Move. Feel the lovely hard thrusts as he filled her and stretched her and made her whole. She was spread, filled. He pumped deep, driving her closer to the edge. She wanted it to last. Needed it to end.

Hunger clawed her, control drawn thin, frayed, her entire focus on the slide and pump of his cock, the joining of their bodies, the synchrony of their souls.

He gripped her buttocks, his fingers sliding between her cheeks, and he drove into her in a fast, hard rhythm.

Frenzied, she sank her teeth into the swell of muscle at the top of his chest, sucking, biting. She tasted his blood, salty, warm, rich on her tongue, joining them in yet another way.

Sharp and wild, she spiraled out of control. Crying out, she came, her whole body pulsing with her release.

NAPHRÉ SCREAMED HIS NAME and scored his back with her nails, her hips writhing wildly beneath his as she convulsed around him, so tight. So wet.

So damned hot.

With a last, deep thrust, Alastor came, his orgasm crashing over him in waves, ripping away the last pretense of his control.

He hung there, his release rocking through him, going on and on. Shuddering, he let the pleasure score him, marking him, freeing him.

Her arms were wrapped around him, and her legs tight, like she never wanted to let him go. He dipped his head, let his mouth move along her jaw, down to her neck. Tiny bites. Open-mouthed kisses. Anything to keep the feel and taste of her vibrant in his senses.

He closed his teeth on her, hard enough to leave his mark, because he'd liked the way it felt when she did that to him.

"I'll start a war before I let him have you," he murmured. And the second the words were free, he knew them for the truth. He would. He would rally his brothers. He would go against Sutekh. Screw politics. Screw—

"Him? You mean her…Izanami."

No, he didn't. And here was his opportunity to tell her. It was no demon that owned her soul. It was Sutekh. But the admission stuck in his throat.

He'd only just found her. He didn't want to lose her. He didn't know how she would react to the news that it was his father that had turned her into a killer.

Alastor felt like he was running blind, having no idea how or why Sutekh had claimed her. No idea what Izanami wanted with her. No idea how Naphré would react when he revealed all.

Telling her that he'd known almost all along that she was indebted to Sutekh was not a risk he was willing to take. Not at this moment, when their very lives hung in a tenuous balance. This place was anything but safe.

He wasn't even certain where this place was.

Too many variables. He would tell her. But not here. Not now.

Let him get her back to the world of man, to a place where he was at full power. A place where he felt in control. He'd tell her then.

"I would never let you start a war over me," she whispered, clearly mistaking the source of his tension. "There's a way out of here, and we'll find it, but it won't be at the expense of innocents. I only kill killers. That doesn't change just because on this job I'm my own boss and the payment is that I get to stay alive."

"Bloody hell."

She laughed. He could feel the vibration in his own chest where it rested against hers. Then she sobered, her expression grown serious.

"Why didn't you open a portal?" she asked. "Why didn't you set yourself free?"

"It would've been a one-way trip, pet. Once I left, I wasn't going to be able to come back. Izanami would never allow it." He leaned up on his elbows and held her gaze, willing her to understand. "And I wasn't leaving without you."

She took a slow breath. "And now?"

"And now we'll have to find another way home." He shook his head, hating to have to give her this answer. He didn't like to admit his current weakness even to himself; admitting it to her made him feel...out of control. But that was just it. He wasn't in control. Not here. He had to face that, accept it, turn it to their advantage, or they didn't stand a chance of making it out. "I'm tapped out, love. It takes a bit of skill and more than a bit of power to connect realms." He paused. "The skill's there. But I'm a bit low on the power."

Whatever reaction he expected, it wasn't the one he got. *Women.* Despite having been raised by a bevy of them, he had no bloody clue how their minds worked.

Instead of expressing concern that he'd failed to provide a way home, she smiled. Her lips curved, pretty dimples peeking in her cheeks. "I've graduated?"

"What?"

"You didn't call me 'pet.' You called me—"

"Love."

She nodded. "Just checking."

## CHAPTER TWENTY

LOKAN KRAYL STOOD VERY STILL. Around him, the darkness was complete. Not even a pinprick of light reached him. Slowly, he extended his hand. His fingertips feathered along cool, damp stone. Indentations etched the stone. He stayed very still, focusing on the shapes, tracing his index finger over them.

A bird. Perhaps a vulture. What felt like the slope of a hill. A rectangle. He knew that shape. It represented a pool. A semicircle, flat at the bottom. His lips curved. He knew that shape as well. It represented a loaf.

The walls were marked with hieroglyphics. These things he knew. He knew them. Recognized them. For some reason, that made him feel light, even giddy.

A faint purple glow began in the distance and grew and grew until it enveloped everything, both near and far. He saw then that he stood on a staircase. Narrow stairs bordered on all sides by walls so close that he could not fully extend his arms on either side. The stairs went on and on, down and up, with no end in sight. And everywhere, hieroglyphics.

He read them. Frowned. Tried again. He recognized the symbols, each one with individual meaning, but when he tried to string them together to tell a tale, they became simply a garbled mass without connotation or sense.

A vague sense of unease gnawed at him. He needed to move. Now. There was…danger. Not to him. To someone he loved…his brother. His brother was close. So close he could almost touch him.

His brother. He knew what the word meant, but couldn't place it in relation to himself. And then suddenly, he could. Alastor. Alastor was close.

Spinning a full circle, Lokan searched for a way out. His brother was there, right there. He but needed to find the way to reach out and touch him.

"Alastor!" A single cry, and then he fell silent, stunned by the sound of his own voice, rusty and harsh with disuse.

The urgency grew. He needed to find him. Needed to warn him. He should not be here. He should not be this close to the precipice. One wrong step, and like Lokan, Alastor would fall over the edge, into the abyss, drowning in the endless absence of self.

But there was something more. Lokan himself had been put here by…whom? He needed to remember. He needed to tell Alastor to get away.

He turned and looked up. The stairs formed a jagged, convoluted path to the stars.

Again, he turned. The way down was a straight line that led only to darkness.

Choose. He must choose.

And as he stood there, the seconds ticking past, he forgot where he was and why he was there. He forgot *who* he was. There was only darkness and quiet and… nothing.

Nothing but the gnawing certainty that he needed to warn…someone…about…*something*.

NAPHRÉ REACHED UP OVER her head, stretching, feeling like a cat. Except she was a bruised, sore cat who was thirsty and exhausted.

But at least she was a sexually satisfied cat.

She felt Alastor's palm on her skin, skimming down along her arm to her breast, lingering there, then down to the curve of her waist and the flare of her hip. Proprietary.

Closing her eyes, she just enjoyed his touch, let the moment spin out, and regretted its loss when he drew away.

"Get dressed. We need to go." She heard him rise.

She shot him a glance through her lashes. He was standing up now, glorious naked male, long legs, broad shoulders.

"Where, and how?"

He looked to the right, then the left. After a moment, he said, "We'll walk downstream."

"Downstream is good. Walking isn't. We'll get no-where. I noticed that when I was trying to find you. I walked and walked and the scenery stayed exactly the same. The only thing that moved was the river. I think that's our only bet."

"Bloody hell," he said softly, his gaze sliding to the water, a frown creasing his brow. His eyes narrowed.

She wrapped her hands around her knees and gave him a moment to figure out whatever it was he was trying to figure out.

One small part of her wished they could stay here, exactly here, with the red sky overhead and the river running past, lost in time and place, here but not here, time passing but not.

If they took even one step forward, this moment would be lost.

"What are you thinking?" he asked. No, rather, he demanded. He expected her to say.

So for all his loss of control, some things hadn't changed. The thought made her smile. She liked him as he was. Exactly as he was.

"I was thinking there is a certain comfort to this moment. I was thinking…I guess a little wistfully that I don't want to leave it behind."

He glanced around. "I'll gladly leave it behind. Happy to see the back of it. But not you, love. You I won't leave behind."

A promise. A vow. He wouldn't leave her behind.

"What if it's the only way that you can have Butcher's darksoul?"

He stared down at her, eyes gone that cold, glacier blue. And he said nothing. She didn't know if that meant he would trade her for Butcher's darksoul, or trade his chance for information about his brother in order to keep her. She didn't want to ask again. Maybe she didn't really want to know.

Suddenly, his expression shifted. His head jerked up, his nostrils flaring.

"What?" she asked, adrenaline kicking in, making her senses hum.

For a long moment, he said nothing, and then, "I thought I sensed Lo—" He blew out a breath and shook his head. "Nothing."

She opened her mouth to press, but he pinned her with a look and said firmly, "Nothing."

Bending, he scooped up her discarded clothes. The movement cast shadows on his features, and she saw the new lines of fatigue, the exhaustion that etched his mouth and eyes. Her fault. She'd taken what he could little afford to share.

And she had to admit, she felt pretty damned good, all things considered. Thirsty, hungry, sore, but more in the way of an inconvenience than a major liability.

"Do you have more sugar?" she asked.

He reached down again and snared his coat and fished through a pocket. He came up with a mint, held it out to her, his expression solemn.

"Not for me! For you."

He just stood there, holding the candy out to her.

Bounding to her feet, she took it. His eyes dipped to her breasts as they bounced and swayed. She laughed.

"What?"

"I'm thinking that tired as you are…no, more than tired…drained, you still look at me as though you want to tumble me on my back and—" She broke off as he grabbed her wrists and yanked her hard against him.

He lowered his face to her neck, traced his tongue along her pulse. "I do. I want to tumble you back and take my time making love to you. Hours upon hours. But I don't have that luxury right now. Later, I promise."

The paper crinkled as he unwrapped the mint and held it to her mouth.

"Not for me," she protested again, but he pressed it against her lips.

But she'd learned from the master. Why argue, when agreement would suit as well or better? She opened her mouth and let him slide the candy inside.

Then, coming up on her toes, she twined her arms

around his neck and brought her mouth to his. When
he opened for her tongue, she slipped him the candy
and danced away.

He watched her through narrowed eyes. "You'll pay
for that."

"Promises, promises."

There was a lightness to her mood that didn't match
their situation. They were still stranded in the Underworld, still uncertain of how to move forward or how
to get out.

When she said as much, Alastor replied, "We're
together. You'll watch my back. I'll watch yours. We'll
figure it out."

She stared at him, his words leaving her all warm
and glowy.

"What?" he asked again, exasperated now.

"You said 'we,' not 'I.' You said 'We'll figure it
out.'"

His lips twitched. "I wouldn't put much faith in that,
love. I'm merely pandering to your need for equality
in a relationship. Catch." He tossed her her clothes.

She pulled on her pants while he pulled on his
slacks, but her shirt posed a problem. He'd torn it up
the middle.

Lifting her head, she found him watching her with a
hungry expression, his gaze fixed on her naked breasts.
He was shirtless, wearing his slacks and shoes.

Without a word, he held his shirt out to her. There
was a tear in the arm, stained dark rust with his blood,
and a hole halfway down the back, also ringed in a
circle of dried blood. She glanced at him and saw that
those wounds had healed. Not even a faint scar remained. Then she looked back at the shirt. The holes

weren't the problem. The problem was that his shirt was white and when she put it on, the dark rings of her areolas were clearly visible through the cloth.

"Too distracting," Alastor said. "Take it off."

"And that will be less distracting how?" But she slid the shirt off her shoulders and handed it to him.

He snagged her knife and trimmed off the bottom half, folded it double, then cut two holes. She had no idea what he was about until he came up behind her, slid a hole up each arm, wrapped the cloth around to the front, crossed it over, and brought it to the back.

"There's just enough for a knot." His breath brushed the back of her neck and she shivered.

She looked down and realized he'd created a sort of wrapped, cropped top that offered modesty when she slid the remains of his shirt over it.

"Innovative."

He smiled. "When I have to be."

"But you prefer not to be."

"I dislike the unexpected."

She tiptoed up and pressed a brief kiss to his lips. "I'm getting that impression."

He picked up his jacket and held it up before him. She expected him to put it on. Instead, he turned it end over end, and seemed to be measuring length. She watched him from the corner of her eye as she laced up her boots. He cut long strips from the back of the jacket, tied them together, then yanked on the ends to test the strength of the knots.

Apparently satisfied with his handiwork, he looped his makeshift rope around his waist, then hers. "The river tore us apart once. I'm not losing you again, love."

And she wasn't planning on arguing that.

Taking her hand, he drew her to the edge of the water.

"Ready?" he asked.

"Not exactly."

He nodded, then jumped, dragging her with him.


"WHERE ARE WE?" Naphré rolled onto all fours, suppressing the urge to groan. Head bowed, she waited until the vertigo that gripped her eased a little. The absolute darkness was disorienting.

She fought against the shivers that racked her, then gave up and just let her teeth clack together and her muscles quiver. No sense wasting energy fighting the inevitable. Rivulets of icy water snaked down her neck, slithered along her back, adding to the overall feeling of being cold, wet, uncomfortable and so damned pissed-off she wanted to scream.

She looked around, a useless endeavor given that she couldn't see even an inch in front of her face.

"Alastor?" she prodded when she realized he still hadn't answered her question. Then again, a little louder, a little sharper, "Alastor?"

"Yeah." He sounded as surly as she felt.

"Why didn't you answer me?" She turned to her left, toward the sound of his voice.

Again he didn't answer.

"Don't suppose you brought a flashlight," she muttered.

She heard a sound to her right, and she spun toward it, nearly losing her balance as she scuttled on all fours and the makeshift rope at her waist pulled taut.

"Just me, love."

"You move like a cat."

"I'll take that as a compliment."

Her lips quirked. She couldn't help it. "I guess I meant it as one," she said grudgingly. "What are you doing?"

"Searching for a source of light."

"Thought you had eyes like a cat."

"I do. For some reason, that isn't enough. I am completely blind here. Wherever here is."

"*Here* is the realm of Izanami," a voice said from the darkness.

Naphré recognized it. The *Shikome*. She sounded tense, angry.

"Is that not where we just came from?" Alastor asked, sounding neither distressed nor surprised to hear they were no longer alone. He was behind her now. He drew her to her feet and pulled her back against him. He wrapped his arms around her, either to offer heat or comfort, or maybe just to keep her in the shelter of his protection. Maybe a mixture of any and all of the above.

Even though he was as wet as she, just the physical presence of his chest against her back made her shivers subside a little.

The *Shikome* made a sound of dismissal. "You were in *Jigoku*. You may relate it to a sort of purgatory, a place where you cannot go forward, or back."

"And *Jigoku* is not part of Izanami's realm?" Naphré asked.

"It is not."

"Why did you send us there?" she asked, noting that Alastor was conspicuously quiet, and feeling a little uneasy about that.

"She didn't," Alastor said softly. "Someone else did."

"You are perceptive, soul reaper," the *Shikome* murmured.

"Process of elimination. You specifically asked for Naphré. You wanted her here, in Izanami's realm. So while you might send me off to toddle about for eternity in a realm where time passes, but doesn't, you wouldn't have sent her. Which means it was someone else."

"Someone else who knew we were coming here."

"Which actually presents far too many options," Alastor said. "You knew." He addressed the *Shikome*. "Sutekh. My brothers." He tightened his arm around Naphré's waist. "Your mother," he said. *Who happens to be a high ranking member of the Asetian Guard,* he didn't say. She heard it anyway.

"The identity of the one who waylaid you is of little interest to me," a new voice interjected. A beautiful voice, like wind chimes. Like laughter. The sound actually made Naphré want to smile.

"Izanami-no-mikoto," Alastor said, his tone low and respectful.

So this was it. She was here, in Izanami's presence. She would learn why the *Shikome* had been sent for her, why Alastor had been lured to bring her to Yomi.

"Alastor Krayl. Naphré Misao Kurata," she greeted them.

Naphré returned the greeting with a small bow. She had no idea if Izanami could see it, but her upbringing demanded she perform it nonetheless.

"Do you know the law of the Underworld regarding promised souls?" Izanami asked.

"I do," Alastor said.

"No. Not you. I speak to Naphré."

She felt Alastor's fingers close around her upper arms, offering her support. Or perhaps he meant to offer guidance, because he squeezed once as though encouraging her to reply.

"I know that a soul promised to an Underworld deity must go to that deity."

"Yes. You promised me Butcher's darksoul."

She didn't really have a clue of exactly how she'd done that, but she wasn't about to ask.

"Your lover wants this soul. He wishes to trade another in its place. His father offered yours."

Alastor's hands tightened painfully on her arms, even as Naphré tried to understand what Izanami was saying. "Mine? How is my soul his to offer? How—"

She froze, spun in Alastor's embrace, the rope that joined them tugging tight as it wound around her, his hands sliding free of her arms. She couldn't see in this utter blackness, but she felt like she needed to face him.

Nausea churned in her gut. She didn't mean to say anything, but almost against her will, the words spewed free. "I denied my duty to the Asetian Guard. I ran from all I was supposed to be, and ended up killing anyway. I consoled myself, convincing myself that I chose the jobs, that I only killed killers. I lied to my mother. I lied to my friends. I couldn't trust anyone, not fully. Not ever."

*Until you. I almost trusted you. You bastard. You shiftless bastard.*

"Sutekh? Sutekh is the demon that owns my soul? Sutekh is the one I've been killing for?" She felt dizzy, sick. So many thoughts collided at once. Alastor had known the name of the demon she'd described to him: Gahiji. He'd said she still owed her soul to exactly the one she'd owed it to all along.

"You knew all along. You lied to me. You tricked me. You—"

She stumbled away, but the rope that joined them pulled taut and let her go only so far. All her anger, her sense of betrayal swelled, aimed at that rope, that connection between them. She dipped, snagged her knife from her boot and brought it up in an arc, slicing herself free of him, severing the link.

# CHAPTER TWENTY-ONE

ALASTOR CAUGHT HER wrist and wrenched the knife from her grasp. She spun away, but he was faster, closing his fist in the back of her shirt and hauling her up against him. Her rushing exhalation told him he might have been too rough.

Tough. She was his. She wasn't going anywhere. Not until he had a chance to talk to her and explain.

Explain what?

That he was the exact bloody opportunistic bastard she thought he was?

Too bad. Not like he'd ever tried to hide the fact.

"Not so fast, pet." He forced himself to speak in a low, even voice, though he wanted to snarl. "I told you I'm not leaving here without you, and I meant it." Grabbing the severed ends of the rope, he wrapped one arm around her and held her close.

"I could remove her from you," Izanami said.

"Try."

Naphré was stiff and unyielding against him. He knotted the strips of cloth once more, but kept his fingers clenched in her shirt just in case.

Leaning close, he whispered against her ear, "Hate me. Leave me. But let me get you the fuck out of here first."

She didn't say a word, just stood there stiff as a

fireplace poker. At least she didn't pull away. Maybe she figured that of the two evils, he was the lesser.

He was a little startled that Izanami didn't try to grab her. But then, they were on Izanami's turf. She had all the power, and all the time.

"Men lie," Izanami said softly, her words obviously aimed at Naphré.

"And cheat and steal," Alastor cut in. "So do women. Make your point."

"My point is that Sutekh claimed a soul that was never his to demand."

"Right. Butcher's darksoul. We've been through this."

"Wrong," Izanami said. "The soul of Naphré Misao Kurata. She belonged to another first. He has no claim."

"I walked away from the Asetian Guard," Naphré said, her voice taut. "I denied them before the dem—" She paused. "Before Sutekh tricked me into swearing my soul to him."

Her word choice wasn't lost on Alastor. He'd asked her before if she thought the demon had tricked her, and she'd said no, that he'd lived up to the promise to save her father that night.

She'd changed her mind now that she knew the true monster she'd promised her eternity to.

He couldn't say that he blamed her.

"You may have walked away from the Asetian Guard, but that does not change your blood. You always were, and will be, a Daughter of Aset," Izanami said. "But that is not the time of which I speak. I refer to a time before you belonged to the Daughters of Aset."

Naphré tensed against him. "Before?" she asked. "I don't understand."

Neither did Alastor, and he had the suspicion that whatever explanation was about to be forthcoming, he was not going to like it.

"I will tell you a story," Izanami said in her beautiful, melodic voice. "There was a man. A handsome Japanese man, descended from a god who sprang from the loins of a goddess. He fell in love with a woman descended from a very different goddess. She loved him, but she loved her duty more.

"Twenty years, he begged the goddess. Let him love her for twenty years, and then he would let her go back to her duty. She denied him. And so he cried out to me. He beseeched me. And he promised me his daughter, if only I would give him those twenty years with his love.

"I granted his request. But as always, men lie. He lied. He beseeched me when his daughter was born. 'Only let her be. Let her live. Let her know the sunshine and the rain. Only do not claim her, and I will promise anything.'"

Alastor could feel Naphré trembling against him, feel the way each word struck her like a blow. He had no doubt as to the identity of the protagonists of this story. Izanami spoke of Naphré's parents. Naphré's was the soul Izanami laid claim to.

"I never replied to his second set of pleas. And so, Naphré Misao Kurata, your soul is mine by right of birth as my granddaughter, many generations removed, and by right of your father's pledge."

"Take me," Alastor said before Naphré could even draw breath. "Keep me. Keep my soul as forfeit for hers." The thought of her trapped here in the dark, never to see the sun was more than he could bear.

He wanted her to have a life. He wanted her to know joy. He wanted that joy to be with him, but he'd rather she know it without him than not know it at all.

"A trick?" Izanami asked.

"No trick. Let her go. I shall stay."

"You say this with such ease, soul reaper. And I think you even believe it. I know you stayed in *Jigoku* to search for her when you might have summoned a portal and left. But how long would you have stayed? How long before you gave up your search?"

"I would have stayed until I found her."

"So you say." She paused, and when she continued, her voice was so soft, he almost didn't hear her. "Men lie."

He made no reply. No point in wasting breath when he wouldn't be believed. His thoughts spun as he tried to figure a way to prove his assertion.

"Light," Izanami said softly, and the area glowed with a thousand flickering candle flames.

Naphré gasped. He drew her against him and slid his fingers through hers. For one shining second, he felt a measure of hope as she let him, then she drew her hand away and his hope was snuffed.

Not that he blamed her. He had lied to her, and he didn't have much justification for it. At any point, he could have told her about her name in Sutekh's book, could have explained about Gahiji. He'd chosen not to, and at the time, his reasoning had seemed sound. Now he'd have to pay the consequences for that choice.

The *Shikome* stood off to one side, her cloak of living insects writhing and undulating in the light.

Izanami was several feet closer to them. She was not
at all what he had expected. Perhaps five feet tall, very
delicate, draped entirely in white. No centipedes. No
maggots. Just layers of gauzy white cloth draped about
her trim frame.

All around them were bodies in various stages of
decay. They were piled in the corners and up the walls.
There were maggots and centipedes everywhere, crawling through rotting flesh, out an empty eye socket or
through a hole that had once been a nose.

Incongruously, there were massive platters of food
beside the bodies. Fresh food. No maggots—they
seemed to have interest only in the corpses. There
were platters of fruit and meat and bread. Even baked
goods.

Alastor stared at the baked goods and an idea sprang
roots, one that would offer him the window to carry
out what needed to be done.

"Would you take my soul in her stead if I could
prove that I do not lie, if I could prove that I will stay
on?"

"There is no way for you to prove that," Izanami
said.

"But if I could?"

"Then, yes, I would take your soul in place of hers.
But know this, soul reaper, if you were to make such
a bargain, there is no going back."

"Are you insane?" Naphré turned on him, her dark
eyes sparking with fury, her mouth drawn in a tight
line. Strain etched her features, and something else,
some other emotion he dared not hope for. "Go, now,
while you can," she ordered.

She whirled to face Izanami. She was trembling,

her limbs shaking, but she executed a little bow and said, "I respectfully request that you send him from me, Izanami-no-mikoto. I am here. My soul is yours to claim. Let him go. Send him back." She shot him a glance then, and he was both humbled and horrified by the sheen of tears he saw in her eyes.

"Send him back," she whispered. "Please."

And that was all it took.

The sound of her begging for him when she would never beg for herself, his proud Naphré.

He let go of her hand. She cried out as he dove for the enormous tray of baked goods and snatched a petit four covered in pink icing. Pink, because it reminded him of her flannel pajamas. Bloody hell, that felt like a lifetime ago.

*Nice sugar hit,* he thought as he chewed once and swallowed, wanting it inside him as fast as he could get it. Wanting this done.

Naphré stared at him, her face a mask of horror.

"Alastor, no!"

He caught both her wrists and held her as she struggled and pulled. Turning his face to Izanami, he said, "I have partaken of the food of the dead. I cannot return to the world of the living, and having eaten it in your realm, my soul is yours. There's your proof, Izanami-no-mikoto. Now, let her go."

The sugared cake hit his stomach and the sugar hit his bloodstream. He felt the kick. He hoped it was enough, because he wasn't relying that Izanami would keep her word.

Pulling together every bit of energy he possessed, he summoned a portal, the relief almost sending him to his knees when he saw the black, smoking oval appear before him.

With a snarl, he shoved Naphré toward it and let go of her wrists. Her arms windmilled, her back arched and she fell back into the portal, her eyes locked on his.

And then she was gone.

He was left with the aching wish that they'd had more time and the hope that she knew he loved her.

"You did not lie," Izanami said.

Heart racing, chest heaving, Alastor turned to face her. Naphré was gone. The portal was closed. That chapter was ended and he had so many regrets.

"No. This one time, I told the truth."

He looked around as it slowly dawned on him that the *Shikome* was gone, the bodies gone. The only things that remained were the platters of food. He was alone with Izanami in a small room. Really, more of a cave. There was a simple table in the center draped with a white cloth. Along the legs of the table were twining vines with large green leaves and white flowers.

"Moonflowers," Izanami said, and for some reason, Alastor thought she was smiling. "They were a gift. Come." She gestured at the table. "Sit."

He sat. Why not? He had all the time in the world.

His gut churned with the thought of what he'd done. "I have questions…requests…"

"Do you? What gives you the right to have requests?"

He shook his head and answered honestly, "I have no rights here. Only requests. Whether you choose to fulfill them is up to you."

She inclined her head. "Speak them."

"Tell me she arrived safely."

"Neither a question nor a request. More of an order, I should say."

No point wasting breath on argument when agreement would get him farther. "My apologies. Please tell me if she arrived safely."

"She did." Izanami crossed to the table and sat across from him. The gauzy cloth that draped her moved as though she were underwater, and he had the bizarre thought that this was all illusion, that none of it was real. That she was showing him exactly what she wanted him to see. Or maybe what he, on some level, expected to see. "Why did you save her? Why not save yourself?"

He stared at Izanami, trying to figure out exactly how to explain. Finally, he shrugged. "Of the two of us, she's the more important to me."

"You value her more highly than you value yourself, but is she more important than finding your brother's killer?"

"Appears so." Given that he was here for the duration, there was nothing stopping him from searching Izanami's realm for Butcher's darksoul. If he learned anything, he'd find a way to pass that information to his brothers. But more than that, the truth was, when it had come down to a choice, there had been no choice. He would give up anything for her. His need for revenge. Even his life.

"Now you evade, Alastor Krayl. You wish me to provide answers, yet you are stingy with your own."

He scrubbed his palm along his unshaven jaw, the

feeling of those bristles reminding him how unkempt he was.

"Ask," he said.

"No. Rather, I will speak and you will listen. I wish to tell you a story."

Wonderful.

"It is the story of a boy. He catches a turtle and brings it home. In the night, the turtle becomes a woman. She beckons the boy closer and asks him to come live with her by the sea. For three years, he lives with her and then, overcome by homesickness, he asks to go back to his village. She agrees, and she gives him a gift. A box. And with it, a warning not to open the box or he will no longer be able to return to her. He goes back to the village, only to find it is not *his* village. Time is fickle. Three centuries had passed. All he knew is dead and gone. The boy opens the box, and he immediately withers away to dust."

Alastor rose and paced the confines of the cave, feeling trapped, feeling sick. It was his story, wrapped up with a different bow. He had gone to Sutekh's realm. He hadn't understood that by the time he went back, everything would be gone.

"Why do you tell me this?" he rasped.

"That boy lost his village, as you lost yours. Then he opened the box that he should not have opened, and he was lost to his love. Foolish boy."

"Is this some sort of lesson? I lost my family because time passed so slowly in Sutekh's realm. Now I've lost Naphré because I opened the box, I ate the food of the dead. I am as good as dust. Did I get the point of the lesson?" He was angry. At her. At himself. At what he'd been denied. The chance at eternity with Naphré by his side.

But that hadn't been an option. He'd chosen to stay because the alternative was that Naphré would have no life at all, that she would be confined here, as he was now confined here.

"I made a bloody choice," he snarled. "Either I opened the box and turned to dust, or Naphré did."

Reaching down, Izanami lifted one of the cake-laden platters. Like the rest of her, her hands were covered by gauzy fabric. He could see nothing of her face, her skin, her hair.

He could feel her watching him. Judging him.

He felt as though he were on trial, or subject to some sort of test.

"Do you wish refreshment?" she asked gently.

He stared at the platter, his stomach roiling. His instinct was to swipe his arm across the tabletop, to send the entire platter smashing against the stone of the cave wall.

Mastering his emotions, he tightened the reins of his control. He was to spend an eternity here. Best not to set off on that tone.

Besides, who had he to be angry with but himself?

"No, thank you," he managed, his throat tight, the words clipped. "But please, go ahead."

Her laughter was like rain, like a dance, like the wind.

"I cannot eat this, Alastor Krayl. I can eat only the food of the dead."

He stared at her uncomprehending. Then a tiny seed

sprouted. "Explain." He barely managed to get the word out.

"Ah. You are back to giving orders." But she sounded more amused than angry. "This is Topworld food, brought here by the *Shikome* for a specific purpose."

"The specific purpose being me. Testing me."

"Yes. Did you not listen to my story, soul reaper? Did you not hear what I said about Naphré's father? About Naphré herself?"

He thought back, ran her words through his mind. "She's your granddaughter."

Izanami gave a small nod. "Many generations removed, but my granddaughter still." She paused, and turned her head to the side. "You would have saved us both time and distress had you greeted the *Shikome* in the alley and come when she bid. As it is, someone sent you to *Jigoku* in an effort to keep you from me. Or perhaps, an effort to keep you from some great truth. It was not me that did so. And I can tell you that Naphré's mother did not know her destination, so could not betray it to Aset. More than that, I do not know. I leave that to you to discover."

"You're sending me back."

"Carry my greetings to Malthus Krayl. Tell him his choice of flower was appreciated."

Before Alastor could ask, she summoned a portal, the chill reaching through the hole to seep right through to his bones. He thought the temperature absolutely lovely.

"Thank you," he said, pausing before it. Then he turned to look at her over his shoulder. "My father's claim—"

"Is null and void. I had prior claim to Naphré

Kurata's soul, which nullifies anything he might say is due him. But more than that, Aset never revoked her claim, regardless of what Naphré did. Now that she has taken first blood, Aset has even greater claim.

"And finally, Alastor Krayl, I have gifted Sutekh with the return of his son. You. Let him try and insist on my granddaughter's debt. He will deal with me, and while your father is immensely powerful...well, let us say that I would provide him with a challenge.

"But to ensure no questions, no arguments, I give Naphré's soul into the keeping of the one who truly values it. The one who has earned her heart. You, Alastor Krayl, are now the sole claimant to the sins of her soul.

"Go, now."

He went.

NAPHRÉ SLAMMED HARD AGAINST the ground, panting as she tried to get the pain under control. Pain in her shoulder and hip where she hit when she rolled through the portal, pain in her gut from the topsy-turvy ride, but worse, the pain in her heart.

He was gone. Alastor was gone.

He'd sacrificed everything for her, picking her over duty. Choosing her over his obligation as a soul reaper, his duty to his father, his brothers. He'd sacrificed Butcher's darksoul. He'd sacrificed his life. He'd chosen her above all.

And it hurt. It hurt so bad she couldn't breathe, couldn't think.

Rolling to her side, she tucked her limbs tight and wrapped her arms around herself. Vaguely, she realized that the portal had dropped her on her living room floor.

She needed to think. She needed to reach past the pain and loss and *think*. Plan.

She rolled onto her back, her chest so tight she felt like a vise was crushing it.

There had to be a way. There had to be a way to get him back. She could find Roxy Tam. Talk to Dagan. He could help her get to Sutekh. She'd go to Aset. She'd—

The breath whooshed out of her as something hard and heavy landed on her. She struggled, pushed. Instinctively, she reached for her knife.

"I wouldn't bother." Clipped consonants. "With the weapon, I mean. You'll find it of little use."

She stilled.

Time stopped.

"How—" She stared up into incredible blue eyes that were inches from hers. He lay full atop her, his breath warm on her cheek. And suddenly the how didn't matter. The why didn't matter. There was only this moment, and if she'd learned anything, it was to make certain that she didn't let the moment pass.

"I'm in love with you, Alastor. I love you." Hot tears streaked from the corners of her eyes. "I love you. I thought I'd lost you, that I'd never get the chance to tell you. I love you."

"Do you?"

"I do."

He caught her tears on his fingers and put them to his lips. "Just checking." He glanced around her living room. "Nothing's changed," he said, his voice rough.

"Should it have?"

"No."

Dipping his head, he rested his forehead against hers. She could feel his hand moving between them, lowering his zipper, working her tights down her hips. She lifted up, helpful.

"I made it in time." He gave a strangled laugh. "Don't you see? *Nothing's changed.* It's all exactly as we left it. This time, I made it back in time."

Then he nudged her thighs apart and put his mouth on hers and kissed her as he worked himself inside her with gorgeous, slow thrusts that built in depth and tempo.

She clung to him and moved with him and forgot whatever questions she had for the moment.

Time enough later. They had nothing but time now.

\* \* \* \* \*

# REQUEST YOUR FREE BOOKS!

## 2 FREE NOVELS PLUS 2 FREE GIFTS!

### HARLEQUIN®

# nocturne™

## Dramatic and Sensual Tales of Paranormal Romance.

**YES!** Please send me 2 FREE Harlequin® Nocturne™ novels and my 2 FREE gifts (gifts are worth about $10). After receiving them, if I don't wish to receive any more books, I can return the shipping statement marked "cancel." If I don't cancel, I will receive 4 brand-new novels every other month and be billed just $4.47 per book in the U.S. or $4.99 per book in Canada. That's a saving of at least 15% off the cover price! It's quite a bargain! Shipping and handling is just 50¢ per book.* I understand that accepting the 2 free books and gifts places me under no obligation to buy anything. I can always return a shipment and cancel at any time. Even if I never buy another book from Harlequin, the two free books and gifts are mine to keep forever.

238/338 HDN E9M2

Name _____ (PLEASE PRINT)

Address _____ Apt. #

City _____ State/Prov. _____ Zip/Postal Code

Signature (if under 18, a parent or guardian must sign)

Mail to the **Reader Service:**
**IN U.S.A.:** P.O. Box 1867, Buffalo, NY 14240-1867
**IN CANADA:** P.O. Box 609, Fort Erie, Ontario L2A 5X3

Not valid for current subscribers to Harlequin Nocturne books.

**Want to try two free books from another line?**
Call 1-800-873-8635 or visit www.ReaderService.com.

* Terms and prices subject to change without notice. Prices do not include applicable taxes. N.Y. residents add applicable sales tax. Canadian residents will be charged applicable provincial taxes and GST. Offer not valid in Quebec. This offer is limited to one order per household. All orders subject to approval. Credit or debit balances in a customer's account(s) may be offset by any other outstanding balance owed by or to the customer. Please allow 4 to 6 weeks for delivery. Offer available while quantities last.

**Your Privacy:** Harlequin Books is committed to protecting your privacy. Our Privacy Policy is available online at www.ReaderService.com or upon request from the Reader Service. From time to time we make our lists of customers available to reputable third parties who may have a product or service of interest to you. If you would prefer we not share your name and address, please check here. ☐

**Help us get it right**—We strive for accurate, respectful and relevant communications. To clarify or modify your communication preferences, visit us at www.ReaderService.com/consumerschoice.

HN10

# EVE SILVER

---

77482  SINS OF THE HEART          ___ $7.99 U.S. ___ $9.99 CAN.

*(limited quantities available)*

| | |
|---|---|
| TOTAL AMOUNT | $ _____ |
| POSTAGE & HANDLING | $ _____ |
| ($1.00 FOR 1 BOOK, 50¢ for each additional) | |
| APPLICABLE TAXES* | $ _____ |
| TOTAL PAYABLE | $ _____ |

*(check or money order—please do not send cash)*

---

To order, complete this form and send it, along with a check or money order for the total above, payable to HQN Books, to: **In the U.S.:** 3010 Walden Avenue, P.O. Box 9077, Buffalo, NY 14269-9077; **In Canada:** P.O. Box 636, Fort Erie, Ontario, L2A 5X3.

Name: _____

Address: _____ City: _____

State/Prov.: _____ Zip/Postal Code: _____

Account Number (if applicable): _____

075 CSAS

*New York residents remit applicable sales taxes.
*Canadian residents remit applicable GST and provincial taxes.

# HQN™

## We *are* romance™

### www.HQNBooks.com